Advance ...

WITHOUT A HITCH

"Put a ring on *Without a Hitch*—a sweet, Southern confection of a book about what it takes to orchestrate everyone else's happily-ever-after when your own heart has been broken. A sneak peek into the world of high-end wedding planning will keep you laughing as Lottie deconstructs the fairy tale and finds her authentic self."

—JODI PICOULT, #1 *NEW YORK TIMES* BESTSELLING AUTHOR
OF *WISH YOU WERE HERE* AND *THE BOOK OF TWO WAYS*

"*Without a Hitch* is a delightfully quirky novel that proves the age-old adage 'We plan. God laughs.' Filled with fascinating insights into the world of high-end wedding planning, you can't help but cheer for Lottie Jones as she learns that you can't script your life and that, sometimes, the best-laid plans are the ones you never make."

—EMILY GIFFIN, #1 *NEW YORK TIMES* BESTSELLING AUTHOR
OF *ALL WE EVER WANTED* AND *THE LIES THAT BIND*

"*Without a Hitch* is a must-read. It is absolutely fabulous. As someone who works in the wedding industry, I found this book's brevity, humor, and the glamorous over-the-top world of Southern weddings a true joy to read. This is the book you will be gifting to all your friends!"

—MINDY WEISS, BESTSELLING AUTHOR OF *THE WEDDING BOOK*

"*Without a Hitch* kept me laughing and loving every fun-filled page! Cancel your plans because you will not be able to put the book down once you start! I absolutely loved it!"

—LISA PATTON, BESTSELLING AUTHOR OF *RUSH*
AND *WHISTLIN' DIXIE IN A NOR'EASTER*

WITHOUT A HITCH

WITHOUT A HITCH

A HITCH

A Novel

Mary Hollis
HUDDLESTON  Asher
FOGLE PAUL

HARPER MUSE

Without a Hitch

Published by Harper Muse, an imprint of HarperCollins Focus LLC.

This book is a work of fiction. The characters, incidents, and dialogue are drawn from the authors' imagination and are not to be construed as real. Any resemblance to actual events or persons, living or dead, is entirely coincidental.

Any internet addresses (websites, blogs, etc.) in this book are offered as a resource. They are not intended in any way to be or imply an endorsement by HarperCollins Focus LLC, nor does HarperCollins Focus LLC vouch for the content of these sites for the life of this book.

ISBN 978-0-7852-5870-4 (trade paper)
ISBN 978-0-7852-5871-1 (e-book)
ISBN 978-0-7852-5872-8 (downloadable audio)

Library of Congress Cataloging-in-Publication Data

Library of Congress Cataloging-in-Publication Data
Names: Huddleston, Mary Hollis, author. | Paul, Asher Fogle, author.
Title: Without a hitch : a novel / Mary Hollis Huddleston, Asher Fogle Paul.
Description: [Nashville] : Harper Muse, [2021] | Summary: "Bridezillas meets The Devil Wears Prada in this hilarious romp through the world of extravagant Southern weddings and the most expensive events money can buy"-- Provided by publisher.
Identifiers: LCCN 2021031106 (print) | LCCN 2021031107 (ebook) | ISBN 9780785258704 (paperback) | ISBN 9780785258711 (epub) | ISBN 9780785258728
Subjects: LCSH: Event planners--Fiction. | Weddings--Planning--Fiction. | Weddings--Southern States--Fiction. | LCGFT: Romance fiction.
Classification: LCC PS3608.U3223 W58 2021 (print) | LCC PS3608.U3223 (ebook) | DDC 813/.6--dc23
LC record available at https://lccn.loc.gov/2021031106
LC ebook record available at https://lccn.loc.gov/2021031107

Printed in the United States of America
21 22 23 24 25 LSC 5 4 3 2 1

"A lady's imagination is very rapid;
it jumps from admiration to love, from
love to matrimony, in a moment."
—JANE AUSTEN, *PRIDE AND PREJUDICE*

"You know how those who can't do, teach?
Those who can't wed, plan."
—*THE WEDDING PLANNER*

"The right man for you might be out there right now
and if you don't grab him, someone else will, and
you'll have to spend the rest of your life knowing
that someone else is married to your husband."
—*WHEN HARRY MET SALLY*

PROLOGUE

What kind of person would plan her wedding without a proposal? The kind who ended up single, sweaty, and salty on the intended date, that's who.

I took another gulp of chardonnay, inhaled the scents of fresh-cut grass and Harper's Marlboros, and watched my three best friends dance on the sidewalk. An iPod and Bluetooth speaker blared "Since U Been Gone." Brightly colored Mexican muumuus stuck to their backs in the humid night air.

They toasted Cinco de Mayo, graduation, and the future, shiny as a new penny. I leaned back on the cool concrete steps of the Texas Christian University chapel and closed my eyes for a moment. The screw-top bottle dripped condensation between my bare feet.

On loop in my head ran the inescapable thought: *This was supposed to be my wedding day.*

"Lottie, get your butt over here!" Natalia, one of my soon-to-be-former housemates, yelled.

I waved the chardonnay at her in dismissive reply.

"Suit yourself," Megan said with a shimmy of her narrow purple hips and a toss of her dark-brown curls. "But this may be the last night we're all together. Like, forever."

"Quit being such a party pooper. It's graduation," Harper said. "You have dancing to do, drinks to consume, and an ex to get over."

"One day, four years of dating will feel like nothing," said Natalia, ever the optimist. "This will just be a blip on your radar. A step on your way to your actual fabulous life."

"Preferably with someone rich and famous who loves you, Jesus, and his mama." Harper winked.

"Maybe someday you won't even feel like such an idiot for planning your wedding years before Brody ever, I mean never, proposed," Megan said.

"I don't think it's idiotic—just very, very committed." Natalia smiled broadly, albeit unconvincingly, teeth white against golden-brown cheeks.

"Maybe more like deserving to be committed," said Harper, arching a thin brow.

"Lovely. Very funny. Thanks, y'all." I knew they were trying to be helpful. However drunkenly.

Three years, nine months, and three weeks prior, I had met Brody Stevens during freshman orientation. The football team let the players out of two-a-days long enough to figure out where their classes would be and to meet enough cute girls to stay motivated during muggy predawn practices.

Funny, I couldn't remember the exact moment we met. Only that by the end of my third day of college, his six-foot-three frame had hauled all my textbooks to the freshmen girls' dorm from the campus bookstore.

Brody was hilarious, ambitious, and smarter than most guys who had their heads bashed every day for a decade. Confident in the way all handsome men were confident, but with the endearing hint of insecurity that remained when your growth spurt hit at the tail end of puberty. He behaved like the gentleman his Baton Rouge mama intended, and he kissed with a certain . . . well, expertise.

We bonded over both being from the dodgy suburbs of our respective towns and scholarship students in the middle of a country club set. He worked hard to earn his spot in the starting lineup—and somehow found time and energy to push me to excel too. I'd spent our first couple of months together wondering why he picked me.

If I scrolled through my social media profiles or mental images of the last four years, his goofy grin appeared in nearly every frame. Every friendship, every club, every milestone was shared. We were Brody and Lottie. Campus sweethearts. All-conference quarterback and student association vice president. We had shed our working-class histories quicker than we dropped our heavily twanged accents.

Okay, yes, we'd even won homecoming king and queen. I knew deep down that it was due to our ethos, the aura surrounding our relationship, and not because I was especially beloved. But Brody was. All of campus and the entire alumni association got to fall in love with him every fall Saturday for four years.

I certainly did.

Sophomore year, my sorority great-grand-big (yeah, I know, I know . . .) got married in the TCU chapel, and I manned the guest book. Daydreaming through the vows, I imagined us at the altar instead. We'd been saying "I love you" for several months and using phrases like "after school" even though it seemed on some distant horizon. But two weeks later when Brody mentioned "our kids," I called the campus wedding coordinator.

I looked at the calendar and found a slim window between the NFL draft, graduation, and training camp. As every undergrad hopeful knew, if I wanted to get married in the chapel, I'd need to book it well in advance. Two years was plenty of time for him to get around to proposing. I could even deduct the $200 fee from my on-campus spending account. Genius. Thus, with little fanfare or effort, May 5—the Saturday after graduation—was on the books.

I slowly and systematically tied my future to Brody's with the subtlest of threads. By junior year the planning had gone well beyond our vows. He'd play in the NFL, and I'd be a card-carrying member of the wives-and-girlfriends club. Law school could wait. It had to since, of course, he could be drafted anywhere.

I channeled all my organizational skills and energy into this new plan. I continued with my English and poli-sci double major, minoring in women's studies, but never took the LSAT, stopped applying for honor societies, and subscribed to *Martha Stewart Weddings*.

Good thing Brody never knew about the wedding date I'd set for us—which I had quietly let go a couple months prior, promising to call the campus coordinator again when the time was right. At least I was spared that particular humiliation. And since I'd caught the roommates eyeing BHLDN bridesmaids' dresses a time or two, I took small comfort that I wasn't the only one who felt confident that the day would come.

Instead, I had no grad school, job, fellowship, internship, or relationship on the horizon—and no clue what to do next. Incredible.

And now it was May 5.

So here my girlfriends and I danced. We'd donned muumuus from our spring break trip to Acapulco, feasted on Tex-Mex at Joe T's, and eventually ended up wandering the campus. We found ourselves at the site, and on the night, of my imagined, intended nuptials.

As I sat on the chapel steps, itchy from mosquitoes, I replayed how a week ago—two days before we donned our caps and gowns—Brody had come over to do the deed. No, not *that* deed. The one that involved tears and a lot of "I just don't think I can balance our relationship with my rookie season." And "You'd be so bored while I played and traveled all the time."

I pathetically tried to explain how low maintenance I was. It wasn't like he'd have to babysit me. I could work, get a job in whatever city he was drafted. We could make friends and build a life there together. I groveled. Basically did everything short of lying prostrate. It wasn't enough.

Natalia ripped a handful of roses from the bush next to the chapel doors and bunched together a sloppy bouquet. "Hold these." She thrust them into my hand. She tucked a long dark lock behind her ear, yanked me from the steps, and led me to the end of the sidewalk near the street. She cued my tipsy band of maids, who began to hum, "Here comes the bride."

"It was supposed to be *Canon in D*," I mumbled, walking with her down the sidewalk aisle. Right, together, left, together, right. Arm in arm we strolled, summer locusts whirring in accompaniment.

As we reached the steps Harper clambered to the top to lead the ceremony, a cigarette dangling from her lips, bouncing as she spoke and nearly igniting a few chin-length blond strands. "We are gathered together tonight to celebrate the union of Lottie and her freedom.

"Lottie, I mean, Charlotte, do you solemnly swear never to go back to that jerk, to, um, find somebody better, to—"

"Never to let him touch her forevermore!" Natalia said helpfully.

"Yes, yes, that *for sure*, and also to find someone else richer and handsomer and just all around better?" Harper finished.

"I do," I said solemnly. I raised my right hand, pale in the glow of the streetlight.

"By the powers vested in me by the state of Texas and this fine college of arts and sciences, I now pronounce you a single lady. You may now . . . take a shot."

With that, my three housemates cheered.

Brody is *a jerk*, I thought, while Harper and Megan began to dance some tequila-infused semblance of the Macarena across the chapel porch. As I stood on the stoop clutching my crumpled bouquet, my friends moved to the bottom, mock wrestling for a chance to catch the toss. Sticky, disheveled, mostly shoeless, some holding half-empty bottles. All perfect. I guess I'd known on some level they would be by my side today no matter what. I blinked, the click of a shutter, framing them in my memory.

I slowly turned my back to my friends, inhaled deeply, and let the tattered flowers fly.

ONE

Seven Years Later

An azalea branch jabbed my thigh, and my heels sank into the mulch. Sweat trailed down my back, and I realized wearing a black silk dress to an outdoor wedding in July was a mistake as I squatted behind the ornamental shrubbery of the Dallas Arboretum and Botanical Garden.

Guests filed past our hiding spot. They fanned themselves as they searched for seats, oblivious to our presence.

At my left hunched the groom. His pale face flushed and dripped while he yanked on his stiff collar. Good. This whole debacle was his fault anyway.

I could hear my new boss, Cedric, squawking orders at the caterers over the walkie-talkie. Any minute now he'd give me the go-ahead to dispatch the groom, Cole Parker-McNeil.

"All planners need to be in position for the ceremony. I repeat, all planners in position," Cedric's voice boomed over my walkie-talkie. "Operation Wingman has officially begun. We're five minutes and counting from go-time."

The groom's only job was to show up on the big day, on time, with a big smile plastered on his face and, if possible, sober. Most would probably have preferred to have a stunt double stand in at the altar so they could keep sipping their flasks in the green room with the groomsmen. But Cole actually *got* his very own stunt double. Instead of walking down the aisle, Cole had a vision of arriving by helicopter. Yes, a helicopter. But he didn't want to do the jumping himself.

Unwittingly, Cole was also starring in my first official wedding at The Firm, known to outsiders as Cedric Montclair Celebrations. The scent of my anxious desperation mingled with my body odor.

Abigail Benton, my former boss at a floral design boutique for nearly six years, had sold her company to Cedric Montclair's megaevent production and planning conglomerate that summer. Architecturally inspired floral design was her specialty, and Cedric wanted to stop outsourcing that segment of the business. She made bank, but all I got was a $500 bonus and a "You're welcome to come too. I'm sure Cedric can find a place for you." It was a no-brainer, as my massive student loans weren't vanishing anytime soon.

So I hunched in the bushes, tasked with helping pull off one of the spring's biggest Texas nuptials.

The bride, Gemma, was practically Southern aristocracy: her ancestors had turned West Texas cotton farming into a global textiles business. But the company recently halted production due to rising US manufacturing costs, and her family had high hopes for this union with the Parker-McNeil venture capitalists.

Despite drawing shrubbery duty, I'd been in awe most of the day. Both the bride and groom wanted to make an impression, which a million-dollar budget could achieve. Every last detail for their five hundred guests had been customized and special ordered from all over the world.

The clients donated a six-figure sum to the botanical garden in order to secure the space for their ceremony and reception. It was almost impossible to shut down the entire gardens for an event, but an exception was made since Cole and Gemma had been so very generous.

The ceremony was set outdoors in one of the more secluded areas. Guests would leave the "secret garden" and move to the reception in a multilevel tent—a structure that had been under construction for almost two weeks leading up to the event.

The vast majority of these elaborate details fell to Gemma, her mother, and Cedric's team. Usually this arrangement was ideal for all parties involved, I'd learned. Most men—grooms and fathers alike—were best left out of the planning process entirely except for occasionally being allowed to help with stocking the bar, selecting the band, and of course, signing the checks. Most men were relieved by this. But not this groom. Cole wanted to make a grand gesture of his own.

Typically, the *bride* was supposed to steal the show with her dramatic entrance, but she surprised us and acquiesced. If I had to hazard a guess, after a childhood of boarding school, equestrian lessons, debutante balls, and other requisite activities of the Southern gentry, she'd had enough of feeling like a stuffed turkey and was happy to concede the spotlight. The planning team was slightly worried Gemma would be a letdown after the groom made his impressive entry, but we always tried to accommodate the clients' wishes. In this case that meant aviation.

The processional started as usual, but at the moment when the groom would typically walk out, the music suddenly stopped. Cedric approached the microphone at the front of the ceremony and announced that the groom was "missing." Muffled sounds of dismay reached our perch.

A precisely plotted fifteen seconds later, the *Mission: Impossible* theme song blared through the speakers, and the whir of a hovering helicopter filled our ears. I stuck my head out of the hedge just enough to see the stunt double jump from the chopper, two hundred feet above us.

"Are you ready?" I handed the real Cole the helmet and checked his parachute backpack.

"Huh, what?" He startled from staring at the guests through the branches. "Wow, we're really doing this." He gulped.

"Are you ready to run out there? We have about sixty seconds, give or take."

He stood, dazed, his eyes as terrified as if he were actually being forced to leap out of the chopper—sans parachute.

"Listen, Cole, I know everyone you know is out there. But focus on this one thing: you're marrying Gemma. If the band doesn't show or her mother throws a fit or the food is terrible, none of that matters. It's all just details." (Obviously, Cedric would never allow *any* of that to happen regardless.)

"I know," Cole said softly.

"My mamaw used to say that the only thing that will last other than pretty pictures is a marriage . . . So, do you love Gemma and want to marry her?"

"Absolutely. She's my . . . well, my everything." He straightened his shoulders as much as the overhanging branches would allow and turned to me, resolve in his eyes. He grabbed the helmet. "Let's do this!"

The stunt guy we'd hired from the skydiving school in McKinney landed on the path right behind us and ran to our hiding spot, disconnecting his parachute and abandoning it on the ground for effect. I grabbed the jumper and shoved Cole out the side. He jogged to the altar, arms raised in victory, to the cheers of family and friends.

Would Cole ever confess that he hadn't actually jumped from the helicopter? Doubtful.

I had no idea where that pep talk had come from. I was the last person to pass along inspirational quotes and starry eyes. Deep down, I still hoped some people found their forever—and it looked like I'd helped make that happen for Cole and Gemma, at least for today. Plus, I really needed things to go according to plan.

For years Abigail and I had designed Cedric's florals and even assisted with day-of details—setting up arrangements before his long-standing team descended for the ceremony and reception—but this was the first time I'd worked on the main event. If anything, it was an audition to see if I could cut it with Cedric's pros and survive the merger. I'd unfortunately gone from Abigail's almost junior partner to a rookie in one fell swoop.

Barring disaster, I'd be assigned to Mary Ellen Bovander, Cedric's number two in the planning division. Her most recent assistant had gotten married and stopped working entirely—right after Cedric did her wedding, of course. Rumor had it that the girl put in two years at The Firm just to secure her premier date.

Now Mary Ellen needed help, and she didn't have time to train someone new with wedding season in full swing. When Abigail suggested me for the job, they were intrigued by the fact that I'd worked with Cedric's team in the past. They opted to throw me straight into the role and see if I could survive. What they didn't know was that my entire financial survival in Dallas was also contingent on surviving at The Firm.

As I stood on the path, admiring my coordinating handiwork, Mary Ellen marched over and grabbed my arm. "Lizzie, you look disgusting. Have you seen yourself? You've got a sweat line down your back and circles under your arms."

"Uh, it's Lottie. And sorry?"

Mary Ellen, however, seemed impervious. Her brunette blowout was shellacked in place, and her brow remained a dewy peach in contrast to my dripping flush. Ugh.

"Don't you know how to prevent that? You live in *Texas*." She handed me two thin panty liners she'd whipped from her bag. "Here, stick these inside the pits of your dress and it will sop that right up."

With that she sauntered back to her original destination, and I crept to the bathroom while the ceremony continued. Baffled, I tried to figure out how the things worked. Horizontally or vertically? I finally stuck them inside my underarms and hoped they didn't show.

"Lottie, please report to the tent," crackled over my earpiece. With panty liners in place I dashed out of the bathroom.

The reception tent was rigged with a custom lighting system that projected twinkling constellations in an evening sky. Every table had a massive floral centerpiece draped in lush white flowers and dripping with crystals. The china, crystal, and sterling silver were brought in from England. Fun fact: just *one* sterling place setting cost roughly $800. The gilded custom stage for the orchestra-style band would have been suited to a Roaring Twenties New York City ballroom. Ornamental bushes dotted the room, trimmed to resemble the constellations brought to life, from the Hunter to the Big Dipper.

However, the crown jewel was the head table, a round mirrored table underneath a huge hanging ring of white orchids, peonies, and crystals—and in front of a solid wall of five thousand white roses and ranunculus. The sight was truly breathtaking.

Just then, Cedric ducked over to check on the space. "Oh, Libby, there you are. I desperately need someone with floral expertise or this tablescape will be *ruined*. One batch of hydrangeas must have been left in the truck or something and have already started wilting."

"Um, it's Lottie . . ."

"Whatever. Come help me fix these centerpieces. They're positively tragic."

A flair for the dramatic, brilliant design chops, and impeccable diction were not Cedric's only distinctive qualities, I pondered as I trailed him. He wore a fedora and designer sunglasses both day and night, indoors and outside, along with at least one Hermès accessory. This time, it was an ascot. His salt-and-pepper hair was luxuriant; his designer clothes impeccably tailored. He also carried a tiny Yorkie—Prince Charles, or PC for short—anytime he wasn't at an event.

In my years around Dallas's wedding world, I'd heard all about Cedric. He could execute parties that most people would never even imagine. Dallas socialites heaped hundreds of thousands, if not millions, of dollars upon Cedric to plan and design their dream debutante ball, birthday soiree, wedding, or even the occasional baby shower (and not always in that order). His wait list, while choosier than the Vaquero Club, still stretched longer than traffic on the Turnpike.

Cedric employed a large staff of "minions": the project managers, floral designers, and production workers who made his visions come to life. Working for Cedric guaranteed a job anywhere in the event industry. He'd built a business from scratch to become the best of the best in our part of the world—and was poised to join the ranks of the country's most prestigious planners.

No wonder Abigail had leapt at the chance to go from his occasional floral contractor to a full-time team member—but I felt woefully unprepared for this level of "eventing." Still, it was time to prove myself proficient to Cedric in the one area of wedding details I already understood: fixing expensive flowers.

All the tables were named after constellations, and we faced the offending centerpieces at the Big Dipper and the Little Bear. In the scheme of big-day disasters, this was minor. Cedric waved his hands at the bothersome bouquets and winced.

"Don't worry, I can fix this." I grabbed the closest caterer and sent him for a cup of boiling hot water from the kitchen. I pulled out the wilting hydrangeas one by one, recut their stems, dipped them into the boiling water for about thirty seconds, and then placed them back into the arrangements.

It took a few minutes, but this trick would perk the flowers right up, at least for the next hour or so. Didn't people know hydrangeas were the absolute most finicky flowers? I also grabbed some floral wire to prop up some of the worst offenders. At least they weren't dead. There was no resurrecting a bloom once it had completely wilted.

As I worked, half forgetting that Cedric was breathing over my shoulder, rearranging the most leafless to the inside and plucking petals off the seats, the arrangements started to resume their intended shapes.

Clapping sounded right next to my ear. I almost knocked over the closest vase, I was so startled.

"Bravo, Libby! Those look *marvelous*." With that he hustled away.

I wiped the sweat from my forehead—*Thank you, Mary Ellen, for my armpit panty liners*—then returned to my post at the rear of the tent.

As the ceremony ended I stood by Abigail, waiting at attention. Her long braids piled atop her head—and off her neck. Smart. And her dark-brown complexion, I noted, was as unaffected as Mary Ellen's. What *did* these women know that I didn't?

Guests streamed in from cocktail hour to the seated dinner. We were on table-directing duty for the moment.

To accompany the theme of "*The Secret Garden* meets *The Great Gatsby* in outer space" (with James Bond parachuting vibes thrown in), the seating cards were vintage paddle fans for the men and vintage lace folding fans for the women, both dotted with Swarovski crystal constellations and the names embossed in gold script. The constellation table names, while clever, meant that no one could look for the numbers near theirs to find the right spot. Lots of rich people wandered around, holding fans up to table centerpieces and appearing puzzled. We tried to help when we could.

"Thanks for handling those flowers." Abigail nudged my shoulder. "I've told him over and over for *years* that hydrangeas can't take the heat, but he believes they will magically bend to his will one of these days."

"Seems like most things *do* bend to his will."

"Ha, very true. The trick with Cedric is to pick your battles—and don't be afraid to fight the ones that matter. I've known him since he first came to Dallas. When you know what's right and it could make a difference, push back. His bite is pretty bad, but he rarely does more than bark."

"Thanks, I'll try to remember that next time," I said with the frantic hope that there would be a next time.

"Lottie, you're doing great. Don't stress so much about screwing up someone's wedding and just do the tasks in front of you."

Working with Abigail had truly been a dream. She had the kind of warm aura that you want to snuggle up to. I was anxious about no longer being her direct report but was grateful she'd still be around the office.

"Yes, ma'am." I nodded.

"How many times do I have to tell you, don't call me *ma'am*!" She laughed, brown eyes twinkling. "Now go help those poor guests find their way to their constellation. Next time I'm going to insist on regular table numbers."

I headed over to the seating assignment table to gauge guests' progress and see how many people had yet to pick up their fans. As my eyes scanned the names, they stumbled upon one I'd hoped not to see for a long time: Mr. Matthew McKenzie, in calligraphic flourish. *Crap.* I'd have to avoid him at all costs, which wouldn't be a problem. Blending into the background was a primary reason why we wore black at weddings.

Once guests finally found their seats, dinner service was prompt and the catering team operated like a well-oiled machine. Three-course gourmet meals to five hundred people was no small feat. I watched in awe as Mary Ellen seamlessly directed the happy couple through their cake cutting and first dances, while also instructing the necessary vendors involved. She was clearly a pro; I had a lot to learn about wedding planning.

An hour later, I spotted Matt across the tent near a group of guests on the dance floor. Wavy brown hair, tall, with deep-set hazel eyes and the shoulders of a swimmer under his crisply tailored tuxedo. Yep. Still made my stomach clench. I ducked behind a screen.

From my hiding spot, I strategized how to avoid him all night. Matt started to turn in my direction, so I jerked my head back—right into cold, hard metal.

"Ouch!" I pivoted to face what turned out to be a camera lens, then gazed up into a scruffy dark beard and wide, horrified brown eyes.

"Gosh, I'm so sorry!"

I frowned and rubbed my skull. "Couldn't you have given me a heads-up?"

"Sorry, I'm supposed to stay out of sight, so this is one of the best angles on guests without being in their way. I thought you saw me when you came back here."

"Obviously not," I interjected.

"Well, when you leaned out, it meant I could too. I didn't expect you to jump back like you saw a ghost."

I sized him up while I checked for blood. Heavy work boots and dark not-quite-skinny jeans. (In Dallas, straight men are known to walk a fine line between slim fit and too tight.) Tight black V-neck that belied a solid, albeit lanky, frame. Thick, unruly black hair. Puppy-dog eyes behind retro glasses and enviably tanned, tawny skin. All in all, the prototype of a Dallas hipster-nerd. Of course he was a photographer.

"I'm Griffin." He extended the hand that wasn't wielding the camera. "I work with Val."

Like most other wedding vendors, good photographers came with a team of their own. This couple had hired one of the top photogs in the state: Valeria Trujillo. She had started shooting for magazines before most of these brides and grooms were born. After a climbing injury on a *National Geographic* shoot, she'd scaled back to covering events. Her rates were still upward of $25,000, but the health risks were far less. But when couples got photos "by Val," they were usually getting a mixture of her takes and her entourage of promising young photographers, eager for the chance to learn from a master. While she prominently roamed an event, her assistant's job was to sneak around and capture candid shots. I only knew all this because of a feature in *D Weddings* I'd thumbed through during a slow night at Neiman's, my side hustle workplace until recently.

"I'm Lottie." I took his proffered hand. "When I'm not having my skull beaten in, I work with Cedric." I crossed my fingers and hoped that was the truth.

"So you're one of the trust fund girls who parade around with clipboards while the grunts do all the work, huh?"

Before I could craft a dismissive retort, I got a call over the walkie to come out behind the main tent. "Nah, you couldn't be more wrong, but excuse me, I've gotta go be one of those 'grunts' now," I said as I waved a hand over my shoulder and hustled away. I was absolutely going to have a knot on my head. *Many thanks, Griffin.*

One of the new interns, Claire, paced outside the tent, freckled cheeks pale and terrified. I had just met Claire a week ago when she was assigned to help me help Mary Ellen. I didn't know her well yet, but she seemed competent enough. My adrenaline started pumping when I saw her face.

"Lottie, we need you down at the dock," she said, close to tears. "There's been an accident."

I didn't bother asking what kind of accident, just hustled down the path to the water as fast as possible in heels. An elderly grandparent could have tumbled down the steps—or something worse—so I barely noticed my surroundings in the mad dash. The night smelled like wet moss and roses. Hidden ground lights lent the path an otherworldly glow. No wonder people found this place magical.

Cole and Gemma were supposed to end the night floating across White Rock Lake in a vintage wooden rowboat that cost more than most people's cars. The fireworks would burst above them—and a few subtle spotlights would make it possible to snag a final round of photographs as they rowed into the moonlight.

Cedric's new batch of interns had been tasked with tying a Just Married sign to the back of the boat and getting it into position. But the boat came untied (probably while they all took selfies on the job) and was now floating away. All the other helpers were back in the main tent, wrangling guests and getting the bride and groom ready for their final dance. The interns freaked out, unsure how to fix the situation. So they called me. I'd like to think it was my Zen-like unflappability, but more likely they hoped that as a fellow low rung on the totem pole, I might berate them less for the mistake. They weren't necessarily wrong, but only if we could fix this.

All the pleasure boats available for rent on a normal day at the arboretum had been hauled away for the event. I scanned the shoreline, hoping for a stray canoe or something.

As I stood there, Griffin, who had followed me down from the tent, spoke up. "When I was scouting the angles earlier, I saw some of the kids' boats docked not too far from here."

With no other option presenting itself other than swimming out into a dark lake in the middle of the night, I turned in Griffin's direction. "Lead the way, buddy."

As we rounded the corner I saw the "boats" Griffin had referred to. He'd neglected to mention that they were paddleboats—and they were all shaped like swans. *Swans.* White textured "wings" flanked the sides, and a long neck and head arched over the passengers. The paddle itself, ignominiously pedaled by said passengers, was orange and made to look like webbed feet. The overall effect was hideous and tacky, and I could understand why Cedric had mandated they be completely out of sight of the guests.

Nevertheless, I was out of options. I untied the closest bird boat and climbed in, then slipped off my heels so I could paddle. Before I could push away, Griffin hopped in next to me.

"You really don't have to—"

"It's no problem. We'll go faster with two."

The hipster had a point. We pointed the bird across the moonlit water and pedaled as hard as we could. We had about thirty minutes before the wedding party trekked down to the water, ready to send off the happy couple. Once again, I was grateful for the panty liners soaking up my sweat.

Too polite and Southern not to make small talk—a religion in its own right—I spoke over the sound of splashing paddles. "So, what's your deal? Where are you from?"

"I'm from Austin. You?"

"Memphis, but I came here to go to TCU."

"Very cool. I went to A&M."

It was hard to get enough breath to speak, but I managed. "So, how did you get into wedding photography?"

"Well, I'm not really 'into' wedding photography," he wheezed. "I'd rather shoot nature or editorial stuff than these"—inhale—"overpriced brouhahas. Like, it's a lot of money to blow on a party. Why bother? But I've always been a fan of Val's older work, so when I got the chance to work with her, it seemed foolish not to take it."

There were about three points in there to address—starting with why people might bother getting married—but before I could interject, he continued. "How did *you* get into weddings?" He smirked. "Just biding your time until your own big day?"

Did *everybody* in town know that that was a thing for Cedric's staffers? "No." (Yes, but I could pretend that zero marital prospects meant I just loved the work.) "After college I started working with a florist who ended up becoming one of Cedric's partners. I followed her here. It's not really where I thought I'd end up either, but here I am."

He nodded, then quietly gazed at the water.

I tried not to quietly gaze at the way his shirt pulled tight across his shoulders as he leaned into paddling. Or to inhale too deeply as his woodsy cologne floated on the breeze, which was a challenge amid all the huffing and puffing. Just because I'd sworn off dating, refocusing my priorities didn't mean I couldn't appreciate the rare opportunity to be, you know, near a man.

After what felt like eons, we finally pulled up next to the wooden boat. How had it gotten so far in such a brief amount of time? Thank goodness we hadn't tried to swim out. We'd have needed that helicopter back for a lake rescue.

We gingerly stepped inside, grateful to be out of the paddleboat that was beginning to make my calves burn. I sat in front while Griffin tied the swan to the back of the boat. Then he picked up the oars to row us back to the dock. I glanced at my watch: ten minutes left.

Cedric timed his weddings with the precision of a drill sergeant. There would be no extra time.

I covertly watched while Griffin strained at the oars. Lugging around a heavy camera had certainly done his biceps good. Had I not been sweating profusely, this could almost feel like a date.

We pulled up to the dock just as the revelers reached the top of the path. Their sparklers glittered in the shadows cast by the trees. I tied the wooden boat to the pylon, shooed Griffin into the bushes, and made a mad dash there myself.

Guests lined the path as Cole and Gemma made their way through the row of lights. I could barely see them from my perch behind some ornamental shrubbery, my MO for the night apparently. Griffin's job was to document their progress. Music played from hidden speakers. The overall effect was magical, celebratory, and thanks to a bit of quick aquatic prowess, seamless.

The newlyweds climbed into the vintage boat. Cole grasped the oars, something he couldn't fake this time, and Gemma arranged her skirt just the way Mary Ellen had instructed her. They shoved off the dock, waving at their guests. It was the perfect good-bye.

Then it hit me. I tried to run out onto the dock, but it was too late.

Panicked, I glanced around. Maybe no one noticed my mistake. But then I saw Cedric and Mary Ellen at the top of the stairs, pointing toward the lake and looking bewildered. In my haste I'd forgotten to untie the swan boat from the back of the getaway watercraft. As the bride and groom made their way to the center of the lake, under a canopy of fireworks, the hideous plastic bird trailed them.

I moved my gaze across the group of guests starting to disperse now that the send-off was complete. Many of them were chuckling as they headed back up the stairs. Of course, my eyes landed directly on Matt's face. He waved. *Double crap.* I was zero-for-two.

I heard the sneaky *click* of a shutter, then whirled around. "If you so much as show those photos to your boss—or anyone—then I will *end* you. Pretend you missed the moment or something."

"Are you kidding me?" he scoffed. "The light and the fireworks are perfect."

"Can't you Photoshop the bird out? You people are always editing stuff in and out of photographs, right?" It might not save my job, but it felt good to direct my frustration at someone.

"No way. Plus, my job is to capture the truth. Yours is to keep stuff like this from happening. Even though, I gotta say, it's pretty hilarious."

Ugh. Maybe I'd need to find yet another backup plan if wedding coordination didn't work out. But as I gazed at the happy couple holding hands under the fireworks and their contented guests waving from the shore, I hoped deep down I'd get at least one more chance.

TWO

If any space could perk a girl up, it was the Cedric Montclair Celebrations office. I hadn't heard anything from Cedric himself, but Mary Ellen had pulled me aside during the postwedding teardown to tell me we would discuss the swan fiasco Monday. I considered not being fired on the spot a win.

Big Saturday weddings compressed our entire weekend into one "off" Sunday and a late start on Monday. So around noon, I crawled through the oversized red lacquered doors, triple-shot latte in hand. Months into the job, the space still felt to me like a beautiful Fifth Avenue boutique. One with glass desks and gold MacBook Airs. Everything was chic and sleek, white, and red—Cartier red, to be exact.

The ambiance made one feel sexy, like a million bucks, which was probably the precise intention. I, however, usually just felt reminded that I was, as legally defined by the IRS, broke.

Cedric held court from his office near the two front meeting rooms. Lined with brass bookcases and featuring a velvet chaise longue for "brainstorming," it was immaculate and intimidating. A tiny white linen cushion rested on the floor next to Cedric's white desk, the only concession to his tiny Yorkie, Prince Charles. PC traveled in his own tote bag most of the time but was allowed the cushion when he was "working" with Cedric. From his domain Cedric could witness the comings and goings of his staff and clients—and he didn't have to walk very far from the front door. If the man sounded a bit like a cliché, well, he leaned into it, God love him.

But the man truly guarding entry to the palace of parties was Travis. He only worked "for fun," whatever that meant, as his partner was a top stylist who made a fortune dressing the wealthiest Dallasites. Travis had two Birkin bags, clearly gifts from his partner. It drove Cedric crazy with jealousy. One of the bags was white, which was a total power move because white said, "I don't care if I get dirty," despite costing more than Travis made in a year.

Though Travis was a glorified secretary, he was the most important person in town if you were planning an event. He had the power to book a meeting with Cedric tomorrow or in two years, depending on his mood that day and whether or not he liked you. He'd been around, seen it all, and could shut you out before the social season even started. Those bright-blue eyes could laser in on a fake Louis Vuitton from fifty yards. He was invaluable as The Firm's gatekeeper.

Travis was at his post, bushy tailed as always. "Ohmigod, how was your first wedding? I heard that the helicopter went off like a *dream*."

"Yes, I managed not to screw up anything with the ceremony at least. Though I did send the couple across the lake dragging a swan-shaped paddleboat, which will be documented in Dallas's society pages forever. But they got married, which is a win, right?"

"If you say so, puffin." He patted my hand.

Despite my lack of Saint Laurent handbags or Valentino shoes, Travis had taken an instant liking to me. He was always willing to help out at least one of the new minions each year, especially those who, in his opinion, lacked a sense of personal style and taste. As offended as I should have felt by this, I considered myself lucky. Travis was always willing to give me his opinion on my attire and ask a million questions about my love life, or lack thereof. And despite my being somewhat of a pity project, I took pleasure in knowing he cared about me, in his way.

"Thanks, Travis."

I trudged down the hall to my desk.

Behind the meeting rooms was a large common area where most of the project managers and upper-level planners worked. Mary Ellen and Abigail were both ensconced there. Each had a glass desk, a white lacquer filing cabinet, and a few small clear cubes in which they could store pens and pencils but not much else. Forget about a family photo or any personal knickknack. If you put out anything remotely sentimental, you might as well start packing. Cedric wouldn't stand for it.

From her perch Mary Ellen could keep an eye on the junior staffers—and Abigail. It was rumored that Mary Ellen had pitched a fit when Cedric brought Abigail to the team instead of simply buying her inventory and client list. Abigail had told me, grudgingly, that she and Mary Ellen had a bit of a fraught history. They'd disagreed over publication credits a couple times over the years.

In the small, fiercely competitive world of high-end events, they were two alphas trying to survive—and working for Cedric was a dream job for those aspiring to make a career in the business. It might not have been personal, but the fact that Cedric put the two of them in a shared office showed that (a) he didn't know about their tension, (b) he had a wicked sense of humor, or (c) he simply didn't give a rip. My vote was option C.

Cedric definitely had a type. He preferred the ultra-polished girls who showed up in *Chloe* over us average, off-the-rack gals. When I got to college, I had highlighted my hair within an inch of its life in an attempt to fit in with my sorority sisters. (I worked two nights a week at Neiman's to afford the dues.) Jeans and a cute top—with heels, of course—were once the weekend uniform, but these days, my weekend uniform tended more toward Nordstrom Rack funeral chic, and my hair had darkened back to its natural dishwater state. Only once had Cedric ever commented on how much he liked my outfit, and I considered those clothes sacred.

Cedric was known for gifting his favorite employees with a pair of the latest Louboutin pumps, and it was painfully obvious who was "in" or "out" at the time based on the soles of their shoes. I would be waiting on mine for a long time, maybe forever—especially after the swan incident.

Past the common area was another open space, this time with fewer windows and a half-dozen Parsons desks. Here sat the assistants. I slipped into my shared cubicle, thankful for a moment of quiet. Intern Claire, my newly assigned desk mate, likely wouldn't be in for hours. She and the other "Trusties"—as I liked to call the trust fund girls from Dallas who frittered about the office, biding their time until their big payouts at twenty-five or thirty—typically didn't show before 2:00 p.m. on Mondays.

As Trusties went, Claire didn't seem as bad as most, and I was trying to withhold final judgment. Slim and smartly dressed, she had, like almost all of the other Trusties, long blond hair that was blown out every day. My midlength dishwater mane got washed every three days at best. *Thank you, Lord, for dry shampoo.* However, unlike the others, Claire had a constant smile and one of those annoyingly cute faces (adorable dusting of freckles included) that drew you in. It could have been worse.

Every day at Cedric Montclair Celebrations was like stepping into the abyss. No one ever knew which version of Cedric would be waiting. Or what other wildcards would walk through the door. Even Mary Ellen cringed behind her desk most mornings as he swept into the office, and they were supposed to be friends. In this case, the devil wore ascots.

I sat at my desk, determined to work and not think about either of them. An email popped into my in-box. From Matt. He'd seen me at the wedding and was disappointed we didn't get to talk.

Oh, Matt . . . I recalled how two years ago, Natalia and I were celebrating Cinco de Mayo, as was our tradition, at a Deep Ellum bar. I typically marked the night with questionable amounts of alcohol and even more questionable decisions. I'd just turned twenty-seven (hello, late twenties and spinsterhood). Harper was married and Megan had just started dating her now-fiancé, making Natalia and me the last of our college group with no rings and no prospects. For the girl who was supposed to beat everyone else to the altar, it was the perfect recipe for wallowing in self-pity and desperation.

I vaguely recalled sidling up to Matt's broad shoulders to order my third or fourth margarita. (I usually fell asleep after two.) Matt remarked how cute my muumuu was. He had just finished business school at UT and was back at his parents' house for the summer before taking a big sports agency job in Miami.

My memory got foggy. I was already three margaritas in, and He. Was. Really. Hot. As our respective groups whittled down and my drinks accumulated, a sloppy makeout in the corner was inevitable. I wished I could say we had a deep connection or even that the night was especially steamy. But all I really remembered was kissing at the bar, followed by an enormous hangover the next day.

Less inevitable were the late-night drinks at Capitol Pub a few nights later. (My mamaw used to say, "A gentleman always calls within two days of the first date." Oh, Mamaw. If only you'd known what dating looked like in the 2000s.)

We went on several sober dates that summer, but he was leaving for Miami in the fall, so we both knew what it was—and what it wasn't. By mid-August I quit answering his texts and phone calls and put him on limited Facebook access. He eventually stopped checking in with me.

Replying to him now would have required facing my own personal shame, which I was comfortably wearing like a sweater, thank you very much. Delete.

I scanned through a couple vendor invoices and then spotted an email from griffinflo86@gmail.com.

Dear Ms. Jones,

I regret to inform you that there seems to have been a snafu at your recent event at the Dallas Arboretum and Botanical Garden. Somehow, a rogue swan attached itself to one of our delightfully rustic-chic rowboats. We're investigating the matter. In the meantime please accept this altered version of reality, sans swan boat.

Sincerely,

Griffin Flores and the DABG,

probably

PS: I'm sorry for what happened and hope you don't get into too much trouble!

I chuckled quietly, saved the edited photo to send to Gemma, and fired off a reply.

Dear Mr. Flores,

While your skillfully modified photograph might not be sufficient to save this lowly assistant planner's position, I am certain that the happy couple will appreciate your documenting the day as it existed in their imagination.

Gratefully,

Lottie Jones

PS: Thanks for helping me paddle. And for this. ☺

I looked up, and Mary Ellen was hovering over my desk.

"Lottie, let's chat."

Before she could tear into me, I tried to explain. "The boat had come untied from when the interns put it into place, so I had to go get it before everybody came down there."

"I still don't understand how a giant bird got stuck to the back."

"Well, that was the only other boat left on the lake, so we used it to bring the dinghy back . . . And then forgot it because we were so focused on getting the boat tied up and ourselves hidden before the guests arrived."

"Who was helping you?"

"One of Val's new assistants." *The one with puppy-dog eyes and great hair.*

"Hmm. I see." She pursed her lips a moment. "Well, fortunately for you, Gemma's family thought the whole thing was some *hilarious* prank by the groomsmen. I started to explain that it was a mistake, but they were so charmed by the whole thing that I decided not to burst their bubble. Cedric played along, too, when they handed him an extra tip for the added amusement. Go figure."

I couldn't believe what I'd heard. "So I'm not fired?" *Did I say that out loud?* I'd just said it out loud.

"No. Just try to keep waterfowl out of the picture from now on. Literally. With a less-weird family, this could've been a real issue. It ruined the final image of the wedding that will be ingrained upon every guest's mind. With these kinds of clients there can be no more slipups. They pay us a small fortune to provide perfection, or at least the illusion of it."

I assumed the extra tip would never make its way to my pockets and considered it the cost of not losing my job. Mary Ellen wasn't known for her magnanimity or collegial attitude, to put it mildly. She'd made multiple assistants and vendors cry. One of our rental companies wouldn't work with her because she'd made too many of *their* assistants cry as well.

But she was an amazing saleswoman. She could, as they say, sell oceanfront property in Arizona, which was good and bad. It became clear very quickly that Mary Ellen, like Cedric, would tell clients that *anything* was possible and then expect everyone who worked for her to deliver on that promise—no matter how ridiculous. Of course, the weddings always came together. Promises were delivered. And not one bride below the Mason-Dixon line didn't want to work with them.

⁓⚬⁓

Two days later, I was making phone calls at my desk. Finding a baker who could make a gluten-free, vegan wedding cake that didn't taste like earwax was proving futile. It shouldn't be impossible in this day and age. But telling Mary Ellen I'd failed to track down a bride's must-have wasn't an option either. As I started to dial yet another dead end, Cedric stormed into the open office area.

"Attention, ladies." He rapped a Baccarat crystal tumbler against the wall of the nearest cubicle and anxiously shuffled his blue suede Hermès loafers. Always with the Hermès. "I need everybody to come in here. Chop chop!"

He led the way to one of the two large client meeting rooms in the front office. Each room was wrapped in gold Gracie hand-painted floral wallpaper that cost as much as a luxury vehicle. White velvet curtains embellished with red-tassel trimmings framed large frosted windows; natural light poured in, but no one could see the parking lot. Massive flat-screen TVs displayed images from Cedric's past events on a constant loop and often helped banish any hesitation—if the on-hand Piper-Heidsieck hadn't done the trick—before signing a contract.

Once satisfied that the team was assembled, Cedric cleared his throat so gratingly that I almost offered to give him the Heimlich maneuver.

"Now, everybody knows that my partner, Geoffrey Berry, is opening a new luxury spa-retreat center near the Chattahoochee National Forest." Yes, Cedric, we all knew because you pasted copies of the *Garden & Gun* article in the break room and both bathrooms.

"As he begins to spend more time in that area, I've decided to do so as well. The time at the spa and with Geoff will do me good, seeing as I stress too much and work too hard and run myself ragged with this business." He paused to stare pointedly at each of us. "I'll be able to unwind and get in touch with nature, like hiking and things of that sort. And I can focus more on building our dream home there and establishing our social calendar."

I struggled to envision Cedric hiking through the hills, a dust-covered Hermès cravat at his throat.

"But because I'll be down there more, I've decided to expand our business. Atlanta is exploding. Now, it's no Dallas, but many big companies are based down there, not to mention the movie and TV people, music execs, and tech billionaires who have also come to town. They may not have tickets to the symphony or a box at Truist Park to watch the Braves, but they have private jets and houses in Malibu—and the best *Real Housewives* franchise, in my humble opinion. And they want weddings to rival Sean Parker's or Beyoncé's. So, what this means for you darlings is that we're opening a second office of Cedric Montclair Celebrations in Atlanta!"

He paused for dramatic effect. No one clapped; we just looked at each other, unsure how to respond. Cedric shook his head as if we were children whose development was significantly behind expectations, then continued. "We're aiming to launch the office next spring, so over the next couple months, we will begin the process of setting everything up and utilizing our existing vendor relationships.

"None of this should really trouble you all. But I am going to be restructuring how we run things around here and making some big hires, including a lead planner to run that office. So everybody be sure and bring your A-game to our current slate of clients. I'd much rather promote from within and avoid having to completely retrain everyone. God knows I spent enough time turning all of you into functional humans. Well, that is all. Any questions? Good."

He clapped twice and retreated to his office.

I stood, mind racing. Sure, the lead planner job in Atlanta would go to Mary Ellen if she wanted it. But I looked around the room and could see the staffing dominoes that would fall after her promotion. By spring I could be in a position to move into one of the lead planner roles here. After that, the boost in salary (and actually keeping the clients' tips) could make a big difference for my student loans. Plus, a girl had needs, like sensible shoes and cash for tacos. I might even be able to move into my own place.

I loved living with Natalia, but if I really wanted to prove that I could make it on my own, even that would have to end eventually. In my mind's eye I imagined purchasing a new wardrobe, signing up for dating apps that cost money, meeting the husband of my wish list, and finding my life completely changed by my thirtieth birthday.

Later, I sidled up to Abigail at the sleek marble countertop bar in Cedric's version of a break room. The Nespresso machine gleamed. (I credited him with teaching me the difference between a latte, an Americano, and a flat white.) The fridge was stocked with nine different types of milk and dairy alternatives, although the skim and cashew were not-so-subtly positioned at the front of the shelf and more frequently restocked as an encouragement. I usually used a splash of half-and-half out of spite. This Memphis girl didn't do nut milk.

Abigail perused the snack basket, her dark braids today plaited down her back in typical laid-back-yet-impossibly-chic style. Kashi bars, chia seed packets, fresh fruit, and ethically sourced turkey jerky were the day's offerings. I often made a lunch of whatever was available. God knew the Trusties weren't indulging, so I felt it was my duty to make sure the food didn't go to waste.

We often had thank-you gifts of food sent to us by clients, and they invariably made their way to the break room counter too. Magnolia Cupcakes and Jacques Torres Chocolates were a current favorite, but I wasn't picky when it came to sugar. I grabbed a local baker's crispy rice treat and leaned against the bar next to Abigail.

"So, big news today, huh?" I said tentatively.

"Hmm . . . yeah. I guess so." She sounded distracted.

"This is great news for you and the other partners, right?" I crunched too loudly into my snack.

"Yes, if it succeeds in bringing in more business. It's also a lot of additional overhead, so I'm worried about how everything will work out. Cedric will have a new lease, staffing needs, insurance, and so on. A lot of logistics to manage."

"Have you thought about who you'll ask to go there? I hope you know how much I've appreciated getting to work with you and learn from you. It's meant a lot that you were willing to bring me with you when you came to Cedric's team." There. I'd probably shown my hand too quickly.

"Lottie, you know I think you're a fantastic asset to the team."

"But?"

"Do you want my honest advice?"

"Yes, I think so?" Honesty was one thing I had always been able to count on from Abigail.

"You're a hard worker; you're more organized and reliable than anyone I've ever worked with, which is why I promoted you at my shop. But you just started here. There's a whole staff of junior and senior planners and even assistants who have been here years longer than you. So you've really got to stand out between now and next spring. I'm your biggest advocate, but Cedric will make the call.

"You've also got to work to impress his other key people, like Mary Ellen. She's not usually inclined to like staffers she didn't directly hire or groom herself, so you'll have to really hustle to win her over." Abigail started reaching for a Snickers bar, cut her eyes at me, and put her hand back on the counter.

"Thanks for the insight." I recognized my cue to let her get back to the snack tray. "Please let me know if you think of anything else or have other tips between now and then."

"You know I will. I'm rooting for you."

It sounded like I shouldn't start looking at studio apartments just yet, but at least I had a road map.

I walked back to my desk in the pod, musing. I passed Claire and the other Trusties huddled together still gossiping about Cedric's news. Savannah, a redhead from Houston, painted her nails carelessly on the clear acrylic of her desk. Those girls had no idea what was coming for them.

THREE

The Blue Bell ice cream selection at Kroger was pretty thin, which wasn't what I wanted to see after a long day at the office. We'd been ironing out details for a big wedding in New Mexico and come across some construction snafu. As a result Cedric had been especially snippy, which traveled way down the food chain to me.

I threw in a pint—okay, a gallon of Cookie Two Step and another of mint chocolate chip along with the leafy greens and other organic produce I'd virtuously placed in my cart. I grabbed a couple grocery store bouquets to rearrange for our table at home. Fresh flowers had become my version of sparking joy.

While standing in the epic line, I glanced at the rack of magazines to my left and eyed the healthy cooking tips and wedding planning guides. Speaking of joy . . . ah, *People*'s Sexiest Man Alive issue. My annual reward for good behavior slash celibacy. This year, one of the Hemsworths was back on the cover. But then my eye caught on the cover chip, the small inset photo. "The NFL's Hottest QB" read the caption below, and my heart sank as I stared at Brody's wide grin and uniform.

I grabbed the issue and shoved it in my cart, too, as my number on the overhead screen popped up. What could I say? I was a glutton for punishment. And a snoop.

It had been years—well, at least six months—since I'd gone on a news-clipping deep dive into what Brody was up to. He no longer had personal social media, so I had to read celebrity news like the rest of the world.

That night, over two flavors of ice cream, I allowed myself to snuggle up on our plaid hand-me-down sofa with the magazine. I read the brief Q&A about his hobbies (riding dirt bikes and cooking barbecue), his favorite charity (Make-A-Wish), and his love life (currently single but with a few famous exes mentioned in parenthesis), and it didn't hurt the same way. I looked at his goofy, handsome face and mostly wished him well. Our relationship felt like a lifetime ago, and I supposed it was.

But as my eyes started to glaze over, I briefly imagined that alternate version of my life. The pang was enough confirmation that I should probably avoid celebrity news on the internet for a while.

Years later, it still stung to recall our final conversation. After I tried to explain why we could make things work—a desperate, embarrassing showing on my part—he finally cut off my objections with a torrent.

"It's not just that, Lottie. When we started dating, we were like a team. Two scholarship kids pushing each other, reaching for our dreams. It was all I could do to keep up with you. You were . . . hell, a steamroller. You had all these crazy-big plans for law school and politics, family and 'having it all' or whatever. And no one was going to get in your way. Now it feels like if I asked you to just follow me around to games and practices, you would."

"That is unfair and untrue," I sputtered. "I just—"

"You've changed. Or maybe I have. But I'm tired. Tired of being the only one who really wants something, who's motivated. What if I got hurt? Would you still want me without football? And what would we do? It's a lot on one person. I don't know . . . I care about you, always will. But maybe we've stayed together because we're good together and it's easy, not because it's right."

I thought he was overthinking it. And I preferred *loyal* and *devoted* to *unmotivated*. But it cut. I'd still wanted those things. I just wanted him *more* than all that. Apparently, that wasn't enough.

I could admit to myself, with the wisdom of an, ahem, almost-thirty-year-old, that he wasn't *entirely* wrong. I'd finished school with no real experience, no plan, and no fallback option.

For the first six months after graduation, I had picked up extra shifts at Neiman's, but that wouldn't cut it once my lease ran out. With pretty meager savings and student loans coming due, I had the choice to find a new job or move home to Memphis. Boomeranging wasn't really an option for my brother, Tom, or me after the recession wiped out our parents' savings and tanked their home equity.

Tom had joined the navy and planned to stay through retirement, which meant his living expenses were practically covered in perpetuity. No oil magnates or tech entrepreneurs had lined up to marry me yet, but fingers were still crossed.

Like a good roommate, Natalia had swooped in to save the day. I'd been griping one day, per usual, about my lack of career prospects, boredom with LSAT study prep, and general poverty and heartbreak. I'd signed up for the next test date, figuring three months was enough time to get back in the legal mindset—and find a useful activity to pad my skimpy résumé before I applied to law school.

"Lottie, shut up. We all know you spent the last two years actively *not* trying to become a lawyer or any other useful member of society."

"Yes, but—"

"No buts," she quipped while filing her nails short. "You basically wasted a four-year education because you were busy scrapbooking wedding collages and making secret Pinterest boards. Don't pretend you don't have file folders of wedding décor clippings that could work for each major market Brody could have been drafted to. There's gotta be a California bohemian beach wedding in there, as well as a Southern rustic-inspired barn reception . . . But that's just it."

"What?" I was clueless.

"You've spent all this time planning your dream wedding and fantasy life—that's literally the only experience you have right now—so why not use it? Didn't you even take that series on wedding planning or home ec or whatever they called it?"

A lightbulb went off. I called Abigail, who'd taught a couple sessions of A History of Weddings and Ceremonies (a *very* important sociology class that counted toward my political-science major), and asked if she ever needed an assistant or extra set of hands. Turned out, she wanted help for a bridal shower she was throwing the next week in Highland Park.

I figured I had nothing to lose, so I hopped on I-30 from Fort Worth a few days later, with no clue as to what I had agreed to do. I helped create a large bassinet covered in white rose petals (the classy alternative to a diaper cake) and mixed pink peony-and-tulip centerpieces. My only prior "experience" was helping with my dad's landscaping business and arranging flowers for our sorority alumni events.

That first day working for Abigail, I pulled off perfect centerpieces and even managed not to drop any champagne flutes. Afterward, she handed me $200 and offered to call the next time she was in a pinch. She hired me a couple other times for the standard bridal shower or birthday party, and eventually I got her to bring me on full time as an assistant.

Mom and Dad weren't totally thrilled with my new job, given that it was about as far away from practicing law as I could get. (I'd never confessed my premature wedding plans, or how they derailed me, so my parents' befuddlement got a pass.) However, they *were* thrilled I was getting paid while I figured things out. My mother had said one evening over the phone: "I guess that silly wedding class you took senior year wasn't a complete waste of your time."

As Abigail's business expanded, she trained me on event logistics, floral competency, and the ins and outs of the planning world, at least from the perspective of a boutique firm. Most of the work wasn't especially satisfying, but I discovered that the skills I'd assumed would rocket me to the top of a law firm—being quick on my feet, problem-solving, and managing people in stressful situations—also came in handy at events. Even my tendency to envision the absolute worst-case scenario was an asset.

Apparently, I'd also convinced Abigail of my competence, and she was a tough sell. I even surprised myself. I helped digitize her systems, pitched her to be on a few Black female entrepreneur lists, and expanded her social media presence. Abigail's event company was soon landing bigger clients—and attracting the attention of Cedric Montclair. There I was: Lottie the wannabe lawyer, turned wannabe bride, now florist extraordinaire.

A year or so into the job, I'd tried to muster some of the fire I used to have about law school, cramming for yet another LSAT date and saving up my party tips to pay the entrance fee. The whole Elle Woods vibe. But my college memories of torts and court opinions were a bit rusty, and after taking—and bombing—it twice, I admitted defeat for the foreseeable future. Elaborate baby shower and ladies' luncheon flowers might not be my passion or even really engaging

97 percent of my brain, but they paid the rent in a city that didn't include Graceland.

Working in weddings was a bit torturous for someone who still secretly hoped her big day would arrive. I couldn't help feeling like I had lost my best chance at a happy ending: husband, kids, domestic bliss, the whole enchilada.

But nothing to do about that tonight. Tonight, I needed to turn off my brain, savor the Blue Bell, pop a melatonin, and get a good night's sleep. I had a rehearsal dinner to work tomorrow, and Abigail was right about stepping up my game with Mary Ellen. I also knew I'd never make it through cake cutting if I didn't rest, and there was no way I was missing out on cake.

FOUR

One of the first things any planner did the morning of an outdoor wedding was to check the forecast—again. We typically stalked the weather radar on thirty different apps ten days out from any event, especially in Texas, where the climate was unpredictable. (Yes, I was more active on my storm-tracking apps than husband-finding ones.)

Fortunately, the forecast for this wedding predicted sunny skies and a high of ninety degrees, which was a bit warm for September. But at least no rain was in the picture. As soon as I finished watching The Weather Channel and downing a triple latte, I dashed over to Highland Park to help with wedding-day preparations.

The groom, Alfie, was marrying for the third time, and his bride-to-be, Camila, was younger than one of his daughters (and me, for that matter). Alfie was a wannabe rock star in his early sixties who had amassed a fortune in the hospitality business. His efforts at starting a rock band proved fruitless, but his latest hotel's signature martini was famous in Dallas and a legend in the food-and-beverage world.

Alfie's personal style aspired to a Mick Jagger but ended up a Joe Exotic. His long, greasy ponytail did little to conceal his bald pate, and he never failed to show up to our meetings wearing the same rainbow-colored paisley silk shirt, unbuttoned halfway down his chest. The effect revealed both patches of chest hair and also that his future bride must be in this for reasons other than his physique.

Camila was a stunning midtwenties Latina woman. After moving to Dallas, she met Alfie at one of his hotels, and "the rest was destiny" (clearly the words from their wedding website, not mine).

They came to us only three months prior to their desired date, at the end of September, one of our busiest months. But once they told us that the sky was the budget limit, we managed to rework our schedules.

We spent eleven intense weeks planning a gorgeous garden ceremony and reception for 125 guests. The couple would wed beneath a canopy of white orchids and thousands of lavender garden roses on the terrace, nestled between their expansive grounds and glittering pool, which featured Alfie's initials engraved in gold like buried treasure. After the ceremony everyone would move to the back of the garden for drinks, dinner, and dancing under a large open-air tent full of expensive catering, candles, and crystal chandeliers.

Cedric's advance production team had arrived much earlier that morning, so by the time I showed up, the backyard was just about ready. Mary Ellen was, of course, running the show, so I touched base with her.

"Oh, hi, Lottie," she said without looking up from her clipboard. Sometimes I thought she recognized people by scent. "You're *finally* here."

"Sorry to be a little late," I fumbled. "There was a wreck on—"

She held up a hand to cut me off. "It doesn't matter. Now, I have all the outside preparations well in hand. I need you to go inside and do the wedding party head count, then check on the cake and the caterers."

Mute, I turned and headed off.

First stop: the wedding party. We typically took attendance at multiple points the day-of. You never knew when a bridesmaid would sneak away for a brief errand or a groom might get cold feet. So we checked in as often as possible while still giving them the illusion of privacy.

Because Alfie was older than our typical grooms, the groomsmen were also older and didn't seem to care much for formalities by this point. They had showed up to the rehearsal last night boozing and smoking cigars and ready for dinner. It was like the typical frat-boy antics without the pliability of drunk young men, who could at least usually be flirted with or bossed into submission. I saw that today was going to be much of the same. Normally, we wouldn't allow this to happen, but Cedric wasn't here, and those "good ol' boys" clearly weren't going to listen to two "sweethearts" tell them what to do.

"Excuse me," I said with as much sugar as I could muster. "Are you gents ready to line up when the time comes? Does everybody know their spots, or should we go over them again?"

"Listen, darlin'," said one gem of a man. "I've been in more weddings than years you've been alive. Why don't y'all just go grab us a few beers and let's call it a day."

Before I could even think of a reply, he turned his back to me and resumed playing cards with the best man. Well, at least he didn't smack my backside as I turned to go. Lucky me.

The groom's daughters from his first marriage were also wild-cards. At the rehearsal Alfie informed us his two "little girls" (both women in their twenties) were still deciding if they would make an appearance at the wedding. They were extremely unhappy with their father's choice of new fiancée and had cut all communication with him the last few weeks.

I couldn't blame them. We saved them seats in the front row, if for no other reason than an "in memoriam" moment.

Next stop: the cake. The couple had ordered theirs through one of Alfie's hotel pastry chefs, and it was three tiers of buttercream-frosted flowers that cascaded down all sides. One thing Cedric taught his planners was to consider where a wedding would take place and what was most appropriate for that setting—especially when it came to the cake.

For example, if the couple wanted their wedding cake displayed at an outside reception, they were limited to the type of frosting since many varieties melted in warm temperatures. Obviously, ice cream cakes were almost always out of the question, not only because they melted but also because they should only appear at toddler's parties, as Cedric was quick to say. Meanwhile fondant, while gorgeous, wasn't always the tastiest but could withstand a nuclear attack.

We gave Camila and Alfie the gentler version of this spiel, but they insisted on savory buttercream regardless—and agreed to leave the cake inside on the big day. I had doubts about how much the bride actually loved cake anyway, given that she looked as if she maybe ate one piece of lettuce a day. But, "A wedding without a cake isn't really a wedding"—another one of Cedric's truisms, this one inspired by the Candy Bar Craze of 2009 and the Great Doughnuts of 2013.

As I moved closer to the elaborately decorated table where their cake was displayed, I noticed something was amiss. The cake was too close to one of the massive windows, with sunlight streaming directly onto it—ninety degrees of direct Texas rays.

I froze in horror as the cake pulled a Wicked Witch of the West and melted on top of itself. One colossal piece of floral frosting dripped off the side of the cake, landed smack-dab on the table, and then fell to the floor. Phrases like "not good" came to mind.

Claire had just shown up and was handing out bouquets and pinning boutonnieres on groomsmen, so I radioed her to join me at the disaster.

"Quick! Help me pull the cake away from the window," I said once she arrived, her mouth dropping open at the sight. We heaved the mushy monstrosity a couple of feet into the shadows and turned down the air-conditioning to about fifty degrees—no need to take any more chances.

Frantic, I dialed the baker to see if he had time to come back to the house and fix the dilapidated tower before guests arrived. But no, he was stuck on a shift at the hotel.

Claire and I worked like mad to fix what we could, using toothpicks we found in the kitchen to fasten the frosting back to the cake. It was a pathetic effort, but we didn't have many options. Thankfully, only one side of the cake had been in the direct sunlight, so the other side seemed a bit droopy but was at least not the stuff of nightmares. We pinned up and smoothed out as much as possible, then turned the cake around. With one crisis semiaverted I headed upstairs.

Camila, our blushing bride-to-be, was running extremely late, and the glam squad was moving at a snail's pace.

"Hi, Chaz, Gloss." I nodded sweetly at the hairstylist and then the makeup artist who frequently worked events for us. "Could you two speed it up a teensy bit?"

Two pairs of heavily lined eyes blinked owlishly at me.

"My love," Chaz purred after a pause, "you cannot rush perfection. We are creating a *masterpiece*." Then he turned back to Camila's brunette mane dismissively.

"Do not worry, Lottie." Camila patted me on the hand as she

perched on a stool. I always love to be patronized by someone younger than me. "They can't start without me, right?"

Nevertheless, I offered to gather the items she would need to get dressed and put them all in one place to speed up the process.

As I moved about the palatial bedroom, I noticed a few key bridal objects were missing.

"Excuse me, Camila?" I didn't want to interrupt the methodical application of eyeshadow. "I can't seem to find your shoes and tiara."

I have long believed that only a true princess should wear a tiara at any time in life; I don't care if a bride thinks she is God's greatest gift, even on her wedding day, a tiara is just tacky unless you're Queen Elizabeth.

"Oh! They're in a bag from the last fitting out in the car. My keys are in the Louis Vuitton purse." She gestured toward a shelf of handbags.

I went to fetch the car keys, but after ravaging through her closet for a good ten minutes, we discovered that her purse was in the Range Rover too.

"Do you think we could do the ceremony without the tiara? I also see at least ten pairs of gorgeous shoes in your closet that would work," I pleaded.

She looked at me like I had three heads. "No, absolutely not! I've waited my whole life for this moment, and it took me forever to decide on those exact ones. I'm not walking down the aisle without them."

The ceremony start time was quickly approaching, and I now had a bride with no shoes, tiara, or jewelry. For Camila, this was the biggest tragedy of her life. For me, this was one calamity too many, too soon into my new job.

"Doesn't the car have a service where you can call the company and a satellite will unlock the doors for you?" My mom once used similar technology when she locked my little brother in the car.

"Yes, yes, it does!" Camila mumbled as the makeup artist tried to put on her lipstick.

"Where is the information on who to call?"

"Oh. It's probably with all the other registration documents . . . in the glove compartment."

I pressed my face to the bedroom window. The $200,000 special-edition car sat in the driveway, taunting me. A casual wedding gift from groom to bride, it had Wi-Fi and satellite long before such things were imagined by other car owners. The fully customized interior featured details such as *Camila* inset in Swarovski crystals in the steering wheel and headrests.

I wanted to handle this situation without Mary Ellen, so I sprung into action. I called a locksmith, making thinly veiled threats of bad Yelp reviews if he didn't get over to the house ASAP. Then I booked a second locksmith, hoping at least one of them would show up fast. As a second backup I dispatched Claire to one of the nearby Preston Road boutiques to buy or borrow a replacement tiara if it took too long for the locksmith to arrive. I then headed downstairs to wait and monitor the situation in the garden, where Mary Ellen was still supervising. Guests would be arriving shortly.

At 1:45 p.m. sharp our first guest pulled up to the home for the ceremony, which was scheduled to start at 2:15 p.m. I glanced out the window of the home to check on the valet. Only three parking attendants were waiting to park cars, and a massive line of cars was forming in front of the home.

As I'd learned in Cedric's wedding binder of rules and ratios, for a residential wedding with 125 anticipated guests, you usually wanted to book ten valet parkers to keep traffic moving and avoid any kind of wait, which was what we'd told the groom. However, Alfie had insisted on using his regular parkers from one of his restaurants, so he booked directly and only hired three.

One of the reasons clients hired a planner was to help them make smart decisions. It was always fun to get paid for your expert opinion, only to have the client decide you were wrong and they were right. Admit it or not, they always wished they had listened to us in the end.

It was too late for us to find additional attendants, so I ran back to the catering tent and grabbed a few bored-looking servers and sent them to help with valet. I crossed my fingers that none of them would drive off with one of the many Porsches or Teslas that showed up. I might have, given the chance. Then after dealing with the valet situation, I raced back to Camila's car to await the locksmiths.

From the driveway I could see through the back gate to the lawn, where most of the guests were already in their seats, positioned in direct sunlight. Usually, guests could be seated in the sun for a ceremony as long as everything started on time. If there was a slight breeze and a short ceremony, all was good. But as our start time came—and went— the more delicate Dallasites began to wither. Wedding-planning 101: don't make guests wait—for anything.

Finally, I caved and radioed Mary Ellen.

"Lottie, *what's* the holdup? Where is Camila?"

"She's refusing to get married without her tiara and her special sparkly shoes . . . and unfortunately, she locked those in her car. But don't worry," I said before she had a chance to say anything. "I've already got two locksmiths on the way, and Claire is out looking for alternatives as we speak."

"Oh, blessed mother, I'm heading up to you both. She's got to get down here *now*." (I pulled the blaring walkie away from my ear.) "I'll talk to her myself. This is ridiculous."

I waited. Would Mary Ellen actually talk sense into her? It seemed futile. Sure enough, twenty minutes later Mary Ellen radioed me back. Her efforts at bartering with this bride had failed too. I felt slightly vindicated.

This princess wasn't going to budge without her tiara, and she seemed completely content to make her poor guests sweat it out while we waited for the locksmith.

"I don't care what you have to do—jimmy a lock, steal a crown from the queen—but we need a tiara for this bride *now*!" Mary Ellen half shouted in my earpiece. "I give this crowd another twenty minutes before pure mutiny begins and we lose all control. Stay downstairs and I'll keep working on Camila."

I tried to stall guests as best I could. Not much could be done when everyone was already seated and there was nowhere to escape the heat.

Things really started to go south when Alfie ambled over, sweating in his tux, thirty minutes after our planned start time. His lanky ponytail, which had been nicely groomed at the beginning of the day, was beginning to glisten from more than pomade. "Ma'am, my eighty-seven-year-old mother is about to have a heatstroke, and if this were a concert, we'd have to start giving refunds soon. Where's Camila?"

Sure enough, the mother of the groom was perched precariously on the edge of the pool, her dress hiked up around her knees, her orthopedic heels sitting next to her. The lady had the right idea. Valentina, the flower girl, was splashing her bare feet in the water beside Alfie's mother, likely soaked but content. Begrudgingly, I explained to him about the tiara fiasco.

I hated having to let clients know about something that had gone wrong since usually the issue could be resolved without their knowledge. However, I thought maybe he would want to try and convince her to get started, and selfishly, I didn't want him to blame us either.

Alfie didn't miss a beat. "Break. The. Window," he said. "Just get that tiara out. I know my baby wants what she wants, and I give you permission to do whatever it takes. We'll deal with the window later."

"I really don't think that will be necessary, sir. The locksmith is on his way—"

"Just bust that window and get her the crown thingy. I mean it." He spun on his heel to check on his mother at her poolside perch.

As I hustled past the guests to the driveway, I radioed Mary Ellen, explaining my new orders to make sure I wouldn't be fired for destruction of property.

"Sounds like the situation is rapidly deteriorating," she said. "If he gave you the go-ahead, I say go for it. Keep me posted."

In all my years working for Abigail, I'd never been told to so much as break a floral stem. I battled the sense of wrongness while walking over to the pricey Range Rover. *Please hurry, locksmith.* As I moved toward the offending motor vehicle, I realized I needed a weapon strong enough to break the window.

The catering tent stood next to where Camila and Alfie parked their vehicles, so I stuck my head inside to see if they had anything that would work. As soon as the staff figured out what was going on, they were more than happy to assist me. Three young men darted off into different directions in search of the perfect tool for the job. What was it with men and breaking things?

The first server came back with a nice garden brick, and the second came back with a poker iron, presumably swiped from a fireplace inside the house. The third server didn't come back at all. (I began to believe I'd gotten stuck inside a very bad joke.) The brick seemed like the best option to try first.

I reared back but couldn't quite bring myself to let the brick fly, wilting like a daisy. I asked the server if he would be willing to throw it, and he acted like he'd won the lottery. The bag of bridal goods was in the passenger seat, but we decided to bust out the back window so we didn't get glass all over the front seats.

The first server reared back and, with more enthusiasm than I would've preferred, hurled the brick. I braced myself for the sound of shattering glass. But the brick bounced right off the window and back in our direction.

We ducked to avoid a direct hit and watched in amazement as the brick fell to the ground without leaving so much as a scratch. What the living hell?!

Were Alfie and Camila somehow involved in the Mafia or a drug cartel and riding around in cars with bulletproof glass?

I allowed the second server to take a stab at it. He smiled at the opportunity and moved toward the same window, poker iron in hand. Once again, I braced myself but then watched in horror as he smacked the window as hard as he could with his metal rod.

The iron bounced right back off of the glass too. The waiter was so shocked he released the poker and it soared off into the bushes. What a joke. I might have expected this from a Hummer, but not a British car known more for needing replacement parts than actually keeping people safe. I was at a loss as to what to do next.

Operation Destroy the Car Window had failed, but then a beacon of hope appeared in the driveway: a locksmith. I was so happy to see him that I almost jumped into his arms.

After examining the vehicle for a moment, he turned. "Ma'am, it's a good thing you couldn't bust out the window."

"Pray, tell me why?"

"This particular beauty's alarm system would have gone off, for starters. Lasts for at least four minutes."

The car was quite close to where all the guests were seated for the ceremony. They would've been hot, sweaty—and deafened. Even if we were able to send the bride down the aisle, I'm not sure if Pachelbel would have had the desired effect when paired with a squawking car alarm. And Alfie or Mary Ellen would probably have had my neck at that point.

Before I could respond, he delivered the final blow: "And I can't get in either. This tricked-out new model has too many antitheft features for my tools . . . That will be one hundred sixty-seven dollars, please." He held out a hand.

It took everything I had to keep from pulling the poker iron out of the bushes and whacking him with it.

Panicking, I radioed Mary Ellen. The car was Fort Knox. No one would be getting inside it today or ever again, for that matter. At least she hadn't made any progress upstairs either. But she would keep trying to talk Camila into getting her highness to the garden.

My whole body drooped. What would I do with my newfound freedom once Cedric fired me? I had $400 in savings and a hefty monthly loan payment. But maybe I could run away to the Bahamas and waitress at a beach bar? Sell sarongs at a dive shop? But then the sight of a slightly familiar lanky frame creeping around the fence interrupted my reverie.

"*Hey, you!*" I yelled at Griffin, who had just ducked behind the garden fence.

"Fancy seeing you here on this lovely day, nothing to do but enjoy slowly evaporating."

"Yes. About that. Any chance you know how to break into a Range Rover without setting off its alarm?"

He moved in my direction. His dark curls seemed unaffected by the humidity that had left my hair as frazzled as I felt. How annoying.

I quickly explained what was going on, including the bulletproof glass, but when he burst out laughing, I gave up.

"Never mind." I took a deep breath and turned to go update Alfie.

"I'm sorry, I'm sorry," he gasped between laughs. "You have to see how ridiculous this is though, right? Also, sounds like something that should not be covered under your job description."

I gave the Range Rover one last glance-over before I abandoned it.

"This is insane," he said. "And the bride really won't come down?"

"Trust me, we've tried everything, but there's no reasoning with her. At this point you might as well go up there and give it a try . . ." But I trailed off when Claire's red Jetta rounded the driveway like a ray of light in a storm. She stepped out of the car with a large bag in hand. *Could it be?*

I left Griffin in the dust and ran to the front of the house. Hallelujah! Claire quickly unwrapped not just one but three new tiara options for Camila, on loan to us from one of the couture bridal salons in town.

I gave our heroic intern a giant hug, grabbed her arm, and dragged her up the three flights of stairs to the bride's room. While holding our breath, we presented Camila with the new tiaras and, to my surprise, she was more than pleased with our selections. Though it wasn't hers, it was a tiara, nonetheless. She probably felt impatient herself, finally ready to get this show on the road. Praise be.

We shoved the new headpiece on top of her head, threw on one of her two hundred existing pairs of shoes, and whisked her downstairs to the ceremony.

As we began the processional, a few of the guests actually clapped. I avoided looking toward the fence, where I knew Griffin was perched, for fear he was still chuckling under his breath. The moment the ceremony ended led to a mass exodus of sweaty socialites. I'd never seen so many people sprint to the bar after a service just for water.

Alfie and Camila were finally legally wed and bound for their version of happily ever after. But we still had hours of work ahead.

"Hey, Lottie?" asked Claire. "Who are *those* girls?" She gawked at the entrance to the reception tent.

I followed her gaze and we both laid eyes on two extremely tall and gorgeous women who had just strolled in. Who came to a wedding after the ceremony? (Tacky people, that's who.) The glamazons were dressed from head to toe in Valentino and looked like they came straight off the runway.

I approached one of the young women, hoping to sniff out whether she was a wedding crasher or not. "Are you a friend of the bride or the groom?"

"Neither!" she said with a toss of her thick, dark-brown hair. "We're Alfie's daughters. We weren't going to come, but we decided it would be more fun to actually show up and ruin the wedding."

Talk about literal. Subtext and these girls were not friends.

"Oh, hi," I replied. "Well, you missed the ceremony, but cocktail hour has begun. The first dance will be starting soon."

"Perfect." She walked between Claire and me like we were a pair of black curtains.

In truth I felt a little scared. Claire and I exchanged worried looks.

"Why is it that hot, mean girls are still intimidating, even a decade after high school?" I winced.

We watched them march off, determined to keep an eye on Alfie's spawn. After about thirty minutes of cocktails and hors d'oeuvres, we pulled Alfie and Camila onto the dance floor.

The DJ was yet another vendor booked directly by the groom. As a "musician," Alfie was pretty patronizing about our ability to distinguish a good disc jockey from a lousy one. How hard was it to plug in an iTunes playlist? All this from a man whose primary musical references involved men in velour wide legs or crop-top tees.

I gave the DJ a nod, which was his cue. Mary Ellen had gone over the announcement and song list with him countless times that morning, and for the first dance, he was supposed to play "Amazed" by Lonestar. (My first dance was always going to be something Coldplay, but Lonestar is a classic choice.)

The DJ announced the couple. As Alfie took Camila in his arms and spun her around, the strains of Kanye West's "Gold Digger" blasted across the tent.

Camila and Alfie stood paralyzed on the dance floor, staring at us with horror on their faces. Mary Ellen just about leapt on top of the DJ's equipment in an attempt to shut it off. He immediately understood he was in huge trouble, and after a few seconds of fumbling, Lonestar started to play.

Although we tried to recover the best we could, the damage was done. The couple danced together, but Camila's face was ashen as she clearly fought back tears.

Mary Ellen and I cornered the DJ to threaten his life, but he told us the groom's daughters had given him the orders, telling him it was a funny joke that their future stepmother would love. How could anyone believe jokes were ever appropriate at weddings?

Apparently they had also given him $500 to play the song, which really sealed the deal. There was nothing scarier than a mean girl with a boatload of cash.

"Well, let's just stick to the schedule from now on, okay?" Mary Ellen said through her teeth while staring him down.

"Yes, ma'am," the DJ replied, realizing he would probably not get the balance for this gig. After all, Mary Ellen could be scary too.

We moved on with the schedule and hoped to gloss over the incident. (Though I was pretty sure that if the heat hadn't given Alfie's mother a stroke, the musical selections probably had.)

Mary Ellen sent me to set up for the cake cutting since I was the most familiar with maneuvering "two-faced triple cream." I wasn't going to let the glamazons screw that up, even though it would be difficult to make that cake look any worse.

As I headed inside the house I noticed that every single picture of the couple was missing. The two beautiful assassins were nowhere in sight, but in their wake were gaping holes on the wall.

After taking a second look at the cake, I radioed Mary Ellen that it was probably best if we just brought Alfie and Camila inside and left the guests out of it. The icing on one side still looked like molten lava.

We turned the wonky side toward the newlyweds—and away from the camera—and Alfie and Camila assumed their positions, Mary Ellen instructing them on which tier to cut and how to hold the knife.

Before Griffin started snapping away, I leaned over to whisper, "Hey, I meant to thank you for the swan-less shot. I hate to sound pathetic, but would you mind trying to keep all the pictures from this side? We had a bit of an icing incident earlier."

"Sure, not a problem. Nobody really wants to see the insides of a cake anyway," he whispered back. "But now you have me curious. Please tell me that one of the guests grabbed a handful while waiting for the ceremony."

"It would be more likely that Alfie's daughters used their fingers to write *whore* across the flowers."

He laughed. "They *terrify* me. So much tall and hair and evil eyes."

"I feel like most guys go for that," I said without thinking.

"Nope, not me." He winked.

"Really? All tall, dark, and brooding, like—well, like you."

"Nah. They seem uptight and mean."

I reined it in before the conversation could digress further. "So, the *icing* . . . The cake got left too close to a window and now closely resembles Two-Face from the Batman movies."

"Oh gosh, that's almost as horrifying to imagine as this wedding night," he quipped, and I couldn't help but snicker. Mary Ellen shot daggers at me.

The couple finally got their hands sorted out and he raised the camera to his eye, back on duty again. I stepped back and tried not to grimace at the traditional spectacle of two adults shoving cake into each other's faces and licking each other's fingers.

Remarkably, the next hour went smoothly. Two more hours remained before the bride and groom's scheduled departure, and though it was a weird crowd, they seemed to be enjoying themselves. But I clearly had relaxed too soon. Out of nowhere I heard a noise from the sky. No way. Nothing in the weather report had suggested bad weather today. Seconds later, the entire sky opened up.

That's what we got for living in Texas. Hot as blazes one minute and drenched in rain the next. Total mayhem erupted. Guests squealed and rushed into the house to take cover. It was like a wet T-shirt contest at the Bellagio.

As the rain came down sideways, the tent did little to shield anything from the storm. Camila burst into tears, and we dragged her and Alfie into the home. Mary Ellen took Camila upstairs to help her dry off, and I headed into the kitchen to find towels for the guests.

Instead, I found seven of the guests eating the remaining wedding cake with their hands. Griffin had called it. Man, he was good. They looked like *Survivor* contestants who hadn't eaten in weeks. Cake littered the counter and floors, and the guests seemed to think it was perfectly natural to behave like Neanderthals.

I chuckled and grabbed a handful of towels to take to the rest of the guests who were packed in the front foyer of the home.

Most everyone looked like they were trying to leave—or escape— and the storm had ended this party early. It felt like a blessing. I hadn't spotted the daughters since the first dance, and this wedding was clearly cursed.

Without enough valet attendants to accommodate this kind of situation, a cluster of cars was trapped on the street. The caterers were frantically trying to move everything out of the main tent and salvage what they could. As to be expected the pathetic DJ was huddled in a corner room smoking and drinking, and Griffin and the other photographers busily captured every moment of the wreckage. This event was not going to wind up in the local wedding magazine, a mantel portrait, or anywhere else, for that matter.

"You know, you don't *have* to take a picture of everything that goes wrong at one of our weddings." I sidled up next to Griffin to peek at his camera display.

Sure enough, he'd captured all the high points: the melting cake that resembled a monster, the grandmother about to die of heatstroke, the cringy ex-bandmates, even the devious and leggy stepdaughters. I thanked the Lord he wasn't nearby while the waitstaff and I pelted the car with blunt objects.

"I told you," he sighed, "my job is to capture the truth. And like they say, 'Sometimes the truth is ugly.' Your job is to manage that ugly and try and make it pretty for just one day. I don't envy you a bit."

"No, my job is to create the ideal circumstances to make two people as happy and relaxed as possible on the greatest day of their lives."

"Who are you, Walt Disney?"

"Lock it up, Griffin." *Good one, Lottie.* "Actually, never mind. It's too soon to joke about anything getting locked up. Just, cut it out, okay?"

"No prob, and kudos to you for creating these ideal circumstances for the lovely couple. I'm sure they're destined for a lifetime of genuine happiness."

"What's that supposed to mean?" I huffed. "I know they're a bit of an unusual match, but . . ."

"I'm only saying these things don't work out more often than they do, right? And it seems the odds are stacked against them even more in this case."

"Sure, you may be right there, but you don't have to be such a cynic."

"Maybe I am a cynic. That's why you'll never catch me on the other side of the camera at one of these." He began to pack his lenses into the bag.

"Really? What do you mean?"

"Absolutely. The odds are never on your side. Hard pass."

Before I could splutter my halfhearted defense of the institution, Mary Ellen buzzed in my ear. "Lottie! I need you! We've got to find more towels!"

I waved a hand at Griffin as I walked back up to the bridal suite. Surely he hadn't meant all that. But the fun ones were usually fatally flawed, so I shouldn't have been surprised. He could still be a good person to work with, and Lord knew I needed a solid list of allies in this business. That was for sure.

Mary Ellen and I decided it was best to move up the departure and get Alfie and Camila on their way to the nearby hotel they'd booked for the night. Alfie's friend had agreed to chauffer (naturally), so we lined up the few guests who remained and pretended to shout in delight as the couple raced through the foyer to their car, leaving their dumpster fire of a reception behind. Good riddance to one of the most disastrous weddings in the history of Cedric Montclair Celebrations.

The valet took another forty-five minutes to clear everyone out, and then it stopped raining. Typical. Mary Ellen, Claire, and I went back to the garden to survey the mess that awaited us and to send all the vendors home. Mary Ellen called dibs on sending off the DJ, but by her expression when she met back up with us near the pool, we could tell something bad had happened.

"Well, the DJ isn't going anywhere, but we certainly are," she said.

"What do you mean? He isn't leaving?"

"While we were dealing with this train wreck of a wedding, Alfie's daughters convinced the DJ to stick around and play for a party they've arranged inside the mansion."

"You've got to be kidding me," I said.

"Nope. He told me that he doesn't work for me and that we should just go. I'd almost say screw them and let's just leave, but we've got to pack up, so we might as well see what those little she-devils are up to."

We stepped into the foyer to find the entire men's soccer team for the nearby university toting bottles of liquor up the giant circular staircase. Right behind them were the evil daughters, who informed us the party was just beginning for them. Not only did they pay the DJ to stay, but they also took all the remaining liquor from the caterers. Apparently, the girls were resetting the house for a party of their own while Alfie and Camila were gone for the night.

"We are *so* not getting paid enough to deal with this," said Mary Ellen.

"Agreed." I watched five frat stars stumble out of the kitchen with more half-eaten cake in their hands.

After all, these girls were of age, they technically "lived there," and it wasn't our gig anymore.

"Let's make sure everything from the wedding is accounted for and then get the hell out of this house of horrors," she said.

As we left we could hear the bombastic strains of the DJ blasting "Gold Digger" again. This time, no one cried.

FIVE

After another harrowing wedding weekend—the bride's stomach got upset after putting on her $8,000 Reem Acra gown, and guess who had to help her keep her skirt out of the splash zone?—I needed a day to unwind. To put it mildly.

And, unlike my coworkers, I didn't use my lunch break to squeeze in a Pilates class. All my exercise, if any, took place on days off. Today I really wanted a workout and the resulting endorphins, ideally followed by Whataburger, of course.

Natalia was training for a triathlon fund-raiser for colon cancer because that's the kind of optimistic masochist she was. She also had three bicycles, which I could never understand, seeing as she only had one butt. But she was always offering to let me borrow one, so that Sunday we put on as much off-brand athleisure as we owned, attached our bikes to the back of her car, and headed to White Rock Lake.

Late September in Dallas was too sweltering to do anything stationary, so biking was perfect. The cool breeze, the sweat wicking away from my skin, and the impossibility of keeping up a conversation as we wove in and out of pedestrians. Just what I needed.

We headed east toward the arboretum. Soon White Rock Lake

lazed by us on my left. It was nice to be here for a reason other than work, and I marveled at how dramatically it had improved in the years since I'd moved to Dallas. The lake used to be full of trash and the paths overgrown and beat up. But the city had decided to improve its green space now that everyone had become so crunchy—or at least pretended to be—making the area a mecca for cycling, jogging, and myriad water activities like canoeing and paddleboarding. It was an oasis just ten minutes from downtown, with clean, sparkling water and lush vegetation.

The lake glistened, blue as the reflected sky, and I started to lose myself in the rhythm of pedaling. My thighs started to ache. My back tensed. Sun beat on my forehead and the backs of my hands. Sometimes I wanted a do-over, a restart. Something to wash me clean. Reset opportunities not taken, paths not pursued, love lost. And, not to add to the cascade, if something washed away my student debt, too, I wouldn't have complained about that either. I churned over scenarios for Cedric's new office and how that could play out. Doors that could open, ways my life could get back on track to my ideal future.

But if I couldn't wash, I could burn the mistakes and missteps away. I pressed into the pedals, deep in my own thoughts, and I almost slammed into Natalia as she stopped suddenly.

"Whew! Let's take a break." She sounded way too cheery for someone who'd clocked a dozen miles.

My lungs heaved too much to answer her, but I nodded, flinging sweat into my eyes. Nat was always the Sporty Spice to my Baby Spice. (I wish I could claim Posh, but as Cedric had reminded me twice last week, my sense of style was still nascent.)

We dropped onto a patch of grass facing the lake; our bikes lay flat next to us.

"Almonds?" She held out the bag.

"Are they Marcona or regular?"

"What do I look like, Whole Foods?"

"Are they salted?"

"Easy there, bougie." She lay back on the grass, long black ponytail fanning around her head.

"Listen, I may have low standards for my dates or, ahem, my friends, but with food at least, I'm old enough to know what I like and not waste my time on the gross stuff. Which is why I prefer over-indulging with Blue Bell and decent rosé."

Natalia Vargas, my best friend of over a decade, was the person who knew my favorite pizza toppings (pepperoni and olives), my first kiss (Rory at a youth group lock-in, where else?), and which vintage *Tiger Beat* poster came with me to college (Devon Sawa, obviously). We could tell when the other one needed a nudge.

"Fair, Lottie. Fair." She closed her eyes, sun on her golden-brown face.

I often coveted Natalia's boundless optimism, even if it got her in trouble on occasion for being ill prepared. I, for one, packed a daily tote bag of anxiety and gloom along with my ChapStick and extra cardigan. I liked to believe it gave me a knack for foreseeing obstacles, but it also gave me a recurring prescription for Ambien.

I pulled out a bottle of sunscreen from my fanny pack and started to douse myself with it.

"Good call, you're starting to look pink," she confirmed, half opening one eye. "Missed a spot on your jaw. I *did* contemplate not telling you."

"You're a real pal, huh? I can end up crisping like bacon on these long rides." I rubbed in the remaining white smears.

"I happen to love bacon. It's one of my great passions." At this, I lobbed my sunscreen at her exposed stomach. "Oof! Okay, I'll stop."

We sat in silence for a beat, watching couples paddle across the lake in kayaks and canoes, none of which were swan shaped.

Since I'd started working at The Firm, I often came home with stories about the latest bridezilla or covert pictures of Cedric's latest Hermès accessory. This week it was an orange leather belt with a polished gold *H* buckle that one could see from space.

To fill the quiet I started in on the event from the day before. "Someone should have warned that bride about barbecue the night before a wedding. I swear the poor thing washed it all down with jalapeños . . ."

Silence.

"And then you should have heard her mother tear into her. She started to ask if the groom had seen her attack a slab of ribs before he proposed, but that was when Mary Ellen cleared the bridal suite. With a mom like that, who needs Jenny Craig? Oof."

"Hey, that's a doozy, but how's everything else?" she said without looking at me.

"Yeah, yeah, it's all fine. Work is good, family is crap, romance is dead—the usual."

"Don't give me 'fine.' What else is going on? You've seemed distracted today."

"I don't know. Been thinking a lot about college lately, which is weird. You ever just wonder how things could have been different?"

"Yeah, all the time. That's why I watch *Sliding Doors* and read all those books about parallel universes."

"You're such a goober. Give me at least one moment to be earnest."

"I am too. And the truth is, everybody has things they'd change about college and their twenties and probably for the rest of time. That's just life," she said, smug in her wisdom. "But on the subject of changing things, have you heard from Matt again?"

I think Natalia held some small hope that Matt would hoist me over his swimmer's shoulders and carry me away, vanquishing all residual regrets. And if I was unavailable, I was pretty sure she'd be amenable to a similar hoisting situation.

"Well played." I laughed. "And the answer is nope, not since the first three unreplied emails."

"Charlotte Louise Jones, you have got to answer that man. He could be the *one*. You never know. He's better than most of the ogres on Bumble."

"I don't know about that. You've found some real winners there."

"Ugh. Don't get me started." She shuddered. "You know, you working every single weekend is really killing my—I mean, *your* social life."

She had a point. We barely saw each other because of our schedules. "Yeah, I'm not exactly on the prowl these days."

"I'm only one girl. I can only join so many kickball teams or singles' groups on our behalf. You've gotta do your part. How else do you imagine ever meeting somebody?"

"I mean, maybe I never will." I fiddled a long stem of grass between thumb and forefinger.

"Don't say that. It's literally been one of your biggest dreams since I've known you. I remember when you read that *Cosmo* editor's book for a freshman seminar and it became your mantra: I *can* have it all. It makes me sad to think you'd give up on that, especially if you've given up on law stuff too."

"I couldn't get in at this point." Ironically, or perhaps fittingly, I struggled to muster a defense. The grass was now braided into a chain. "Even if I could, I'm already drowning in debt. There's nothing left to go to more school. That dream fizzled out a long time ago."

"Well, I have to admit, I'm glad you went for it, but I certainly never thought you'd stay in event planning."

"Me neither. But it's better than I thought, I think. Don't get me wrong, Cedric is like Dr. Jekyll and Ms. Wintour—you never know who is coming to work. And his number two, Mary Ellen, is more of a pit bull in a Milly skirt. But the events are spectacular and the clients, while über rich, are also mostly sweet, if a little much."

"That's good. It would be a bummer if you spent all your time planning parties for terrible people."

"Touché. If I stay with the team, there may also be some solid room for advancement."

"So, then, is that the new dream?" She backed off. For the moment.

"Heck if I know." I half lied. I didn't want to admit that I had recently started dreaming about running Cedric's new office. I certainly couldn't say it out loud yet. "Find a handsome oil baron client of ours and then pull a runaway groom sort of situation? We could escape on his private jet, and no one would know where we went. That should be my next plan. I dunno, what's *yours*, Nat?"

Natalia did something in sales, but truthfully I had no idea what. She worked for the US headquarters of a Chinese manufacturing company that made buttons, shoelaces, and other garment minutiae. It was a testament to the recession that her company was now building a plant outside Dallas to utilize cheap American labor, instead of the other way around.

"I don't know either," she said. "You know I got moved into the marketing department last month, which is great, and there are more women here than when I was in sales and client relations. Those departments at my company are a total mix of good ol' boys from multiple continents, all equally uninterested in my opinions. But I was so excited to be on this senior VP's team. Elizabeth was made VP at thirty-three, the youngest person ever. She has a reputation for being a generous mentor and for putting her assistants up for great jobs in the company. Her former assistants are all junior execs now. I thought I was going to get promoted right away too."

I was so proud of Natalia. She had found a path at this company and stuck it out. Her enthusiasm and drive seemed limitless. Her indecision and self-doubt were, well, significantly less than mine.

"The thing is," Nat continued, "the longer I work on her team, the less I see the path ahead. As women we need to see it to be it, right? We have to see someone with a life and a career that we want. Elizabeth is forty-two now and has never been married, other than a broken engagement in her twenties. That's par for the course for all the female execs. They work late during the week, go to the gym in our building, and then work on the weekends too. None have any semblance of a personal life. No kids, at least none that I know of. No functional romantic relationships. So, I'm not saying marriage is the be-all, but I look at the women ahead of me, and no one has a life I want. And we're not in New York or LA, for Pete's sake. This is *Dallas*. If you can't have it all here, then where can you?"

"Well, I'm probably not the one to give advice on that. Where I work, the people who have the lives we want pay us to make theirs possible."

"And you're happy with that?"

The question hung in the air.

"If we're going to make it back before noon, we should probably get going, right?" I stood abruptly.

I pedaled back around the lake double-time. My feet clanged with every turn of the chain. *Ding. Ding. Ding. Ding.* Measured and precise, my feet worked as I mulled over our conversation.

Trees clinging to their leaves whirred by. In Dallas the seasons didn't change in graceful, vivid colors. Leaves simply exploded in a riot one day, fell off the next. Spring arrived with the same urgency and violence. Want to tell winter good-bye? *Boom*, cherry blossoms.

I started thinking about the rest of fall, our craziest wedding season. We had six megaweddings in October alone.

"*Lottie!* Look—"

I focused my eyes just in time to notice the narrow concrete pylons in the middle of the path—and slam into one.

All I was aware of next was lying on the path, grit and gravel stinging my palms. I rolled onto my back and did a quick inventory. My knees were bruised but protected by the Spandex. My neck? Not so great.

Nat knelt by my side. Her bike fanny pack had gauze and antiseptic pads. She helped me back on the bike. Somehow we limped back to our apartment, where I spent the rest of the afternoon propped on the couch with an ice pack pressed to my knee.

Later, Megan came over for wine-and-movie night. I let her in the door and waited while she took off her shoes. There were too many errant dogs and horses in Dallas to let anyone track sidewalk microbes inside our place. Plus, it kept us from having to clean as often.

I turned in the light of the hallway. From her position on the floor, she looked through her dark-brown bangs and spotted my mangled appendage at eye-level. "Wow, Lottie, what happened to your leg? It looks hideous. I mean, painful."

"Nice to see you too." I laughed. Megan was never one for subtlety. "I fell off a bike. Long story. Actually, that's it. That's the whole story." I winced as I tried to walk.

"Geez. Good thing you've still got nine months before my wedding pictures."

Yes. That's exactly what I'm worried about, Megan. With all the

*dramatic brides and crazy bosses in my life, I am stressing about your
wedding.* "I know, right? It should be fine in a couple weeks."

I regaled her with the tale of my haplessness as we walked to
the living room. We sprawled on the overstuffed sofa, an egregious
plaid, rolled-arm hand-me-down from Natalia's big sister. We'd found
a couple of chairs from Craigslist that walked the thin line between
modernism and the 1980s, but they worked too. Frames with our
sorority logos had slowly been phased out in a concession to our late
twenties; an array of metal frames with friends and family sprinkled
the wall above the couch. The apartment was a far cry from the
grown-up home either of us thought we'd be living in by now, but
we also didn't mind when someone spilled red wine on the furniture.

To save ourselves from hearing more about just *how hard* it was to
plan Megan's wedding, we decided to look to the expert. No, not me,
but Jenny from the Block. The divine Ms. Jennifer Lopez. The super-
woman who could run away from a dumpster in Manolo Blahniks,
wear that slick ponytail for the duration of multiple couples' engage-
ments, and still manage to win Matthew McConaughey.

Yes, *The Wedding Planner* was on tap for the night.

As J. Lo planned the perfect million-dollar wedding without
breaking a drop of sweat, all I could think was that planning a wedding was hard—super hard. While she spent an entire film hoofing
it in stilettos, I'd never worn a pair of pumps for an entire wedding.
(Thank God for ballet flats stashed in my emergency bag and glove
box.) And the panty liners plastered inside my dresses were really the
only things keeping me from looking like a thirteen-year-old boy in
gym class.

The screenwriters also must have thought it was best to cut the
scenes where Lopez held up the bride's dress in the toilet, helped the
groom's mother with her Spanx, or broke up a fight in the hotel lobby

between two inebriated bridesmaids. They also omitted the dramatic boss who often sent his minions closer to the edge of their sanity than the brides ever did. Kathy Najimy certainly made for a sweeter film, even if none of her scarves were Hermès.

"Ohmigod, Nat! Massimo is like the guy from Prague but with a different accent!"

"You're just saying that because he's supposed to be foreign," Natalia said, sliding down the sofa cushions.

"You're right. The guy you went out with—what was his name, Megan? Simon or something like that? Nowhere near as hot as Justin Chambers."

The pillow smacked me in the arm. "At least I got out and had a good time! You just spent your time and money paying for phone cards to call Brody."

She had me there.

We launched into reminiscing about who still talked to her flames from our European summer abroad.

While I was too busy pining over my jock back home, Megan and Natalia were having the time of their lives dating rugby players we met on our first weekend getaway to Prague. The easyJet flight was just the three of us and a whole team of the most beautiful university men with English accents. Megan truly believed she'd died and gone to *Love Actually*.

While my best friends were enjoying their youth abroad the way I had always envisioned, I was standing watch to make sure neither one of them was abducted or drugged. Natalia dated her guy, Adam, for several months after we returned to the States, but an international long-distance relationship proved impossible. Since then, she'd had about as much luck online dating as I had.

"I still think about our last date," Natalia shouted as she half spit out her wine. "I know it's crazy, but we really had a connection. I just can't eat fish and chips or whatever passes for food over there my whole life. I'd miss margaritas and my grandmother's tamales too much. At least we'll always have Hampstead Heath."

"And grass stains on your dress!" Megan chirped, as she opened another bottle of nine-dollar Trader Joe's pinot.

As if she possessed a sixth sense of when we were together, Harper's perfectly symmetrical face popped up on my screen. I paused the movie, accepted the FaceTime, and showed her Megan and Natalia, who waved.

"Hello, loves, do you miss me?" Harper quipped. "Hudson, Zoe, wave at your aunties!" Her four-year-old son and two-year-old daughter gave the obligatory wave before dashing off to eat a snack in Harper's pristine, all-white kitchen in the background.

"Of course," Nat said. "How was the big interview? I saw it got picked up on CNN!"

"It went well enough," Harper said. "Our new mayor is a total boss, and I liked her a lot. Everybody's interested in what she'll do next. But I definitely didn't expect the national stations to pick up our little local TV news interview. Hudson, put that down!"

Harper had become an anchor in New Orleans after stints in Little Rock and Tallahassee. Along the way she'd met and married her accountant husband, Liam, who worked from home and mostly played Mr. Mom. I was as unsurprised that she'd become a successful journalist as I was stunned she'd gone for the stay-at-home dad and two kids. I guessed some women could actually have it all.

"And how is wedding planning going?"

Before I could answer about my job, Megan jumped in. "It's soooo stressful but really great! Josh is the absolute best and my parents have been really supportive. We're planning on booking the Oklahoma City Zoo—you're still holding that weekend, right?"

"Yes, of course," Harper said. "But I was talking to Lottie about work, hon."

"Oh, right." Megan handed my phone back sheepishly.

I filled her in on some of my latest projects and the prospect of Cedric's new office.

"That's amazing. You totally deserve one of those new roles if you want it. How's the competition from that team of nuts you work with? Still no straight, eligible men in the mix?"

"Nope, just trust fund girls and ineligible slash uninterested men . . . except there's a new photographer guy who has been working some of our events. He's just a friend, but it's been fun to mix things up some."

Of all my friends, Harper was usually the last to pressure me to get out and find a boyfriend. Probably because she knew firsthand the extra time they consumed.

"Oh really? Do tell!" I could sense Megan's and Natalia's ears perking up too.

"There's not much to tell, honestly. He's a photographer who works with one of our most frequent collaborators. Name's Griffin. But he seems pretty anti-relationship right now, so it's a nonstarter. But he's funny, at least, and it will be nice to have a guy friend around."

"He can be your work husband!" Megan had been watching too much Bravo TV again.

"Oh, and tell her about Matt," Nat said unhelpfully.

I knew I couldn't escape this inquisition, so I filled Harper in on seeing him at the wedding and his follow-up emails.

"And I think she should *answer* the man and give him another chance," Nat practically shouted.

"I agree," Harper said. "I'm actually amazed he would give *you* another chance after last time. What have you got to lose? It's not like you've got other eligible, non-sociopaths knocking on your door, right?"

"Not to mention he looks amazing on paper—and in person—so you might as well," Nat added again from the background.

"Aww, thanks, peanut gallery!" I said over my shoulder.

I agreed to think about it, and then Harper had to jump off the phone to deal with a toddler emergency, which was fine since we had important romcom viewing to get back to.

Overall, my dating life had been sparse—I liked to believe it was because I focused so much on work. I'd had a couple other weeks-long relationships in addition to Matt, but nothing ever stuck. And approaching good-looking people, unless they worked behind a bar and had a happy-hour menu, was never exactly in my wheelhouse.

Brody had fallen into my lap in college. So while everyone else perfected their dating skills, I lost my edge and probably some confidence. Not to mention that was before all these dating apps existed; my brief bio likely pegged me somewhere between exhausted, puritanical, and prehistoric. It was near impossible to meet someone face-to-face in any "normal" situation, for which I 100 percent blamed the iPhone.

When I looked at Tinder, Bumble, Coffee Meets Bagel, and the slew of apps I hid in a folder marked "Fitness," I felt like a pathetic, habitual "left swiper." I wasn't actually doing anything or making a real effort, but scrolling through countless potentials felt like it counted for something.

"You should do it," Megan said gravely. "I'm so grateful to have met Josh because it's a dark scene out there."

Natalia cringed and nodded. "Dallas is like a wasteland for straight women past a certain age—as in, like, twenty-five. I should know . . .

The odds are decidedly *not* in your favor." Nat loved dystopian fantasy, which was why she kept attempting online dating.

"Yeah, most men aren't in a rush, it seems." I nodded. "When they hit their thirties, they know there'll be a bevy of successful, desperate women their age—and a lot of twentysomethings too."

"One of my coworkers pointed out recently that the instant she turned thirty, she stopped getting matched with anyone younger than forty, presumably because all the men her age clicked the Under 30 tab. Because they could," Nat said. "Jerks."

"And in the South, when these men do inevitably get married, they want a woman, ideally five to twenty years younger, who will keep house, pop out two babies, and join the Junior League." I envisioned nearly all our girlfriends from college at this point.

"I mean, my sister did that and seems quite happy." Megan was obviously imagining her own immediate future.

"Of course she is, sweetie." Nat smiled kindly.

Maybe Natalia was right, and I just needed to get back out there regardless of how much it scared me. Matt seemed like a safe enough place to start, even if he fit the typical Southern frat-star profile. I'd gone to college with too many guys like him—only interested in one thing despite rapidly showing signs of early middle age. Yet, for the moment, these men had good looks, money, and no reason to rush into marriage. They almost always turned out too good to be true.

I couldn't deny that the Matt I'd known years ago seemed different than the other guys, but his background was so similar, it was hard not to make assumptions. Hence, the unresponded-to emails. I was avoiding the inevitable heartache of another short-term dalliance that would be fun but also a waste of valuable time off my biological clock.

We turned the movie back on. Megan tried to talk over the scene where Bridgette Wilson-Sampras's onscreen parents get drunk, so I turned up the volume, then went into the kitchen for another Dr Pepper. Everything was grating on my nerves.

It even annoyed me that, at the end, the whole point of the movie was that Jennifer Lopez stole the perfect man right out from under the billionaire-businesswoman-but-down-to-earth beauty. Was that really the kind of ending I wanted? But I felt energized by the new possibilities before me and by J. Lo's gumption. I could do this. I would carve out my spot at The Firm.

SIX

I am *loving* this capsule wardrobe! That green top really sets off your eyes."

I didn't have the heart to explain to Travis that "capsule" was code for "limited budget" in my case. Instead, I smiled and handed over a Monday morning iced double-tall blond almond latte from Starbucks, part of my weekly bribe for his good graces. Since none of the other planners arrived before ten, he was, as usual, watching episodes of *Queer Eye* on his computer and taking notes.

I had a lengthy list of things to check off before Saturday's wedding at the Dallas Zoo. My first appointment of the day was a site visit with Cedric and Mary Ellen at eleven, so I answered emails and tried to look busy.

I had another one from Griffin.

Dear Ms. Jones,

We at Land Rover of North Texas wanted to apologize again for the strength of our security system. Your efforts have revealed to us the distressing lack of remote-opening options should a moron be able to purchase one of our vehicles. We promise to remedy this in the future, and while we cannot promise you'll ever be able to afford one of our cars, we can promise they will always be pretty enough to make you feel bad about your choices.

I chuckled and left the message unread to reply later. Out of the corner of my eye, I could see Cedric in his glass office. He was on the phone, grinning like the Cheshire Cat while he paced the carpeted floor. He hung up after twenty minutes and frantically summoned Mary Ellen to his office. They sat on his chaise longue, heads together, conspiring.

At eleven Cedric and Mary Ellen made their way to the parking lot. I hopped into the backseat of Cedric's new Audi, and we headed to Preston Hollow.

I watched the pointed Tudors and imitation Italian villas roll by. Somewhere in these sprawling manses lived people like Mark Cuban, Ross Perot, a host of billionaires, and half the Cowboys and Mavericks players. Most of Cedric's Dallas clients were from Preston Hollow, Highland Park, or the like. I imagined our tiny, cheap Memphis house, tried to envision it sitting alongside a particularly grandiose Greek revival. The bittersweet image made me smile. What would it have been like to grow up in this world?

I'd been in Texas more than a decade but still often felt like an outsider. Tennessee and Texas had a lot in common. Neither was technically part of the Grand Old South, yet they liked to pretend that made them superior. But Texans had some inherent host of contradictions I was still learning to navigate.

How did one population pride itself on being both hospitable and fiercely territorial? Entrepreneurially self-made and accidentally oil rich? More populous than almost any other state and yet as stubbornly independent as the Wild West? Even the accent wasn't precisely Southern. Texas was just "off" enough to be unique.

The idea that everything was bigger in Texas, though, I understood. My experience with Cedric had proven this. His events featured big crowds, big hair, big budgets, and bigger drama.

On the drive Cedric took advantage of the opportunity to quiz Mary Ellen and, by default, me.

"Libby, in your years in flower-land, you must've learned something useful? Let's do some fun facts. Like, why do we use lilies so often—aside from the obvious: they're white."

Don't blow it. "Um, they mean purity and innocence, just like white dresses."

"Bingo."

"And hey, it's Lottie, not Libby," Mary Ellen interjected. I was shocked.

"Of course, my apologies. Now, what would you tell my bride who just asked for a bouquet and centerpieces of calla lilies, though?"

"That she better not have any kids around since they're poisonous."

"What about a bouquet of daffodils?"

"Does she want to have a hand rash in all her pictures?"

He kept at it for thirty minutes until we pulled up to a limestone fortress. I thanked Abigail silently for making me brush up on the language of flowers—and give every potential flower in her inventory a test run to see what could happen in case of heat, cold, tornadic winds, and sweaty palms. I had apparently been trained for this car ride.

As we entered the ginormous iron gates surrounded by a fence that put the Berlin Wall to shame, I couldn't help but gasp at the sheer magnitude and might of the home. Was this guy a Russian dissident or a Saudi prince?

The compound was nestled in the middle of one of the most

prestigious and sought-after streets in town, so it was surprising to see armed guards at each corner of the fence, along with several others piled in a gatehouse looking bored. Palm trees lined the drive. As we parked outside the main doors, a valet greeted us, then quickly whisked Cedric's Audi out of sight so as not to congest the picture-perfect façade towering overhead.

Cedric, intimidated by no one, waltzed right up to the massive carved-wood door and pressed his ring-adorned forefinger against the gold-plated call box. A voice with a thick New Jersey accent asked who was calling (as if the armed forces at the front gate hadn't already run a complete background check), then informed us someone would be out to greet us soon.

The three of us stared at each other, waiting on pins and needles to meet these people. A lock clicked, but much to our surprise, it wasn't the main door that opened before us. We had failed to notice a smaller, narrow door that was cut into the larger door. We stood slack-jawed as the tiny door opened, and a diminutive man stepped out to greet us.

"Hello, my name is RJ," he said with a low bow. He wore a vivid sapphire-blue suit and Yoko Ono glasses. "If you would please follow me, I will take you to see the mister and missus of the house." With that, he turned crisply on his heel and walked back through the small door.

Thankfully the larger door opened, too, and we stepped into an unexpected foyer. If the outside looked like a medieval fortress, the inside was a dystopian fantasy. The foyer's white marble floors and walls housed a staircase befitting an art museum. The stairs were made of glass or Lucite—completely see-through—and led to an equally impressive and equally transparent "sky bridge" that connected the two upstairs wings of the home.

I was suddenly terrified at the thought of having to use the stairs, given that I had worn granny panties and a skirt to work. A man undoubtedly had designed this house.

Thankfully we marched right past the stairs and through at least ten cavernous rooms, all of which housed the strangest art-deco furniture and art. Brightly colored wooden chairs with large modern faces painted on the backs sat under yellow glass chandeliers that were over six feet tall. White carpet covered every floor. Black limestone cougars and jaguars perched atop white marble consoles and columns. An overpriced Dallas decorator with very questionable taste must have had a heyday in this place.

Suddenly Cedric's insistence on wearing dark-tinted Gucci sunglasses everywhere, including indoors, made perfect sense. He could hide the sheer horror in his eyes without offending potential clients. As I remembered to close my open mouth, I wished I'd kept my shades on too.

Our guide led us to an outdoor terrace that overlooked a private beach. Yes, a private beach in their backyard. Apparently the bride-to-be was a regular at La Pelosa Beach, which Mary Ellen stage-whispered was somewhere fabulous in Italy. So, of course, when they built their lavish estate, the couple completed the project with a replica of her beloved beach for her to enjoy privately every day. This was probably the closest I would ever get to a beach in Italy, unless some undiscovered rich relative named me their heir—or one of Cedric's brides booked a destination wedding in Capri. A girl could dream. So I soaked in the magnificent view as long as I could until we finally sat down with our new mysterious clients.

RJ sat in his own chair that had a little extra cushion so he could reach the table, and he nodded to a man who came out from a door at the end of the terrace carrying a tray full of drinks and various bites to eat. Mary Ellen and I pulled out our notepads, each took a San Pellegrino, then waited for what would happen next.

I was beginning to think this was all some sort of "hidden camera" show when we were finally introduced to the bride- and groom-to-be. They entered the terrace from yet another door (the house that never ended) and strolled over to the table.

Oksana was a petite, beautiful Eastern European woman with piercing gray eyes and thick brown hair that curled all the way down her back. Her heels were at least six inches tall with a platform that gave her the height she lacked. Her skin-tight Versace green dress had a slight sheen, and it barely covered her torso, exposing her slender legs and D-cup breasts. (Who wore Versace during the daytime outside of Vegas—or at all?) Her chest was highlighted by a very large gold-and-emerald necklace that coiled up right around her cleavage like a snake peering into its den. It was as though she'd stepped straight out of The Wynn casino at 2:00 a.m. Given the surroundings, though, she fit in.

If this wasn't enough to test my skill at maintaining my composure, the groom-to-be was a sight to take in as well. David, a Bill Gates lookalike, was also wearing a bright-blue suit with circular glasses like his mini-doppelgänger. He carried what my male peers referred to as a pimp cane. I doubted David *was* actually a pimp, but if I'd seen him on the street, it would have been hard not to label him as such. He was clearly Oksana's senior, and by exactly how many years, I couldn't be sure. At least twenty. Once again, I coveted Cedric's sunglasses.

We all made introductions. David sat next to RJ, and again I couldn't believe this wasn't some kind of dream or alternate universe. They were dressed to match. The couple gave us a quick background of how they'd met, which had Mary Ellen, Cedric, and me on the edges of our seats by this point. A whole new world existed on this side of the gates, and we couldn't wait to see it all.

David had amassed his fortune in the energy drink business. He started one of the earlier popular drinks that he eventually sold for a fortune to a company based overseas. He no longer actively worked for the brand, but he sat on the board and enjoyed the perks of his nine-figure deal.

Less than a year ago, he had been in Las Vegas for an energy beverage convention. One could only imagine the people watching there. Contemplating mortality, as one did while gazing out the windows of the Encore, he decided to meet with a millionaire-matchmaker to help him find love, which had evaded him all these years.

"I'd never married, didn't really have the time for it, with the work of starting the business and all." He added that he had a grown son from a "brief liaison in my twenties."

Yep. Not the first—or last—client who married someone the same age as their child.

"The next day, the matchmaker emailed me Oksana's picture and instructions on where to meet her, inside the MGM."

"I just love Vegas," chirped Cedric as he took a sip of his Pellegrino. "I get so inspired there. Anything can happen, and there's such a zest for life."

"Exactly." David smiled. "It's like a shot of oxygen, and Oksana and I go back at least every other month."

At that moment Oksana looked over at David and smiled at him while rubbing his hand. I sat frozen, not wanting to seem anything other than normal, the opposite of how I felt.

I also started to wonder about Oksana's side of this story. Why was she in Vegas with the millionaire-matchmaker in the first place? Did no one think about this but me? My mind ran through a range of possibilities, from sex trafficking to visa security. But maybe she was independently wealthy and simply liked older rich guys. Time would tell, I supposed. Although appearances could be deceiving, she didn't seem under duress. In fact, she looked pretty happy.

Anyway, David and Oksana hit it off. He proceeded to tell us an awkward account of their incredible first date, and I tried to listen without actually taking it all in because I did *not* want the visuals stuck in my mind. "And the next day, I dumped all my Viagra in the sink. I knew I wouldn't be needing it anymore, and I haven't since. That's how I knew Oksana was the one."

"How sweet," Mary Ellen added in the highest pitch I'd ever heard from her. She appeared to struggle not to spit out her sparkling water. I'd gone mute by this point. Cedric, however, carried on like a champ. He just continued reeling in the clients.

"Oh, that's just wonderful! The sweetest story I've ever heard!" Cedric gushed. "Now, tell me about your big day. Did you have any idea of what you want it to feel and look like?"

As we discussed details of their impending nuptials, it became clear their wedding would resemble their home: over the top, flashy, and in a very specific taste. The budget continued to climb, so Cedric pressed forward, even though I knew he died a little inside every time they mentioned a red lacquer heart-shaped dance floor, painted models to resemble Greek statues, and tables made of ice with vodka shots for everyone. They met in Vegas, fell in love in Vegas, and by God, they were going to bring Vegas to The Ritz-Carlton, Dallas no matter what it cost.

After about an hour I came out of my note-taking fog when Cedric asked me to pull out one of our contracts.

"Sign here," he said. And with the stroke of a bright-red pen, Cirque du Love was in planning phase one.

We said our good-byes to the bizarre but happy couple and headed back to The Firm to regroup for our next round of meetings.

I spent the first hour back at the office filling in Claire and a few other interns about our meeting. Although none of them actually believed me. "I couldn't make it up if I tried," I said.

Later that afternoon Mary Ellen rang my desk phone and asked me to come to her office. It was unusual to have any one-on-one meetings with her, but perhaps the team had noticed I was the only assistant who didn't miss entire days due to emergency cosmetic procedures or too-frequent headaches.

"I'm sure you haven't fully recovered from our meeting earlier today—I know I haven't—but our brides wait for no one. We've landed a new major client, and although you're already bound in an ironclad NDA, we can't trust any of the assistants or other interns with more information than we have to give." She drummed her French-manicured nails on the Lucite as she spoke. "So, we'll be giving you details on a need-to-know basis, and right now, all you need to know is this: The bride is a Hollywood actress whose movies you've definitely seen, and the groom is a public figure too. Nobody even knows they're dating as they only met a few months ago, and they're hoping to do one of those things where they just casually drop the news that they're married into a *Vanity Fair* article, the same way Taylor Swift releases albums these days. Or, I guess, how Taylor dates people these days too. Anyway, they want to get married soon to ensure the news stays under wraps. We have to jam on this one, which is the only reason I'm looping you in now, Lottie."

"That sounds great. Thank you. What do you need me to do first?"

"Well, first you can go get some fresh highlights. You're getting a little brassy, and we can't have you representing The Firm looking like we found you wandering the Dallas Fairgrounds in denim cutoffs." Ah, there she was, the Mary Ellen we all knew and loved. "Then I need you to start pulling together a list of luxury Mexican beach venues for early May that include proximity to a decent airport, accommodations for a hundred guests, and the ability to block off visibility—so no all-access public beaches. I need the list by the end of the week. Got it?"

"Yes, of course."

"It should go without saying but with high-profile clients, don't fangirl or get all weird on them. I don't care if she starred in your favorite movie ever. You must treat them with absolute professionalism, or we could lose the contract."

"That shouldn't be a problem at all."

"Good. This is the kind of opportunity that could really put you on Cedric's radar. I haven't seen him this excited about a client since we did Jessica Simpson's birthday party. Anyway, just don't bomb it like the botanical garden swan show."

My mind raced to the possibilities. These clients sounded like they had a pretty elevated sense of self-importance, but that might be a good thing when it came to our bonuses. Cedric cared about money, of course, but he cared more about cachet, about social capital, because that led to growth and more lucrative events. Whoever these people were, they sounded like his dream clients. Young, famous, undoubtedly beautiful. I was determined to do all I could to wrangle my way onto this wedding and then absolutely crush it.

"Now, when you're scoping out venues, I can't emphasize enough how important it is that there be private areas on the property. We'll also need to come up with a strategy for guests, including how we get everyone there, set up NDA forms, phone confiscation . . . There'll be a lot to do and much to discuss before their wedding—less than seven months away. But for now, hustle up. And don't worry about the venues' availability. Any place in the world would kill to host this couple's big day." Then she handed me a sealed manila folder.

I did as she said and dashed back to my desk. I prayed to the Mexican beach wedding gods that this would be my big break.

With everyone but Claire gone for the day, I had some privacy. I tore open the folder and laid it on the desk.

Inside, a shot of Harriet Devore from the Oscars red carpet practically shimmered. Her hand rested on her hip at a jaunty angle and the slit in her glittering silver skirt almost met the one down the bodice, revealing underboob and more than a little of her hip. Clearly, the woman wasn't wearing underwear and didn't require underwire. I involuntarily clenched my abdominal muscles. My mother had spent years harping on me to improve my posture, to no avail.

I skimmed the stats but didn't really need to. I'd just watched Harriet, or "Dirty Harry" as *GQ* had dubbed her years ago, star in the remake of *Thelma & Louise* opposite Naomi Scott two weeks ago. She had that perfect mix of innocence and sex appeal that drove guys crazy and yet left every woman in the theater thinking, *Gee, we'd totally be best friends if I could just meet her*—instead of thinking they'd like to murder her in her sleep for being impossibly perfect.

I vaguely remembered that she was from a town in Kentucky dubbed the Bourbon Capital of the World, which only made her more relatable. Her brand of Southern charm popped up in roles when convenient. She'd also just broken up with her A-list boyfriend last summer, and the last *Radar Online* article I'd read had them secretly back together. No wonder Cedric wanted to keep this one under wraps.

I felt a quiet thrill at working with Harriet. But as I turned the page, my heart stopped. Brody Stevens's face stared back at me, in his Los Angeles Rams football uniform. He looked so handsome, so *him*. I could feel both adrenaline and anxiety surging. My pulse raced. I could hardly breathe. I unconsciously shook my head. *No, no, no, no.* The words in his brief bio barely registered.

He'd met Harriet at a charity fund-raiser this spring. The gorgeous actress and the strapping, in-his-prime NFL quarterback. Sparks flew, according to Cedric's notes from his initial call with the happy couple. I couldn't bring myself to read the rest.

I pushed the dossier back into the folder and stared at it. What in the world was I supposed to do with this information? I couldn't wrap my head around Brody getting married, let alone to a movie star. There was no way I would be looking into venues for them today. Absolutely not. Was I really about to embark on planning a wedding that I'd, in a way, already planned? This was some sick, sad joke. Such a gut punch. I felt embarrassed, not knowing precisely why. No one would know—no one at The Firm *could* know—but I'd have to carry this.

Mercifully Travis informed Mary Ellen that one of our afternoon meetings had been rescheduled. Cedric was the only one needed for the remaining meeting, which was made solely for the purpose of picking out flatware for a different wedding over a year away. All I had to do was answer a few emails from clients, book bands for a few smaller events, and then make sure our files were in order for the next day. It took everything I had to finish those tasks because I couldn't wait to get the hell out of the office.

I needed a drink and a platter of overpriced sushi. I was going to eat my feelings while I attempted to process them.

"Claire," I called across the row of mostly empty desks. It was after five, after all. "Want to grab a bite at Yutaka?"

Her eyes lit up like I'd offered her Willy Wonka's golden ticket. Poor little rich girl must have even fewer friends at The Firm than I did. "I'd love to!" She practically jumped out of her desk chair, clearly not working much and just biding her time until a respectable hour to leave.

I didn't fault her. My personal go-to trick was to leave an open email draft while also browsing Anthropologie in a smaller window.

We drove separately to Yutaka in Uptown, and I left the car radio off, lost in my own thoughts.

I'd known intellectually that Brody would find someone else. And although I'd done my best not to obsessively track his career, that was difficult when my ex often appeared on Monday Night Football. But it never crossed my mind that his move to LA last season would lead to something like this. I shouldn't have been surprised. He'd been playing—and earning—well, and I knew he wanted to have a family. But why couldn't he have married some sweet, slightly ditzy NFL cheerleader or one of his agent's assistants? Even a former *Bachelor* contestant, or, at the very most, a personal trainer with a sizable Instagram following? I would have taken that.

More than anything, though, I guess I wished I'd figured it all out before he did. I wished I'd found my own happy ending first.

Time hadn't fully put me in the place yet to look back and see it was all for the best that we didn't work out. And, really, *was* it for the best? Because in that moment, it felt like the best thing might actually be for *me* to have a lavish Mexican beach wedding. Not lovely, rich, unblemished Harriet. Brody had become exactly who I always believed he could be, and that made the part of me who would always care about him happy.

But the me who had only just recently started to feel like I knew who or what I wanted again was sent into a tailspin. No amount of wishing him well could take away the questions, and nothing could quell the gnawing what-ifs about the separate paths we'd chosen.

I wasn't even sure how I ended up in this job, sitting across from billionaires planning weddings better suited to Bravo shows. If someone had told me growing up in the suburbs of Memphis that I'd meet people like Cedric's clients, I would've thought she was delusional. But after college, I was in survival mode. Heartbroken and lost, I fell into this career that offered some security. What did I know? The girl who'd put her dreams on hold to plan a wedding was now planning weddings for a living. I'd already given up too much for one future plan that disintegrated. I couldn't fail again. But was I really happy? Seeing the image of Brody with his dream job, marrying some dream girl brought all these feelings and questions to the surface.

"What am I *doing*?" I gripped the steering wheel harder than needed.

Most of my friends from high school had stayed in state, picked a job, and then settled down for the long haul. I didn't want that either, but I didn't need to stick around this gig any longer if it wasn't for me.

"Calm down, Lottie," I repeated like a mantra. *Breathe.* I exhaled and relaxed my hand on the wheel.

I was doing okay. I paid my bills. I had amazing friends. I wasn't going on dates, but I was at least browsing the app selection. And that had to count for something. I was no Mary Ellen (or Harriet Devore), but I hadn't been fired yet. I could plan the heck out of Brody's wedding and earn myself a hefty raise. I was a *professional*.

Sure, I might want to stick a boutonniere pin in my eye at the image of him marrying Harriet. That might not change. But in the meantime I'd have an overpriced cocktail and some delicious sushi to fortify me for another week, another wedding.

SEVEN

Nat, can I borrow your blue Zara dress?" I called down the hall.

"Yes, seeing as you're already wearing it."

I'd hoped she wouldn't step outside her room and notice. "Thanks, you're the best!"

"I'm just letting you because I want this date to go well," she said. "When you guys get married, will you name your firstborn after me in tribute?"

"Yes, if it's a girl." I put on mascara in the hall mirror. I'd finally replied to Matt's third email, weeks later. The girls were right. Why not give him a second chance? It had absolutely nothing to do with the fact that I'd just found out Brody was getting married. Matt answered within the hour and asked me to Thursday night dinner.

"Nat works great for a boy too. Sounds sophisticated. We can quibble over baby names later tonight when you're groveling about how much you owe me for making you go in the first place," Natalia said. "Or we can discuss in the morning, if you find a reason to stay out too late. Just promise to take care of my dress." She mock shuddered.

"You're disgusting!" I laughed as I ran out the door, still buckling the strap on my favorite wedges.

Matt and I were meeting at Bistro 31. I was impressed with the choice. Refined but not too fussy. Cedric always said, "You want them to try, but not too hard. If he takes you to The French Room right away, he's clearly hiding something or making up for a shortage, if you know what I mean."

Cedric, the love guru. Apparently he would assist your love life *and* plan your wedding. If the price was right.

I spotted Matt leaning against the bar, dressed in crisp, tailored navy slacks and a button-down with the sleeves rolled up over his forearms. He ran a hand over his light-brown hair—not a strand out of place—and waved. Lord, he was gorgeous. Even if we didn't go out again, the night would be worth it for the free food and the chance to stare at him across the table.

I decided right there to give Matt a fair chance.

Matt had been a Sigma Chi kinesiology major, which meant our paths rarely intersected in college, save for an introductory psychology class sophomore year and the occasional party. He used to have a longtime girlfriend, too, some Pi Phi. But that night a few years ago, we bumped into each other downtown, with our few friends still in the area. Feeling like leftovers in that awkward space between beginnings and endings, college and what one hoped was real life. The attraction was certainly there, beneath all the tequila; it was rather natural to open up to him. Nothing deep that night, of course, but I felt at ease. And he made me laugh. Maybe I had given up on him too soon.

"Hello, Lottie." He dipped his head at me like a cowboy. "You look fantastic."

"Thanks, Matt. You don't look so bad yourself." Classic date line. Wow, I was so good at this banter stuff.

We went in for an awkward hug, and he ran his hand from my

shoulder down to my lower back. I hoped he didn't notice the resulting chills all over my body. I needed to get out of the house more.

"So, how've you been?" I continued.

"You mean this week or in the last two years?" he said, but with a smile.

I couldn't believe it had been that long since he and I, um, went our separate ways. "Well, when you put it like that . . . both. Last time I saw you was before you moved to Miami."

"And you were heading to law school."

"Actually, I was just applying to law school. But that obviously didn't work out."

"Oh? That's what you told me before you stopped answering my calls." He winked.

I felt a twinge of guilt for ghosting him after that summer, but it seemed like there weren't too many hard feelings. I told him about the meandering path that got me to this point: still living with a college friend, working for Cedric, and not dating anyone.

"Yeah, sorry about that again. I just wanted to try for a fresh start. You know the cliché: new city, new job, new everything . . ." I trailed off.

"Listen, it's just good to see you. I love Dallas, and it's been great meeting new people. But I guess I'm a bit nostalgic about college these days, and you're one of the few friends I have who's still living in the metroplex."

"Friends?" I asked.

"Yeah, friends." He gave me another wink and took a swig of beer.

I tried to hide my blush as I shoved a dinner roll from the bread basket in my mouth and laughed like an idiot.

"Well, so how's the big, fancy job?" I asked after finally swallowing the last piece of said roll.

"My guess is that the only divas in this town bigger than your brides are my clients." He chuckled. "I knew managing athletes wouldn't be as sexy as it sounded, but there are nights I'm cleaning vomit out of one of the pro-baller's cars and then driving them home so they don't get a DUI and suspended."

"Wow, I guess our jobs have way more in common than I ever imagined. Between the sloppy groomsmen, treacherous extended families, and tightly wound brides, I feel like I've become an overpaid, actually underpaid, babysitter of sorts."

Matt laughed, and we continued to swap "war stories" from our growing careers through the first and second course.

"However, despite any similarities, I get the sense you probably make five times what I do," I said as the waiter brought out the dessert menus.

"Well, I'm definitely not complaining about that. The money makes all the annoying clients worth it. I actually just started looking at houses in Devonshire."

"Oh gosh, I can barely afford rent, and you're already working on a down payment. That's impressive."

"Well, I'm not exactly going to open houses yet, but I've got some money saved. Trying to plan for the future."

"But isn't it all families and young kids over there? Not quite the 'swinging bachelor pad' I always imagined you in."

"So you're saying you fantasize about me?" He snickered.

I blinked. "You know what I mean. Don't get too cheeky with me yet. I've only had one glass of wine."

"We'll have to fix that." He signaled the waiter to bring me another.

"Ugh, just one more, but don't get any ideas. You're basically a stranger to me right now. Plus, you're dodging my question. What's up with the suburbia house hunt vibes?"

"Well, don't get me wrong, I love being single."

My eyes just about rolled all the way back into my head.

"But my parents are starting to breathe down my neck about settling down, or at least finding just one person to date with long-term potential. And frankly, I don't think I'm that far off from wanting the same." He chuckled at my expression of surprise. "Come on, Lottie. Don't *you* want that for yourself?"

"Of course, obviously. Yes. But I got so thrown for a loop the last time I thought I knew what my life would be like, and then it didn't pan out. I've always wanted love, marriage, kids, but for years it's felt only further away. It's taken me a while to find a new path. Now, even if it were within reach, I'm not sure that's what I want."

"I imagine it's more within reach than you think," he said kindly.

"Maybe, but I'm also just now starting to really find a groove in my career. You've definitely got me beaten there. Things still feel so uncertain. And even if I was more stable, the Dallas dating pool isn't exactly packed with successful, never-married men looking for an almost thirty-year-old junior wedding planner with student debt and premature stress wrinkles."

He was quiet for a minute, and I hoped he wouldn't bring up Brody. We'd talked about him that summer a couple years ago since they knew each other, but thankfully he let it lie. I didn't need that specter outside the office too.

"You're too hard on yourself. I'm just glad you agreed to have dinner with me. You look beautiful, and there's just something about a Southern woman these Texas women don't have."

"Like what?" I replied. "Grit and sass?"

We both laughed, and something inside me fluttered a bit. *Traitor.*

"Sure," he said. "And since I'm clearly the big earner at the table, how about I buy us one more round of drinks?"

"Ugh, fine." I blushed yet again.

We finished our nightcaps at the restaurant. "I'm traveling to Houston next week, but I'd love to see you again soon," he said, helping me into my Uber.

"I'd like that." I flashed him a flirty smile that I'm sure looked sloppy thanks to our final round.

"Then just answer my texts." He shut the door with a grin.

Natalia's dress would be safe for tonight, but Matt had won himself at least one more shot. She would be thrilled. I guessed I would have to let her gloat for a minute, but that was it. After all, it was just a second date.

EIGHT

Brody and Harriet's wedding became my albatross. So many details, so much secrecy, so deep the heartache. With all the work to do, I was working alone one late afternoon in October, which made me a bit of a pariah. My coworkers frequently ducked out early for SoulCycle, Pilates, hair appointments, or something equally "important."

Aesthetic standards were not in my budget, though, so I fired off a response to Griffin's latest email. He'd sent me a couple funny stories about Val's crankiness, and I recounted a recent wedding where the couple had insisted on a clear aisle laid across the swimming pool like something out of Indiana Jones. With hundreds of lotus blooms floating on the water, all looked magical—until one of the brides-maids had slipped off the slick surface straight into the pool during post-ceremony pictures. It would have been funnier if she hadn't been wearing an $800 dress. Having a guy friend again felt refreshing. Every time griffinflo86 popped into my in-box, I smiled.

After finishing up emails, I browsed beach venues. Imagining myself there helped assuage the sting from reading about romantic honeymoon packages and envisioning my ex ensconced with his svelte, famous fiancée.

My office phone rang. "Lottie, I have a, um, very special client here for you," Travis chimed.

We met with clients by appointment only to keep from going insane from all the random bridal drop-ins that would occur. ("I just wanted to check in and show you this centerpiece I saw in *Martha Stewart Weddings*. Oh, and how are my invitations coming?") If we were available to brides twenty-four seven, we would do nothing but answer their questions and talk them off whatever ledge they were perched on at that particular moment. For absolutely no reason, I might add.

"They don't have an appointment? Shouldn't they come back when someone with actual authority is here?"

"Yes," he whispered, and I could tell he turned around in his chair so the clients wouldn't hear. "But she's carrying a limited-edition alligator 'Diamond Forever' Chanel purse. She said they are only in town for the day, and they want to meet now, or they will find someone else. If this turns out to be a client of substance, that's not unhelpful to you."

"Won't I get in trouble for going rogue?"

"You can blame me if that happens. Tell them I foisted it on you because I didn't want to lose a potential client. Just feel things out. Then we can schedule a real meeting with Cedric or Mary Ellen if it's legit. No need to waste their time if it's not."

Confession: the only word I understood was Chanel, but it was safe to assume he meant they were visibly rich. I wasn't in a position yet to take initial client meetings on my own, but Travis was right. I could sure use a share of the hefty commission if I helped bring them in.

In the waiting area stood an extremely tall woman holding her $260,000 purse and a live chicken. Yep, real live poultry in our office. It was nestled against the Chanel, which was slung over her shoulder.

Next to her stood her presumed fiancé. The top of his balding head barely hit my shoulder, so on his statuesque bride-to-be, it was right at the level of her ample St. John–clad bosom. I had a mental flash of him tucked in at night by her side. Shuddered. Then asked how I could help.

"My name is Jonathan Reilly, and this is the love of my life."

Okay, but what did her mama call her? Before I could respond, he launched into how madly in love they were, how he had just proposed the night before, and how they couldn't wait another moment to start planning their dream wedding. "We drove straight to Cedric Montclair Celebrations as soon as the rooster crowed because dad-gummit, we knew y'all could plan the perfect wedding for us. We're so excited, you see."

"Well, we're so happy for you and glad you came in to see us. Unfortunately, the offices are closed for the day," I said politely, trying to get a better look at the Chanel. "I'd be happy to schedule an appointment for you at a later date, though."

"Sadly, that just won't do. We are heading to England next week for Poultry Club of Great Britain's annual festival. My love has a couple chickens competing, you see." I saw, again, she was still holding a chicken.

But when he mentioned they would be sparing no expense on their wedding, that settled it.

Now, a note about Cedric's Rules: All was generally fair in love and wedding planning. When customers booked appointments in advance, they were divvied up among The Firm's lead planners, using some rubric that took into consideration things like experience, overall workload, timeline, and how the budget fit into company-wide and individual compensation. The formula had just enough secret ingredients for Cedric to justify redistributing clients on a whim (aka, as punishment), but most of his team felt like business was pretty equally shared.

However, when a client had the audacity to walk in sans appointment, all bets were off. I wasn't a lead planner taking a meeting that had been blessed by Cedric, but no one else was in the building. And Travis gave me *his* blessing, so this bizarre duo's nuptials were technically mine. *All* mine.

"Why don't you come right on back then?" I said. "We will just clear the schedule for the rest of the day, won't we, Travis?" He winked at me and pretended to clack away at his keyboard to empty my nonexistent schedule.

I led them into one of the meeting rooms and then offered to grab some sparkling water. As soon as I stepped out, I dashed into the bathroom, splashed the back of my neck with cold water, and put on my game face. *Get it together, Jones. Landing a wedding of this size could raise your profile, or at the very least teach Cedric your name.*

As I walked back in, I needed that game face. The happy couple was blissfully making out on the red silk sofa—he was literally perched in her lap—while the chicken proceeded to pace along the seat back. I shook off my cringe as visions of chicken defecation dripping down raw silk flashed before my eyes. I lunged for the bird just as it started to lift its little tail feathers.

I lunged again, but it dashed off the sofa and onto a high shelf on the floor-to-ceiling gold-leafed bookshelves. Who knew chickens could fly that fast? These shelves housed box after linen box of decadent fabric and ribbon swatches, design books, a Russian Fabergé egg on a stand, a pair of Chinese ginger jars, and various other objects of "inspiration" that could be drawn upon to show clients.

I grabbed, missed, and then had to catch an antique Moroccan vase I'd sent plummeting to the floor below. The chicken walked along the top edge of the bookcase, coolly assessing me.

The couple continued, unbothered.

I was hoping Travis could see at least some of the commotion through the frosted-glass wall separating us, but the traitor had already left once we were inside. Let's be honest. Even if he had seen all this, in no universe would Travis have touched live poultry anyway. I was on my own.

"Um, excuse me, miss . . . I hate to interrupt . . . but your chicken seems to have . . . escaped," I said in between futile jumps to reach the top shelf.

Finally the future Mrs. Jonathan Reilly slowly stood, as if she'd just noticed another human was in the room. Maybe she saw my distress, or maybe she simply cared about the chicken. Either way, she calmly reached high above my head, grabbed the creature by its feet, and pulled it down into her arms again.

With the chicken safely returned to her lap, we settled in for our meeting. It took me a minute to compose myself and get my heart rate down. I started with a bit of small talk about our business and then moved to basic questions as I'd seen Mary Ellen do at each initial meeting. I, of course, looked at the bride-to-be to answer, but she said nothing. Her five-carat diamond ring flashed as she smiled and stroked the chicken's feathers, never saying a word.

Mr. Reilly explained that "the love of his life" (gag) owned a property about an hour outside of Dallas where they wished to be married. The house sounded like Tara from *Gone with the Wind* with a touch of *The Addams Family*. The old Victorian sat on nearly a thousand acres, once used for farming and now pretty much plowed under and drilled into for its crude oil—and thus worth a Sultan's fortune.

They were comfortable spending up to $800,000 on the ceremony and reception. For only 250 guests, this was a solid budget. Jackpot. To think I almost hadn't let them in.

This strange couple had met when he was assigned by his oil-and-gas company to manage her property's mineral rights. This meant she lived on a large field worth a boatload (literally an oil tanker's worth) of money. The future Mrs. Reilly—Sarah, I finally learned—spoke for the first time when she told me she first fell in love with Mr. Reilly over her message machine.

"It was like something out of a movie." Sarah grew even more dreamy eyed, if possible. "He said, 'Ma'am, I'd like to take care of you. I mean, I'd like to take care of your mineral rights.' It was the most sensual sound I'd ever heard. The chickens ran out of the room; they could tell I was not myself. And when he explained all the stuff about the land, all I could think about was the way I tingled as he said his name and 'ma'am.' I replayed that message a hundred times."

Of course, playing the message did not translate to returning the phone call, so the next day Jonathan Reilly left her a second message. At the end of a week, his messages had ranged from goading to demanding, petulant to "I know you can hear me." Finally, he threatened to come out to the ranch himself. "And I knew, right then, that we would get married."

I would have known right then that I was going to be kidnapped and held for ransom, but to each her own.

Finally, when Jonathan came over to talk oil rights in person, she asked him to stay for dinner, and the two wackos hit it off.

After a few weddings, a planner became a military-grade drug dog trained to sniff out gold diggers. I could smell one by my second month at The Firm. But despite all indications, I didn't think Mr. Reilly fit the bill.

Still, Sarah was not what I would call a babe. The couple were both in their late forties or early fifties. She spoke so slowly at times I thought I might fall asleep between sentences. It was clear she was on medication. The upside was that despite her chicken, she seemed to be a laid-back type of bride. *I owe you one, Vicodin.*

We'd long passed the start of my nightly TV routine, so I concluded our first meeting with a signed contract and a hefty deposit and set up a site inspection to view their property with Cedric. I was quickly learning the value of having a big budget combined with clients too stoned to be choosy. I headed home, excited at what had transpired, albeit a bit befuddled by this couple. I supposed there was someone for everyone, as Mamaw used to say.

The next morning Travis briefed Cedric and Abigail about the clients before I had a chance to say anything. Their reactions could've gone one of two ways. I sincerely hoped they would be excited—and forget how I took a solo meeting without their approval.

"Travis said you nailed the consult," said Abigail, perched on the edge of my desk. "Look at you go, girl. Cedric was thrilled to secure another big event for this quarter. You're really making moves."

"Thanks, Abigail. I keep thinking nothing else can shock me, but then someone walks into the office with a chicken."

"Well, you'll certainly never get bored in this place, that's for sure. Cedric won't say this to you, but you're doing a good job here. Mary Ellen seems way less stressed, which is a miracle. And even though we've had some hiccups at a couple recent weddings, it sounds like none of it was your fault. Thinking on your feet to handle issues that come up isn't always something you can teach. I should know, as the person who taught you most else! Very few people can plan weddings at this level and survive for a decent period of time."

"That means a lot," I said. "Although I miss getting my hands on the flowers sometimes, the planning side can actually be fun—or at least entertaining."

"Well, keep it up," she said, then headed back to her desk.

A few days later, Cedric and I set off for our first site visit to see Mr. Reilly and Sarah. Since I'd booked the wedding and Mary Ellen had other clients to manage, it would be the first time Cedric and I went alone together. I didn't know what to expect, but I could hardly wait for someone else to bear witness to the characters I had just met.

To break the silence as we drove south on I-45, I mentioned my excitement to see this oil-spurting Victorian estate. Cedric adjusted his red beret and decided to enlighten me. "You really never know what kind of client you're working with until they pony up the cash to pay for things. Always remember that, Lottie."

"Yes, sir, of course."

"Dallas is known for being the land of the 'forty-thousand-dollar millionaire.' That's a real thing, swear to Jesus and Jehoshaphat. Everyone acts wealthy with designer clothes and luxury cars, but in secret they live in tiny studio apartments—albeit in Highland Park— with no furniture. Then they eat mac and cheese every night for dinner. I should know. So beware of the fakers, and don't waste your time with them. I'm fully prepared for this couple to be all talk and no offshore accounts."

I personally didn't think that was the case, and Mr. Reilly and Sarah would prove him wrong. Cedric spent the majority of the drive on the phone with the office approving final decisions for clients. He also discussed booking flights and hotels for his next personal trip with Geoffrey. His life sounded so glamorous, and I found myself putting a few notes into my phone about some of the exotic locations he described.

As we drove through the charming main street of Corsicana,

Cedric sighed. Loudly. This was not unusual, but then he released another big sigh and slowed the car absently.

"Um, is everything okay?"

"Oh yes, quite all right . . . This place just reminds me of my hometown."

"Which is?"

"Canyon, out near Amarillo. Our downtown square looks a lot like this. Or it did. I haven't been back in years." He gazed at a cute mom-and-pop shop out the window.

"Oh, I always thought you were from Dallas or some other big city. You seem to"—*how do I say it?*—"fit in so well here."

"That, my dear, is the result of an SMU education, on scholarship. Plus years of close observation of rich Dallasites in their natural habitat. You get very good at listening to people and then giving them the version of you, of life, of whatever, that they want . . . Even if they never say so directly."

He paused for a moment. The car turned onto a county highway as we exited town. Pillowy cotton fields looked ripe enough to burst. A herd of black cattle dotted a distant brown hillock.

"To little Panhandle high school me," he continued, "SMU sounded like the most cosmopolitan place—I'd never been anywhere then—and theater was my way in. I came on a scholarship after spending my youth performing in *Texas*, the musical. It's like *Oklahoma!* but better, and bigger, of course. And the whole thing is set in a canyon outside town. We basically rode horses through Palo Duro Canyon and fired cap guns and sang songs about state history. Not exactly my aesthetic, but still quite fun and *highly* dramatic."

Whodathunk. If I squinted, I could imagine a young Cedric, hair not yet peppered with gray, enthusiastically riding on a horse in full cowboy garb. In a way, it worked.

"Well, everybody comes from somewhere. Case in point." He briskly gestured between us. *Isn't that the truth?*

We finally arrived at Sarah's home just outside of town. The car rattled over a cattle grate and bumped past several oil drills on the unpaved road to the house. Our jaws dropped as we drove down the gorgeous tree-lined driveway and pulled up to a stunning historic mansion.

"I feel like there should be someone waiting on the porch to serve me sweet tea as I put my feet up," said Cedric, always a class act, as he pulled his Goyard bag from the trunk. Today's second signature accessory was his belt with a large brushed-gold double *GG* buckle.

He was already casing the joint as we walked to the front door. The extensive land surrounding the home provided plenty of room to accommodate a large wedding. We couldn't see much past the house, but several other structures on the property seemed to go on and on into the horizon.

Cedric gingerly knocked on the front door, and Mr. Reilly greeted us. "Welcome to our slice of heaven. We're so glad you're here." This sounded like a recording as you enter a carnival fun house, which I soon discovered was totally appropriate.

The first thing we saw, as Jonathan stood aside to let us in, was a massive dollhouse. Dollhouses and tiny dolls *everywhere*. We were in the middle of some Granny-meets-Chucky hellscape. Every table, bookshelf, sofa—even the grand piano—in their sprawling home had a tiny house, café, zoo, or some sort of miniature on it. Each miniature was decked out to look just like its real-life structure. This was the stuff of Zillow listing nightmares.

Mr. Reilly, I presumed, was waiting for us to say something out of admiration, like when one walked into a home with priceless artwork.

Cedric blurted, "Wow, what interesting dollhouses you have here. Look how many there are!" I mean, what else was there to say?

I might've tried to run right back out the front door at this point, but Cedric had a firm hold on my elbow.

Just then Sarah clomped down the stairs, clad in a ruffled dressing gown and still holding a chicken, and it was Cedric's turn to work to keep a straight face. I don't think he believed me about the chicken in the office until this very moment. He hid his surprise by bowing low to kiss her free hand in greeting. Sarah was too heavily medicated, though, to notice.

"Why don't we start with a tour of the property first, and then we can sit down and discuss details?" said Cedric.

I was still a bit in shock, but I managed to pull out my notebook and measuring tape to document everything Cedric dictated as I followed him.

On our tour we learned the full extent of Sarah's love for dollhouses, chickens, and roosters. (As if her bringing poultry to our meeting wasn't an indicator.) She led us to their kitchen, where a rooster named Miguel, with a cast on his tiny leg, held court. He had gotten himself into a cockfight and broken his leg and was thus recovering indoors. Naturally. Chicken feces scattered the floor, and it smelled like it. I started to gag thinking about anyone cooking in this mess. We were clearly going to need a catering tent for the reception as there would be no way to get this kitchen up to code.

To let us pet "sweet Miguel," Sarah began chasing the rooster. She stumbled around, grabbing at Miguel but missing him every time. Even with a broken leg, that rooster valiantly outran her. On her tenth lap around the kitchen island, Cedric couldn't take it anymore.

"Oh, don't worry about us, Sarah darling," Cedric crooned. "We will have plenty of time to pet the poultry. Why don't we move outside now to see the grounds, since that's where everything will take place the day of the wedding?"

Thankfully Sarah gave up, left Miguel hobbling, and led us out to the back of their property.

After about twenty minutes it became clear we would be poultry experts by the time the Reillys said "I do." Sarah toured us through countless coops that housed over 150 chickens and roosters. And Sarah didn't use the fowl for their eggs or their meat. No, they were just Sarah's pets—and every single one had a name. They even had themed families. The rest of Miguel's posse had Latin-sounding names, including Rosita and Josefina. Another brood, led by the rooster Shakespeare, featured chickens Ophelia, Rosalind, and Juliet.

Each bride deemed one element as essential for her wedding. For some, it was making sure they had a great band or the perfect favor for their guests. (For me, it would have been wearing Mamaw's amethyst necklace.) For Sarah, it was including a chicken-coop tour during cocktail hour. Each coop would have a handmade sign for guests who wanted to peruse the grounds. This was ridiculous but nonnegotiable.

Cedric couldn't help himself and whispered a couple terrible cocktail-hour cock-and-hen jokes at me while we walked the coops. Each time Sarah turned to recite the names of each chicken for me to write, his face went innocently blank. I couldn't take it anymore. This lady was out of her chicken-loving mind. The hefty commission was the *only* reason I was willing to jot down all of those names for one of those adorably illustrated maps—this time for a barnyard—but I did. New addition to résumé: chicken coop organization skills. Cedric was always trying to get us to improve ourselves, and voilà! Mission accomplished.

After measuring the open spaces for the tents we needed and escaping any more proverbial and literal crap, we headed back into the home to discuss some of the basics of design and the general list of to-dos. Cedric and I reluctantly sat side by side on a floral chintz sofa with dollhouses all around. Sarah basically sat on top of Mr. Reilly in the matching sofa across from us.

"In addition to the coop tour, I would like elements of the chickens to be incorporated into the wedding theme," said Sarah.

"Yes, but with a contemporary spin to it, of course," said Cedric. "We already have the note about naming the tables after the coops."

I could tell that he'd already conceded enough and was going to push back on this one as much as he could, without completely ignoring her. He really was magnificent at convincing a client that they were getting exactly what they wanted, while really steering them toward his own vision.

"Yes, I could see hanging large panels of chicken wire with white peonies woven through," he mused. "They'll be reminiscent of feathers."

"And some coxcomb and actual feathers could be bold to try in the centerpieces," I suggested.

"Great idea, Lottie," Cedric said with surprise. "Miss Sarah, we will come up with a *divine* scheme for your big day. Lottie or I will call you next week to discuss more details and to schedule our design presentation."

After going over our proposed vendor list of suggested photographers, bands, lighting specialists, and more, we managed to wrap things up easily. Sarah really only cared about her animals and paying homage to them. Other than that, she deferred all decisions to us. We said our good-byes, including what felt like an obligatory pat of one of the indoor chickens—then booked it out of there as fast as possible.

We were mentally exhausted after our time with Sarah and Mr. Reilly. I'm sure Cedric's feet hurt as much as mine did from wearing the wrong shoes to what turned into a trek through the poultry fields.

"I must admit, I didn't believe Travis when he told me your initial description of these clients," Cedric said. "But I'm certainly a believer now. And people say *I'm* eccentric. *Please.*"

"I'm still trying to figure out how one finds room for a passionate love of not only chickens but also dollhouses. I've found that one all-consuming hobby is usually enough."

Cedric grinned. "But regardless of how 'unique' this couple is, the wedding will be absolutely stunning, I assure you. And I'm sure you can handle it, Lottie."

I was excited by the mere fact that he knew my name, let alone that he already seemed to trust me. But before I could say anything, he whipped the car across two lanes.

"Thank God," Cedric said. "Next exit, there's a Chick-fil-A!"

We both died laughing, and I realized this wacky wedding might have forged a bond between Cedric and me. If so, it might actually be, given the chicken of it all, worth the cuckoo.

NINE

With no chickens and no other drama, it was remarkable how much I could accomplish. I ticked off details for a few local events; I coordinated a construction project for a ceremony in New Mexico; and I winnowed down possible venues for Brody and Harriet's wedding to an appropriately alluring few on the Mexican Pacific coast. I was an ice queen. I was a machine. I was a *professional*. And I'd gone to dinner and a movie with Matt before he left for an endless series of scouting trips.

The week of Halloween, several of us were shuttling off to Houston for a costume-filled fete. Griffin would also be there, which I knew because we were still emailing each other regularly with "war stories."

I still can't believe you ate chicken right after spending an afternoon with hundreds of them. Sarah would never forgive you if she knew. The whole thing totally freaks me out. I'm not a vegetarian, but man, that story's enough to make me only eat beef for the foreseeable future. Sounds like it was a good bit of one-on-one time with Cedric. Val usually just hands me her (heaviest) gear without speaking, lol. I swear she brought nine cameras to our last wedding, and of course, I got to lug them all. Perks of being me! ;) —G.

I fired off a reply:

Haha, fortunately Cedric doesn't trust anyone else to carry his designer satchel. It was quite a trip in every sense of the word, but yes, good to be with him alone. He's got some surprises for sure. Oh, and nothing in this world will stop me from eating those Chick-fil-A nuggets. Don't worry, though, we're only serving local beef and fish at the couple's wedding. So if you work that one, you won't starve. —L.

I could admit a slight hope Griffin would reply that he was scheduled to shoot Sarah and Jonathan's wedding. He could be entertaining—and helpful in a pinch. I certainly enjoyed working events more when he was there, but I chalked it up to fun flirtation now if nothing else. At least it gave me something to look forward to besides leftover cake.

I'm not sure yet if I'll be assigned to that one, but I'll be in Houston in the meantime. Sounds like it's going to be an epic party to shoot. See you soon. —G.

On Friday we headed south to Houston, another city of energy sources, astronomical wealth, and exorbitant parties. This time, for a teenager.

I'd worked with some spoiled clients by now but never one this young. Alice Marcus, the youngest granddaughter of the second-oldest branch of a department store dynasty, was turning sixteen, and a normal sweet sixteen party Just. Would. Not. Do.

So they called Cedric.

The theme was "Alice's Wonderland." Cedric believed that sometimes the most obvious was best: "Don't fight a good theme if it's staring you in the face, darling."

For birthdays and other celebrations, Cedric often let his imagination loose, unrestrained by the conventions and traditions of a wedding. Even the most creative and nontraditional bride had her boundaries. However, birthday parties, quinceañeras, and bat mitzvahs were a completely different story. Cedric loved to claim his mantra was "More is more and less is a bore."

This was no exception. For this event Cedric required us to dress up as Wonderland characters "to add to the ambiance" of the party. And the venue had a bylaw that their staff never, ever dressed up in costume. Lucky employees. However, we were a couple characters short because Cedric, Mary Ellen, and a couple Trusties were working The Firm's wedding at Rosewood Mansion on Turtle Creek. So I recruited Natalia to come.

After a lengthy road trip we arrived at the legendary River Oaks Country Club. We took over the entire venue for what Alice's mother, Octavia, described as an "intimate" party of 350 people. I'd be lucky if fifty people showed up at my wedding (once I was finally able to find a husband), so the idea of a teen knowing 350 people well enough to celebrate her birthday was mind-boggling.

The advance production team had already begun transforming the hunting lodge–inspired golf club ballroom into the Mad Hatter's tea party. A hall covered in mirrors distorted you in every possible way. You felt drunk, despite only having bubbly virgin cocktails in champagne flutes with pink straws and a tag that read: *Drink Me*. The cocktail napkins had the words *Eat Me* written in gold-foil lettering, also on-brand.

Once partygoers reached the ballroom foyer, a life-size leafless tree had been spray-painted gold. Hundreds of playing cards with names and table assignments dangled from the limbs by long strands of red satin ribbon. The cards were all from the suit of hearts, of course, for the "Queen of Hearts." Somewhere, I imagined, a dumpster overflowed with discarded spades, diamonds, and clubs from countless decks.

The flower arrangements for this party required specific skills. Half of the dining tables featured large arrangements of origami roses and tulips that appeared to be comprised of oversized playing cards. And since no water was required, they were folded weeks in advance, which was apparently how long it took to make over eight hundred origami flowers. If learning origami wasn't enough cause, Abigail's team would never forgive Cedric the paper cuts suffered for this project.

On the other half of the dining tables, giant clusters of white roses had been messily dipped in red paint and left to drip-dry so they looked like someone had tried to paint the roses red. It was brilliant.

I nudged Abigail as we walked by. "How did you get the paint to stay on there without ruining the flowers?"

"I've been experimenting with that paint recipe for *weeks*." She shook her head. "We usually use spray-paint, but it needed to drip, so I've been playing with it in our garage. I finally found the right consistency, but I've also probably ruined the front of Doug's car."

"Well, color me impressed." I waited a beat.

"Lottie, have you ever thought about a career in comedy?" She and Natalia both rolled their eyes at me.

We were stopped short by Alice's seven-layer birthday cake, an artistic masterpiece of scenes from the story in icing. So many artfully decorated cookies, petit fours, and macarons surrounded the cake that the surface of the table was barely visible. Every time Natalia and I walked past the table, we would stealthily grab a cookie or two (or six) and shove them in our mouths—a perk of the job.

Curved buffet tables covered in green linen—to hold the actual food—snaked around the room. At the very end they were connected to a live model, wearing the same shade of green and body painted to look like the smoking Caterpillar from the story. She even had a hookah to blow large puffs of smoke into the air.

Abigail went off to check on the sound crew and take a lap to more closely inspect the various arrangements. Natalia and I were in charge of checking in all the interns, which was a bit like herding cats, but I secretly enjoyed bossing them around.

After making sure all the little Trusties were accounted for and in place, Natalia and I slipped into our ensembles in the staff green room. Occasionally at events I was given quasi-sexy outfits to wear, but this time I was the White Rabbit, clearly a male character, to no one's concern but mine. No Playboy Bunny spin allowed either, given this was a party for "kids." Instead, I was dressed in a frumpy-looking vest with brown trousers, suspenders, a red bow tie, and an oversized pocket watch. A stage makeup artist was hired to paint our faces to match our characters. With whiskers, a black nose, white bunny ears, and matching bunny tail, my costume was a complete catastrophe. Making it even worse? Natalia was assigned the role of one of the singing flowers with a green leotard, a "leaf" skirt, and a beautiful floral headdress. She looked like a garden goddess, while I looked like a fat rodent.

Abigail, of course, got to be the Cheshire Cat, and I glared at her as she also looked adorable in her purple velvet jumpsuit, fluffy tail, purple cat ears, and cute little whiskers across her flawless brown cheeks.

Griffin, true to his email, was also working this event, and I couldn't wait to see what character he was assigned.

He walked out of the changing room, and we locked eyes. He was given the "honor" of dressing up as the Mad Hatter himself because he was the most involved with the guests, constantly in their faces taking pictures. I'd clearly drawn the short straw.

"Okay, you have a knack for catching me at some truly suboptimal moments," I said to Griffin as he walked over to where we stood. "This whole situation," I pointed to myself, "is off-limits as far as pictures are concerned. Just like the swan and the Range Rover incidents. I mean it—if a picture of me in this costume surfaces, I will *end* you."

"It's good to see you, too, Lottie."

"Hey. This is my roommate, Natalia." He looked at her with interest. *Maybe I should set them up.* I wasn't sure what his status was, but if Natalia got a boyfriend, she might stop trying to hack into my dating profiles to find matches for me. She'd have to figure out his deal about relationships, obviously, but she was welcome to try. Or she might at least get free dinner out of the gig. Dallas daters seldom went Dutch.

He admittedly looked kind of cute in multicolored striped pants and an oversized blue top hat that set off his dark hair. He looked almost dashing. For a fictional character, of course.

"I like your costume." I gave him an exaggerated eye roll at the same time.

"Yours could be worse."

"How?" I scratched at my wool trousers. I was beginning to sweat in rather inconvenient places.

"Well, he could've assigned you two Tweedledee and Tweedledum. Or the Walrus." He popped a cookie into his mouth.

Natalia snickered. I ignored her. "I guess you've got a point. When the Walrus eats all those baby oysters, it is so depressing. Even Cedric drew the line at offering an oyster bar tonight because that part of the movie devastated him."

"Glad to know he will draw the line somewhere." Griffin laughed.

"You seem awfully comfortable in that getup," I said.

"It's not too bad. And you actually look pretty cute. That little tail is the best part."

"Excuse me?" I choked. My face flushed. Thankfully I had enough makeup caked on to hide my reaction.

"Relax," he said. "I'm just messing with you. Don't call HR."

"As if The Firm has HR. I mean, good to hear it. I mean, thanks?" Wow. What on earth was wrong with me?

Natalia smirked and gave me a little nudge, which I also ignored. I needed more practice talking to live human men my age.

He graciously moved on. "If you're not busy yet, why don't y'all come with me to check out the photo prop area? I need someone to help me test out the lighting."

"You go help him, and I'll go find that cat-lady boss of yours to see if she needs anything before the party starts." Natalia nudged me yet again.

"Okay, but I'll come find you in a sec." My look conveyed certain death if she nudged me in his direction one more time.

Griffin's work at this party was supplemented by the "photo booth." Gone were the days of an actual photo booth—the retro kind where you ducked behind a curtain and out came four quickly snapped photographs. Instead, most clients requested an interactive "photo experience," complete with a million props. Holding on to the memories or inspiring FOMO on social? Not mine to judge.

For this party a custom-painted enchanted forest served as backdrop to an extra-long wooden table, jam-packed with stacks of vintage teapots and teacups (all glued together and stacked on hidden metal rods to prevent them from tipping). Small vases were bolted to the table in clusters overflowing with pocket watches. The trick was, this table was actually only two feet off the ground, so guests could appear to be dancing on the Mad Hatter's fantasy tea party table.

"Jump on up there, Rabbit, and strike a pose." Griffin reached out his hand to help me up onto the table.

"If Abigail sees me doing this and has a conniption, you get to explain that I'm working." I gripped his hand and hoisted myself onto the table. His hand felt solid in mine, and I ignored my traitorous racing heart. *Not now, Jones.*

I proceeded to stand on the table, then posed in various unflattering, goofy positions using the props, while Griffin took test shots and adjusted the lighting.

"Let me remind you, if any of these see the light of day, you know I'll have to kill you. I know a guy." It was truly hard to be threatening while holding a Cheshire Cat smile on a stick.

"You got it, boss. But I might keep just a few as blackmail. You never know what we might get into in the future." He grinned.

I started blushing—again. Okay, he was definitely flirting. Either that or I was desperate for any male attention. Regardless, I hopped down before I could say or do anything awkward. Well, anything additional.

"I better go check in with Natalia," I said once my tongue resumed function. "I left her alone too long, and Abigail's probably searching for me."

"*You're late! You're late! For a very important date . . .*" he sang as I sailed away.

Ugh. He's actually pretty funny, I thought as I almost ran into the guest of honor herself.

Alice walked into the building dressed as the eponymous heroine in a poufy blue dress, starched white apron, and—since this whole party felt as if Walt Disney and Tim Burton had a baby—an enormous black bow that streamed down her back and held a flashing light "diamond" in the middle.

She proceeded to walk around, critiquing the vendors and sampling the sweets. One of the poor caterers trailed her around the room with a tray of petit fours (Alice's favorite), filling in the holes left in her wake.

Natalia and I took our places by the tree of place cards, looking busy while we scoped out the room and the guests who had started to arrive. I'd never seen such a crew of teenage Trusties in my life. Most of the girls were costumed as flowers or queens, with a few elaborate Cheshire Cats and Dormice included for good measure. And almost without exception, they managed to find a coordinating Judith Leiber crystal-encrusted handbag in the shape of a flower, insect, teacup, or animal, which each cost about $2,000. No big deal for Daddy's Black Card. The boys were Tweedledee and Tweedledum, the Mad Hatter, or the Knave of Hearts. A local costume shop must have been handing out bonuses right about then.

Natalia gawped at a scantily clad March Hare who walked by.

"Nat, you can't stare! You're supposed to act aloof and unaffected by what's going on around you. We're in character."

"Well, in the movie the flowers were very judgmental, so I'm just playing along!"

We both laughed, and I watched as Griffin mingled among the teenagers—and their wealthy parents. They engaged with him, smiling and posing. He moved around with ease, capturing several angles on each party guest. It was a shame Val made him hide in the background most of the time. He seemed great with people.

"Don't think I don't notice what you're staring at," whispered Natalia.

"Please don't make me pluck off your petals in front of all these people," I whispered back.

"Mmm-hmm." She winked.

Time flew, and before long it was time for the seated dinner to begin. We ushered the guests out to the back lawn of the clubhouse. Outside, Cedric's team had built the party's masterpiece: a field of twelve-foot-tall giant mushrooms. Mimicking the scene in the book where Alice shrank, the overall effect was pretty trippy. Mushrooms were built from wire frames covered in plaster and fabric that was then painted. Gauzy tents draped between the mushrooms to cover the dining tables scattered below. Each table had more vintage teapots strewn about the tops, but these overflowed with vivid flowers and trailing vines to create a lush, colorful runner. Abigail had outdone herself yet again—and made Cedric's reputation solid gold.

Once guests were seated, we ducked back in the air-conditioning. Even in the fall, Houston was hotter than a ghost pepper. My rabbit's vest and suit were sweltering, and Natalia's leotard was darkening in places. I whipped out a couple panty liners from my vest pocket. "Here, take these."

"What in the world would I do with those?" Natalia asked.

"It's one of our tricks." *Ours? Wow.* "Stick it in your armpits so you don't sweat through your clothes." Mary Ellen never had to know I was taking credit—something she did *all* the time.

While we stood watching the party through the windows, Griffin ambled in, wiping the sweat off his brow with the back of his hand.

"Whew, it's miserable out there." He nodded at us. "Hey."

"Hey, yourself."

"I tell people all the time they can't make up the stuff I see through this lens, but no one believes me."

"Well, I do," I replied.

"After all this, I do too," added Natalia. "I don't know how the two of you do this every weekend."

"Well, we usually aren't in costume or surrounded by rich high schoolers." I laughed. "Some of our weddings are actually about two people in love getting married and not about all this teenage fantasy."

"I must have missed those weddings," he mused, staring through his lens at the crowd.

Natalia and I exchanged a look.

"This set is pretty amazing though," he added, breaking the silence.

The dinner was wrapping up, and the DJ, dressed as yet another Tweedle Dee, picked up the mic for the first song. He was given *very* specific instructions by Abigail for this event. There was no way we would take any chances with a DJ after the "Gold Digger" incident.

"Now, my fairy-tale creatures," he said in the same obnoxiously smooth voice that all event disc jockeys have. "To kick things off at this sweet, sweet sixteen is the sweetheart dance. So, Alice Marcus and Kevin Basker, please come to the dance floor. Nothing like young love—right, everyone? Alice and Kevin, it's your turn to take a spin as the happy couple!"

A lanky auburn-haired specimen—dressed as the King of Hearts—sauntered to the dance floor. Alice practically skipped toward him. They pulled each other close in a graceful move I was positive they'd learned at cotillion or whatever finishing class these sorts of kids went to. Or, I supposed, on TikTok. They swayed to "At Last." Of all the songs in the universe, this teen princess picked a song about waiting a lifetime while dancing with her high school sweetheart. Ah, young, stupid love.

As if he could hear my thoughts, Griffin leaned over and whispered in my ear, "I almost feel a little bad for them."

"Why?" I said without turning, acutely aware of his face next to mine.

"They think this is it. True love. Forever and ever, amen."

"You're so mean."

"Yeah, but am I wrong?"

I couldn't disagree with him, no matter how hard I wanted to believe.

"Fifty bucks says it doesn't last through high school."

"No deal," I said. "The odds are on your side on that one. But I still think it's sweet, even if naive."

"Suit yourself. This could have been your moment. You gotta bet on someone sometime, Lottie."

"Look who's talking, bud."

I glanced around. Abigail had moved inside, presumably dealing with details for the grand finale—fireworks over the golf course followed by a performance by the Houston Rockets' Power Dancers, also in costume as some sort of tacky bunnies. Alice was a superfan. All the money in the world, and the girl still had the taste of a teenager.

Griffin moved closer to take pictures of the teen couple, and I hopped back to Natalia.

"Hey, you want to go watch the fireworks?" I asked.

"Ooh, yes! Can't we see them from here though?"

"Yeah, but I have a better idea."

We snuck around the side of the clubhouse, quite a feat considering we looked like a rose and a rabbit. We slipped inside one of the golf carts waiting there. Cedric's team had reserved a few to run errands, reach the far parking lot, and mitigate other emergencies. The keys were sitting in the cup holder.

I put it in gear and drove toward the green, giving the clubhouse and festivities a wide berth.

We cruised along the manicured grass, past a rock-edged pond and a grove of elms. I pulled over on the other side of the trees, out of sight of the clubhouse. I still had my walkie-talkie if Abigail or the Trusties had an emergency. Ten minutes until fireworks.

Natalia and I had been potluck college roommates who melded like peanut butter and honey—so much so that eventually we accepted the inevitable and proceeded to create our own platonic domestic partnership. We'd learned to cook together, traveled the world, and been in and out of our first serious relationships. She was my ride-or-die. Even on a golf cart.

Junior and senior years we rented a house with Harper and Megan. And as Natalia and I hopped out of the cart to sit on the manicured grass, I thought about our last week all together with a pang. My wedding-that-wasn't and the end of an era.

Of our group of friends, Nat was always the encourager. She was the rock. But I'd been so busy working for Cedric—and complaining about it—I had no idea how she was really doing.

"So, how's work been?" I started awkwardly. "Is your boss still refusing to promote you?" I now understood that Natalia worked in marketing for the manufacturing company, but I still had zero clue what she actually did on the daily, so this seemed safe.

"Yep . . . A couple weeks ago she hired a new girl over me to be my supervisor. Which feels like a clear sign. I think I'm being replaced."

"No way. Can she even do that? You work so hard; I can't believe this."

"I can't tell if I just haven't made an impression or if she wants somebody schmoozier, especially with clients," she said, dejected. This was not going the way I'd hoped. "I have great relationships, but I'm not a suck-up. I kind of suck at it, actually . . . Anyway, that's why I took this gig. Anytime Cedric needs help, let me know because I'm trying to save money in case I need to find a new job."

"Absolutely, of course. But geez, I wish you'd told me!"

"I didn't want to stress you out, Lot. You've got enough on your plate working for Attila the Hun and his merry band. I'll be fine. Maybe a change would be good for me. And if I have to start an online pyramid scheme to make rent, just promise to buy lots of essential oils and protein shakes, okay?"

"You're ridiculous! But of course I promise." As I leaned back on the grass and stared up at the darkening sky, I felt like a selfish brat. I'd been so worried about my own debt and about impressing Abigail and now Cedric that I hadn't even bothered to really keep up with my roommate. With my frequent late nights and weekends and her early mornings at the office on Chinese hours or training for rides—our schedules still often didn't overlap. We could go days without seeing each other. But that was no excuse. "Be a better friend" moved to the top of my to-do list, which I was clearly crushing these days.

"Have you seen Matt since your date at Bistro 31?"

"Yeah, we grabbed a drink at the wine bar after work last Thursday. I think you were at that training seminar all evening."

"So . . . how was it?"

"I mean, he's charming and hot and really smart. He travels a lot, but sounds like he's at least based back in Dallas for a while now that he's working at a sports agency that reps guys from the Mavs and the Rangers."

"Does he still kiss like he used to? And did he try to take you home yet?"

"Natalia!"

"Don't get mad at me. I need all the vicarious action I can get after my last couple weirdos and squidgy specimens."

"I plead the Fifth. But obviously, I would tell you the instant something happened . . . Please tell me about *your* date this week. I've been *dying* to know," I said. Natalia always had the worst luck in online dating, but she walked away with the best stories.

"Well, it was fine. He went on and on about how he went to Rice, like I should be impressed by his academic credentials. I just about fell asleep during dessert. And, of course, he made me split the check with him. Buh-bye . . . *Wait,* have I told you about the other guy, my 'soul mate'?"

"Um, no, but what's his deal?"

"The other day, I got a high-alert email from Match," Nat began. "The subject line said they had found me a 100 percent match. I clicked, eager to meet Mr. Right.

"Instead, I met MrConfident469. He looked to be about forty, with curly reddish hair and eighties wire-rimmed glasses. In one of his pictures, he's riding the mechanical bull at Billy Bob's—'Look! I'm brave!'" She waved her fists in mock excitement. "In another, he's snorkeling in the Caribbean in a T-shirt—'I'm adventurous and still sun conscious.' In my favorite picture, though, he's wearing a safari hat with no explanation. In what looked like a Chili's."

"Gosh, I think I'm obsessed with him."

"Well, you may have him. Here's my favorite part of his profile." Natalia pulled out her phone and opened the app.

"Brace yourself: '*I hesitate to write this next paragraph . . . but, speaking of compatibility, don't judge a book by its cover! Looking at my pictures, you might have noticed that my build is on the thin side and wondered if I will be able to please you. Don't let wrong assumptions stop us from meeting, if you know what I mean. Of course, some* women don't care about that, and it's only one part of me you will get to know in the future. Also, I've been told that I have magic hands. I love to cuddle. I'm also very good at cooking Italian food. But that is all down the road.'"

"Then, he went on to explicitly describe some of his favorite sexual acts before he described his bald spot," she finished. "Just as a disclaimer, you know?"

I was rolling on the ground, wheezing too hard to summon a sufficient response.

"So I deleted my account." She crossed her arms. "I mean, what does he think women are on Match for? I literally have no idea."

"I . . . have . . . no words . . . for you," I gasped. "Please, please stay on there. What if your real soul mate is joining right now and you'll never meet him? What if I get bored or sad and need more stories?"

"I'll consider it. I also got asked to join a new flag football team—those are usually full of athletic single guys."

"Good, please let me know if you find any decent contenders for either of us or need someone who kicks left footed."

"Will do. But, Lot, while we're on the subject, do you really want me to start on all the things you're *still* not doing to meet anyone?"

Crickets.

"Um-hmm. You're the only person I know who signs up for every possible dating site and never actually matches with or messages anyone. Forget about trying to meet them in person."

"I just haven't found—"

"Nope, save it. It's like your confidence and your libido went on vacation in the early 2000s. Do you think Matt could help you find them?"

"Ouch. Harsh."

"That Griffin guy was also cute."

"I don't really know what the deal is there, but I think it's a no go . . . so if you want to give it a try, I can pass along his number."

"No thanks, I think I'm going to see where things go with Mr. Confident. Not to mention I think you're the one Griffin's interested in. I saw him looking at you across the room more than once tonight. And not through the lens of a camera."

I found myself blushing for the third time tonight over this guy. But I wasn't in the mood for more in-depth conversations about him or anyone else. At least not while dressed like a stuffed rabbit.

"Ugh, can we please be done talking about guys for tonight? Unless, of course, you want to share more of your Match stories."

"No way. It's funny for a while, but then it just gets depressing."

"Oh, look!" I pointed. "Fireworks are starting!"

We lay back on the grass next to the golf cart, watching the explosions above us. It was magical and probably unsafe. But I was grateful for the moment. I resolved to help Nat find her happy ending—or at least her next step.

As the fireworks ended I heard the radio crackle. "Lottie, come in, Lottie!"

"Yes, Abigail?"

"Hey, where are you? We need help handing out the gift bags."

I crossed my fingers and felt bad as I lied. "I'm just around the corner helping guests."

"Sounds good, just come around to the front."

We sped back to the clubhouse, careful to keep the cart out of sight. Natalia and I each grabbed a box of favors and stood on either side of the front entrance, passing out bags to guests as they left. During a lull I snuck a peek inside. A vintage teacup rested on a folded Gucci scarf, for the sake of padding, no doubt. I recognized a jewel-encrusted selfie stick (as if these kids could possibly take any more selfies than they already did), a Kylie Jenner lip-plumping kit, a bunch of Flash Tattoos, and a Le Labo candle set, which cost at least $200. And rounding out the goodies of the Gen Z zillionaires was a $50 gift card to Whataburger. Now that's a gift even I could appreciate. Taquitos at 2:00 a.m. transcended class and generation.

After the last guest departed, Natalia and I each claimed two of the extra bags for ourselves, then stumbled over to Abigail's car. We leaned against it, half-asleep from being on our feet all day.

"Did you get to say good-bye to the Mad Hatter?" Natalia asked through a yawn.

"No, but I'm sure I'll hear from him Monday."

"Oh really?"

"Good grief," I said. "We just email. We trade stories a few times a week while we're at our desks, that's all."

"For now." Natalia grinned.

"Just get in the car," I said once Abigail joined us.

As we drove to the hotel, I itched my sweaty skin, grateful to be out of the costume. I leaned my head against the door, trying not to nod off. Maybe if I earned a promotion, next time Cedric would let me be something less humiliating. Doubtful, but a girl could dream.

TEN

My phone rang three times before I woke enough to answer it. It was noon on Sunday, but I was exhausted from the drive back from Houston the day before, followed by a wedding that night. I couldn't imagine what Cedric or Mary Ellen could possibly need, but I rolled over to check the screen. Mom. On the fourth ring I picked up.

"Mom, what's going on? Is it an emergency?" I tried to force myself awake.

"Sorry to wake you up, honey," she said, clearly not that sorry. "I just wanted to talk to you about Christmas."

I slumped back onto my pillow. "Christmas is still two months away."

"Yes, but your brother's deployment is ending, you know, and he'll be back stateside starting in February."

"I know, we've been counting down. It's so hard slash annoying to FaceTime him with the shift he's on in Japan."

"Yes." She took a breath. "With him coming back, we thought we should go over and visit him at least once. Your dad has been saving the credit card points for something special, and we haven't been out of the country since Aunt Norma took us on that cruise. Tommy gets a little leave over Christmas, so we're going to Japan for the holidays!"

I blinked. "Oh."

"Obviously we would *love* for you to come, but we understand about time off work and flights. We wish we could fly you there ourselves. We just don't want you to feel abandoned or like you don't have anywhere to go."

I mean, *of course* I felt like that, but I also understood that many of my peers were alternating with their in-laws or hosting family gatherings at home. That just wasn't my life stage yet. So I mustered what little grace I could find.

"Mom, don't worry about me. I get it." Nope, did not get it. Family Thanksgiving had stopped when Tommy was in boot camp because three people and one turkey felt like a sad ratio. Now I was losing Christmas too?

"We have a couple of events between Christmas and New Year's, and Cedric is always offering bonuses to employees willing to stick around and pick those up. I'd been meaning to talk to you about that anyway. I can FaceTime y'all while you do gifts, and it'll be just like I'm there."

"And we can mail you presents!"

"That would be great."

If it were possible to unintentionally make me feel any lower, my mom would find a way. Sure enough, she did.

"Okay, wonderful. Whew, what a relief. I'm so glad it will work out." She exhaled, then continued at speed. "I also wanted to let you know I just got a notice in the mail that there's another LSAT test coming up after the New Year, and I can't stop thinking that you should take it at least *once*."

My two LSAT attempts happened shortly after college in a spurt of desperation to reclaim my prior life plan. As I was more focused on my heartbreak than on torts or any studying, suffice it to say they did not go very well—and I had still never told my parents I'd blown it twice.

"Mom, I don't even want to be a lawyer anymore, or at least I don't think I do. Plus, I'd have to spend the next three months doing nothing but studying for it. I can't take that kind of time off from work and still keep my job."

"I know it's a lot to think about, but it's been years now since you first put a pause on law school, and if you do decide you want to take it, you're running out of time. Maybe you could use the extra time over the holidays to study?"

"I appreciate your checking on it, but they also don't just give you an unlimited number of tries at it either."

"Well then think about your biological clock."

"My biological clock?" I yawned. This was going to be a longer conversation than I thought—and one I couldn't avoid. We were hitting all the high notes today.

"Yes, Lottie. You're well into your childbearing years. I've held my tongue and given you space and time, but I just found out that Laura Lee is pregnant, and now I'm worried about you." Mom huffed. "Your cousin's your age, and the last of your friends to get pregnant, and—"

"Nope," I interrupted. "That is literally just not true."

"Lottie, please take this seriously."

"You want me to take law school or having a baby seriously?" I asked, now starting to get annoyed.

"Both."

"Well, pick a lane. And I'm not the only woman without kids. Natalia isn't even dating anyone either!"

"Her mother is equally distressed by this fact too." Mom was sounding sanctimonious. "You don't have to go to law school. You don't have to get married or have children, but you can't stay in limbo any longer. I just want to know that you're pursuing the life you want for yourself."

"Well, Laura Lee isn't exactly the pillar of inspiration for me. She married her high school boyfriend, has had three failed careers—remember when she wanted to be a hairdresser so she dropped out of nursing school? And I have no idea where they're even going to put that baby in her apartment."

"You know what I mean, Lottie. You had such big dreams growing up. It's impossible as a parent to sit and watch your kids settle for a life they don't really want. I just want you to find something that makes you happy and stick to it."

"Listen, Mom." I needed to calm her down. And myself. "It's totally my fault you feel this way right now. I admit I'm not the best at calling home or keeping you updated on how I'm really feeling at the moment, but I'm not floundering. Yes, I'm sort of starting from the beginning again, which sucks at almost thirty, but things are also progressing. And not just with my job. I have friends here, good friends, and we take care of each other."

"I'm glad to hear all of that Lottie," she said. "It's just that your dad worked so hard to build the landscaping business. It took years for him to get where he is now, and he started when he was a lot younger than you are. And he had me to help. It's not easy making money. You know that." Ah, there it was, the constant struggle of the middle class.

"Oh, trust me, I do. I remember exactly when you told me we couldn't afford the seventh-grade trip to Dollywood. After I got that job at the library, shelving dusty books after school, I pretty much never stopped working through high school—you guys taught me that."

"I just don't want you to have to work yourself to death when you don't have to. You still have options, but they won't exist forever. That's all I'm trying to say."

Some days, as I dealt with the problems of the über rich, it was actually good to have a reminder that the so-called crises we handled didn't compare to the reality for the rest of the world, my family included. Amid all the pomp and circumstance, I needed to remember what was really important.

"I need you to trust me right now, Mom. I get this isn't what I said I always wanted."

"Oh, I know. I remember very well all the episodes of *Law & Order* you and your brother watched on the weekends. It gave him nightmares for life, but for you, it became everything." I had come to college with the theme song as my ringtone for my parents. My girlfriends got *Sex and the City*, naturally.

"Remember when I'd reenact the courtroom scenes with my Barbies?"

"Yes." She chuckled. "Poor Ken got locked up every time."

"The perp was almost always a man, what can I say?"

"And I almost went blind proofing all those boring papers you wrote for school about Supreme Court cases. Which were brilliant, I mean."

We both laughed.

"I just wanted to be the female Atticus Finch."

"And you earned every bit of those scholarships to TCU, even if they didn't cover it all," she said.

"Thanks, yes." I ignored the unintended dig. "What I'm saying is that I know the value of hard work and time. I also know money isn't everything and that dreams can change. Sometimes they have to . . . I mean, look at what happened with Brody."

"Oh, Lottie. I know you understand. It's just my job as your mom to make sure you have as few regrets as possible. You always wanted to be a wife, a mom, and a lawyer, and it just hurts my heart to see you not bein' any of that."

"I promise you, I'm doing pretty well . . . In fact, I just got assigned my first wedding to plan on my own."

"Why, you don't say!" Mom rallied. "That's great, sweetheart. Way to save the big news."

"Yes, really. And you'll never guess what the bride is obsessed with."

I couldn't tell her everything about sweet, befuddled Sarah, but we laughed at the wackiness of a wedding full of dollhouses and chickens.

"If all goes smoothly, it could mean bigger things for me here . . . I finally feel like I might have a real future in Dallas."

"Well, I'm so glad to hear that, and I'm sorry if I scared you when I called," she said. "Time is flying by, and all of a sudden I have grown children who have full lives of their own."

I guessed I was lucky to have someone who cared enough to call me in a panic on a random Sunday afternoon to discuss my aging ovaries.

"Do you need me to come home so you can see for yourself that I'm okay?"

I only had a couple weeks back in Dallas before the team headed out of town again for yet another destination wedding. This time it was in the wilds of New Mexico, and the last thing I wanted to do was drive all the way to Memphis.

Not to mention my life in Dallas looked absolutely nothing like my old life.

"No, honey. You keep doing what you're doing, but maybe just check in a little more frequently."

"For sure."

"I've got a little money I can send you if you need it."

"Thanks, but I'm good." It felt awesome to say those words and remotely mean them.

"Lottie! Want to go grab a drink with us?" yelled Natalia from the other room.

Apparently Megan had stopped by to show us the latest issue of *Brides* and get our feedback on linens. She knew texting links to articles was no way to verify we actually read said articles. Megan's wedding was rapidly becoming my pro bono side hustle.

"Yes, just hold on a second!" I called to my friends. "Sorry, Mom. Gotta run."

"Well, I love you. Better call me again soon. Maybe your dad and I could come for Thanksgiving this year. We'll see. I could use a good Tex-Mex meal and a margarita."

Getting Dad to leave the business unattended twice in one year was unthinkable, but I said, "Just let me know. Love you too."

"C'mon, let's go!" shouted Megan as I hung up. "We're going to try and make the brunch happy hour at Mattito's."

"Give me five!"

I thankfully hadn't taken off my makeup from the night before, which, while disgusting, made getting ready the next day a breeze as long as eyeliner didn't run down your face overnight. I pulled my hair into a topknot and grabbed a T-shirt from my dresser.

As I pulled it over my head, I realized it was the one TCU football shirt I'd held on to after Brody. It'd definitely been too long since my last Laundromat trip.

I paused. I didn't rip it off instinctively as I once might have. It was just a comfortable old T-shirt that felt familiar and nothing more. I chose to be okay with it. This T-shirt would not win. I could be a pro, a boss, a tin woman, an automaton who could do what she had to do. I pulled on my white jeans, threw on my flip-flops, and headed toward the door.

⌇

I tried to carry that Zen attitude about Brody's wedding into the next week. On Tuesday I had a lengthy call with Tasha, Harriet's assistant who lived in Los Angeles. Cedric had conceived the top-line elements of the celebration with the couple in some early conversations, so it was up to Mary Ellen, Tasha, and me to iron out the details and keep them in line with the overall feel of the wedding. I liked Tasha. We traded sarcastic comments and jokes about all the miniscule details under our purview.

"What do you think about these linen dinner napkins? Do they communicate 'I'm elegant but also casual enough for a poolside supper'?" she asked.

"Absolutely. But what about these letter-pressed tags for the individually boxed chocolates at each place setting? The monogram needs to be big but not too big so you can see some of the chocolates inside, but not too much so it's still a surprise," I replied.

We got along, which made the process of selecting specific shades of ivory for ribbons and many other fussy details somewhat pleasant.

"I know these details matter for some people, but they will be completely lost on Harriet. That's not her vibe. And Brody wouldn't know what a charger plate was to save his life," Tasha said.

"I know, I remember when—" I stopped myself. I assumed Brody's and Harriet's respective teams knew about my history with him and role in their wedding, but since my name wasn't on the contract paperwork, perhaps it had gone under the radar. I wasn't about to flag it and risk getting myself booted off this plum, essential assignment.

"Oh, sorry, I've got to go—my noon appointment is here." I pivoted. "I'll call you back this afternoon to finish going through everything else if that works for you."

"Great, I've got to get my midmorning coffee. It's only nine o'clock," Tasha joked.

"Sounds good, talk soon." With that I clicked the flashing light on my desk phone. "Hi, Travis."

"Hello, Lottie. I have Miss Ledoux here for your meeting." He was always so much more mannerly when clients were in the lobby. He sent her to the larger conference room to look at fabric swatches and mood boards while I gathered her wedding information to take into the meeting with me.

Cassie Ledoux was sitting pretty in one of the tulip conference chairs, ankles crossed in her custom Miron Crosby boots. Immaculate makeup, sleek brown blowout—the former rodeo queen façade was always on point. She was the cowgirl version of Kate Middleton, and I loved her. Mary Ellen and I had worked with Cassie and her mother for many months now planning her upcoming nuptials, and she was by far my favorite bride.

Cassie was the queen, or more accurately, the princess of natural gas, and her wedding would take place in New Mexico in a few weeks. Her father owned thousands of acres in Texas that produced invisible gold every day. However, the family no longer lived in Texas. Instead they enjoyed their private compound in the mountains of New Mexico, and I was excited to see it in person next month. Cedric and Mary Ellen had attended the previous site visit to the property, and the client's Gulfstream G150 jet was provided for them as easy transportation to and from New Mexico. I'd never stepped foot on a private plane, so I could only imagine how fabulous it was.

However, for a gagillionaire, Cassie was an extremely laid-back bride and could not have been more enjoyable to work with. She was a former barrel racer, which was all she really spent her time doing when they still lived in Texas. Had a lifetime spent mucking stalls helped put things in perspective? Horses couldn't have cared less how much money her daddy had. Either way, she was a hoot and a half, and I appreciated her off-color sense of humor.

Cassie was coming in today to finalize a few last-minute details and also hand over a couple sentimental items we wanted to ensure were incorporated into the design.

"Daddy wants for me and Paul to bury a bottle of bourbon upside down near where the ceremony will take place so supposedly it won't rain the day of the wedding. He said it needs to be a month out. Do you think that's crazy?"

I laughed. "No, it's actually a common tradition in the South. The groom's supposed to dig it up on his wedding day to drink with everyone." I smiled. "Some couples will actually save some of it to keep on their bar as a reminder of their wedding day."

"Well, now I guess that's kind of sweet," she replied. "There's so much to remember for this wedding, and I'm so thankful to have y'all helping us. Mama and I would never be able to do all this on our own."

"You make my job enjoyable. It all becomes second nature to us, but that's because we work on weddings every day. When it's your first one to plan, I'm sure it seems completely overwhelming. Especially if it's a larger event like yours."

"I blame Daddy for that," said Cassie. "I wanted to elope with Paul and skip the production, but my father wouldn't have it. He's got more friends coming to the wedding than I do."

For Buck Ledoux's only daughter's wedding, no expense had been spared. Many of The Firm's clients would initially tell us we had unlimited funds, but then everyone had their "do not go a penny over

X dollars" moment somewhere along the planning process. However, this one actually had *no budget*. Cassie's mother, Patricia, just asked that we keep it "around a million dollars," said with a conspiratorial wink. Needless to say, we didn't complain about the blank check entrusted to us for the event. I was pretty sure our tab was up to $1.2 million and counting.

"Cedric has thought of everything," she said. "Every design rendering he showed us in our meetings looked like a movie set. Paul just about lost his mind when I showed it to him. We both think this is all a bit too much, but it makes my parents happy so we're going along with it. It will be one heck of a party."

We started thumbing through the fabric swatches for said party. We were bunting this bash up in as many pinks as possible, which had been Cassie's primary design objective all along.

"When I was little, my granny trained me to say, 'My colors are blush and bashful,' which was adorably cheesy and from *Steel Magnolias*, of course. Now my colors are more like fuchsia, sunset, and blush, but I've remained a clichéd pink girl for life." Cassie fingered a piece of linen best described as bubblegum pink. "I've avoided Pepto-Bismol at least, so that's a win, right?"

"For sure, and Cedric would never let you go astray. In my experience I've found it's best to tell Cedric what you want and then step back and let him work his magic. I'm excited to work this wedding for you."

"You've been so fun to work with too," Cassie said. "Afterward, I'll be so sad not to see you as much as I do now."

"Thanks, Cassie. The door is always open." This marked the first and only time I'd ever say that to a bride.

"Please let me take you out for drinks once Paul and I are home from our honeymoon. I'll be in Dallas for one thing or another."

"I'd love that," I said, and I really meant it. "Now, let's talk about the handkerchiefs you brought in to wrap around your bouquet. And did you bring your family photos to frame for the guest book table?"

We spent the next hour checking off the rest our to-do list. Before Cassie left, she gave me a giant hug and made me promise to answer her texts after the wedding to set up a time to get dinner.

In moments like this a surprising affection for my job smacked me like a wave. Could I even imagine doing anything else right now? Who would have thought I'd end up here—and happy-ish? Who knew if Cassie and Paul's marriage would last? But I desperately hoped they'd make it, for all our sakes. And helping bring her the day of her dreams, or of her dad's dreams, felt more like a joy than a job.

ELEVEN

On Saturday night Megan texted our group thread:

> Well, I'm going to have a nervous breakdown. My engagement photographer bailed on our session tomorrow, and we need the photos for our save-the-dates to go out on time. Kill. Me.

For once I realized I might actually be able to help, so I called Griffin. I would normally hesitate when calling a guy, even at my age. While my generation grew up with landlines, I now had entire friendships based solely on text or DM. However, Griffin was a vendor, I reminded myself as I dialed, even if this wasn't exactly a work call.

"Lucky for you, Lottie, I'm free tomorrow," he quipped. "But I'll only take the gig on one condition."

"And what's that?"

"You have to tag along as my assistant."

"I hope you have deep pockets. My help doesn't come cheap."

"Well, it's actually more of an internship . . ." He laughed.

I found myself more excited to "work" on my day off than I'd imagined I would be. I couldn't tell yet if it was because I'd saved the day for my best friend or because I got to see Griffin. Regardless, I didn't hate the feeling.

The next morning, he pulled up outside our building. I ran out to his truck and we set off for the West Village, just a few minutes away.

A little district in the middle of Uptown, the West Village was super walkable and packed with shops and restaurants. It was often where my friends and I found ourselves on rare weekend nights I wasn't at an event. Cork Wine Bar was also the scene of Megan and Josh's first date two years ago. ("Never commit to dinner if you can avoid it, just in case he's a narcissist or a sociopath" was one of single Megan's former truisms.)

We were too early for wine, but the area was full of cute spots to act as a backdrop for the pictures.

"Hi, y'all," I said as Megan and Josh approached, hand in hand. "This is Griffin."

"Griffin!" Megan jumped in for the hug, per usual. "I really can't thank you enough for rescuing us. It's so good to finally meet you!"

"Yeah man, thanks." Josh extended his hand.

"It's no problem. Happy to help. Where do y'all want to go first?"

Local artists had been commissioned to paint murals under several of the overpasses and on the walls of businesses around the area. We stopped where cinderblocks had been transformed into rainbow-hued hexagons that looked three-dimensional.

As always Megan was in perpetual motion. Even when trying to pose, she bounced. But Josh grounded her. He put a hand on her back, not to tell her where to go but just in affection, and she instantly stilled. She remained an anxious, rubber ball of a bride-to-be, but around Josh at least she was calm.

Griffin put them both at ease too. I held the light reflector as he seamlessly made small talk and instructed their poses.

"Tell me how you guys met." His hands continued to adjust the lens, snap a picture, find a new angle as he chatted. "Now, Josh, put your hand on her waist. Lean there."

Megan launched into their story: I was running late after a rehearsal dinner (typical) to meet her at the wine bar, and Josh bee-lined over to where she was sitting alone with a glass of wine in one hand and a book in the other. "I'm old-fashioned about books, so I always keep a physical copy of one in my bag," she said. "I'd never been approached in such a not-creepy way before. He just exuded confidence. And he'd actually read the book. So I decided not to tell him to scram."

Soon books turned into backstories, and by the time I had arrived, girls' night was officially canceled. They went to dinner, and I'd had to play second fiddle to Josh ever since. "I've never been so grateful to Lottie for being a workaholic slash bad friend," Megan added. My version might have been *slightly* modified from how she told it, but still.

A fleet of restored vintage trolleys ran from the West Village to Downtown. They had adorable names like Rosie, Betty, Petunia, and the Green Dragon. They dinged cheerfully down the green median of a cobblestone path. Griffin took a few shots of Megan and Josh in front of the Green Dragon before we all climbed aboard.

As we looped around the neighborhood, I looked out the window and felt the breeze on my face. The West Village was a great cross section of urban Dallas life. Yuppies, families, and empty nesters comingled on the streets. Most days a breeze blew down the corridor, making it bearable, even enjoyable, to sit outside the cafés year-round. A dog-friendly café with an adjoining dog park was down the block, and a parade of pups dripped down the street, tails wagging, sopping wet from doggie pools. A couple on roller skates did tricks for pedestrians before they skated away, hand in hand. It felt vibrant and magical. Homey.

Griffin captured a few more angles of Megan and Josh cuddling on the trolley bench, and then we got off to head to our next stop nearby: Klyde Warren Park. Walking up to the park, I found myself so grateful for the urban planner who dreamed up building a park on a highway overpass. Dallas's distinctive skyline glinted overhead as we strolled the grassy acreage between Downtown and Uptown.

Megan and Josh had adorable retro townie bicycles they'd secured nearby before meeting us, which they now rode under the white arches of the dirt path that encircled the park. I grabbed a seat at one of the green café tables, unnecessary for the moment.

Griffin in his element was something to behold. Gone was the wry, withdrawn demeanor. Instead he was cracking jokes and giving compliments as Megan and Josh attempted to smile widely, look natural, and not fall off their bikes. He was jogging backward to stay ahead of them, and his backside was decidedly *not* unenjoyable to watch. When he paused to wipe a little perspiration from his forehead, our eyes met. He grinned widely and winked. This was clearly a lot more fun for him than photographing wedding parties—or at least he was good at pretending.

"Hey, gang, want to take some pictures at the food truck next?" I suggested, solely for the photo op and not at all because I was ravenous.

"Good idea, Lottie!" Griffin said loudly. Then as an aside to me: "You're looking a bit hangry over here."

"You better look out. I bite."

Today was the fruit truck's day and not pizza as I'd hoped, but the colorfully Instagrammable bowl still took the edge off my hunger.

Our final stop was the Dallas Museum of Art across the street. On the way we passed under a canopy of magnolia trees, their blooms long gone. With the red steel of a Mark di Suvero sculpture in the background, Josh picked Megan up and twirled her around. The shutter clicked. I had to admit, she looked deliriously happy. A little bit of a bro, Josh might not have been my cup of tea, but he was kind, cute, and gaga over my friend. I found myself just genuinely thrilled for them.

My new guy friend, on the other hand, remained an enigma. He'd never mentioned a girlfriend, and I liked to think we got along well. But he also seemed pretty negative about relationships, or at least marriage—and the lavish weddings we worked. I'd never asked him what he meant about never being on the other side of the camera at Alfie and Camila's wedding. Regardless of his attitude, he was certainly skilled at working with couples. I had no doubt Megan would be thrilled with the outcome from today. This should buy me at least a year's worth of good-friend brownie points.

"Now, kiss her like you mean it," shouted Griffin as they posed in front of the Chihuly flowers inside the café of the DMA.

"I'm good at that." Josh leaned in to kiss Megan. She squealed, pretending to be shy and putting up the most pathetic fight I'd ever seen.

"And let's go ahead and get that clichéd leg pop, Megan," Griffin said as he continued shooting. "The cheesier it feels, the better the images will be."

I couldn't help but smile, listening to him coach the couple. He was really funny, if you liked sarcasm, which I did. Megan and Josh looked so natural together, so happy.

"You know what they say about marriage?" he asked. "Marriage is about three rings: the engagement ring, the wedding ring, and suffer-ing."

"Griffin!" I yelled. "Don't scare Josh off!"

"Oh please." Josh smirked. "That's a great one. Hadn't heard it yet. And don't worry, Lottie. If I haven't been scared off before now, it's never going to happen."

Megan planted a giant kiss on his cheek and winked at me as they headed up the long hallway of the museum.

"I've got way worse jokes than that one," Griffin deadpanned. Then he laughed and fell into step alongside me.

"Oh, I'm sure." I rolled my eyes but grinned despite my best efforts.

"Let's grab just a couple more pictures outside in the garden, and then we can call this a wrap," said Griffin. "I've got some really great images from today."

"Sounds good," said Megan. "And please let us take you to dinner to thank you for doing this on such short notice."

"Yeah, we'd love to buy you dinner and drinks, man," said Josh. "I was secretly dreading today, but it turned out to be kind of fun."

"Thanks guys," replied Griffin. "I've got to edit in the studio later tonight, but I'd love a beer first."

"Perfect." Megan shot me yet another wink.

Great. Now I knew what, or I guess I should say *who*, we would be talking about later.

We pulled up to Mia's, one of our favorite Tex-Mex joints not too far from the museum. While we waited to be seated, the guys went inside to order a round at the bar while Megan and I snagged seats on the patio.

"Oh my gosh, Lottie! He's so cute! Why didn't you tell me he was so cute?"

"As a matter of fact, I think I did."

"Well, I like him a lot."

"So do I—as a friend. I've told you all this."

"Yes, but that was before I got to meet him and experience the hotness in person. What's the holdup?"

"For starters, he's never given any indication that he's interested in anything more than friendship."

"Are you kidding me?" She put a hand on her hip. "Obviously you missed all the longing looks he gave you while we were walking around today. He kept sneaking glances while he was supposed to be focused on yours truly. But, I get it."

"You have always had an overactive imagination." I needed to put a stop to this before the guys came back. I would *die* if Griffin overheard us. "Plus, I told you, I don't think he wants to get married. That's the attitude anytime it comes up, which is a lot when you work in weddings. So we're just going to be friends. Sure, flirty friends, but just friends. I can get into that."

"Do you think he wants to be a priest?"

Before I could reply, Josh and Griffin returned, deep in conversation about Texas college football teams and too engrossed to pay attention to what we'd said.

I took the frozen margarita from Griffin, savoring its chill in the warmth of early evening. "Thanks." I nodded at him.

He smiled back, and I found myself staring at his lone dimple, which I'd never noticed. *Focus!*

"I think our table's ready if you want to come." He stepped aside for me to go first, and I felt his hand rest on my back as I passed by.

Keep walking, Jones.

The hostess led us to our table near the bar and a neon sign that said, If Mama Ain't Happy, Ain't Nobody Happy! Megan and Josh grabbed one side of the booth, Griffin and I the other. I tried not to notice the gentle pressure of his leg resting against mine. Freaking Megan. I had been fine before she started asking questions.

"So, we've been talking a lot about ourselves today." Josh opened his menu. "Tell me about how you guys met."

"We know you're not together, he means," Megan said, only making things more awkward.

"No worries," Griffin replied. "We met at a wedding at the botanical garden. Lottie had to chase down a rowboat that escaped for the bride and groom to use."

"No, that's not it at all—we first met when you whacked me on the head with your big, fat camera. He was creeping behind me in the reception tent."

"In my defense, you had the best view of the guests."

I picked at the vinyl tablecloth with a fingernail.

"I'm sure you see all kinds of crazy things at weddings behind that lens," said Josh.

"Oh, the stories I could tell," said Griffin. "But I think Lottie should tell some of her stories instead. I want to know what really goes on behind those giant red doors at The Firm."

"Well, it took every ounce of strength I had to keep my composure when one of our brides-to-be pulled a live chicken out of her handbag in the middle of our meeting."

"No way," said Josh. "That didn't happen."

"Sure did. And that was just the start. Their house is covered in dollhouses, and they own 150 chickens with better living quarters than any of us."

"Shut up." Megan smacked the table. "I would've freaked out."

"I guess I'm conditioning myself to have the best poker face in town, if nothing else." I devoured a few chips.

"Cedric really holds it all together, which amazes me," I continued. "He's over the top in his attire for sure, and the hours are starting to get to me. But if you want the naked truth about anything, he will tell it exactly like it is."

"That sounds horrible," said Griffin. "He terrifies me when he swoops into weddings like a Dementor."

"I'm somewhat used to it now," I replied. "And at least there are no games with him. Mary Ellen is the one who's tough to read. But I guess you can't love everyone you work with."

"Tell me about it," said Griffin. "Val isn't the easiest boss either, but she's crazy smart and talented. When she first hired me, I didn't want to work in weddings, but I jumped at the chance to learn from her."

"I guess you have to take the bad with the good as long as you love what you do."

"I'm going to order us all a pitcher." Josh thankfully lightened the mood.

"Don't forget the queso," I said.

"Get the bowl—not that pathetic little cup," added Griffin.

"Well, y'all just go ahead and pig out in front of me," said Megan. "I'll be over here with my sad salad at the best Tex-Mex in town. I'll be so happy when this wedding is over and I can eat carbs again."

"Me too," said Josh. "Babe, you know you'll be gorgeous no matter what. It's no fun being the only one eating something other than green leaves when we go out now. And no matter what, we'll stop at Whataburger as soon as we leave our reception and get you the cheeseburger of your dreams."

"And this is why I love you." Megan kissed him.

We enjoyed a really fun dinner together, and later Griffin dropped me off with a reminder to bring my boots for New Mexico. It had been so long since I'd gone on anything that even remotely resembled a double date. But I could get used to it. Even if only in my head.

Apparently I wasn't the only one thinking that. Moments after I crawled into bed, my phone pinged. It was Megan.

> I stand by my earlier assessment. *Why* are you not *all over* that?? He's cute and funny and creative and sweet and I could go on.

She was relentless. I appreciated that once friends found their "person," they decided their new mission was to help you find yours. Before, it was every woman for herself. Now, Megan was like Cupid and Santa rolled into one.

> And I stand by mine. He's not interested, and I'm not wasting my time any longer. We're getting too old to mess around if there's no possibility there.

After a few minutes, she replied:

> Blerg, you're right. We're too old . . . thirties here we come! Not everyone can find their cheeseburger Josh lol. But a girl can hope! Sweet dreams (of boys with brown eyes and dimples)!

TWELVE

Puffs of red dust clouded the windshield of our rented F-150. We rattled over a cattle grate and jostled down long-dried tracks through ochre New Mexico clay. A particularly jarring bump tipped the truck, and I smacked my forehead against the window frame. I winced, rubbing my head, praying it wouldn't bruise.

Mary Ellen kept her foot heavy on the gas, lumbering along, unconcerned with me, the peon, riding shotgun. We'd spent almost a week prepping the site, but this morning we got to sleep in as a "special treat" from Cedric after last night's rehearsal dinner. Lucky us.

Soon we turned a corner and the shrubby excuses for trees parted. Down a narrow gravel drive stood a giant pueblo-style estate covered in greenery. A hundred yards behind it was a crisply painted barn that one could only assume held the barrel-racing horses Cassie, our bride-to-be, was famous for riding in her misspent youth. Behind that were stunning views of northern New Mexico's mountain ranges, including snow-capped peaks.

Our wilderness location could best be triangulated using Santa Fe, Albuquerque, and the North Star. But despite not really appearing on Google Maps, it was absolutely breathtaking. The property boasted three thousand lush acres courtesy of underground irrigation. Even more spectacular in person than what Cedric and Mary Ellen had described upon their return from the site visit. By the time I arrived, our team was well into transforming a massive two-tiered tent in the middle of this desert oasis into a pink fantasy wonderland.

We rolled up to the tent where Cedric busily barked orders to the floral underlings. Shades of pink bunting were draped throughout the main tent—from deep magenta to the palest blush—to give it an overall ombre effect. In stark contrast to the frothy sorbet overhead, custom wooden chandeliers made of sliced barrels hung down over every dining table. Cassie had hoped to pay homage to her days in the Houston rodeo circuit, and this was as close to that look as Cedric was willing to get. Even this was a stretch.

Hundreds of pink tulips and roses spilled over the tops of each barrel. You'd likely get kicked to the curb if you ever mentioned the words *shabby chic* in our office, but I couldn't help smiling knowing that this event was exactly that. A little piece of Cedric died while designing this one. I just knew it.

Three smaller tents fanned out behind the big one, each adorned in a singular shade of pink. One held a lounge area, another several rows of carnival games, and the third, an elaborate photo booth—complete with a mechanical bull (with a floral wreath around its neck, of course). This was what a million-dollar dream wedding looked like in New Mexico, folks.

The tents were set in a grove of well-manicured blue spruce trees. From the branches hung matching chandeliers of wood and steel, festooned with bunches of pink and white peonies and long sprays of pink astilbe. Cocktail tables were packed with tea candles and miniature arrangements of matching pink spray roses, so it seemed as if the hanging and blooming stems reached out to each other.

After a few hours of arranging place cards and menu cards and making certain not a rosebud was out of place, we finished our prep work. With both the ceremony and reception space ready for action, Mary Ellen and I headed back to our Airbnb to change before we had to start wrangling up the wedding party for the ceremony.

We had been wearing more casual work clothes for the past week as we raced about preparing for the weekend. Everything on the property was covered in a thin layer of dust, and if a guest ventured out into one of the open fields near the tents, they would likely step into a steaming fresh pile of horse manure courtesy of one of Cassie's prize-winning ponies. Needless to say, it wasn't a place for Manolos (not that I could afford them), but my cowboy boots from college sure came in handy.

Kudos, Griffin, for the reminder.

Now that Cassie's big day had arrived, we swapped out our ranch-hand attire for more formal black wedding planner clothes to finally transition to running the show. I changed as fast as I could to find Cassie and wish her well before our prefunction company meeting. She was already dressed and ready for the ceremony when I entered her palatial bedroom suite in the main house. It was a mere five times the size of my apartment bedroom. Rustic wooden beams and a kiva fireplace contrasted beautifully with more glam touches like a canopy bed and an antique mirrored chandelier. Her equally grand closet housed the largest collection of custom boots I'd ever seen.

"Lottie!" Cassie yelled as soon as she saw me come in. "I can't believe today's the day."

"I know," I replied as she gave me an endearing hug. "You look incredible, and this day is going to be so perfect."

"Cedric wouldn't let Mom and me go into the tent today since he wanted all the final details to be a surprise, but I'm so excited to see everything later."

"It's magical out there, a vision of pink," I said while fluffing her skirt. "I won't be with you leading up to the ceremony, but Mary Ellen will take great care of you. I can't wait to see you walk down the aisle."

"Thanks, Lottie." She took a deep breath. "I hope it goes by slowly. I don't want to miss anything today."

"No matter what, you've got a great photography team to capture all the details," I said, thinking of Griffin. "You just enjoy your time with Paul and try to relax. We've got everything else covered."

With that, Cassie gave me one more hug. As I walked out of her room, I smiled. My own dreams might have been indefinitely postponed, but I was finding joy in making her fantasy come to fruition. It was the first time I felt on an emotional level—not just a financial one—that my wedding journey might not be wasted. For today, that was enough.

Once I arrived back at the reception tent, Cedric and Mary Ellen were ready to rally the team on the dance floor to go over the schedule just before the guests' arrival. Everyone received their marching orders, and then we all moved in various directions to prep for the start of the ceremony.

As low woman on the ladder, I'd been relegated to wrangling the members of the Texas Boys Choir. Now the crown jewel of this particular wedding was hands down the chapel we'd constructed on the estate. The whitewashed wooden structure sat about a hundred yards away from the house—in the opposite direction and intentionally upwind of the barn. Complete with stained glass, a steeple with a working bell, a narthex, pews, and a multileveled choir loft, large enough for the boys to draw guests to tears with their magical prepubescent voices.

An antique brass bell from a Santa Fe monastery hung in the steeple to ring as Cassie and her new husband ran out the door—all built solely for the wedding. Crews had spent a month constructing what would be torn down in less than forty-eight hours.

I gathered the flock of angel-faced boys and corralled them toward the chapel. We marched up a small staircase, and they filed into their places in the elevated loft behind the altar. A stained-glass window—presumably imported from some European church demolition—cast a multicolored glow on their downy, comb-slicked heads. Their choir director silently counted kids, then turned to me, horrified.

"We're missing two!" he whispered before he turned sternly to his members. "Where are Jaden and Cody?"

Eighteen cherubic faces gaped at him. Finally, after an eternity, one tiny hand shot up from the middle row.

"They were playing with a corn snake earlier, Mr. Taylor."

"How do you know what kind of snake it was? It could be poisonous! Never mind. Where were they, Declan?"

"In the trees just past the barn."

I looked at my watch. Cassie was set to walk the aisle in ten minutes, and guests were starting to come in. One of the missing boys was the first soloist on "Ave Maria," so his absence would be pretty obvious. Not to mention that playing with snakes felt—well, unsafe. I sprinted down the staircase and toward the horse barn.

Sure enough, around the far side stood the boys, ivory choir robes grass stained at the knees. One held a small red-and-brown-striped snake in his hands. But before I could yell at them, I spotted Griffin, lens aimed at the little cretins, who were hamming it up for the camera and showing off their prize.

"What are you doing?" I yelled, livid. He must have been trying to ruin my life. I took back all the positive thoughts I'd had toward him

after Megan's engagement shoot. "They could get bitten any second! And aren't you supposed to be stationed somewhere? The ceremony is starting *now*."

"Easy there, it's not poisonous," Griffin said, turning to me. "Sorry guys, we gotta go!"

I told them to drop the reptile, grabbed each boy's arm, and dragged them back to the chapel.

With the aspiring herpetologists back in the choir loft, I snuck around the corner to check in with Mary Ellen, who was standing in one of the side aisles hidden behind a faux column. *What in the world would these people do without me?* I wondered. For a moment I felt the comfort of job security.

As Cassie began her stroll down the aisle, the boys' beautiful soprano filled the vaulted ceiling. Once the vows began, though, I noticed a ripple going through the otherwise still children. Then, I *knew*.

I slipped away from Mary Ellen and walked stealthily up the side stairs (out of the guests' view) to get a better look at what was going on. Those little devils had ignored my orders and somehow managed to sneak in their slippery friend. I had visions of what Mary Ellen would do to me if the snake got loose in the ceremony. Probably flay the snake—and me.

Griffin spotted it as well but I proved to be faster. Without deigning to acknowledge him, I yanked Cody into the hall from the side. He whispered that he'd brought the snake inside in his pocket, and of course, it had slipped out to go exploring. Snake wrangler was *so* not part of my job description, but the stakes were too high to screw this wedding up. As the one in charge of managing the choir, I'd be to blame if things went south. My adrenaline took over. I felt no fear.

To hunt the snake without being seen by the guests below, I

needed to crawl underneath the risers built to make the back row of boys visible. Fortunately, the chapel was too new for any dust bunnies, but I was pretty positive that on all fours, Griffin would be able to see way more than just the missing snake.

"Lottie, stop. I'll go under there," Griffin whispered, putting a hand on my arm.

Okay, so he could be chivalrous. All righty.

"Thank you." I sniffed, relieved I didn't have to flash him or touch a snake, no matter how small it was.

After what felt like an eternity, he found the snake, casually wrapped around an unsuspecting boy's ankle. Good thing it really wasn't poisonous. Griffin unwound the creature, motioning to the boy to keep *very* still. He crawled out, triumphantly holding the reptile out to me as the recessional march played. Mission accomplished.

"Well, thanks for that," I said. "Guess I'll forgive you for encouraging them to play with that nasty thing in the first place."

"You know what they say, 'Red touching black, safe for Jack . . .'"

"No, my Girl Scout training apparently skipped that one. I should go check on the reception. Where's your next posting?"

"I'll be lurking through the dark corners, per usual."

"I'll see you around then, I guess." I scooted past him and went to find Mary Ellen.

Soon guests settled into their respective dinner tables. It was a huge relief to see first courses served because it meant the planners and most other vendors got a brief respite before dinner ended and the party wrangling resumed. I usually took the opportunity to sneak into the kitchen, throw off my shoes, and stuff a few leftover appetizers in my mouth before round two began.

Clients always provided us with vendor meals, but they were usually revolting—and, regardless, band members tended to eat everything before the rest of us saw a crumb of food. Smart vendors shoved granola bars in their pockets so they could at least keep from passing out from starvation before the reception ended. Every now and then a client fed us what the guests ate, but I learned not to count on it. Leftover appetizers it was.

Between the first toast and the steak and branzino pairing, I was snacking away and looking around for Mary Ellen. Suddenly a loud *boom* followed by a series of loud *booms* practically shook the catering tent. It was either thunder or an impromptu shooting contest.

I dashed out, barefoot and with a mouthful of tuna tartare, and saw smoke on top of a hill. The fireworks, which were supposed to be the pinnacle of the reception when all guests moved outside after dinner, had accidentally gone off.

Mary Ellen had run out, too, and we jogged up the hill to see what had happened. Meanwhile Cedric radioed the sound team to blast the music so guests wouldn't know what was happening. Once a preprogrammed firework show started, it couldn't be stopped. About $20,000 went up in smoke, and only we were there to see it.

This was not good. Like, really not good. At least this mishap wasn't even remotely my fault.

I caught up to Mary Ellen just in time to overhear her yelling something about a "bubble lady" to one of the groundskeepers. A bubble lady? I thought we'd be yelling about the premature firework debacle.

"How could this happen? Where is she? I can't even see her!" Mary Ellen was still trying to catch her breath from running up the grassy hill in heels.

"That's her? Over there in the bushes? Well how do you suggest we get her out?" Mary Ellen barked out.

Then it hit me. She was talking about the entertainer we'd hired to perform to music on the client's man-made lake during the fire-work show. The lake sat directly beneath the hill we stood on and would be in clear view of the guests once they moved to the tent deck following dinner.

In an ideal world, the female acrobat was to be encased in a large plastic bubble—like a hamster in a hamster ball—and dance around as it floated across the top of the water. Cedric had seen this done on a pool at some gala he'd attended in the Hamptons, and when he mentioned it to Cassie's mother, she said she just *had* to have it at her daughter's wedding.

The bubble dancer's show coordinated with the fireworks display; the first *boom* was her cue to begin. So when the fireworks launched for a crowd of zero, her show started early. Then the pre-sunset winds had gusted and blown her into an overgrown corner of the lake. Not only was she now a hamster trapped in her little hamster ball, but she also looked to be hurt.

Mary Ellen radioed the lighting tech to shine a spotlight on the situation, but her priority was to check on guests postexplosion. All it took was one pointed look in my direction for me to know I was going fishing for the bubble lady.

My pride had been decimated long ago, so as I picked my way over through the shrubbery filled with God knows what, I decided to call in my own backup. Still barefoot, I might add.

"Griffin? It's Lottie. Are you still on break, or are you back on?" I breathed heavily into my cell. (No way was I going to radio him for the whole team to hear.)

"Yeah, I'm eating the pathetic scraps the band left behind. Why do you sound so winded?"

"Well, we have another situation down by the lake, and I could really use some help . . . That is, if you're not busy and don't mind. And swear not to take one single picture or I *will* break your camera."

"Gee, how could I pass that up? Way to sell it. Wedding planning sure looks like a real gas."

"You're hilarious. But I could use the help. And don't talk about gas at the moment. There are live pyrotechnics going off. Just shut up, come outside, and follow the spotlight to the lake. Can't miss it."

With that I hung up the phone and approached the bubble in the bushes.

Tavia, the performer we'd hired from Reno, wore a shiny gold Spandex unitard that captured the light and thankfully made her easier to spot in the brush. She was polite but clearly in pain—and desperate for assistance.

"Hold on, I've got someone else coming, and we'll figure out how to get you out of that thing."

"Thanks," she said, holding her ankle. "I think I twisted it when I bumped into the rocks near the shore. I don't know if I can dance tonight."

"Don't worry about that at all." I tried to stay calm and hunt for a branch to push her closer to shore again. Her bubble floated just out of reach, but I couldn't find anything around me to help guide her to the side.

Just then, Griffin—by now a regular hero—showed up. He assessed the situation.

"Grab my hand." His palm was warm, and I was suddenly aware of my clammy palms—until he almost pulled me with him into the lake.

"What are you doing?" I shrieked.

"Just hold on. I'm going to lean in and try to push her to the side."

He was pretty lean but pushing six feet, I imagined. As we made a human rope, it took both my hands and every ounce of strength I had to keep us both from going in the water.

"There! That should do it," he said as though he had just won the 5A state championship. His stock was growing by the minute, and I had to admit, I was impressed.

The bubble floated to the shore. "How do we get you out of there, Tavia?" I asked.

"There's a watertight zipper over here," she gestured. Griffin grabbed the zipper, and as soon as he started pulling down, the air released and our injured mermaid was free.

Though we had rescued Tavia, this was still a *big* problem. We now had nothing left for the after-dinner show. Not that the infinite stars overhead weren't enough to gaze at, in my opinion, but Cassie's parents had paid for pizzazz.

"Thank you, Griffin." I shooed him on his way. "Dessert should be served soon, which we know means cake cutting." A photographer who missed a cake cutting would be blacklisted from any future wedding business.

"Good call, don't want to miss the traditional face-shoving-of-the-cake." He turned to leave, and I took a moment to breathe and admire the view of his taut backside in his jeans. Mary Ellen and Cedric showed up just as Griffin was out of sight (thank goodness).

"Don't panic. We can fix this, or at least part of it." For someone so outwardly dramatic, Cedric was calm and collected at events—but I wasn't sure even *he* knew how to bring already detonated fireworks back to life. "Listen, there's no way to salvage the firework show, but by God, there will be a bubble dance performance."

"How?" Mary Ellen and I asked in unison.

I could guess what he was thinking. No way I would say it aloud, though, let alone offer myself as the sacrificial lamb.

"Lottie, I'm going to ask more of you than I normally ever would." *Okay, here he goes.* "But I'll promote you to junior planner and give you an extra week's worth of paid vacation if you put on that unitard, get in that bubble, and do your best to move it around the lake."

Mary Ellen started to say something—hopefully to stand up for me—but I interrupted before she could get a word out. "I'll do it. But I can't promise I'll look anything like Tavia or be able to stand up in that thing at all."

"Deal."

Just like that, I was climbing the ranks. Also probably about to embarrass or gravely injure myself.

"Mary Ellen, help her change and get into that contraption. I'm going to go smooth over the firework situation with the couple." Cedric puffed out his chest, ran a hand over his thick hair, and marched back to the reception tent.

I looked at the deflated bubble, which slumped on the ground. "What did I just agree to?"

"To becoming tonight's entertainment, but don't worry. I'll help you get through this," Mary Ellen said in a tone I'd never heard her use before. Were we bonding? Who knew, but I'd take the help and think about the rest tomorrow—if I actually survived the night.

We dragged the bubble and helped Tavia limp back to her dressing area, a curtained-off space near the other side of the lake. She took off her costume, and I pulled it on, refusing to look at myself in the full-length mirror in the room. At least the Spandex adjusted to my body's shape, which was in the ballpark of Tavia's but not near as voluptuous or toned as her performance-ready figure.

Tavia gave me a few tips about keeping the bubble stable and moving without tumbling every second. "And if you do fall, make it look intentional and no one will ever know," she added with a thumbs-up.

Perfect. This was going to be a total disaster.

Mary Ellen radioed Cedric that I was ready as she and Tavia gently pushed me out onto the lake. I took a minute to gain my balance, but navigating wasn't so difficult if I moved around slowly.

Thankfully the guests were far enough away that some of my clumsiness would be lost on them. Their after-dinner cocktails would also help. The wind had also completely died down. The lake was as smooth as glass, and I began to feel somewhat peaceful. Until the spotlight hit me like a bolt of lightning.

The music started. I couldn't see the guests, but I knew I was "on" and needed to try and move around somewhat elegantly. By elegantly, I meant walking very slowly in my hamster ball while waving my hands about and pretending to know ballet. In recent years I had spent more time bouncing off random strangers at bars than trying to dance gracefully to anything. But I faked it.

The lights faded after five minutes of music, my cue to exit the water. Zero clue what I actually looked like, but I felt so proud for not wiping out and smashing my face on the side of the bubble that I did not care.

As I approached the shore, I could hear Mary Ellen and Tavia clapping.

"Great job, Lottie!" Mary Ellen yelled.

"You're quite the natural," said Tavia as they tried to pull me in.

"Thanks! Now please get me out of here before I wipe out!"

Cedric radioed Mary Ellen that the guests loved the water show, and the bride and groom had already moved on from the fact that we would be sans fireworks for the evening. None of the guests ever knew what they'd missed, given the whole thing was supposed to be a surprise anyway. I'd missed most of Cassie's reception but felt like I'd personally done her a solid.

"I'll need everyone to report to the cocktail tent to prepare for the departure," said Cedric.

"Lottie, can you change and meet us up there?" Mary Ellen asked.

"Yes, I'm good. I'll see you soon." I stepped out of my plastic prison and headed toward the dressing area with Tavia.

"Take your time. You deserve a break," Mary Ellen said.

Wow. All this time, all I needed to do to gain an edge in The Firm was to sport spandex and dance like a circus performer.

I stripped off the unitard and donned my black dress, then arrived back at the reception area just in time to see guests waving their sparklers and shouting good-byes.

As Cassie and Paul climbed into their horse-drawn carriage and rode off into the cooling night, she looked so happy. Crickets chirped as I meandered back toward the tent. A few minutes later, Griffin fell into step beside me. Before I knew it we were strolling under the stars.

I broke the silence. "Thank you for all your help today."

"I aim to please. A one-stop shop for bubble wrangling, snake charming, and charming in general."

"Easy there, ego."

"Is it ego if it's true? You should see me around grandmothers of the bride. I still can't believe you danced in a bubble."

"Why? Did I look completely ridiculous?"

"No, it was pretty cool, actually. But I'm just shocked you were game to get out there and do it. You don't exactly seem like the type."

"What on earth is that supposed to mean?"

"Relax, sorry. I just mean that it was a pretty ballsy move. A little bolder than I would have guessed from the responsible, uptight, type-A planner I've gotten to know. And you're not exactly as ruthless as some of the trust fund girls I've seen. But from what the kitchen-tent rumor mill had to say, it paid off. Congrats on the promotion."

"Thanks. I also got an extra week of vacation that I'll never have time to take, in case the rumor mill didn't include all the fine print. Also, what do you mean by 'uptight'?"

"Um, just that you can be pretty straitlaced, like you have an idea about something and aren't the most open to changing your plan." He paused. "Forget I said anything."

I bristled. "No, tell me what you meant. I feel like my whole life right now is a testament to my ability to change my plans."

"Lottie, we probably worked no less than four or five events together when you were with Abigail. You just didn't notice. No offense, but an artsy, skinny nerd who works with the grunts doesn't exactly fly on your radar. But it doesn't matter. Forget about it."

"Wait, really? I don't think you're a nerd! I mean, I'm one of the 'grunts' too," I spluttered. "But I get that that's not what you're saying."

As we stood there under the chandeliers hanging from the spruce trees, I mulled it over. I'd always thought of myself as one of the nerds or overachievers in school; I had to be. Always a bit of an outsider. But the fact remained I hadn't branched out from my sorority or the friends Brody and I shared in college, and in the years since, I'd mostly stuck to my small-but-mighty crew. I wondered what—or whom—else I'd missed.

The band transitioned from Beyoncé to Rat Pack to slow things down and encourage the remaining guests to gather their designer clutches and go. The candles flickered in a docile breeze.

"When was the last time you danced at a wedding?"

Surprised, I had to think about the last time I went as a guest. "Probably my cousin's, a couple summers after college."

Without asking he reached for my hand and took a little bow. A conciliatory gesture, if there ever was one. I dipped a small curtsy before he pulled me close, in the trees where the lights were dim. The bandleader did his best Sinatra.

I had always envisioned a simple reception for myself. No acrobats or fireworks, certainly nothing as tacky as Laura Lee's dollar dance. Not even a garter toss. Just a top-notch big band with a classic catalog. When it was going to be Brody, our song was always Coldplay's "Green Eyes" because of *my* eyes. Never one for subtlety, Brody—like Cedric—always thought obvious was, well, best. I'd mentally choreographed every detail of that first dance with him. Now, years later, I was at a different wedding, spinning in someone else's arms.

Griffin's hand rested on the small of my back. I prayed I wasn't sweating through this stupid dress as I caught a whiff of his lemon soap and Tide detergent scent.

"Relax, Lottie."

"I am relaxed." Well, maybe I *was* looking around, paranoid that Cedric would jump out from behind a tree trunk or Mary Ellen would come calling for me. "I'm sorry, I'm just trying to figure out what the next crisis is going to be . . . and how it's inevitably going to be my fault."

"I've noticed you're often the one scrambling to save the day." He spoke close to my ear.

"Ha, more like I'm the one who keeps screwing up, then tries to fix what she's broken."

"Why do you worry so much about it? None of the other assistants—I mean junior planners—seem so stressed."

"For starters, they all have trust funds to fall back on. And instead I have like eighty-seven thousand dollars of student loans left to pay off. You know how pricey TCU is. I really, really need this job."

"That part, I completely get."

We continued to move beneath the trees, and my body settled

against him. "And it's the first time I've felt like I was doing something that, you know, helped people," I continued. "I realize that's silly because they're bagillionaires and don't need—or always appreciate—the help. But for someone like Cassie, that actually does mean something. In some small way I get to be a part of making their life, well, better. Their memories better. Their dreams come true. Their marriages start on the right note.

"I don't know why that matters to me, but it does. Maybe it's because I thought my life would go differently or be further along by now. I thought I'd be the one up there instead of back here . . . Anyway, I'm rambling and probably boring you and should just shut up."

"No, not at all. Just . . . being the one up there isn't always all it's cracked up to be," he said softly. We danced for a minute in the quiet, each lost in our own thoughts. I blamed the warm New Mexico air, the twinkling lights dancing on the lake, and the feeling of grass on my bare feet for the heat in my stomach. I became conscious of his thumb slowly rubbing my lower back.

Griffin leaned in closer to whisper in my ear. Chills ran up my arms. *Cool it, Jones.* "You were great tonight, Lottie. You certainly surprised me, and it sounds like Cedric too."

"Thanks, Griffin," I said, afraid to turn and look at him.

"I also think you should probably wear a gold unitard more often. Do you get to keep it?"

"Shut up, you weirdo," I said, the moment broken.

Mary Ellen's voice blasted from my earpiece. "Lottie? Lottie are you ready to go?"

I snapped back into reality. "Yes, I'll be right there. I . . . I just need to find my shoes."

"See ya 'round, Lottie. Thanks for the dance." Griffin slowly released me from his arms.

"Anytime." I awkwardly turned toward the catering tent to retrieve my shoes, trying to keep what little dignity I had left.

No surprise, my shoes were nowhere to be found. That shady waitstaff. Thankfully they were old Nine West pumps that I'd found on sale for twenty-five dollars. Joke was on them. Well, on me, too, as I had to walk across the property barefoot again, which was less than pleasant. Mercifully, I managed to avoid any warm horse manure. That would have done me in.

I passed out on the ride back to the Airbnb, and Mary Ellen had booked us on a later flight back to Dallas with the interns, so we got to sleep in a bit. Cedric, of course, took the client's private plane.

When I entered the office Tuesday, much to my surprise, a red box with a black bow sat on my desk. I assumed it must have been a mistake until I spotted the card:

Lottie, great job this weekend. You're one of the girls now, and your feet should look like they belong here too. Kisses, Cedric

Wouldn't you know it. My first pair of Christian Louboutin 100mm black patent Pigalle pumps. He even nailed my size. I was getting somewhere.

THIRTEEN

It had been almost a week since I danced with Griffin, and I hadn't heard from him. Not a text. Not even our usual email banter. And I wasn't about to be the one to initiate nonprofessional contact. Well, I guess we had already initiated contact ages ago, but whatever. I wasn't going to reach out. Maybe it had just been a silly, friendly thing, but then I remembered how flirty he was about the unitard. Geez.

I knew he wasn't working the wedding the next Saturday at Brook Hollow Country Club because the bride's friend was the photographer. Never a good idea, by the way.

But on Friday night I breathed a sigh of relief—and annoyance—when his number showed up on my phone.

"Hello?" I pretended I didn't know who it was. That game was admittedly easier in middle school when we didn't have caller ID.

"Lottie, it's me. Griffin."

"Oh, hi."

"How are you? Sorry it's been a minute. I was out in Marfa with Val doing a shoot."

I feigned disinterest.

"Anyway, I wanted to know if you'd like to go to a concert with me and some buddies tomorrow."

"Griff, tomorrow is a *Saturday* during the fall." Some people had college football; I had event season. "We've got a wedding. Don't you?"

"Oh, right. I don't this week. Want to meet up afterward? Natalia could come too."

A late-night hang is never a good idea, especially after a twelve-hour workday. But maybe this time it was a *great* idea. Plus, it would be nice to have someone besides a drunk groomsman appreciate my new Jason Wu LBD from Neiman Marcus.

Natalia was making it an early night because she was training for a charity bike race all weekend, but I could still go. We made plans to meet up in North Oak Cliff, a hipster clichéd part of town that fit his aesthetic. But if he was buying drinks, I wouldn't complain.

Thankfully that day's wedding was uneventful. For one of Cedric's fetes, it was rather cookie-cutter, but most of that was due to the bride's unoriginal taste. She'd held on to too many decade-old issues of *Brides*. (My own box of back issues was purely for nostalgia and not inspiration, obviously.) Anyone who still asked for a candy bar station and mac and cheese in martini glasses was bound to be basic—at least according to Cedric and Travis. Still, the checks cleared.

As I was heading to my car, Abigail texted to let me know there were extra cases of wine left over from the wedding that the bride's family was giving to the staff.

Free booze? Yes, please. Natalia would be thrilled, as I rarely contributed to the apartment stash of communal wine. A haul like this would last us awhile.

I booked it to the bar tent and grabbed a box that appeared to have a good mix of red and white. Twelve bottles of wine wasn't a light load, but with no attractive, muscular kitchen staffer in sight to help, I picked up my goodie box and wobbled across the cobblestones in my new heels toward the car.

As I tried to open my trunk, balance in the new "Loubs," and hold the cardboard box, it tipped out of my hands and hit the pavement with a terrible crash. Three bottles exploded onto the pavement, splashing red wine all over the bottom of my dress and both legs.

"Are you kidding me?" I said to the soaked box.

Everything had gone smoothly tonight, so I had this coming. My black dress concealed the red stains for the moment, but my legs looked like something out of a horror movie. I grabbed an old beach towel I had left in my car after a day at the apartment complex pool and rubbed myself down. After cleaning up all the glass and drying off as best I could, I put the remaining bottles in the back of my car and fled the scene. The only thing keeping me from calling it a night and getting to bed as quickly as possible was the thought of a nightcap with Griffin.

I drove along Jefferson Boulevard toward North Oak Cliff. My new shoes were killing my feet, so I reached down with one hand to take them off and slip on the ballet flats I kept stashed in my glove compartment. I must have been weaving while trying to finagle my shoe swap because before I knew it, lights flashed in my rearview mirror.

"Oh, for crying out loud," I said, again to no one, as I pulled over to the shoulder. I just couldn't catch a break.

I rolled down the window and put on my best smile. "I'm sorry, officer, I was just—"

"Are you aware that you were crossing back and forth between lanes?" he said. Then his face pinched. "Ma'am, I need you to step out of the car."

As I did so, it dawned on me that he'd caught a whiff of my car—and me.

"I need you to walk in a straight line for twenty steps," he commanded.

"I'm so sorry, I was working a wedding tonight, and it's just that I'm tired from being on my feet all day and then this box of wine exploded all over me, and I haven't even had a sip to drink," I pleaded, turning toward him.

"Just walk in a straight line please."

This man was not having it, so I attempted to "walk the line." Between the blisters on the ball of my foot and my general exhaustion, I must not have been quite as balanced as he wanted, or he just got a better whiff of my pinot-soaked skirt.

Next, he shone a flashlight into my eyes. "Now can you recite the alphabet backward?"

On a good day that would've been tough to do. But I tried not to cross my eyes and recited the letters. I must have spoken too slowly or acted too nervous—which I was—because he seemed unconvinced.

"Can't I just take a Breathalyzer or something?"

He also had one of those handy but said the field test was standard. After an eternity of waiting on the results, he came back to my window again.

"You passed, but I'm giving you a citation for reckless driving. You could have caused an accident swerving across lanes like that."

Humiliated, I didn't bother arguing anymore. I took the paper from him without a word.

"You're free to go, ma'am." Thank God. "Do you have anybody who can come pick you up?"

Wait, what? "But I'm not drunk? We just went through all that."

"The way you were driving, you should call somebody. It's late. I won't boot your car, and it should be safe here until the morning."

I sat there, shaken, on the side of the road. Natalia was already in bed and notoriously kept her ringer on vibrate all the time, and Megan was at her parents' place for a weekend of wedding planning. I swallowed my pride, took a big gulp, and straightened my big girl panties. Griffin was either done for the night or still out and about. Either way, I owed him a call to explain.

"Hello?" He sounded drowsy. It was almost midnight; he was probably heading to bed.

"It's me, Lottie," I said in a rush. "Funny story, but I got pulled over for drunk driving even though I wasn't drinking. I dumped a case of wine on myself. But I'm so sorry for flaking tonight. I didn't want you to think I'd bailed."

I waited. Silence.

Then Griffin burst into the loudest, howling laugh, and I had to pull the phone away from my ear.

"Glad to see you're awake after all," I sniped.

"Sorry, couldn't help myself. Are you okay? Do you need a ride?"

"I'm okay. I was going to try and get an Uber, but I'm worried they won't let me in smelling like I might puke on their upholstery."

"That's silly. I'm up now. Where are you?"

"I'm on the side of Jefferson Boulevard near the Bishop Arts District."

"Great, I live nearby. Drop a pin in your location. Be right there. Hold tight."

When he showed up fifteen minutes later, I was listening to an audiobook and trying to think about beach vacations with handsome men. When I got out of the car, I almost attacked him with a hug, I was so excited to see a friendly, non-law-enforcement face. "Whew, you reek," he drawled.

"Thanks. You would, too, if you'd taken a bath in red wine!"

"So where do you want to go?"

"Wait, really? It's after midnight and I smell like a walking bar."

"You promised me we'd hang, and now I'm wide awake. I'm not letting you end the night, or I guess the day, like this."

He wasn't wrong. Despite the exhaustion it would be a bit before I could sleep. There were certainly worse ways to unwind. "What do you have in mind?"

"If you don't have any suggestions, I've got an idea."

We drove through the west part of town, mostly in comfortable silence. I may also have napped a little against the window of his pickup truck. We stopped at a gas station, and while the car was filling, he ran inside and came out holding a brown paper bag.

Back in the car, we drove ten minutes more and then turned onto a frontage road and wound through some industrial streets until he pulled over at a bizarre-looking hill. I couldn't tell for sure, but it looked like the ground dropped off about thirty feet from the truck.

I followed Griffin as he strolled purposefully into the darkness. Then we stopped in front of a chain-link fence.

"What is this place?"

"Just trust me," he said.

"Well, you were a reliable roadside assistant . . ."

"Good." He quickly scaled the fence and dropped down on the other side. "C'mon!"

This better be worth it. I managed to climb over, thankful it was too dark for him to see how I flashed him.

He took my hand and led me through what felt like a disaster zone. Or a construction site. We dodged debris, and as my eyes adjusted, I could see we were on a path next to the Trinity River. The lights of Downtown flashed behind us. "Um, Griffin, is this safe?" I stammered.

"For sure," he said. "We're not supposed to be down here this late, but it's one of my favorite places to go at night. It's peaceful."

"Do you happen to be armed?"

"Lottie, I have a BA in fine arts. Do I look like the kind of guy carrying a concealed weapon?"

"Well, no, but this *is* Texas. You never know."

"I cross my heart to stave off any attackers long enough for you to run away if it comes to that."

He mockingly flexed, and I was surprised by the hardness of his bicep. There was more meat on those bones than I'd thought.

"Meh, it'll do," I said instead. Reassured, but not very, I followed him down the path to a grassy spot near the river. He sat. I sat too. From the paper bag he pulled out a cold six-pack of Dr Pepper, a bag of chips, and a jar of salsa. Perfect.

"I figured you've had enough of the hard stuff for one night," he quipped, handing me a can in the dim light.

My legs brushed the grass as I opened the soda. The city lights flickered magically. This guy was good. *Really* good.

A lone bullfrog bellowed, long and low, near the water. Muted traffic sounds occasionally wafted over. The crisp early December night was, otherwise, silent.

"Since most of what I know about you is that you're good behind a camera and you seem to hate weddings, tell me something else about you."

"For starters, I don't hate weddings. I just have trouble wrapping my head around some of the crazy ones we work. It's a lot of fuss and money blown over a risky proposition."

"I guess that's fair. I definitely would have 100 percent agreed with you a couple months ago. But for most of our clients, it seems like the investment is worth it. They're all so full of hope and love . . ." I sighed.

"I dunno, I'm no expert. But I'm starting to at least enjoy the events. At least some of the time." I blushed, thinking about our dance, grateful for the cover of night.

"And that is your prerogative, Lottie Jones." I liked the way my name sounded on his lips. "I just don't have to be all starry eyed about it is all. For me, it's just . . . work. A job."

I left it for the moment. "Tell me, what's your story, Griffin Flores?"

"That's a pretty big question. What do you want to know?"

"Give me the elevator pitch. I vaguely remember you're from Austin?"

"Yes, ma'am. My dad's family is in ranching in West Texas, and my parents met at college. Dad went to UT like his dad, got his MBA at the business school, and was ready to take over the family business when he found out my mom was pregnant with me. They'd met in statistics class and been together for a couple years."

"Were they married?"

"No, and my abuelo never really got over it, even though my parents had both just graduated and were adults. He's deeply Catholic, so I get that babies before marriage was a big deal. They got married eventually, but he still isn't super nice to my mom. On top of it all, I think he saw her as a leech to my dad instead of an asset. She's smart, worked hard ever since I can remember. He's gotten over it some in the last thirty years, but they chose back then to stay in Austin and work in real estate.

"Enough about that mess. The rest of my family is amazing. I have two younger sisters and then my little brother, who was another 'accident.' And lots of tías and tíos on my mom's side we're pretty close to," he said. "Okay, your turn. Tell me about your family."

"Ah, the Joneses. Not much to tell—it's just my mom, dad, my brother, Tom, and me. Your family life sounds extremely exciting compared to my small, somewhat boring clan in Memphis. No one is trying to 'keep up' with these Joneses. We've basically been caught and passed by . . . Maybe that's why I've liked living in Dallas so much. There's so much going on here."

"It's certainly, um . . . an interesting place." Griffin took a swig of Dr Pepper.

"Well, looking back, I think I always wanted something bigger, more unpredictable. I wanted to be a trial lawyer, if you can believe that."

"Really? You do seem to have a knack for dealing with intense clients. And you're quite argumentative."

"Thanks, I guess," I said laughing. "Who would've thought the skill sets would be interchangeable?"

"What do your parents think about your job?"

"They're supportive but waiting for me to figure it out. They thought I was going to be a lawyer, too, then a wife and mother as soon as possible. Then I became a floral designer. And a wedding planner now seems like just another thing I'm trying out—so I'm not sure how seriously they take it. Plus, it's hard for them to understand clients blowing a million dollars on a single event."

"I get that. Mine also harp on me for 'bouncing around taking pictures,' as they like to call it. I don't tell them about most of Val's events because they'd be baffled."

"This world couldn't be further away from what I've known. Growing up in Memphis, things were really tight financially, and both my parents worked like crazy. In some ways I felt like just as much of an outsider there as I do here."

"Why's that?"

"Well, our middle school fed into a much richer district's high school. It was a great education," I went on. "But a few of us stood out like sore thumbs. I think that's when I got really motivated to push myself. I was determined that nobody would know I was a girl from a prefab with a chain-link fence. I ran for student government—just class secretary, nothing flashy—and won. I went out for track and French club. I spotted the prettiest group of girls who seemed smart but not 'fast' and methodically befriended their leader."

I shook my head at the thought, then paused, punched with sudden nostalgia. "At fourteen, fifteen, you feel like your life has finally started and that everything that happens from there on out will dictate your entire future. It's why first heartbreaks feel crushing, first defeats seem insurmountable. Even though it will all pass, you don't believe that yet."

"Man, I remember that feeling," Griffin mused.

"Right? Every tiny occurrence is a way bigger deal than it needs to be."

I told him about getting into TCU but decided to leave out any Brody details since this wasn't about our previous love lives. And, of course, Griffin hadn't exactly asked.

"I got the job with Abigail because I didn't actually prep much to be a lawyer after college—and when graduation came, I found I hadn't wanted it enough to really pursue it as a career after all. I let other things get in the way. It all had lined up so perfectly that I just went along with it, and then when it fell apart, I didn't chase back after it."

"Sounds like you mostly liked the *idea* of it, the clear path—you go to college, go to law school, do some clerking, then you find a firm and go into practice. It's very straightforward. Obvious."

I shifted in the grass. "Please excuse me while I put my body armor back on, which you have so ruthlessly destroyed."

"Sorry, I just call 'em like I see 'em. Gets me in trouble sometimes." There was that one-sided dimple again.

"No, I get that. Occasionally the thoughts in my head come out my mouth and it doesn't go well either. Not that this didn't go well, but you know what I mean." I was getting stratospherically good at ruining good conversations. I moved on.

I told Griffin how, as the oldest child, I still felt responsible to try to help my parents in some way. I was still working to pay off my student loans, but I dreamed about being able to send money their way so they really wouldn't worry about me.

"So, even though this is somewhat of an 'accidental' career for me now," I said, using tortilla chips to make air quotes, "it's turned out okay. Maybe even better than okay. I can't believe I've been working for seven years in events. I started working for Abigail without any other idea what to do. Then Cedric bought her out, and I came too . . ."

"There you go again with the going along with whatever the next obvious option is."

"I mean, isn't that always how life works?"

He shrugged. "Maybe. I guess. Just seems like there's not much of your own choice involved, not much asking what you really want."

"Well, in one way or another, all my 'choices' have led me to this moment. And now I'm here, sitting in what seems to be a landfill of sorts with you." I gave him a small nudge with my shoulder.

"Touché." He nudged me back with a grin.

We sat in companionable silence, dipping chips straight into the jar and eating them with a crunch. I could faintly smell his woodsy cologne-and-detergent scent on the cool breeze. The outlines of his face were faintly visible in the night. I couldn't really tell where this was going, and I started feeling fidgety. "Enough about me. What'd you do after A&M?"

He paused for a moment. Worked his jaw. "It took a while after school for me to figure things out too. Eventually I ended up taking a job with Mercy Ships, an NGO that gives free medical care, as their photographer. We traveled around several African countries for a couple years. I took pictures of the work they were doing and the communities impacted by the surgeries, wells, and other projects. Stuff like that. But I also got to travel around the coast of Africa a lot, and I submitted some of those photos to Val, back when she was still doing nature photography. We stayed in touch. When I was ready to move back, she was hiring. It just wasn't in quite the same subject area I envisioned. You and I have that in common."

"I imagine it's a bit of a culture shock to go from nonprofit work to million-dollar weddings."

"That's putting it mildly."

"I've seen you crush it at weddings. Your images are incredible, and the couples lose their minds, even if Val gets the credit. You're good at it, even if you say your heart's not in it. I'd love to see you shoot something you actually cared about."

OMG, I'd said *heart* and *love* in the same breath. I was that girl. *Don't be that girl, Jones.*

"I mean, I'd miss getting to harass you at events, but if you don't like the industry, you should try to get back into something you're passionate about," I told him.

"And you should try to get a job you actually enjoy too. But we can't have everything."

"Hey, that's not fair," I said. "I just told you how much I like it." I *did*, right? "I actually like working with the clients," I elaborated. "And I like the feeling of helping people be happy and make great memories. I also like solving problems, which I do just about every weekend as you have now seen."

We spent the next hour or so laughing and sitting side by side near the water. He never tried anything, but it was nice to be with someone and not feel the pressure to be overly ambitious, affluent, or even flirtatious. I could get used to that.

"Lottie?" He turned to look at me. Those dark eyes were warm, and his golden skin practically glowed in the faint light.

"Yes?" I felt the blood rush into my cheeks. Was he going to try and kiss me?

"I really like hanging out with you, even more now that I know something about you other than your penchant for fluffing dresses. But I just want to be up-front that I'm not looking for any kind of serious relationship right now. Wow, that sounds horrible. I'm not looking for anything 'casual' either. I mean, I just, I want to be friends with you. I've—"

"Wow, I've never been friend-zoned so hard by someone I barely know."

"Sorry, I just find that Southern women—especially at our age— often jump to conclusions and go down that road. Before you know it, she's already looking at china patterns—"

"Well, consider me concluded," I said way too quickly, with an attempt at a laugh. "No worries, of course, we're good."

"Great. It's just that things are complicated for me right now, and the last thing I'd want to do is lead you on."

He babbled on, but I didn't hear anything else he said. I was a little embarrassed, but mostly mad that he had beaten me to this conversation. If anyone was leading someone on here, it was *me*.

"Griffin," I interrupted, "let's not make this weird for us. After all, I just need someone to act as my Uber home when I've bathed in a box of wine. I don't want anything screwing that up."

He laughed, relieved I'd broken the tension.

"Tell me more about your time in Africa," I said, changing the subject. Solid pivot. "So many countries there on my bucket list, and it may take a while, but I'm definitely going one day."

He smiled and dove right into telling me stories.

Soon the sky started to turn pink. Griffin stood, pulled me up, and walked me back to his car so he could drive me back to mine.

As I shut the door of my Prius a half hour later, I caught a pungent whiff of wine. But if I smelled *just* the right spot on my shoulder, I could smell his cologne too.

A few hours later, Sunday morning, I dragged myself out of bed at eleven for our bridal party work session with Megan. She'd brought over the save-the-dates to stuff into envelopes and bribed Nat and me with mimosas and Shug's Bagels.

I could barely keep my eyes open after the full day of work and then late-night excursion with Griffin, but I was determined not to bail on my bridesmaid duties.

"Lottie, tell me what happened last night!" Nat chided. "You weren't home when I went to bed and didn't call, which isn't like you."

I explained the wine, the citation, and then Griffin coming to pick me up.

Once the girls got over the fact that I could've gotten arrested without their knowing, they shifted their focus to Griffin.

"Wait, wait. Go back," Megan interrupted. "Tell me what happened in New Mexico!"

"Oh, right. Forgot I hadn't filled you in. Well, he helped me problem solve a few times, which now seems to be our MO." I told them about the snake and the bubble and my eternal shame slash pride over it. "Then he asked me to dance under the stars at the end of the night. I thought he was going to kiss me—which would have been a terrible idea. But then he didn't, and I didn't hear from him for a week."

"So, did he finally make a move last night?" Nat asked eagerly.

"No! Instead we spent this random romantic night together, and then he basically tried to break it off with me before anything ever really started. The most annoying part is that I wasn't even wanting anything to happen. At least, I don't think so."

"Wait, why?" Megan asked.

"For the same reason as always—he's pretty blunt about his disdain for weddings, cynical about romance, you know the drill. Maybe that's why he thinks he needs to let me down easy. But I'm too old to waste time on a fun fling or something that's not going there. Mom was so kind to remind me of that a couple weeks ago. Yes, he's funny, sexy, easygoing, and smart, but there's no future with him, so it shouldn't go further than it already has."

"That makes sense," said Nat. "What a bummer."

"I don't want friends with benefits or another relationship that wastes my prime time. Not to mention a broken heart. We seem to have a lot in common and some crazy chemistry, but if he doesn't see this going somewhere, we need to stop acting like it is."

"See, this is how we know God was a man," Megan quipped. "He made our prime childbearing years line up so perfectly with the ages we're expected to be building a career and a life for ourselves." Engagement had made Megan unusually insightful.

"Like they say, you can have it all, just not all at once," Natalia added.

"Or as my mom says, 'Diamonds are forever, but ovaries are for ASAP,'" I said.

"Okay, we need a fun diversion while we stuff envelopes." Megan grabbed my phone. "Let's do one of those flashback memory slideshows. My photos app always suggests old pictures from college where we look like total idiots. Our fashion sense was beyond terrifying."

"I can't believe we're stuffing the actual save-the-dates for your wedding," I said, as I begrudgingly handed over my phone. "Good news for you is that I'm a pro at this now."

"I will say, Lottie, you've certainly been an engaged girl's best friend with this job of yours," said Megan.

"I'm glad someone can appreciate my skills." I laughed as I started lining up all the invitations, reply cards, envelopes, and stamps.

"Just don't change jobs before I get married," added Natalia.

"Oh, Nat dear, whenever that blessed day comes, I'm charging a fortune to help with yours." I chucked an empty invitation box at her.

Megan looked up from the phone. "Any outrageous new clients or sexy, sunny destination weddings? I'm dying to go on a trip, but Josh and I are saving all our points for the honeymoon."

"Actually, I'm going to Mexico after New Year's on a site visit for a high-profile client." This was my moment. Brody and Harriet's wedding was shrouded in secrecy and NDAs, on top of keeping my connection to them under deep cover. But I knew I needed to tell my friends something now or they'd be livid when they inevitably found out. I exhaled.

"Listen." I set down a save-the-date. "I need to tell y'all something, but you must *swear* you won't tell a soul, or I could get fired, sued, or worse."

Megan looked like a dog who was about to be given a new bone.

"Y'all also have to promise not to yell at me for taking this long— and you can't stop me either, as I've already decided I'm working this one."

"Just spit it out," barked Natalia, who was also now staring me down.

"So, the groom getting married in Mexico is Brody," I blurted. "Yes, *my* Brody. And on top of that, he's marrying a very famous, practically perfect, A-list celebrity."

Silence. Both their mouths gaped. It was the first time in ages I'd rendered them speechless.

"Oh. My. Gosh," said Natalia finally. "That's . . . a lot. I mean, what are the odds? And are you *sure* you can't tell us who the bride is? Please, Lottie!"

I shook my head. "NDA rules."

"Well, then, are you sure you're okay working his wedding?" asked Megan. "I know it's been forever and you've dated other people, but it's a whole 'nother level of 'over it' to help him marry another woman."

"Especially when, you know, *you* wanted to marry him so much yourself that you practically planned it. Well, actually did." Natalia winced. "You sure you're okay?"

"Trust me. I know all of this, and I've thought about it way too much," I said. "It's too big of a wedding and opportunity at The Firm for me to pass up. This could almost guarantee I get promoted in some way when Cedric opens Atlanta. Not to mention, it's got to be some huge personal-growth milestone to be so happy for your ex that you're fine planning his wedding to someone else, right?" Yep, totally fine.

Megan looked pensive.

"It could actually be good for you," said Natalia as if trying to also convince herself. "Like you said, it's a huge opportunity, and maybe it will be cathartic or something to watch him profess his love for someone else. Talk about a closed door."

"No way," said Megan. "Maybe I need more time to digest the

news, but sounds like a bad idea. I couldn't imagine planning Josh's wedding to another woman."

"Well, that's a totally different situation." As ever, Natalia came to my defense. "Lottie's long over Brody. Of course you can't imagine Josh with someone else."

"Thanks, Nat," I said. "And it's true, Megs. Don't worry about me. I'd never volunteer to help with his wedding. I'm not that mature. But there has to be a reason it fell into my lap. I'll be okay."

"Well, you're a better woman than me." Megan sniffed as she stuffed another envelope.

"Thanks, y'all," I said. "We'll see how much better I am when I'm actually in Mexico crying behind a palm tree. Or, like, pathetically trying to steal him back from his gorgeous fiancée."

They both laughed and dropped that conversation for the rest of the evening. We continued to work like an assembly line, sitting on the floor of the apartment. Periodically, a particularly choice photo from college would come on-screen and we'd crack up at our younger selves. Various pics of us dressed as preppy tennis pros, cowgirls, or gumball machines for fraternity theme parties would pop up. Ridiculous, yes, but we had a blast.

I loved these women, and I hoped that one day we would all be sitting together again, stuffing invitations for my wedding. And if that day never came, at least I could count on these two women to be there for me.

FOURTEEN

January arrived. I survived the holidays on take-out Chinese food, Blue Bell ice cream, self-pity, and the promise of a sunny beach. By the time the site visit to Mexico for Brody and Harriet's wedding arrived, I was ready for a little "vacation," even if it was really a work trip to facilitate my ex-boyfriend's nuptials. It wasn't Dallas. I'd take it.

Cedric, Mary Ellen, and I were checking out the resort four months before the event took place. This was protocol for every destination wedding Cedric planned; he believed you had to physically lay eyes on anything you selected for a client. I was, presumably, brought on this trip because they needed someone to haul suitcases and apply sunscreen in hard-to-reach places. Plus, I'd found the venue, and as a newly minted junior planner, my presence was justifiable to all the jealous Trusties and assistants.

But first we had to get there. Why we didn't have a direct flight to Mexico from Texas was *beyond* me, but I shut my mouth and packed my passport. We made it to the Los Angeles airport, which I'd refer to as the Armpit of America from then on, and it was a complete madhouse. At LAX no matter how early your flight got in, there was never enough time to get to your connection, which was always in another terminal. So, of course, we were running late.

Cedric was freaking out about missing the plane, so he abandoned Mary Ellen and me in the middle of the terminal with all six carry-ons. We'd each taken a roll-aboard and a garment bag of essentials in case our luggage didn't make it. Cedric, of course, refused to relinquish custody of his precious designer clothes to the airline—though it was fine to abandon them to our mercy. He ditched us with the luggage plus eight shopping bags he'd purchased duty-free and fled to the gate with the excuse he was off to hold the plane. What a saint.

LAX was full of rude people in a hurry. Left alone to manage the largest bags, and struggling up a steep set of stairs, I heard a loud scream and turned around to find Mary Ellen flat on her back, spread-eagle, sliding down the stairs completely tangled in Louis Vuitton luggage.

Not one person stopped to help or even look at her, which was odd given she was yelping like a sad puppy. I couldn't believe my eyes. She became airport roadkill at the bottom of the stairs as the masses continued to step over her as though she didn't exist. Like I said, Armpit of America.

In the midst of her wailing in pain (visibly, she only had a scratch on her knee), I did my best to peel her off the stairs, wipe Lord knows what off her back, and help her limp to our gate. With me carrying five out of six bags, naturally.

I tried to hurry Mary Ellen along, but she refused to put pressure on her leg and clung to her knee like she would never walk again. *For. The. Love.* We arrived as they began boarding the last group. Cedric was nowhere in sight, so I let the gate agent assist Mary Ellen onto the plane and followed behind, dragging our bags.

As we passed through first class, I caught sight of Cedric, nestled in his luxury seat and smugly sipping a cocktail, oblivious to the peons passing by him. He never asked why two male flight attendants escorted Mary Ellen to her seat. If he wasn't going to acknowledge it, I sure wasn't either. Needless to say, I loathed LAX, I mean the Armpit of America, but Mary Ellen will always credit me for saving her life there.

One bag of ice, one large narcotic pill, and two Bloody Marys later, Mary Ellen could magically walk again.

We arrived in Mexico without further incident (thank God) and were picked up by a black Hummer with blacked-out windows sent by the resort. The Hummer was equipped with cold towels and Perrier bottles for us to enjoy as the driver sped through the busy streets of Los Cabos. Soon we arrived at a towering adobe wall with two enormous wooden gates that opened to the resort.

Down a long palm tree–lined drive, we were dropped off in front of a white stucco fountain and large archway leading to paradise. Upon exiting the car, we were each handed a colorful fruity cocktail.

I deserve this, I thought as I followed Mary Ellen and Cedric, who waltzed into the lobby like he owned the place.

"Cedric Montclair, reservation for three, please." He fanned himself and sipped his pineapple libation. "This place is *everything*, and I get so inspired by all the color and energy here. I think it's the best sleep I've gotten in my life." Cedric poured himself onto a royal-blue settee covered in pillows in various shades of blue.

When I had suggested this particular resort, I had no clue Cedric frequented the place, but that only made him trust my decisions more. I was feeling as confident as ever.

"Let's all get settled in our rooms, then I'll buzz you both to go over plans for the afternoon." He then sauntered off behind one of the three butlers who would escort us to our individual suites.

That afternoon I did indeed settle comfortably into the hotel. When I say comfortably, I mean it was so luxurious I never imagined sheets could be so soft or a view could be so stunning. I even had my own room on the second floor of one of the villas. I lay on top of the bedspread and closed my eyes, soaking it all in.

We were staying at one of the nicest resorts in Los Cabos. My suite alone cost $1,500 a night, and I was lowest on the food chain. The resort was situated at the tip of the Baja Peninsula, with one of the area's few sandy beaches, and the Sea of Cortez sparkled outside my window. Instead of the humid urban stank I was used to, the hot air wafting in my window smelled like flowers and spices. Despite the niggling knowledge that I was here to plan my ex's wedding to a global superstar, I felt like this moment almost validated my life choices. Almost.

Soon I snuck out for a walk through the grounds. Cedric had a strict schedule for us that involved scouting locations and triple-checking that the food and beverage orders were correct. Because Brody and Harriet were not coming on-site before the event, we had to preview most details on their behalf. The tragic irony was not lost on me.

It was also a complete crapshoot as to when and *if* shipped flowers and décor would arrive for an event in Mexico as they had to pass through the dreaded customs department, which was notorious for delaying and losing almost everything that came through. Cedric's solution was, naturally, to bring a suitcase of cash—and Mary Ellen, whom I learned spoke fluent Spanish. While they were both at the customs office confirming proper receipt of the wedding items shipped in thus far, my schedule was technically open for a couple of hours.

The sand squished between my toes as I walked along the beach. I thought about my friendship with Griffin, as I hadn't heard from him in almost a month. Sure, it had been the holidays, so he got a free pass. But, frankly, I missed him.

What the heck was I doing? I enjoyed being around him and appreciated his passion and sense of humor. Didn't mind his face either. But he was pretty hard to read—and had made it abundantly clear that he wasn't interested in starting something romantic. More than that, though, maybe we wanted very different things in both life and in love.

And then there was Matt, who had his life so together. Sweet, successful, stable. His face was acceptable as well. Ready for marriage and interested in me. He was Mr. Perfect on Paper, like he'd been since we'd reconnected.

I trudged back up to the pool deck and found a sunny lounge chair with a good sightline to the lap pool. There were a couple nice-looking men doing rounds, and why waste a great view?

Cedric and Mary Ellen found me, and they sat at a nearby table to also enjoy the view while we ordered a quick lunch. The resort's on-site event staff met with us to iron out a few remaining details about the schedule. I listened in awe (while frantically taking notes, of course) as Cedric and Mary Ellen chimed in about what would happen every last minute of the weekend. Between the staff's flawless service, the resort's luxurious accommodations, and Cedric's exquisite designs, this truly would be a dream weekend.

"Next step," said Cedric once our meeting ended. "Swing by the ceremony site."

We made our way to the resort's white stucco chapel, niches on the front façade peppered with statues of saints. It predated the hotel construction and was too small for the ceremony, so it would serve as backdrop while the vows took place at the stone courtyard.

"I'm having a vision," Cedric said, facing the stairs that led to rustic wooden double doors. He gestured at us. "Y'all go up there so I can see the light this time of day. It's just about right."

We climbed the stairs. Mary Ellen veered right, then turned to face me.

"Lottie, you be the bride." *In this instance, I'd wanted to be. Way to rub it in, Cedric.* "Hold your hands like you've got a bouquet. There. And Mary Ellen, take a step to the right." I fought to keep my face blank. He jotted a couple notes in his sketchbook. "I'm seeing an arbor, larger than what we originally discussed with Harriet's team. Palm fronds, the biggest orchids we can find."

He closed his notebook with a flourish. "Okay, thank you. I'll make sure to fill in the floral team. Now, let's go sample the drink menu. Chop chop."

We spent the rest of the afternoon sipping the resort's signature cocktails. We talked about everything from The Firm's biggest upcoming events to the latest Ryan Reynolds movie. No one got too deep into their personal lives, which was ideal considering the drinks were all very, well, relaxing. I couldn't be counted on not to blab that I had dated this particular groom, which wouldn't have been a good look. I was still off-kilter from our ceremony reenactment. Too close to home.

By sunset Cedric decided to forgo a group dinner and head back to our rooms, which I was thrilled to do. I collapsed on the bed in my suite, unable to bother with room service.

The next morning, Mary Ellen and I trudged the grounds, sweating as I lugged a bag of "necessities"—aka bottles of Acqua Panna, sunscreen, and Sakara bars—from one end of the resort to the other. Cedric had sent us on a scouting mission. The resort had standard locations for wedding events, but Cedric was certain that if we just explored the acreage enough, we would find an uncharted spot with a perfect view of the sea. Apparently, when you're a celebrity, your wedding portraits can't look like anyone else's on the planet.

Cedric, of course, had informed us he would wait at "mission control"—most likely located on a floating flamingo in the pool, iPhone wrapped inside the Swiss Army knife of waterproof phone bags so he could see location photos as we texted them to him.

We schlepped through what felt like a freaking rainforest, hiking narrow trails I was pretty sure were intended not for resort guests but groundskeepers. Glittering cerulean water peeked through the thick trees, and sticks and tropical leaves crunched underfoot. I had intended to marry Brody a mere two blocks from my off-campus housing. Oh, how far we'd come.

When one was sweating bullets and hiking in flip-flops, conversation was sparse. Mary Ellen and I gasped for air at each other or gesticulated to indicate when we should stop and snap a picture.

"Over there," she croaked at me, pointing to an opening in the thick foliage. We trudged over to what turned out to be a rocky promontory over the bay. We could see the distant mainland, across sea that sparkled with the dazzle of midday. By mutual consent we each sat on the large, flat rocks that lined the clearing.

"Some . . . times . . . I hate . . . that man," she wheezed. I nodded, unsure whether I was supposed to acknowledge the comment or pretend it was just the sound of the breeze.

"He wasn't always like this." Mary Ellen started to breathe normally.

"What do you mean?"

"He wasn't always so entitled or intense. I mean, he still works hard, but he used to be the first person to get his hands dirty, as hard as that is to believe. When I first came to work for Cedric, he still sounded like a hayseed from the Panhandle—and had the salt-of-the-earth work ethic to go with his original accent."

"Yeah, he told me a little bit about his hometown on our way to Corsicana. I was shocked. I always thought he was from somewhere up north. Or at least Kansas."

"That's the point of his careful, nonspecific diction. He only drawls when he thinks it will help make a bride's mother feel more comfortable."

As someone who had amped up her accent—and slowed her speech—a time or two to get what she wanted, I couldn't fault him for that one.

"So, what changed?" I asked cautiously.

"Well, I met Cedric right after he moved to Dallas from Canyon. I had just graduated from SMU and wasn't sure what to do. I guess I should have thought about that before majoring in art history, but alas." She shrugged. "My mother's friend from the Dallas Junior League board had hired Cedric to plan a retirement party. He still handled such boring events filled with 'ordinary' people at the time. She went on and on about his creativity, his artistry, and his prospects, and I overheard her talking about how he was trying to build out his team.

"The next day, I called him up. We connected over SMU. He, of course, made me go through the most ridiculous tests to see if I could cut it. He quizzed me with all kinds of random questions about design and décor to get a read on my taste levels. He knew he could teach me how to plan a party, but good taste? Unteachable. Apparently when I mentioned my affinity for hand-painted Gracie wallpaper and chinoiserie porcelain, he knew I was 'the one' to help him build his burgeoning business. It *has* disappointed my mother that I've become the hired help, but every year I buy her a Chanel purse for Christmas, so she overlooks where the money comes from. At least I'm not draining the trust fund like my sisters.

"But I digress. Like I was saying, back then he would stay and help once guests left instead of booking it back to the hotel and leaving the rest of us to clean up. We would go out for drinks after big events, just the two of us, and gab about clients. He was so much fun. He'd already changed his name by then."

"Wait, what?" This was all blowing my mind.

Mary Ellen cackled. "Do you think someone named Cedric Montclair would have survived high school in Canyon? Or worked in a literal canyon? He was born Clyde Murray."

"Doesn't have quite the same ring."

"Honey, when he moved to Dallas, he even pretended to date women for a couple years."

"That must have been unfortunate all around."

"I think he found his niche with wealthy divorcees. They were more interested in his help picking new curtains than new lingerie."

This camaraderie felt good. Hopefully she'd really start trusting me and notice all the work I was putting in instead of keeping me second string. Or maybe she'd at least, you know, share the tips. A girl could dream.

Both of our phones buzzed with a text marked urgent. Apparently we hadn't checked in with His Highness in a half hour and he was getting worried that we'd fallen off a cliff. (I assumed he had insurance policies on us on the off chance. He hated to be inconvenienced without proper compensation.)

Our gal palling over, we continued along the trail, stopping only to snap pictures of various vistas.

That afternoon we met up in Cedric's palatial suite to go over our photos of the potential locations. I internally lamented not dining at the Michelin-starred restaurant's seaside terrace when we instead ordered room service.

Still, I grudgingly munched the most delicious tacos on earth and got to work.

As we neared the end of our photos, Cedric stopped us. He *would* pick somewhere as far from the main resort as possible.

"There, that's it." He pointed at a small clearing that opened up to a drop-off. Rocks and boulders dotted the grass, and thick tropical trees were interspersed with indigenous flowering bushes. He was right. It was perfect.

"Imagine Harriet standing there for portraits," he added, pointing. "They could do a first look here too. Mary Ellen, I saw a picture of the dress Vera is creating for her, by the way. You'll love it. Her groom will just die when he sees her."

I, also, wanted to die. But I smiled and took notes. *New office means new job means more money and new life. Be a robot, Jones. Repeat.*

Next, we looked at the chairs, tables, linens, and lounge furniture provided by the resort. Cedric had already spotted hand-embroidered Otomi linens he wanted to use from a local market when he and Mary Ellen went to customs. They cost a small fortune and would most likely get ruined at dinner, but of course that didn't matter. He decided the resort's luxe linens were not up to par, even if they were good enough for Oprah, who had just checked out.

While we were thumbing through the wine list and making notes about what we would need to smuggle in, Cedric stopped.

"Now, ladies, this is *very important*," he said slowly. "Harriet Devore and her sports guy aren't my biggest celebrity clients. I've worked with Beyoncé, after all." I was not about to point out that it had been a party for Solange in Houston. "But they're still very high profile. Don't believe for one second they actually want privacy. This is about the control and the money—always is. I would expect the images to land at *People*. Anyway, clients like this can be freaks about guests taking and leaking or posting photos. We will need to have phone-check stations at every event to manage any potential leaks over the weekend.

"My belief is the guests kind of like it when we do that because it makes them feel like they're *really* important to be here. But it's so essential"—he pronounced the word as if the *i* were its own syllable—"that no photos of this wedding get out there. No Facebook or Instagram or Snapping or whatever the kids do these days. And *definitely* no paparazzi. Lottie, I'll be sending you on sweeps of the perimeter from time to time."

"Okay, I can do that." I was baffled. He spoke as if this were the Brangelina wedding (RIP). This was Brody, after all. A guy who probably still watched Adam Sandler movies and, at one point, owned jorts. But I knew better than to ask Cedric too many questions—or let on that my interest in the couple was anything other than strictly business. We'd now passed the moment when I could confess without consequences.

We split up to tackle a few remaining tasks. Mary Ellen and I took pictures of the welcome-party location, which would take place on a private beach near the front of the resort. Cedric was planning an upscale lobster bake, and we needed to measure the area for custom cabanas that were shipping in from California. Cedric, wearing an orange Hermès caftan, was off to the menu tasting for the rehearsal dinner and wedding reception, which he said must always be done on a full stomach so you aren't "deceived" into liking something mediocre simply because you're starving.

A few hours later, we synced up at the main resort lounge to debrief. Mary Ellen and I had scoped out the beach, and Cedric was sufficiently stuffed from his ten-course tasting.

We sat at a low table near the panoramic windows with our drinks. "So, Lottie, how's your sex life?" Cedric said, as casually as if this were a conversation about the weather.

"Excuse me?" I choked on my skinny margarita on the rocks.

"Well, you're beautiful, and after working with us a few months, you've finally started to figure out how to dress properly and highlight your hair. It's been quite the glow-up, so I'm sure you're not short on suitors."

"Thanks? I think."

"Oh, come on. There are no secrets in this job, no room for embarrassment. After all, I've held up at least a hundred wedding dresses for clients while they used the restroom during their reception. I'm sure you have visuals you'd rather forget."

He and Mary Ellen both cackled while my face positively scalded.

"Okay, well, if you must know, my dating life is . . . sparse. I'm seeing someone, but just casually. I don't have much time to go out, not to mention I don't really think I'm cut out for app dating either. Every man on them seems like a total basement dweller or he's just sending unsolicited pictures of his nether regions, which is just—"

"Don't worry, sweetie," Cedric chimed in as he ordered a round of shots for us all. "I'm very happy with Geoffrey, but I'm not one to dole out love advice. Sex, on the other hand . . ."

Thank God he ordered shots. We had officially crossed over into a conversation I was not prepared to have with my boss, let alone anyone else. I think he'd missed the point of what I was saying too.

"Lottie, I can tell you how to have any man you want begging you to marry him."

"Itsso true," said Mary Ellen, who had started to slur a bit by then.

"I've already heard this advice, and it clearly worked for me. How do you think I finally got Tate to propose?"

Oh gosh, he was starting to make explicit gestures and movements with his hands. I quickly looked around us to see who might be watching (like I would remember anything the next morning) and noticed that two stars from *Game of Thrones* were drinking at a table across the bar but paying absolutely no attention to us. We were safe. Well, I suppose that was a relative term at this juncture in the conversation.

"And finally, if you really want to make him go crazy—" Cedric's voice elevated at this point, and he made a couple more motions while Mary Ellen and I both gasped, though for different reasons.

"Wow, so that's how it's done?" I said, shrill.

"Yes. Trust me. If you're going to take advice from anyone, take it from a gay man. We know what we're talking about." He signaled our waiter for the bill.

"So true," repeated Mary Ellen, like she—now three drinks in— had any real clue as to what he was saying.

Cedric swiped the pen across the bill in one dramatic motion and then bid us both good night.

"Well, that was quite the ending to a long day," said Mary Ellen.

"You're telling me." I picked up my clutch and tried to stand up without falling over. "I feel like we should at least cuddle."

"Now don't start getting needy, Lottie," Cedric shouted as he strolled off into the darkness toward his suite. "Straight men absolutely *hate* that."

And just like that, our deranged nightcap was over.

I stumbled back to my room and collapsed on three-thousand-thread-count sheets. After what felt like only a few minutes, I woke up way too early to the sound of the phone ringing.

"It's me," Mary Ellen chirped. Had she laced her coffee with cocaine? "This morning Cedric will be busy with floral vendors, so I think you and I need to do some 'research' in the spa facilities. What do you say?"

"Meet you there in five minutes!"

I threw on my monogrammed hotel robe over my bathing suit, slipped into the complimentary slippers, and headed down to the five-star spa. Mary Ellen had made us appointments: first, hot stone massages, followed by deep-cleansing facials. Then we would test the spa facilities.

I spent a heavenly three hours being rubbed and popped and scrubbed, which was especially helpful given that I needed an intense detox after the night before. I was definitely going to volunteer for every possible site visit in the future, even if I did have to schlep Mary Ellen's bags.

Post facial, I stumbled groggily to the soaking tub, where Mary Ellen sat with her head resting on the edge.

"Oh, hullo," she mumbled.

"So last night was fun," I said as I dropped my robe and melted into the warm bubbling pool of water.

"Yeah, it reminded me of the way things used to be with Cedric. It was the first time we've had fun like that together in a while," she said. "Every now and then he comes back down to earth and I see my mentor, my friend again."

As if the facial and massage weren't enough, this tub pushed me over the edge into complete relaxation, and with that, I also felt like Mary Ellen and I had reached a new level in our relationship.

"So, you've told me all about Cedric, but what's your story?" I asked.

"Way to ask an easy one," she said with a laugh. "Well, I grew up in Dallas. My mom—the one who hates what I do—was everything you'd expect of the wife of a city comptroller: president of the Junior League, involved with the Dallas Museum of Art, Susan G. Komen, Dallas Symphony Orchestra League, and other things that made her seem more altruistic than she really was.

"My favorite part of all of that hubbub was going with her to check on events before they started. She'd go talk with caterers and double-check seating cards, and I would wander around, rearranging centerpieces and adjusting garlands. I loved watching her, too, before she'd go out. As a girl I thought she looked like a queen in elegant gowns.

"Later I attended SMU, where I enrolled in art history with the intention to teach. Sadly, I found out I was completely hopeless as an instructor—you have to actually care that people are learning—met Cedric, and the rest is history."

We were never going to be buddies, but Mary Ellen was at least more human than I'd thought. Especially for a grown-up Trustie. I almost, well, *liked* her.

"And you're engaged?" I asked, now too relaxed to come up with anything interesting to say. She launched into the long tale of meeting her fiancé, Tate, at a Slipper Club social function last year. I started dozing off in the tub, though, and missed all the personal stuff about him. Mary Ellen finally paused her own groggy ramblings long enough to notice that I was getting bleary eyed.

"Well, Lottie, I think we've had enough—time in the spa and of my stories. Let's get back to the suites to change for our last meeting."

That night, after checking final details with resort staff, I settled in for the last time on my magnificent sheets. Seeing the location where Brody would marry Harriet wasn't as brutal as I'd expected. The cocktails helped, of course, but I was grateful for the preparation—and the time with Cedric and Mary Ellen. That would make this torment worth it. As my melatonin kicked in and my mind finally slowed, I drifted off. We all needed some fortifying rest before facing LAX again.

FIFTEEN

Returning to my sad, shared apartment was quite the letdown after my stay in paradise. Especially considering the Brody of it all.

Enter Matt. He was once again in Dallas between scouting trips, and we had a couple dinners on the books. Time with him was a welcome break from work. Although it did sound like some of his athletes could give our worst groomsmen a run for their money.

We laughed our way through dinner at trendy Dragonfly and Public School 214. It was nice to be wined and dined, and per usual, Matt looked (and smelled) amazing. I was always happy to see his name pop up in my text notifications, especially one dreary January Tuesday.

> I'm heading to Fort Worth Friday night to check out a player at TCU, and if you're not working a wedding, I'd love for you to come along.

> It's your lucky day. I do have a wedding, but it's not until Sunday so I'm actually free Friday night. I'd love to come.

> Great. Think you can get off work early Friday? We could hit the road before rush hour and grab dinner at Joe T's if you can.

> Listen, I will move heaven and earth to make sure I'm free to eat at Joe T's.

> Perfect. Me too. I'll pick you up at 3 p.m. then from your place. It's a date.

It's a date. I guess that was what one would call it. But in a world of undefined relationships, it was still weird to see the word *date* show up on my screen.

> See you soon.

Friday afternoon, I had no qualms about leaving work early. I finished everything I needed to get done for the weekend by noon and felt good about Sunday. Claire promised to cover for me should anyone ask, but given that everyone else in the office left around 3:00 p.m. on Fridays, I wasn't too concerned my absence would be noticed.

Claire had turned out to be the best work wife a girl could ask for. She and I were scheduled to work several upcoming events together, as she was a standout and in line for a full-time role. Maybe a promotion would be in both of our futures.

Matt showed up at the apartment right on time. His BMW sedan smelled just like his cologne. I didn't care about the car as much as the smell, which was downright sexy. He filled me in on all the trips he'd taken the past few weeks and how the pro basketball draft worked, since I was completely clueless in that area.

I regaled him with stories about weddings, which made him laugh and cringe a bit. I forgot that not everyone was desensitized to some of the more intimate things we dealt with—such as wiping down a bride's naked, sweating body for her while she was in between changing dresses at her reception.

"You're one tough cookie," said Matt.

"I guess you could say that. But so are you. I mean, not a cookie." *Gosh, I'm awkward.* "I don't know how you handle the pressure of your job. There's so much money involved, and the future of someone's life can literally change overnight."

"Yeah, but you get used to it. I'm numb to it now, just like you're numb to all the wild wedding crap you deal with."

"You're right about that."

"Have you been back to TCU recently?" Matt changed the subject.

"Not in a few years. I'm so excited to see the campus again," I said as the Fort Worth skyline came into view.

"It looks like a completely different place."

I sighed. "It was such a fun four years."

"I totally agree. I loved my college experience and get so nostalgic about it. In a good way, you know?"

"Absolutely. I don't know if I'll stay in Dallas long term, but I could definitely live in Fort Worth."

"I know what you mean," Matt said. "As much as I enjoy going out, which is still a lot because of my job, Dallas is so over the top. It seems like I'd burn out there after a while."

"Whatever happened to looking at houses in the burbs?"

"Oh, I'm still in the market, but now it's more like homes near Tanglewood. Good schools, you know?"

I didn't want to seem too amenable to everything Matt was saying, but I did agree with him again. Something about Fort Worth still felt like home. "Ha, I can't believe you're already thinking about those."

"It's never too early, right? I mean, thirties is a late start compared to lots of our friends from school," he said.

We pulled up to Joe T. Garcia's in the Stockyards, and the moment I stepped out of the car I was transported back in time. Brody and I used to eat at Joe T's at least once a week, and even from the parking lot, I could smell the food.

We sat in the back garden under a heater near the pool and fountains. Twinkle lights lit up the trees, and the mariachi band played nearby. The sun had just set, making it extremely romantic out there.

"I can only have one drink tonight since I'm technically working at the game. Plus I have to get us both back to Dallas safely," he said. "But hey, don't let me stop you."

"I'm good with one too. I've got to run a rehearsal tomorrow afternoon, and there's no need to suffer through it with a hangover."

"Well, it's for the best anyway. If I had more than one margarita, I might try and recreate that night we had at the bar a few years ago."

Blood rushed to my cheeks. "Oh geez. Yeah, that wasn't my best moment." I tried to laugh it off.

"Are you kidding? I remember that night pretty fondly."

Thankfully the waiter arrived to take our orders and break up the conversation. Once our drinks came, Matt offered up a toast.

"Here's to the past, and to a bright new future for us both."

We clinked glasses and proceeded to, quite happily, down an inordinate amount of fajitas.

After that, Matt drove me through TCU's campus so we could see what had changed over the years. The faculty parking lot that connected the freshman boys' and girls' dorms was now a lush, grassy quad. The old student union had been replaced with a high-tech multipurpose building. I bet the food in there even tasted good, which would certainly be an improvement. Despite new dorms and athletic facilities, it still felt the same to me. There was such a good vibe on campus, even if things didn't end the way I'd thought they would.

Driving past the chapel, though, was like having my knees knocked out by a wave. Good thing I was seated and buckled securely. I hadn't seen it in years and could still feel the heartache and fear and tequila of that night. When my plans crumbled and my imagined wedding to Brody evaporated. The moment certainly dampened my reminiscing.

We had a great time at the game and laughed about how I'd never attended a single basketball game when I was actually in college. I was too busy with Brody's football schedule to give any other sport a chance.

Matt was totally in his element. He led me through the back of the stadium afterward and into the area outside the men's locker room. "I've got to go in and schmooze with a few of the guys we're hoping to sign, but I won't be long. I promise."

"I'll be fine here. Take your time."

He gave me a wink and then ducked inside the locker room. It gave me a few minutes to relax and check my phone.

Wouldn't you know it? Two missed calls from Griffin. I hadn't heard from him in what felt like ages, and I hadn't seen him at one of our weddings in over a month. His emails had stopped, too, and I missed those. He, of course, called the minute I was on a date. He didn't leave a message. For the best, though, since he had ruled out our being more than friends. No beating around the bush there. I winced every time I recalled that late-night chat. While I was curious as to why he'd called, I wasn't going to call him back now.

Matt, on the other hand, was consistent and expressly, if not explicitly, interested in me. He came out of the locker room as I put my phone in my purse.

"Ready to head back to the Big D?"

"Ugh, if we have to," I said.

He laughed and took my hand as we headed back to the car through the crisp winter night.

Why did holding hands feel like *such* a big deal? I had no clue, but I was floating as we walked to his car. He might have told me about one of the potential draft picks he saw in the locker room, but I didn't hear a thing.

He opened the door like a Southern gentleman, and I let him. We drove back in silent sexual tension—the kind you could cut with a knife. The radio played, but all I could focus on was if he would try and make a move when we got back to my place.

I'd kissed him before, but this night felt different. Because this time around I was sober, and it was a fresh start. This wasn't some casual fling or a late-night escapade at a bar. If I kissed him, I'd be communicating how much I was into him. And I was.

"I had a great night, Lottie," he said as he opened my car door. "Can I walk you up to your door?"

"Sure." I tried not to throw up from nerves.

We arrived at my door and before I could pull out my keys, he gently took hold of my waist and pulled me into him, giving me the gentlest kiss. His lips were soft and tasted like spearmint gum. I kissed him back, then sheepishly thanked him for a wonderful night.

"I hope to see you again very soon." Matt gave me one last, long hug.

"I'd like that." I bit my lower lip, then headed inside.

I'd barely closed the door behind me when Natalia came barreling around the corner into the living room. *"Well?"* She stared at me with her eyes open wide.

"We had a great time. And he just kissed me." I beamed from ear to ear like an idiot.

"Oh my gosh. Oh my gosh," she screamed. "Tell me *everything*."

Of course I told Natalia every detail from the night, including my random missed calls from Griffin.

"Look at you, love triangle," she said.

"Give me a break. Griffin is just a friend, remember? A complicated, cute one, but a friend, nonetheless."

"Yeah, right." Natalia grinned.

"And Matt is great, but . . . I don't know, for some reason I'm not totally feeling him just yet."

"What part of that kiss are you not feeling?"

"Well, I'm attracted to him—you'd have to be a moron not to be. And he's kind and funny and successful and all that. I just don't know."

"Hon, you've been hung up a bit more than usual since you started working on Brody's wedding," she said. "I'm sure it's a reminder of what can happen when you get carried away. But there's a big leap between seeing where things go and secretly planning to marry someone. You got this. Brody's fully moved on, as you know."

"Yes, I have a daily reminder of that. It's not really about Brody. Work is about to get even busier, and I'm really trying to nail this job. But I do like Matt—more and more every time we go out. I'm only trying to keep it casual."

"Totally," said Natalia. "You don't have to rush into anything. But how *fun* that you're going out with someone who's totally into you!"

"I guess so. At least I can delete Hinge for now, right?"

"Listen, that's legitimately a good enough reason to marry the guy." She laughed.

Matt still wanted that life we'd all imagined in college. And not from a lack of imagination; he'd seen enough outside of our Texas bubble and knew what he wanted. What was wrong with that? At least for now, my love life and career were looking up.

~ ✳ ~

As Brody and Harriet's wedding date neared, Mary Ellen and I began once-a-week FaceTime calls with Harriet Devore's assistant. I'd still never spoken to Harriet, but Tasha relayed her thoughts on the various design elements. I dreaded the moment we'd finally meet, knowing the complete transparency of my poker face. I might have to try and pull a Cedric move and wear sunglasses. Gradually Mary Ellen was skipping some calls and entrusting more details to me. I started to pin my hopes on this wedding being my big break.

With two months as an official junior planner under my belt, I felt like I was finding a new groove at Cedric Montclair Celebrations. After Mary Ellen and Abigail, I handled more responsibility than any of the other planners. The only downside was my relationship with Mary Ellen had regressed to pre-Mexico levels. We hadn't worked together in weeks, and it started to feel weird between us in the office. Abigail seemed to celebrate my growth, but it was hard to tell how Mary Ellen felt about it. Especially after Cedric called me into his office one Wednesday afternoon.

"Lottie, please sit down."

This posed a challenge, as the chaise longue was precariously covered in swatches and dish samples. The other seat was occupied by Prince Charles. I awkwardly pushed the little dog's legs over a few inches so I could squeeze half my body onto the chair.

"Your clients have been raving about you these past few months, and Abigail says you're doing a fantastic job on your own," he said. "She's been—on my instructions, of course—letting you take the lead more, and she says your instincts and composure are improving. Mary Ellen does not disagree with her assessment."

"Thank you." I tried not to sound too surprised.

"I'm going to give you a small raise," he said casually, while also feverishly typing on his computer.

"Thank you so much," I repeated, stunned. "I really appreciate that."

"Well, that's not all. I'm also looking to add a younger and fresher face to represent the company in the Atlanta office. You might just be that face."

"Oh my gosh, thank you, Cedric. I'd never really thought about making the move to Atlanta myself, but wow." Wow was right. After seven years in Dallas, I was just starting to build a life here that I loved. Was I actually ready to give that up?

"Why not?" He stopped typing on his computer and made eye contact, then took a sip out of his Starbucks Venti iced coffee.

"Truthfully, I have just really enjoyed working here and never thought Atlanta would be an option." *Don't blow this opening.* I quickly continued: "But that would be so wonderful. I'm beyond thrilled you're considering me."

I felt like a goober, but I wasn't really sure what to say. I still expected to be called Libby half the time.

"Don't get too sappy. Nothing is finalized. I just wanted you to know that I'm watching you, and we will need strong planners in Atlanta to grow that business, which could be a good option for you if you're interested."

"Yes, yes, I'm definitely interested," I said, beaming from ear to ear.

"Then keep up the good work. And really think about whether you'd want to make the move. We'll talk again soon."

"Thank you so much again, Cedric." I stood and repositioned the Yorkie, who had not moved a muscle since I sat down.

"Oh," he said as I was nearly out the door. "Don't say anything to anyone. We don't need any more drama around here than we already have."

"No problem," I promised, turning on my heel.

I couldn't believe it. Moving to Atlanta felt like a huge step, but I was so excited that I didn't care. Where would that leave Matt and me? Would taking this job be the final nail in the coffin of my aspirations to attend law school? Maybe it was time to be realistic about that one anyway.

I headed back to my desk and felt Mary Ellen's eyes digging into me from the open door of her office.

Did she know why Cedric had summoned me? He'd said not to tell anyone else about the potential Atlanta promotion, but he told Mary Ellen everything. Or at least I thought he did. She didn't come and ask for details, but I could tell something bothered her.

As I pretended to send emails, I continued to absorb what Cedric had said. Atlanta, huh? I'd grown to love Dallas—despite all its flashy flaws. But I'd only come thirty miles since college. Perhaps in more ways than I-35. Atlanta could be a completely fresh start. It was something new to ponder.

SIXTEEN

We were working an early February wedding, and with Cedric's attention focused on prepping for Mexico and the new office, I'd been deputized to run this event with Abigail and a small team.

The couple, Adaego and Mack, were delightful to work with in the months leading up to the event, so I was excited to finally put all our plans into action for them. They'd met in high school in nearby Pflugerville, but Adaego, the bride, was from a big Nigerian family and the groom's side were all Scottish. We'd had fun melding elements of both cultures into an otherwise straightforward ceremony and reception at a vineyard in the Hill Country.

Everything went as planned, aside from a couple unruly groomsmen in kilts. But as we were packing up at the end of the night, Griffin came over to where I was loading Abigail's car. I hadn't really paid him much attention, I was so busy with the day's details—and making sure I didn't blow it while things were going so well for me at The Firm. Not to mention I called him back the day after the TCU game and he never picked up. I wasn't going to give him the satisfaction of letting him know that I cared. Which, of course, I did.

"Hey, Lottie." He thrust his hands in the front pockets of his dusty skinny jeans and kicked the dirt with one toe.

"Oh, oof—hi!" I shoved the final box in the trunk and shut it with a not-inconsequential amount of effort. With that I went to give him a quick hug, catching the scent of laundry detergent under the odors of sweat and crisp cologne.

Did he even care that our friendship was strained due to his sudden withdrawal and the clear boundaries he'd laid out? I was seeing Matt now, of course, at least whenever he was in town. And while we hadn't talked about exclusivity, it seemed to be the case. But I could still miss being able to share silly stories with Griffin and talk to someone who fully understood what I did for a living. I stepped back and looked up at his face. "What's up?"

"I wanted to see what you were up to tomorrow. When are you going back to Dallas?"

"We haven't really decided yet. Abigail is my ride, and she likes to sleep in after weddings. So I imagine sometime around the crack of noon. Why?"

"Well, it's just that my family lives near here, and I'm staying with them. If you wanted to, I'd love for you to come over for brunch with us before heading back. I could even take you to Dallas if she needs to head out." He let out a long sigh.

"Oh. How fun you get to see them." I took a moment to compose myself. I was taken aback given that he wanted me to go with him to meet his family. This felt like a huge deal on multiple levels.

"It's not a big deal, really," he said, reading my mind. *Thanks for letting me down easy, dude.* "Just a casual Sunday brunch."

"Sounds great to me. I'd love to come. Can you come pick me up, or should I take an Uber?" I was very good at playing the easygoing, strictly platonic, no expectations, totally cool friend now.

"I'll come get you at ten tomorrow. Sound good?"

With that he gave me the briefest of waves and hightailed it to his car. He was being so weird. But later, as I drifted to sleep on my Holiday Inn Express one-hundred-thread-count sheets, I tried not to let it worry me. I'd had quite a bit of practice dealing with clients' parents. Not to toot my own horn, but they all tended to love me.

~✖~

Griffin picked me up in his beat-up blue truck, and we drove to East Austin. The drive flew by as we settled back into our easy rapport, and I discovered our shared affinity for old-school country music. When you're from Austin or Memphis, music lives in your blood. I was thrilled not to have to listen to whatever pop sensation was leading the charts. With the windows cracked, and George Strait and Johnny Cash playing, it was the perfect drive after the day before.

Signs and storefront windows we passed were a motley, vibrant mix of English and Spanish. People sat in a circle of lawn chairs outside a couple of the stores, soaking up a Sunday afternoon breeze. We passed modest, well-maintained bungalows as we drove under mature oak trees.

Then we pulled up to a nondescript midcentury bungalow at the end of a quiet block. The only thing that made it stand out from the other neutral-toned homes was the bright-turquoise front door. A concession, I imagined, to someone with taste who could not be constrained by neighbors' opinions or homeowners' association rules.

He'd run me through the family tree and prepped me for meeting everyone. Parents, his younger sister, Olivia, her husband, and their two kids. His other sister, Penelope, was in school at A&M right now, and his brother, Cruz, was at a soccer tournament, so at least I didn't have to face them all at once. I took a deep breath as Griffin slid his key in the front door.

"Hello?" he shouted.

"I'm back in the kitchen," a woman replied. "Everyone else is out back."

We turned the corner to see a beautiful, middle-aged woman pulling a dish from the oven. "Hello, you must be Lottie." She wiped a hand on her apron before she extended it and tucked a stray dark hair behind one ear. "I'm Marisa."

"It's so nice to meet you. Thank you so much for including me. Can I help with anything?"

"Absolutely not. You're our guest, and Griff is completely counterproductive in the kitchen. You just keep him entertained so he stays out of here."

"Hey, that's not fair!" he chimed in. "I can make a surprising array of dishes now that I live on my own."

"Yes, honey, but how many of those require the George Foreman grill or kebabs and an open flame?" She patted his hand.

"Very funny, Mama."

We exchanged pleasantries until we were interrupted by Griffin's five-year-old niece and three-year-old nephew careening inside. His sister Olivia was only twenty-seven, but she'd married her high school sweetheart and started early on kids. I watched Griffin wrestle with the pair on the kitchen floor before his mom shooed us all out to the deck.

Olivia was sitting at a table, sipping a soda and holding a bubble wand. Griffin came over and gave her a big squeeze around the neck. "Where's Ben?"

"Oh, he had to run into the office today to prep for a big presentation tomorrow," she said, turning to me. "You must be Lottie."

Before I could respond she jumped up and gave me a big hug too. None of the Joneses were huggers, so I was a bit taken aback, in the best way possible. His father stood up from the other chair and extended a hand. "Welcome to our home, Lottie. I'm Danny." We chatted for a few minutes before Marisa ducked her head out to call us back inside.

We gathered around a large dining table in a room papered in a faded 1990s floral pattern. Griffin sat to my left, Olivia to my right. She winked at me conspiratorially. His father sat at the head, and his niece and nephew filled in the other seats. I traced the worn scratches in the table with my finger while we waited for Griffin's mom to take her seat at the end nearest the kitchen. How many Sundays had they spent around this table? Easily hundreds.

My parents had stopped really doing daily meals together the year I started running track and my brother, Tommy, began competitive baseball. It became impossible to get all four of us in the same place at the same time. Soon, it became unimportant. This past year, we hadn't even done Christmas.

Marisa finally laid a casserole dish on the table and took her seat. "So, Lottie, you're a wedding planner?"

"Yes, I work for Cedric Montclair Celebrations. I've been there about a year."

"Oh yes, I know them." She turned to her husband. "Danny, they did the Jeffersons' daughter's wedding last summer. Remember? I love his work, Lottie. You must really enjoy it."

"Yes, we get to help with some really beautiful projects. I'm learning a lot for sure."

"But what's *he* like? At that wedding, I only saw him running around the background and looking like the Wizard of Oz."

"Was he wearing something red?"

"Yes! I think it was his shoes. They stuck out because everything else was black."

"Sounds about right . . . But to answer your question, he's a character." We discussed Cedric's eccentricities and some of the craziest weddings I'd worked, though I tried not to completely throw my employer under the bus. The last thing I needed was Marisa telling one of our former clients that I was talking out of school.

"Tell us about your family, Lottie. Griffin says you're from Tennessee? Do you have any siblings?"

I found myself launching into the brief bio, skipping over my parents' financial struggles, of course, and their concern for my new life choices.

The rest of lunch was a lovely blur, full of the gentle teasing, inside jokes, loud children, and extra helpings I often wished the Joneses were capable of.

"Lottie, why did you go into wedding planning?" Marisa asked. "I assume it's not a major at school or anything."

I'd been asked the *how* before but not the *why* so directly. "No, it's not." I laughed. "I guess I always imagined what my own wedding would be like. But I also wanted to be a lawyer. Not for any great reason, mind you."

I wasn't about to tell Griffin's family I'd planned my own fake fantasy wedding. "After college I realized I'd put a lot more effort and energy into planning events than I had into preparing for law school or any other job. So I gave it a shot. That was more than seven years ago, and here we are."

"Wow, seven years. Do you think you'll stay with it?" Marisa said, with innocent subtext that moms were experts at.

I stumbled through a noncommittal answer, aware that the air had shifted.

"It's nice to see at least *some* people in your generation can stick with a career," Danny chimed in pointedly.

"Seriously, Dad?" Griffin said. "You couldn't have waited until at least after dessert to get into it?"

"You've only been back for like a year. How do we know you're not going to jet off again to the other side of the world?" Mr. Flores said, coming in hot.

"Do you really want to get into this here and now? Because I don't." Griffin pushed his chair back and walked straight out the back door.

After a beat, I took my cue to go out after him. His little niece and nephew had also taken the cue that the meal was over and dashed to the old wooden swing set in one corner of the backyard. They whooped as they clambered up and down the ladder and down the slide.

A honeysuckle bush reached its tendrils across the deck railing, sending its sweet scent wafting across the yard. Griffin and I each claimed an Adirondack chair in one corner of the deck, under the shade of a large maple tree.

After a few moments I broke the silence. "What was all that about? Why did you blow up in there?"

"Oh, you know, it's always the same thing with him. We've had that fight a hundred times already. It's no big deal."

"It didn't *seem* like no biggie . . ."

"I don't really want to talk about it. Sorry you had to see that, though." He folded his arms and looked toward the kids. They swung forward and were suspended in midair until the chains caught and snapped them back to gravity, swinging them backward again. Back and forth, up and down.

"I've already told you my parents aren't exactly obsessed with my career choices either," I started. He stilled, listening. "Once I left home, they told everyone they knew in Memphis that their daughter was going to become an attorney. Not that they had any idea what that looked like more than I did. It went on that way all through college. When I bombed my first LSAT and then didn't apply to law school, they tried to be encouraging, but I knew they were just appeasing me. To them I'm just a glorified party planner. Maybe I'm not 'making a difference in the world' like I always told them I would."

"Lottie, I've watched you with clients, and you do make a difference. I see it all happen through my lens, remember?"

"You're sweet, but lately it feels like all I do is manage one potential crisis after another. And look at you changing your tune. I thought you were all doom and gloom about weddings."

"Yeah, yeah. Let's focus on you. You make some of the biggest moments of people's lives possible and perfect. You may not be fighting battles in courtrooms, but you're making something. I'm the one who doesn't exactly make or do anything. I just capture what already exists."

"Oh, come on," I protested. "I may be helping them out, but everybody knows that nobody remembers *anything* that happens on their wedding day. Your pictures ensure that they have some happy memories, even if they're manufactured from photographs and not actual memories. It's really the only thing that lasts forever from any wedding."

"Well, that's true I guess." He turned those inquisitive brown eyes my way. "Does it make me a jerk, though, that I don't really care about the ones I shoot?"

"Ha! There's the Griffin I know. What exactly do you mean?"

"Like, all I can think about when I'm working weddings with Val is how wasteful they are. The amount of time and money spent by the clients we both work for is insane. So much so that the focus is often lost on what the wedding is really about—the couple. Put aside the fact that I personally believe most marriages don't work out. Forget the giant wedding. Use that money for something bigger than yourself. I'm a bit of a hypocrite, I know, since this is what pays my bills."

"You know, I've thought about this lately. Many of our clients, not all, but lots of them are huge philanthropists, especially in Dallas. Some cases, they've given away multiples of what these weddings cost."

"So I should feel better because I'm helping bring joy to generous-but-filthy-rich people?"

"Hey, whatever helps you sleep at night."

"My dad's concerned that I make a good living," he finished, "but I find myself more concerned about *doing* good."

I knew what he meant. It was hard to find meaning in what we did compared to everything else happening in the world around us.

I changed tactics. "But, Griff, your family seems pretty great. I can tell that they at least want you to be happy and find what's best for you . . . What was it they were saying about jetting off again?"

He stiffened and stared out at the yard. He took a big breath in and out. "Yeah, they mean after my ex and I split. I left."

"Oh. You haven't mentioned that before," I replied awkwardly.

"Yeah, because it feels like a long time ago. We filed for divorce after less than three years."

Wait, he meant ex-*wife*?! "Oh?"

"Emily and I met at school and got married the year after graduation. I think we both knew it wasn't the right thing, but our families were close and it seemed like the natural next step," he said matter-of-factly.

I tried to sound both neutral and supportive. "Wow."

"You're not the only one who likes to take the obvious path, I guess . . . You know, you meet in college and date for a while and there's this expectation that college is where you find your 'person,' especially here in the South. So I assumed that because the first girl I really ever dated said she loved me and we did all those things—classes together, football games, campus ministry, you get the drill—that it would work out."

This was sounding disturbingly familiar. "What happened?" *Please don't say you cheated, please don't.*

"In some ways I wish I had some big 'she cheated on me' moment. But one day I came home from work, and she had papers waiting. She'd already packed up a suitcase to take to her sister's house. I appreciate that she wanted to tell me in person and didn't just disappear, for what that's worth. But she said we wanted different things in life. She wasn't ready to be a wife, and certainly not a mom yet, and needed to go figure that out on her own. I was completely blindsided."

"Wow," I said again. I was stunned.

"In hindsight, she wasn't completely wrong. We were so young and had no idea who we were or what we wanted back then. But I still would've appreciated the chance to work on it, to see if we could grow in the same direction. Instead I got the dining table and TV, and she took the couch."

Oof. Could Brody and I have wound up like that? We'd never know. I wasn't ready, though, to tell Griffin that I'd dodged a similar fate.

"That's why I went to Africa for a couple years. I looked at what few marketable skills my art degree gave me, quit my graphic design job, and volunteered as a photographer."

Everything clicked into place. "You started over."

"Yep, I just needed a change."

"But I imagine it was also hard to be alone and away from everybody after going through something like that."

"Totally. They said they understood, though my extended family, of course, has some, um, strong feelings about divorce. But I don't know that my parents have completely forgiven me for running off and not turning to them when everything fell apart. I guess I was ashamed, though. And I didn't need the reminder of their happiness or even Olivia's."

If I had a family like his, the last thing I'd want would be to go halfway across the world and leave them. No matter how heartbroken or shattered, I couldn't imagine thinking that living in a yurt by myself in the Serengeti would be in any way preferable. I said as much.

"I don't think you get it. They don't understand that not everybody finds their soul mate at twenty and sticks it out for the next thirty to fifty years. Or maybe that marriage just isn't for everyone."

Before I could respond the sliding glass door opened, and Danny stuck his head outside. "Hey, you two, want to come in and have some homemade ice cream? Your mom's been running the churn all morning, and it's finally frozen enough. We saved you the paddle if you're interested."

We both stood and returned to the house. I think we appreciated the conciliatory gesture by Griffin's parents—and were relieved that the conversation was forced to an end.

After a bowl, or two, of ice cream, we both said our good-byes to his family and headed back to Dallas. It felt good to be around so many people who loved and supported each other the way his family did—or at least appeared to. I knew Griffin was being hard on them, but I was that way with mine. Family was always more complicated than it looked.

On the drive back to Dallas, we listened to music, but I was disappointed that our earlier conversation had been cut off. If anyone understood heartache and shifting life plans, it was me. Brody and I didn't actually end up getting married, so maybe I didn't understand Griffin's experience. But I did understand now why he hated weddings so much. No wonder he thought they were meaningless, given that his own marriage was so brief.

"Thank you for telling me about Emily," I finally said, crossing my fingers that he wouldn't shut me out. "I never got married, of course, but I totally understand what you mean about how things progress in a certain way, and how there are all these expectations on us that we're going to find someone in college."

"Right. There's this whole idea that our early twenties—or earlier, in some cases—really serve as the time to find a spouse and set up a happily ever after."

This conversation was already hitting a nerve. "When I got to TCU, it was like living in a dorm full of *Bachelor* contestants. Buzzing about the eligible guys, approaching fraternity mixers like hunting parties. And then I met my college boyfriend. All the pieces fit."

"Exactly," he said. "If you haven't met 'the one' in school, there's probably something wrong with you."

"I mean . . . my parents met in college, and so did yours. It *does* work that way for some."

"But it's not the *only* way, or even always the right one, Lottie. Who believes that at eighteen or even twenty-two we know ourselves well enough to pick a major, let alone pick somebody to spend our lives with? How did that work out for you and me?"

"It messed me up, kind of. I don't know if it derailed my plans, my identity, or if I simply bought into this idea, placed all my chips on this one relationship."

"See? Just because you date someone at the 'right' time doesn't mean you should spend your whole freaking life with them. Guys feel that pressure too."

"Sure, but it's hard to really feel the same level of pressure when you've got a two-to-one ratio on campus to choose from, huh?"

"You're gonna get pissed at me, whatever I say." He laughed. "This is a no-win . . . But, yes, almost any college guy who wants to have a girlfriend mathematically, theoretically, should be able to find one. Which messes with how you see the whole equation too."

"I maintain that this is another reason why college women are pretty much screwed. Gimme more debt, less income, fewer potential partners, and a few idiots to choose from . . ."

"Ha, right," Griffin went on. "Well, it's a very big risk to count on the fact that of all the people in this country, with all the colleges to attend, jobs to have, places to live, that you're going to meet the one person with whom you're most compatible—"

"Don't you mean soul mate?" Somehow, I needed to know.

"Nah, I don't believe in those. And before you start saying I'm a cynic, it's not that I don't believe in true love. It's just that people change. The trick is really finding the person who will grow with you. If you don't, then you end up like twenty-five-year-old me, heartbroken, alone, and completely adrift."

"That sounds a lot like twenty-two-year-old me."

"We certainly have that in common. I'm just saying that people don't have to participate in that system at all. Young marriage—or maybe marriage in general—is not all it's cracked up to be. And maybe more of us are better off alone than we might think." He paused. "My therapist calls all of this the Southern Matrimonial Complex, by the way."

"That's interesting." *Noted, will revisit.* I was too wrapped up in our conversation to even begin to sift through how scarily relevant this term might be to my own mental health journey. "Wait, therapist?"

"Yeah, I started counseling a couple months ago."

"Wow, that's great," I said. "I just think it's cool when guys are cool with talking about it that openly."

"Maybe if more people did, then more people would get help . . . and fewer of us would be train wrecks. Evidently, I've still got more work to do." He chuckled and turned onto my street. "What number is your building again?"

I pointed it out, lost in my thoughts.

"Thanks again for today, Griffin." I stepped out of his truck and grabbed my bags.

"Absolutely. My family loved meeting you."

"They seem great. I guess I'll see you at the next crazy-wasteful wedding."

He laughed. "Looking forward to it, buddy."

Ugh. Buddy? He might as well have high-fived me right then and there. I waved good-bye and walked up to the apartment. I felt oddly comforted and yet more confused than ever, and the day's conversations had all hit too close to home.

SEVENTEEN

From the moment the developers snipped the velvet ribbon and opened the doors to the new Ritz-Carlton, Dallas, every event planner in town started complaining about the ballroom décor, which was very, very red with ornate gold accents. In the office Cedric referred to the venue as the "Schitt's Carlton" and was always annoyed when he had to design an event there. Short of recarpeting the entire room and building faux walls, which we'd done before, nothing could be done about the color scheme. Fortunately for David and Oksana, our millionaire match made in Vegas, the ballroom was their signature color.

It felt like forever since I'd last seen the couple at their ostentatious estate in Preston Hollow. Oksana looked exactly the same as she did in our first meeting: head to toe in Versace and dripping in gaudy jewels. David was in a green satin suit but looked like he'd aged another twenty years, making him now at least a hundred and two by my count.

We'd coordinated everything for their ceremony and reception via email and phone as the couple spent half the year at the St. Regis in Bal Harbour. They had odd requests, but Cedric kept designing.

Every time I spoke with them, they couldn't contain their excitement for their big casino-inspired extravaganza. Our team was bringing Las Vegas in all of its over-the-top glamour to Dallas on Valentine's Day—Aphrodite help us all.

The event setup started a full week prior, and by the following weekend, you would've thought we'd ordered every single red rose in the metroplex. Abigail's army of floral designers created sumptuous arrangements that belonged in a ballroom at Versailles.

Even as his inner designer writhed in agony, Cedric followed the couples' wishes and had a special dance floor made that was Ritz-carpet-red and, of course, in the shape of a giant heart. A breathtaking ring of red flowers and candles was suspended from the ceiling above the dance floor. It looked like a burning ring of fire that would've impressed Johnny Cash himself. The ballroom's existing Murano glass chandeliers tied in nicely too.

Dining tables were covered in red and gold silk tablecloths flown in from Japan, and the crystal and flatware had gold accents to match. I was told the couple purchased three hundred Versace red-and-gold Medusa Gala china place settings at $400 a pop just to use for the reception. As such, the guests would be staring at a gold woman's head with snakes for hair for most of their dinner. Every square inch of the ballroom dripped red flowers and suspended crystals.

And as if all this wasn't enough, one of my jobs for the last few months had been securing the main entertainment that evening. Vegas was known for its fabulous shows, so naturally in his design Cedric included two "living fountains," which were to be flown in from Nevada. I had no idea what to expect, but I became an expert.

Dressed in togas and painted from head to toe in various shades of gray, these people were rigged with tiny, masterfully hidden hollow tubes that ran the span of their bodies. The performers stood in pools of water that were built on-site and decorated to look like working fountains. The water was circulated through the tubes, which then came spurting out each of their fingers to resemble a real-life fountain. Once set to Italian music, the result was like a jaw-dropping, miniature Bellagio water show.

As a surprise to his bride, David requested a team of former Cirque du Soleil acrobats. During the entrée course, they were scheduled to do a routine on the dance floor. I was excited to see their thrilling feats—and grateful that Cedric had done the hiring on this one. If an aerialist happened to fall onto the dessert table, it was on him and not me—hopefully both literally and figuratively.

An event like this would set a client back at least $600,000. A bill like this would send most people into cardiac arrest, but the future Mr. and Mrs. Energy Drink didn't bat an eye (likely because of their highly caffeinated heart rates).

When they arrived at the hotel the night before, David and Oksana had nothing but positive things to say about the décor and design, and Cedric was relishing their every word. They had decided not to host a rehearsal dinner, thank goodness, instead opting to dine privately with their intimate family in one of the larger suites in the hotel. One less thing for us to worry about, given that we were practically coordinating a live Cirque show today.

As they came down to take photos before the ceremony, the couple looked spectacular, if over the top. The bride wore a custom satin Pnina Tornai ballgown, complete with diamond-encrusted plunging neckline and massive tulle skirt. An upside-down cupcake with glittering sprinkles.

The groom looked practically dapper in his Tom Ford dark-navy tuxedo, necktie, and signature sunglasses. However, his white dress shirt had layers upon layers of ruffles, just like Lloyd Christmas, and his dress shoes were silver. He'd almost nailed it. So close . . . and yet so far.

The ceremony took place in the courtyard just outside the ballroom. Cedric's designers created a breathtaking white floral arch overflowing with orchids, garden roses, mums, and lilies. The guests sat in acrylic chairs with white silk cushions. The ceremony programs were placed perfectly straight on each chair, and a small but sturdy red glass heart kept each program from blowing away. Along with the program was a packet of white and red rose petals for guests to toss at the happy couple as they came back down the aisle.

As guests arrived it was apparent that many of the bride's relatives had made the trip to Dallas from overseas. One main reason for holding the nuptials in Dallas instead of actual Vegas was that the groom's ninety-year-old mother couldn't travel, but Oksana's side logged enough frequent-flyer miles to compensate for that. More than half of the guests were from former Soviet Bloc countries. The groom's remaining relatives were scarce, and his friends were sixty plus in age. There were, however, quite a few young pieces of arm candy accompanying the older gentlemen. That's Dallas for you.

With the ceremony under our belts, Mary Ellen began organizing the bridal party for the formal pictures, and I scurried off to the ballroom with Claire to make sure our living fountains were ready to start.

Cocktail hour was short and sweet, and an ice sculpture that doubled as a vodka luge kept everyone entertained until the doors opened. So classy.

Once Mary Ellen gave me the go-ahead, Claire and the rest of the interns opened the ballroom doors to reveal the reception space. As if we'd opened the gates to Disneyland, every single guest pulled out a camera phone and began taking pictures. All posing with either a living fountain performer or fire blower, guests took almost forty-five minutes to take their seats for dinner. I was amazed by how many selfie sticks fit inside pillbox clutches.

Mary Ellen's voice boomed across the radio.

"As soon as the couple's announced in the room, meet me by the cake table," she said.

"Roger that." I took my normal position next to the band to make sure they were cued properly for the bride and groom's entry into the reception.

"And now for the first time as husband and wife, please welcome Mr. and Mrs. Humphreys," said the lead singer.

The band started their customary dinner set, though I'm not sure they really knew what to think of the strange acrobats who raced onto the dance floor and contorted their bodies in all kinds of unnatural ways. Oksana, however, was thrilled.

I asked Claire to come with me in case Mary Ellen assigned me any jobs that were meant for more than one person, as she normally did. Together we headed for the cake table.

Mary Ellen stood beneath the six-foot-tall Sylvia Weinstock masterpiece that was flown from New York, first class, for the affair. This wasn't my first Sylvia cake to see in person, but Claire gawked for at least a minute. They were edible works of art; for $20,000, they had to be. Today's masterpiece was white but had streams of red roses, lifelike but made entirely of icing, flowing all the way down one side.

"Lottie, I'm going to let you handle the cake cutting tonight so I can take a quick break and make a call. You got it?" Mary Ellen asked, looking distracted.

"Of course, I'd love to!" I sounded more excited than intended.

"Calm down, it's just the cake. But make sure they cut exactly where one of the bakers marked it, otherwise they could hit a support and topple the whole thing."

"Geez, just show me, and I'll take care of it. I'm sure it'll all be a piece of cake." I waited. She rolled her eyes. I grinned. We'd done this a million times together, albeit never on my own, so I knew it would be a simple task.

"Here's the marker. You know the rest of the drill. After dessert we can start on first dances and everything else." With that she practically ran toward the lobby and her next task.

Entrées almost finished, it was our time to grab the bride and groom from their table, cut the cake, and slice and serve it for dessert. I led them to where the towering confection stood, on a table beneath a rose-covered chuppah-like structure complete with billowing gauzy red curtains.

"Are you two enjoying yourselves?" I asked as we hustled over to the cake. There waited Claire, standing guard.

"I'm having the most wonderful time," Oksana exclaimed in her lovely, crisp accent. "Thank you for bringing my dreams to life!" She and David were both in great spirits and eager to cut the cake—then cut a rug.

"Now let me explain quickly how this works," I said once I positioned them side by side, perfect for photos.

"David, you take the knife, and Oksana, you place your hand on top of David's. You want to cut the cake *right here* and nowhere else. Pull out a small piece to feed to one another for pictures."

Claire brushed up next to me as she brought over two glasses of fresh champagne for the couple to wash down their bite of cake with after their photo. Cedric was always teaching us to think about the next moment and how we could make it better for the clients.

Once the photographer gave us the thumbs-up that he was ready, David and Oksana did as they were told and began the ceremonial cutting of the cake.

But something was wrong because the whole structure shook as soon as David brought the knife down. Before I could grab his hand, he was already slicing down again to free up a piece, which sent the cake even more into motion. He must have sliced right into one of the structural foam layers.

The cake was falling. It was purely instinctual, but my hands flew up as high as I could reach. I shoved both hands into two layers of perfect, thick frosting. A single red icing rosebud dropped onto my shoulder. Sweet.

Claire was quick behind me with her own hands on two other layers. Somehow we had managed to stop anything from toppling onto the bride and groom. However, we were both wrist-deep in icing, frozen in place like two idiots.

I looked over to see David and Oksana staring at me in horror.

Okay, stay calm, Jones. Stay calm.

"Listen, everything is fine, but the cake clearly is a bit 'imbalanced' at the moment. Just put the knife down and head back to your table, and we will try the pictures again after first dances." I tried to project confidence. "Dessert will be pushed back slightly, but we will handle this, no worries."

"Um, all right," said David. "Are you sure everything is fine?"

"Yes, I just don't want us in the background of your beautiful picture, and we need to make sure this cake stays put. Happens all the time. Go enjoy your guests for just a minute longer," I said, now trying to convey urgency so we could figure out how to get our hands out of their cake.

I was grateful the cake was in the corner of the ballroom, and though many guest tables were watching this nightmare, we were one spectacle that wasn't spotlighted in the middle of the room for everyone to see.

David and Oksana walked away looking confused, but at least they were gone. I could commence quietly freaking out to Claire. She had, I noted with some satisfaction, frosting clumped in her usually immaculate blond strands.

"What the hell should we do?" I said.

"No idea. But I may lick my hands clean after this is over."

"So not the answer I'm looking for. We've got to balance this thing out so we can untangle ourselves. And clean it up."

"At least it didn't crash down on the bride and groom!" Claire said. "Could you even imagine how horrible that would've been?"

That would definitely be a promotion killer, I thought. Those sorts of images—a bride covered in her own cake, wedding ruined, etc.— somehow always made their way onto social media, and without fail, someone on the planning side got blacklisted. Not me, if I could help it. Thankfully Cedric had gone home the moment dinner started, and Mary Ellen was still MIA.

Unbeknownst to us, the photographer, who was not Griffin, had immediately gone into the hotel kitchen and grabbed one of the pastry chefs working that night.

"What in the world happened here?" the chef asked.

"I'm not sure, but the bride and groom must have cut into whatever middle support system was holding up the top several layers, and we were about two seconds from a tragedy," I said. "Please tell me you can fix this."

"Let me see if I can stabilize it," he replied.

Claire and I only had to stand there a few more minutes as he somehow secured the top layers back into place, which was perfectly timed given that our arms were starting to shake. Clearly I needed to spend more time at the gym. No more biking. Just weight lifting.

The chef helped smooth out the massive holes we made in the top few layers, then moved some of the roses up from the base of the cake to hide the holes as well. I exhaled. Most of the damage was done to the back of the cake, so pictures could go on as usual. This was now the second cake I'd saved in less than a year.

As soon as Claire and I washed our hands (and did lick a few of our fingers), we retrieved David and Oksana from the dance floor to retake pictures. We had the chef cut out a piece from another layer, which he assured us was safe, and put it on a plate for the bride and groom to use. I wasn't taking another chance at starting this whole mess again by giving the groom the knife.

Soon the couple was happily back on the dance floor.

"Claire, can you watch the room while I find Mary Ellen? She's been gone awhile now."

"Hey, do you think there's a chance the marker on the cake got moved by accident?" asked Claire.

"I don't know. Maybe? Those markers are put in very specific places by the baker. Not to mention it's really hard to knock down a cake that size. David would have had to hit just the right spot. So, it's weird for sure."

"I can't imagine why anyone would do something like that."

"Me neither." I thought about Mary Ellen and all the recent good times we'd had together. Was this about Atlanta? Was she starting to feel threatened by me? "Regardless, thanks for saving my neck. I really appreciate it."

"Of course. That's what I'm here for." Good to see at least one Trustie who didn't mind getting her hands dirty, albeit with frosting.

I darted off to find Mary Ellen wondering if maybe Claire was right. I found Mary Ellen pacing around in the lobby, not on her phone, doing absolutely nothing.

"Hey, Mary Ellen," I said. She nearly jumped out of her dress.

"Oh, Lottie, how'd it go?"

"I just got off my phone call and was about to come back in. Is everything all right?" She asked again before I could answer her first question.

"It was perfect!" I said, trying to analyze her face as I spoke. "The happy couple is dancing the night away now."

"Really? Oh, that's great. Thanks for taking over," she said curtly. "Well, we both can't be gone, so let's get back in there and wrap this thing up."

I'd been trying so hard to impress not just Cedric but Mary Ellen too. I didn't want her job. I just wanted her to like me and maybe even consider me her equal in planning one day. I couldn't tell what had transpired, but my hope was that this was all in my head.

Thanks for planting that seed, Claire.

Mary Ellen was super nice and overly helpful the rest of the night. Claire was dying to know how she'd behaved, but I told her we'd talk about it later. I didn't need any more drama.

As the event was wrapping up, I got a text from Natalia. Her Match date had bailed at the last minute, so she was free and feeling sorry for herself. I'd warned her about the inevitable disappointment of making a first date for Valentine's Day, but she'd ignored me. Instead of "I told you so," I told her to meet me in an hour at the Rattlesnake Bar, over in The Ritz's restaurant.

It had opened a couple years earlier to rave reviews and was considered a hotspot for local celebrities and millionaires. Before college my only experiences with hotel restaurants consisted of breakfasts in the Motel 6 and one trip to Nashville at what was then called the Opryland Hotel. My brother and I had ridden the *Delta*, a small, tacky boat that floated through the hotel, sipping a virgin version of trash can punch—served in ceramic trash can glasses—and feeling fancy.

A half hour later, we waved the bride and groom out the ballroom doors and into the lobby. They'd be spending the night upstairs in the hotel's most opulent suite. I'd never done a wedding where we performed the ritual send-off that ended at an elevator. It felt a little anticlimactic, but they opted for that instead of exiting the building only to circle the block and reenter.

Once the guests filed out, Cedric's breakdown crew went to work clearing the space. I took this as my cue to go find Natalia and a cocktail, pronto. Claire offered to handle packing up the gifts and miscellaneous items we were always responsible for post-reception, and Mary Ellen had left the minute the elevator doors closed. I was free at last to grab a drink with my best friend. Maybe she'd convince me the averted cake crisis was just a simple accident.

EIGHTEEN

Spring in Texas usually starts in February, so wedding season does as well. The Firm was busier than ever. We bounced from weekend to weekend with at least four events every Saturday. Every time I turned my head, one of the florists was running by with an arrangement needing final approval or linens were being tossed around like footballs.

Before I knew it March was nearly over. And I was headed to Sarah and Jonathan's ceremony in Corsicana at the state's biggest chicken resort. (That might not have been patently true, but it felt right.)

Because I had landed Sarah and Jonathan as clients, and because I'd been doing well at work, their wedding was officially mine. Cedric would still oversee production and come down for at least one day, but as for all things planning related, such as the entire weekend's schedule and vendor, bridal party, and guest management, I was the lady in charge. Training wheels were going off. Mary Ellen wasn't thrilled I was already "flying solo"—insert chicken joke here—but she'd also booked a long weekend getaway, her first vacation in almost a year, so wriggling her way out of the trip to usurp my role would have been too obvious.

For her part, Abigail's botanical garden event was canceled, so she offered to jump on for my first solo event. Her clients had gotten fed up with their parents bickering over silly details, so they decided to secretly elope weeks prior. I was relieved to know that Abigail would be around in case I needed backup.

As lead planner I was admittedly scared to death, but I also believed I could handle a wedding of this scale on my own. I'd seen just about everything possible; nothing could surprise me. I'd also have Abigail helping me out. However, no matter what happened this weekend, it was my neck on the line.

So, like any logical human being, I focused not on my fears but on the weather. Which at the moment was, for Texas, particularly dicey.

Our team had planned for the weather to be unseasonably cold, but not *this* cold. In years past, March could be a rather warm month in Central Texas, with highs lingering in the midseventies after what passed for winter ended. I packed everything black and warm I could find and then headed out for coffee with Natalia. I wanted to talk to someone I didn't work with for at least an hour before I was immersed in Cedric's world again.

We grabbed our usual drinks at Starbucks, settled into a corner table, and caught up on the past week. I relished discussing something other than brides, and I never thought that Natalia's talk of office budget cuts would sound so soothing. I was beginning to think that "normalcy" was completely in my past.

Too soon, Natalia had to run back to her office, and I needed to go pick up Abigail. I honked as I pulled up outside her place, a pretty brick Tudor town house off Oak Lawn.

She hopped into the car with her typical dancer's grace. I thought of my mamaw's frequent comments on my "gallumping" everywhere with a twinge. Some of us just weren't born with coordination. Her husband, Doug, waved from their stoop as we pulled away. I didn't know him well, but they were always so cute together whenever he came around the office.

The drive gave me plenty of time to fill her in on the past few weekends' events and all the insanity surrounding The Ritz wedding.

"Cake aside, I'm glad everything else with that one went well," she said. "How are you feeling about taking the lead today?"

"I'm feeling pretty good. A little nervous but not freaking out yet. The last couple months' events have thrown so much at us. I've learned a lot. We'll see, though."

"It all looks a lot more natural for you now," she added. "You don't seem nearly as frazzled as you used to be, and I can tell you're getting good at rolling with whatever issues come up."

"That means a lot, Abigail."

She settled back into her seat. "It seems that you either have what it takes to be a wedding coordinator or you don't. Sure, there are things to learn and you improve with time, but it's either going to eventually become second nature or it's not. You're finding that groove."

"Thank you for not making me feel like a moron while I found that groove these last few months—and for taking a chance on me years ago."

"I'm so happy I did. You've grown a lot, Lottie. And just remember that not even Cedric or Mary Ellen is prepared for every situation that comes up, no matter what they may say." She reached for the radio to turn up the latest Beyoncé song.

"How about you?" I asked over the music. "Is it still weird to be working for someone else's company?"

"Some days I miss being my own boss, but I do *not* miss all the back-office stuff I used to have to handle. That kind of paperwork and pressure are too much, especially right now while Doug and I are trying to have kids. I'm perfectly happy to work on beautiful events and be creative but not have to be where the buck stops."

"So, kids, huh? How is that going?"

"Yeah, we'll see . . . I made this deal for the freedom to focus on it, take some time off when we have a baby, and just get to be around more whenever that day comes." She looked out at the passing fields and twirled a braid around one long finger. I kept driving, falling into my own thoughts.

Raising kids on top of running a business would be incredibly challenging, I assumed, and I appreciated Abigail's candor. She was genuine in a world of artifice. A great mix of total type-A boss and unflappable go-with-the-flow, which I also appreciated. A woman who had carved out her place in the world of highest of high-end events, and yet still had a lovely home and a husband she seemed to adore. One of the few people in our industry who had a life I'd envy. Hats off to her, truly.

We rocked to whatever was currently in the Top 40—most of which I didn't recognize—for the remainder of the drive. It felt good to tap the Prius steering wheel, sing at the top of my voice, and let loose a bit. Lord knew I'd need to relax before I buckled down and faced the flocks of chickens awaiting us down the road.

As we crossed the steel grate, I could see the clear-top tents in the distance. One positive thing about cooler temperatures and events was that you could use clear-top instead of white tents if you wished. When it was even remotely warm outside, those suckers turned into greenhouses. Even without side walls, flowers and guests wilted from the heat.

But when the weather allowed, clear-top tents were my absolute favorite. Cedric was known to string lights across the entire ceiling so as it grew dark outside, the inside of the tent sparkled and looked like a million stars. Out here, away from all the city lights, my guess was that Cedric had actually only ordered enough lighting to wash the tent in a glow so that people had enough light to see, but the ceiling was left untouched so the real stars could shine through. I sighed just thinking about how romantic it would all appear.

"I wish Griffin was working this one," I mumbled, without realizing I was talking aloud.

"Well, well, well. Seems like your professional *and* personal lives are getting interesting," Abigail teased as she started unloading the car.

"Oh geez. I can't believe I said that. Nah, we're just friends. At least I think that's the vibe. He's certainly cute, but I really don't think there's a future there . . . He's a great photographer, and I'd love him to capture my first big solo gig, but I'm sure the photography team working this one will be just as good.

"Can you even believe how many stupid signs there are for all the chicken coops?" I said, quickly changing the subject.

Abigail took the hint and played along. "It's not as if those poor chickens will be outside for anyone to see. It's freezing cold out here." In Texas, anything below fifty counted as "freezing," so in this instance, she was correct. "Don't they snuggle together in their henhouses or whatever?"

"Ha! You're probably right. That poor calligrapher spent hours writing out hundreds of chickens' names no one will ever see. I'm sure Cedric will be more than thrilled if I call off the barnyard tours."

We finished gathering all the wedding-day items we had picked up from the office before leaving town and headed toward the guesthouse, where we would be lodging for the duration of the weekend. It was large and nice enough for the planning team, but not for Cedric, who would be staying in the best hotel in Corsicana: the Hampton Inn & Suites. I thought he'd have a stroke when I told him it was the nicest hotel within a twenty-mile radius, but given the budget of this wedding, he decided it was worth the agony to stay one night nearby in case there were any last-minute production issues and the client wanted an actual appearance from him. His hotel was also where all the guests were staying, which made it additionally horrifying, but the only other option was a Super 8. Cedric informed me that he would rather camp outside than stay there. Hampton Inn it was.

Abigail and I shared a room, and the two Trusties sent down to assist us, one being Claire, had to bunk up together down the hall. I wished I could see their faces when they walked into the guesthouse. Claire was proving to be a hard worker who might actually want a career in the wedding biz. She also had been a very loyal and helpful companion to me personally, but that didn't mean she'd be thrilled with "roughing it" while on the road.

We dumped our things in our room, then headed over to the three tents to see how setup was coming along. The tent for the ceremony stood near a small and charming pond, and the reception one stood about twenty feet away in the direction of the main house. Catering and reception were side by side so waiters could quickly and seamlessly enter and exit the party. A matching clear connector united the tents so once guests entered the ceremony, they never had to step foot out into the cold air again on their way to the reception.

Texas weather could sure make people wimps. After Camila and Alfie's sweltering-then-rained-out fiasco earlier this year, I decided it should be a law you had to use tents at any outdoor event in the Lone Star State.

The ceremony space was only as big as was needed to fit 250 silver Chiavari chairs, as Cedric liked to keep the service feeling intimate. Carpenters had built a stage at the front that was being covered in white carpet as we arrived. The florists were working on the ceremony arch made entirely of manzanita branches, and there were beautiful arrangements of all-white flowers at the end of every row of chairs. It was a dreamy aisle.

Cedric actually decided to turn off the heat as soon as setup was complete so they could leave the flowers out overnight. A tent without heat would basically become its own cooler, and there was plenty of time to warm things up again before the event.

The site was gorgeous, and the best part of all was how little remained for us to do the next day since it was literally frozen in time.

The Trusties had arrived by the time we went back to our room for a change of clothes and a bite to eat. Cedric made sure that the caterer stocked our kitchen with food since we weren't sure how much free time we'd have, not to mention the sparse dining options in Corsicana (although the downtown was rife with cute mom-and-pop shops and boutiques). Claire and her pal Amanda had started assembling the guest welcome boxes when we arrived, which was a pleasant surprise. I knew Claire was the one to thank, as I wasn't sure the other platinum-blond Trustie actually knew how to look for things to do without being instructed slash prodded slash threatened.

"Maybe if we get these finished in a couple of hours, Cedric will let us drive home instead of having to stay here for the night," Amanda said to Claire.

Figured. I knew she couldn't be here without complaining, and I was pretty sure I could hear her navy Range Rover still running, ready to depart at any moment.

"Cheer up, girls," I said obnoxiously loud. "At least this weather means now you won't have to shuttle guests to all the chicken coops tomorrow night."

"Oh geez," said Amanda. "I totally forgot about that. Thank God for the freeze."

Abigail nearly choked on her tortilla chips laughing.

"We're going to grab a bite to eat before checking on the seating assignments in the main tent." I reached into the bag of Tostitos myself and dipped into the jar of Joe T's salsa we'd stashed in the cabinet. "Feel free to eat whatever you want that's here, and let's plan on meeting up in a few hours before you deliver the amenity boxes."

"Sounds good." Claire stayed positive despite her coworker's negative attitude. She kept assembling the various boxes and tying them with a bow.

"I want a farm wedding someday," continued Claire. "But in Colorado. None of this fake stuff. I want a ranch with real mountain snow, carriage rides, beautiful views, and everything else Vail has to offer."

Oh, to be twenty-two, rich, and completely naive again. Well, I was at least *two* of those things once upon a time. Again, Cedric had to know that most of the Trusties were only "working for him" because of the date it secured them for their own nuptials or society party one day. I didn't think that was ultimately Claire's end goal, but it seemed to be Amanda's. At least she could tie ribbons. That was pretty much all we needed from her this weekend.

Abigail and I headed over to the reception area with menu cards, table numbers, and place cards in hand. The long clear tent looked like a snow globe, even more beautiful than the renderings Cedric had created months ago.

Dining tables were dressed in hunter-green velvet linens. Royal Staffordshire Tonquin Brown dinner plates sat on top of hammered copper chargers. Cut-crystal drinkware and hammered copper tumblers glinted in the candlelight and strands of twinkle lights. Vintage brass and low copper vessels overflowed with garden roses, tulips, and amaryllis in various shades of cream, peach, and burnt orange along with lush greenery. Berries and russet feathers peeked out every so often, and antlers interspersed at odd angles. Reminiscent of an enchanted woodland from a C. S. Lewis novel, this was by far my favorite design Cedric had ever created.

"Wow," Abigail said. "Y'all really did a beautiful job on this one."

"Thank you," I said. "It's not hard to see why Cedric is paid so much for his ideas. I know you probably could look at a blank space and imagine this, but I sure as heck couldn't."

She nodded as she looked around the room.

Since the tables were already completely set for the following day, Abigail and I put out the place cards, menu cards, and table numbers, which only took us a couple hours. We were pros, after all. It was fun to work alongside her again like this.

Once we finished up, I texted Claire and Amanda to bring over the escort card supplies so we could finish up most of our tasks for the next day.

The Trusties both gasped as they entered the tent, and I could see them plotting out their own receptions again in their minds.

"Focus, ladies," I said. "If we finish all our setup tonight, we can sleep in tomorrow, and it will be a breeze later in the day."

I think all they heard was "sleep in tomorrow" because they rushed to the escort card table to help.

"All right, that's a wrap in here," I said. "Are you good to take the welcome boxes to the guest hotel in town without us?"

"Yes, we can handle it," said Claire.

"Plus, we might stop and grab something for dinner when we're done," said Amanda.

Abigail and I had, of course, picked up Chick-fil-A to have later at the guesthouse. Just staying on theme.

✗

"That dang rooster." Abigail pulled her pillow up over her head. "I'd kill that bird if I lived here."

"But then you'd have to explain the murder to his chicken harem," I mumbled. "Guess we didn't need to set an alarm after all." I checked the time. It was 5:30 a.m. The sun wasn't even up yet.

"Ugghh. Surely he'll stop soon and we can sleep for a few more hours. It's going to be a long day, and I'm so not ready to start it."

Abigail fell back asleep, and I soon followed suit. Three hours later, when day had fully dawned, we got up and started prepping for the day ahead. Since we were already on-site, we stayed in our pajamas and drank coffee in the guesthouse living room while going over the schedule.

"I vote more weddings start this way, with a charming country guesthouse and easily accessible caffeine."

"Count me in," said Abigail.

Surprisingly, the Trusties were already awake and eating yogurt in the kitchen when we came out. Still in their silk pajama sets, they had already gotten fully made up for the day. Gotta love Dallas women. They never let anyone see them without full hair and makeup.

We went over everyone's tasks for the day and night. Abigail would assist me with the wedding party, the ceremony, first dances, cake cutting, and the departure. The Trusties were in charge of running guest shuttles and herding them to and from the various locations.

"I think the only thing we have left to do is to hang the egg ornaments on the wisteria branch archway near the exit," said Claire.

For the guests' favors, Cedric had suggested hand-blown glass eggs for them to take home. Each guest would select one on their way out of the reception, and Claire and Amanda would be there to label and box them up and send them on their merry way once the grand event concluded.

"Perfect," I replied. "Abigail and I are going to check on the bride after we get ready, and then we'll come help you with the eggs." Unlike the décor inside the tents, we'd decided not to take our chances leaving glass eggs outside overnight where they could blow off or worse.

We arrived at the main house around ten thirty, where Sarah was already in hair and makeup. Her trio of bridesmaids surrounded her, cooing encouragement as her beauty regimen progressed.

"Hi, Lottie," Sarah said, in a half whisper.

"Good morning, Sarah." I was sincerely surprised she remembered my name. "Happy wedding day!"

"Oh, thank you so much," she replied softly.

"Is there anything you need right now? Anything we can help you with?" I asked, as was custom when we saw the bride for the first time.

"Not now, but later I'll need some help getting upstairs into the attic in my dress."

"Oh, sure." While I wondered what in blazes she needed to go into the attic for, I didn't want to seem nosy so didn't ask questions.

Abigail gave me a look from across the room like she was wondering the same thing. With Sarah content for the moment, we headed off to check on Jonathan.

Jonathan and his two brothers—his only groomsmen—were getting ready in the "man cave" over the horse barn. To call it a horse barn really didn't do it justice since the barn was nice enough for me to live in contently for the rest of my life. It was straight out of a *Garden & Gun* issue, and I was a little bit sad for the guests who no longer got to tour the barn due to the weather. However, it did make the logistics easier without a "cocktail hour chicken show."

When we entered the barn loft, Jonathan was pouring himself a drink while his brothers played pool.

"Hey, Lottie." Jonathan sounded chipper as he walked over to Abigail and me. The man was about to officially earn direct access to millions, if not billions, of dollars, so no wonder he was all smiles and roses.

"Hi, Jonathan. Happy wedding day," I said. "We're just checking in to make sure you're on schedule getting ready for pre-ceremony pictures and to see if you need anything."

"I think we're all good up here. How's the love of my life doing?"

Gross. Here we went again with that "love of my life" business.

"She looks like a dream," I replied, thinking of her penchant for relaxing medication. "She seems happy and calm. Everything's going great."

"I'm so glad to her that," Jonathan said. "I knew today would be bittersweet for her without her parents. Mine are too old to travel here, but they're still holding on," he said. "The good news is that her father will still be with us today."

"Yes. I do believe that at important moments in life like this, our lost loved ones are with us in spirit." Wow, my bridal bedside manner had *improved*. Even Abigail looked at me like I was the wedding Yoda.

"But see, Sarah's father's spirit will *actually* be here with us since his ghost lives in the attic," said Jonathan, casually taking his turn at pool.

"I'm sorry, what?" My Zen flew out the barn window.

"Yeah, Sarah's father died working an oil rig when she was a teenager. Some people even thought foul play was involved. Then a few years after he died, the women started hearing noises in the attic.

Sarah moved his favorite rocking chair up there, and it rocks on the old floorboards at all hours of the night. Sarah loves that her daddy is still in the house."

My jaw must have been on the ground. Abigail's certainly was.

"But don't worry, girls. He's a friendly ghost. He's never done anything to bother us. As long as she's happy, I'm happy, and I couldn't care less if she likes going up there to visit with him. I think it's sweet."

I seriously could not believe what I was hearing. As if the dollhouses and chickens weren't enough. No amount of love or money could tie me to someone who not only believed in ghosts but also voluntarily hung out with them. I snapped back into planning mode.

"That's just sweet as pie," I lied through my teeth. "I appreciate you telling us this, and I'm sure today will be wonderful for everyone, both here and in the . . . attic," I said. "Well, we'd better go and continue all the preparations. See you gentlemen in a few hours in the ceremony tent for pictures!"

Abigail and I couldn't get out of the barn fast enough.

"Did that just happen?" She shook her head. "I told you that you'd jinx us by saying nothing weird would happen today."

"Hey, I said it was going to be easy. I never said it wouldn't be weird." I smirked. "We can't tell the Trusties. We need them to help Sarah visit the attic later. No way you and I are going up there."

"Absolutely not," said Abigail. "We don't get paid enough to deal with a phantom father situation."

"At least that's better than a mummy of the bride, amiright?" Abigail didn't even reward me with an eye roll for that one. I personally thought my dad joke–level sense of humor was, if anything, improving.

The rest of the day was normal—or as normal as could be expected at nuptials full of bumpkins and agoraphobes in rural Texas.

Cedric showed up before the start of the ceremony to say his hellos to the bride and groom so they knew he was here, even if it was only for a couple hours. I filled him in on how the other vendors were doing, how the schedule was running (perfectly, I might add), and how he could head out with nothing to worry about. No need to tell him about daddy ghost, of course. He probably wouldn't have believed me anyway.

"Great job, Charlotte."

I continued to be stunned that he knew my full name, forget about using it.

"I'm *abundantly* glad I followed my instincts and let you take the lead here."

"Thank you for the opportunity to run such a large event," I demurred.

"I really need to know I can trust the team for my new Atlanta office. That they can run things smoothly without any additional drama. God knows we already get enough of it in this business, and quite frankly, I get really tired of all the whining and complaining from some of the other staff working for me."

"Oh, I totally get it." He didn't name names, but I had some pretty decent guesses.

"To be blunt, I love that you're young and fresh and pliable," he said. "And I mean that in a good way. You aren't already jaded by the Dallas social scene since, well, you've never really experienced it. I like that you actually want to prove yourself. You're not entitled. You might be just what we're looking for—if you can keep this up."

I somehow played it cool. I'd ignore any jab at my middle-class background if that's what it took.

"My parents led by example," I replied, realizing how important that example had actually been. "They drilled into me the satisfaction and payoffs of hard work. I can't thank you enough for giving me this chance."

"All right then." He tossed his red Gucci scarf over his shoulder. "Enough of the heart to heart. You get it. You're doing well, and you're part of the team now, so keep it up. I'll be at the Hampton Inn hot tub. Call me if anything comes up," he shouted as he walked away.

With that, Cedric was gone. I was in charge, and I'd never felt better.

Once I gathered my thoughts and stopped daydreaming about a chic new office for myself in Atlanta, I radioed Abigail, who was finishing up pre-ceremony pictures with the wedding party.

"Everything's great," she started. "But Sarah has mentioned wanting to go visit her dead dad two more times . . ."

"I was really hoping she would forget about that."

"And apparently," said Abigail, "the Trusties heard about it from one of the bridesmaids while they were helping lead them over, and they've already told me they will quit and drive back immediately if we try and make them do it."

"Son of a bee sting."

"Ditto that," agreed Abigail.

"All right," I finally said, after waiting a moment for Abigail to offer to go with Sarah, which of course she didn't do. She might have been assisting me, but she was still higher on the food chain. "I'll do it."

I can do this. Ghosts aren't real. Not. Real.

"Are you okay making sure the guests get seated and that the musicians and minister are ready go to?" I asked.

"Yes, and I'll have the Trusties help me so there's not one little hiccup." She sounded relieved to be absolved of ghost duty.

"Cedric literally just gave me the most praise I've ever heard him say to anyone, and I'm not going to let some moment out of *The Sixth Sense* screw anything up for me now," I said to her, though it was more of a pep talk to myself.

"That's really great to hear. Sarah just went back up to her room to apply more lipstick and is waiting for one of us to help her into the attic. Good luck! I'm sure it's all just an exaggeration and you'll be fine."

"Thanks, I'll call you when we're finished."

"Roger that, boss."

One of my absolute favorite moments was standing with a bride-to-be and her father right before the ceremony started. That time was often so precious for them—and emotionally overwhelming for me, no matter who they were or what kind of client they'd been up to that point.

Even for someone like me, whose family could never afford a wedding like this, it was usually part of how I envisioned this monumental day. My dad was never super sentimental, unless it had to do with Tom and me. Then came the waterworks. I always imagined he would offer his arm, struggle to say something wise or sweet through tears, and then we'd walk the aisle. Someday, maybe.

Granted, many of our clients had absent or deceased fathers, complicated parental relationships, or sometimes two dads slash father figures. Some even chose their mothers or brothers to walk them. Modern families often threw our traditional ceremony roles for a loop. But the symbolism of the people who raised and shaped the bride escorting her to her future remained poignant. And when one combined all those emotions with the booming organ, trumpet, choir, or sometimes all three, it was virtually impossible to hold back tears.

However, right then, I was not choking back emotion. No, this was full-on *Saw*-level chill bumps. I tapped on Sarah's bedroom door.

"Come in," she said almost inaudibly.

"You look stunning." I always said that the first time I saw a bride fully dressed. It didn't matter if her hair was permed, her face was pulled tighter than a tick, or her dress looked like an oversized cotton ball. You always told a bride on her wedding day that she looked perfect, the wedding was perfect, and the whole day was just perfectly perfect.

"I've come to take you over to the ceremony site." I willed her to completely forget about the whole ghost of it all.

"Oh, yes, but first I need you to help me get upstairs to give a kiss to Dad," she repeated, like hers was a normal request.

"Sure." In a need-to-know world, I did not need to know. Any additional information might make me flee. So I refrained from further questions.

Sarah turned toward the door. I moved behind her to gather her long satin train and follow her toward what I hoped was at least a friendly phantom.

We passed several more bedrooms as we moved down the long hallway covered in black-and-white family portraits before we stopped in front of a wooden door with a vintage crystal handle. As she opened the creaky door, my heart pounded and my palms started to sweat.

"I just need a little help up the stairs, and then you can wait for me back down here," she said.

It was difficult for Sarah to maneuver up the narrow stairwell, and I could only imagine how dirty the sides of her satin dress would be from brushing up against the walls. I'd deal with that later if need be. Survival was first and foremost. I gathered up the train of her dress and timidly trailed her.

As we reached the landing I wasn't sure what to expect, but it wasn't as creepy as I had imagined. A wooden rocking chair sat in the middle of a large, unfinished attic space. A portrait of an older man that looked like it was from the early 1900s sat on a small side table. There was also a vintage record player with a dusty record sitting on top.

"Thank you, Lottie. I'll just be about ten minutes, and then you can come to help me down."

"Sounds good. I'll be back soon." I tried to sound casual as I fled down the stairs.

I closed the door behind me and glanced at the time on my phone, trying to slow my breathing and get my sweating under control. I could do this.

"Abigail, it's Lottie, come in," I said into the walkie-talkie.

"Hey, Lottie, how's it going?"

"Sarah is upstairs now doing Lord knows what, but she will be ready to go in about ten minutes. How's the ceremony seating going?"

"It's all good down here. The tent is warm, looks beautiful, and is filling up with guests just like normal."

"There's nothing 'normal' about this wedding," I replied.

"Well, hang in there. Just get Sarah down here, and it will all be a walk in the park, or in the barn, after that."

"Roger that."

Ten minutes felt like ten hours, but it was finally time to make one last trip upstairs. Then I'd be done with "daddy dearest" and could get this (freak) show on the road.

I tapped on the door. "Sarah?" I said quietly but also loud enough for her to hear me from the bottom of the stairs. "If you're ready, it's about time to go."

No reply.

"Sarah?" This time I said it a little louder.

Still nothing.

I took a deep breath, then eased up the stairs.

As I reached the top step, I peeked up just enough to see what was going on. Soft instrumental music emanated from the record player. Sarah swayed, eyes closed, back and forth in front of the rocking chair, which to my terrible surprise was also rocking back and forth on its own.

I do not *believe in ghosts.* Every hair on my body stood straight up. I couldn't move, let alone speak. What was I supposed to do? After about thirty seconds of paralysis, I shifted my weight to escape, but the step beneath me creaked.

Sarah spun around. "Lottie, you just about scared me to death." *I* scared *her*?

I stood there staring. The rocking chair slowly came to a stop on its own, as though someone had just stood up and walked away from it.

"Bye, Daddy," she said over her shoulder before she turned off the record player. "I guess the time got away from me. But I had such a nice visit. I'm ready to go now. Can you come help with my train?"

"Um, sure," I said meekly.

I don't even remember going down the stairs, but before I knew it, we were outside and walking toward the ceremony. Surely I had just hallucinated all that.

I still couldn't speak, but Abigail saw us coming and cued the processional music. Sarah showed up just in time to walk herself down the aisle.

"Lottie?" Abigail asked, then said it again louder. "Lottie!"

"Oh, what? Sorry."

"Are you okay? What on earth happened up there?"

"Well, it wasn't anything *on* earth," I finally said. "That whole ordeal was the creepiest thing I've ever experienced." I told her what I'd seen, or at least what I thought I'd seen.

"Holy moly. You're still white as a ghost yourself."

But before we could really get into it, the preacher pronounced the couple and the recessional music started.

"Tell me about it," I said. "Let's just get through the rest of this night and hope there are no other specters on the agenda."

"Amen to that."

As punishment for forcing me to confront the ghost alone, I made the Trusties field most of the coordination through the end of the night. They needed the practice, and I needed time to regain my wits. Thank goodness there were no more surprises other than most of the guests didn't dance and left early, which made for an easy departure and wrap-up of the night.

The reception was beautiful but quite boring. I wasn't complaining. I would happily take boring by this point, given that at any moment, Abigail and I expected zombie chickens to stumble out of the bushes.

The Trusties decided to drive back to Dallas since it was just 10:30 p.m. when the last guest was shuttled off to a nearby hotel. Abigail and I, however, waited to pack up everything we were responsible for until the following morning and enjoy one last night together in the guest cabin. I even got a fire started in our gas fireplace, and we both sat up eating cake and drinking a leftover bottle of wine.

Daddy ghosts aside, this soiree went smoothly. My first time running the show was a success, and we were both quite pleased with the accomplishment.

The following morning I received a text from Cedric congratulating me on a job well done—and reminding me that Monday was my turn to bring in lattes. Back to the land of the living and on to the next bride.

NINETEEN

One morning a few weeks later, Cedric rolled in around ten thirty. An earlyish arrival meant something big had happened in his life, and he wanted to gloat about it to everyone in the office. (See: the Atlanta announcement.)

Quite the colony of worker bees swarmed as he burst through the glass doors, latte and designer bag in hand (his Yorkie in his Louis Vuitton carrying case), swaying and humming aloud like he'd just won an Oscar.

"Travis, go ahead and book that flight I mentioned to you earlier," Cedric said in a voice just a hair below shouting so that everyone, including the tenants next door, could hear him.

"I'll need to fly first-class on Emirates, since I'm going to be one of the *keynote* speakers. The last thing I want to do is worry about making a connection like at that horrible airport in Los Angeles."

No one had to ask Cedric where he was going. He continued screaming at Travis so we would all be sure to hear his big news. "I'll be speaking at the Engage! summit this year in Dubai, right after Preston Bailey. We'll need to start working on my presentation *imme-diately*. Please book the underwater suite for me there, the one that

Khloé Kardashian stayed in. I want to be able to take a bath and look at *sharks*."

"Of course." Travis completely ignored the fact that Cedric was still standing there awaiting praise.

"That will be all for now, then," Cedric mumbled as he trudged past Travis and headed to his office, somewhat deflated.

"What's he talking about? And who's Preston Bailey?" asked Claire.

"I'm not sure," I said, "but I imagine he's a wedding planner. Sounds like some kind of convention."

Mary Ellen just about spit out her espresso and whipped around from where she was standing outside her office. "It's *not* a convention," she spewed. "First of all, conventions are disgusting and worthless for anyone at Cedric's level. What he's talking about is a weeklong inspirational retreat that anyone in the event business dreams about attending."

"Oh, my mistake," said Claire, still totally confused.

"Preston Bailey is the be-all, end-all." Mary Ellen sighed. "He is *the* top celebrity and Saudi royal-family wedding planner, and people pay him millions of dollars just to plan an event. He's like the Baz Luhrmann of weddings—he creates the most transportive, gorgeous fantasy worlds." She pulled a coffee-table book from the top shelf above her desk, ignoring Abigail as usual. At least the indifference was mutual.

Claire and I drooled over every picture in the book about Bailey's events. There was a twelve-foot Arc de Triomphe made entirely of rose heads, massive chandeliers hanging from the ceiling dripping in white phalaenopsis orchids and crystals, every kind of animal you could imagine made completely out roses, and that was just the first chapter.

"Okay, he *is* amazing," I admitted.

"Yes, and this retreat is one of the only times he publicly speaks to a group of people. He's too busy for that kind of thing, but he views it as a courtesy to his peers in the business who go just to get away and booze and schmooze with one another.

"This retreat is like a VIP camp basically. The counselors, who are the 'celebrities' of the business, get paid to attend and eat and drink their way through the weekend while pretending to 'help' the campers, aka the attendees," she said. "And Cedric, as one of his closest peers, usually attends."

"I see," said Claire. "Does he take anyone with him?"

"Yes," said Mary Ellen. "But usually just one other person since it costs thousands of dollars if you're a regular attendee. I've gone every year before with him. But he's going solo this year, so he'll have to do all his note-taking himself," she said smugly. Evidently us lowly junior planners and interns would never, ever reach the summit.

"It sounds like this year will be extra fun with Cedric taking on a VIP role himself," I said.

"I guess," she said. "He will be able to live off of this pseudocelebrity status for years." She laughed, twirled around in her chair, and went back to working on yet another all blush-pink and champagne-colored design proposal, ending our conversation.

Almost a month went by without Cedric talking about any of our clients or day-to-day business. His world was prepping for the conference and making sure he had all his outfits planned for each event and that his presentation was at least somewhat comparable to Preston's.

As the date neared I was just counting down to another break from his presence—and a work trip turned family visit back to Tennessee.

One Friday night I was wrapping up some linen orders for Brody and Harriet's weekend. I had to admit that their events were all going to be stunning. The resort was über luxe, as I'd gotten to experience first-hand, but Harriet had also pushed to create a very relaxed, intimate atmosphere. I patted myself on the back (for the forty-seventh time) for being so mature about the whole thing. As long as I didn't envision actually seeing them together, it was *fiiiine*.

As if on cue my phone pinged. I hadn't heard from Griffin in a couple days because he was off on a shoot with Val again. I was the very definition of chill and respectful of boundaries. And I'd gone out with Matt once or twice when he was in town, which gave me someone to text with the odd anecdote or check-in. Matt was reliable (and gorgeous), so I was completely fine with Griffin's inconsistent friendship. Completely. Also *fiiiine*.

> Hey, what's up?

I would never understand why men just threw that one out there apropos of nothing. Like, was he asking how I was, what I was doing, or just saying hello?

> Long time no talk. At work. You?

> Just got back from Utah with Val. We shot a wedding in the middle of a reservation. It was really meaningful and the mountains were gorgeous, but cell service was garbage.

I guessed he could have a pass on his texting absence, then, this time. He texted again before I could reply:

> What are you doing Sunday?

Trick question, of course. A girl never wanted to be too available, but she also didn't want to miss out on a potentially fun hang with her platonic scruffy photographer friend either. This girl opted to play it safe:

> I don't know, I'll have to check my schedule. Why?

> I've got a gig and could use an extra set of hands if you're free. I can almost guarantee it will be more exciting and more inspiring than a wedding.

> That's a high bar there, Mr. Flores. But I'm game. What time?

> Meet me at 8 a.m. in the parking lot of a middle school. I will send you the address. Have a good night.

As I mapped the directions later, I cursed the early morning. What in the world would we be up to?

Sunday morning I met Griffin in Arlington. Orange graffiti had been recently scrubbed off the cinder-block walls of the middle school.

I got out of the Prius and strolled to where Griffin was leaning on his truck, looking at his phone. "Hiya." I nodded at him, unsure whether to go in for a hug.

"Hey, Lottie." He stood, straightening.

"Mind telling me why we're here so early on a Sunday morning?"

"We're taking portraits for the Heart Gallery. Have you heard of them?"

"I don't think so?"

"It's an organization that photographs kids in the foster care system who are eligible to be adopted. We then put the pictures on a website, display them in galleries, and also hold events where the kids and potential parents can meet. Once every few months, I take pictures for them."

"Wow, that's really cool." I was a bit stunned to speak.

"You said you'd *love* to see me shoot something I actually enjoyed helping with." He gave me a wink.

He *remembered*. I'd been so squirmy, so awkward over that last conversation home from Austin but had hoped he couldn't tell. I pursed my lips. Before I attempted to laugh the whole thing off, he continued.

"So if you're up for it, I need you to help me chat with the kids to help them relax. And I need help taking notes so we can use any extra info from our conversations for the website. Is that okay with you?"

"Absolutely, but is there anything I should know before we go in?"

"Well, all the kids know they're here because they want to be adopted. That makes things easier, in some ways. Many of them have been in the system for years and their parents' rights were terminated a while ago. For some, of course, it's far newer."

"Anything I shouldn't say?"

"Yeah, don't bring up parents because in one way or another, their family, for lack of a better word, broke. Any happy or good next step like getting adopted still comes out of a lot of loss. Our job is to facilitate that while being sensitive to wherever they're at in the grief process. I don't mean to be super heavy."

"That's okay, it's all tough stuff."

"Just be positive and ask them about themselves—their interests, hobbies, favorite subjects at school, foods, TV shows—stuff like that.

All of that will help them relax, and it's helpful for their bios on the site too. But otherwise, just act natural."

On a good day my "natural" vaguely approximated a relaxed human being. That sounded like a lot to keep in mind, and I was nervous I'd say the wrong thing.

Always attuned to my mood, Griffin added, "You've got this. They just need someone to be interested in *them*, even for a moment. I've seen you talk to clients and every vendor there is out there—you're great with people." He took my hand, gave it a quick squeeze, and then turned to go inside.

I wished it didn't affect me every time he touched me. Chalk the juvenile flutters up to being back in a middle school. I followed him into a fluorescent-lit gymnasium, where the scents of old sweat and bleach commingled in the air. A board in the wood floor creaked underfoot.

Griffin went straight to a woman with a long silver ponytail and big turquoise earrings. "Jeanette!" he said as she grabbed him for a big hug. When he pulled away, he gestured at me. "This is my friend Lottie. She's helping me out today. Where do you want me to set up?"

"Hi, Lottie," Jeanette said warmly. "You guys can take the blue backdrop today."

Griffin set his camera bag down in front of a large canvas pinned to a stack of pushed-back bleachers. As he pulled out lenses I looked around. Two other photographers were here, and a group of kids had just arrived.

A social worker walked over to us with a tall boy who pulled at the cuffs of his sleeves and stared at the ground.

The boy sat on the stool, his shiny loafers kicking back and forth. When he finally looked up, his deep brown eyes darted around the room. He was like a cornered cat, ready to dash away. "Hey, buddy, what's your name?" Griffin said, camera held down at his side. "I'm Griffin and this is Lottie."

"I'm Craig," a soft voice mumbled.

"You look really sharp today. I like your shirt a lot. Think they make it in my size? How'd it look on me?" Griffin and Craig were almost the same size, but I wasn't about to mention that.

Craig smiled the tiniest of smiles. "Nah, it wouldn't look as good on you."

Craig was fourteen, and he loved to dance—Bruno Mars was a favorite singer—and his favorite book was *Ender's Game*. He played basketball with some kids in the neighborhood but thought baseball would be fun, if he could live in one place long enough to join a team. He liked school, especially English and science. Math was hard, though.

I jotted notes furiously, frantically, hoping I could paint a picture of even a fraction of this boy's hopes and personality. That Griffin's pictures would capture the brightness of his big grin once we finally earned one. That someone would see his picture and say, "*There's my boy!*"

And then it was on to the next. This time, there were three. Somewhere back in my mind, I remembered reading that sibling groups were the hardest to place in homes. The reasons why made sense, but when I saw the way these three kids played together and showed each other affection, I couldn't imagine someone not wanting to make it work.

Devin, Kevin, and Joy were nine, ten, and eleven, respectively. They kept a hand on one another almost the whole time, instinctively staying connected. Knowing they could be pulled apart.

Griffin put them at ease, though, so they gradually let go and started to chat. They loved Barbies (Joy), soccer (Devin and Kevin), and spaghetti (all three). They had learned to swim last summer and dreamed of becoming competitive divers because they watched the summer Olympics. They ate Cheerios for breakfast because their foster mom wouldn't let them have Lucky Charms on weekdays. I tried not to cry.

Later, after Griffin packed up his gear, we walked out the dark school halls to the parking lot. I felt wrung out, weighted by the reality of these kids' situations but also full of hope that this might lead to adoptive families.

"How do you do it?" I asked.

"Do what? This?"

"Yeah, how do you come every month, and sometimes see the same kids, and not lose hope or be frustrated?"

"Oh, I get very frustrated. Every time I hear their stories of bad foster parents or relatives locked in prison, I get frustrated at all the ways we've failed them. I also get pretty frustrated that people spend so much money on stuff like megaweddings when these kids don't have clothes for school. These are probably the only 'nice' clothes they'll get all year. I get frustrated every time my aunts or friends from college go off on social media about some abstract political issue when there are real, live kids here who need help. But this is one small thing I can do. I guess that probably doesn't really answer your question."

"No, it does." I'm struck by how bright his eyes get when he's worked up. They're practically molten. *But focus, Lottie.* "It's a way to make a difference while doing what you do best—taking pictures."

"I hope so. After I came back from Mercy Ships, I floundered a bit. I didn't know exactly what I wanted to do, and everything just seemed so frivolous in comparison."

"Ah, so you went into wedding photography to escape frivolity. That makes sense."

He guffawed. "Fair. Seriously, though, it took me a hot second to find Val and start working with her. Before that, I was about to take a job with a pet photographer. I would have harmed myself. Or someone's dog."

"You would have been terrible at that."

"Yeah, I'm too impatient or cynical for it." He shrugged. "No tolerance for the kinds of people who have strollers for their dogs and *Cat Mom* T-shirts."

Something clicked into place in my mind. "Oh, I get it now . . . Everything makes sense, Griffin."

"What?" He appeared confused.

"You're not a cynic. You're an idealist."

"I prefer to think of myself as a pragmatist."

"No pragmatist spends his weekends taking pictures of teenagers who want to be adopted."

We leaned against our respective cars, quiet for a moment.

"All this," he waved in the direction of the school, "is yet another reason why I just don't think marriage, that whole life, is for me anymore. Maybe I can do more good if I'm not tied down."

I was challenged by his altruism. My sporadic days off were spent in significantly less selfless ways. It was inspiring, and more than a little annoying, that he'd found a way to use his skills to help people. In life, how could one walk through open doors while still pursuing meaning? What if the path ahead didn't lead to an obvious way to make a real difference in the world?

Most people never stop to ask these questions, though. The fact that he had—and taken action on it—was extremely appealing.

We locked eyes, like he could read my thoughts. I liked him. There it was. I've never had a good poker face.

But there was no point in wishing for things that wouldn't happen.

And I was technically, however unofficially, dating Matt. So I chalked the day up to an inspiring-but-devoid-of-romance experience.

"Thank you for the invite. Today was really cool. But now I've got to go do *my* volunteer work—helping Megan find good vendors in the middle of Oklahoma."

"I'm really glad you came." He opened his mouth as if to say more, then closed it. "If you're ever interested in volunteering again, let me know. They also have an annual benefit I imagine they could use help planning."

"Ah! Now I see your angle."

"Just trying to help you see the big picture, be a better person, and apply those mad skills to a more appreciative clientele."

"Thanks, I'll consider it," I said. "So I'll see you in a couple weeks?"

"Yes, have a great trip to Tennessee."

As I pulled out of the parking lot, I kept my eyes on the road. No looking back at him. Only forward.

TWENTY

Exiting the baggage claim area of Nashville International Airport felt like stepping into a steam room, minus the spa benefits.

"Whew! It's hotter than Satan's housecat here." Mary Ellen dabbed her forehead with her silk scarf, a rare concession. "Let's pray the truck with all the portable air conditioners makes it without any issues. If not, the caterer might as well just cook the steaks on the sidewalk next to the reception tent."

So much for trying to tame my hair this weekend, I thought to myself as I followed Mary Ellen toward the rental car shuttles.

While we were looking for our car in Nashville, Cedric was happily ensconced, or submerged, rather, in a shark-themed suite in Dubai at the Engage! summit. Abigail was back in Texas, hopefully ordering a poolside cocktail with her husband, Doug, since she'd ended up in charge of a 350-person wedding at the Four Seasons in Las Colinas. Events at the Four Seasons basically ran themselves, and given there weren't any over-the-top elements added to this wedding, it would be a walk in the park for her and the rest of the team. It had been ages since I'd worked a cookie-cutter wedding. I sort of missed those.

Cedric wanted two planners on the Nashville gig since it was a rather large affair, and since Abigail was already booked, Mary Ellen and I were back together again. I was hopeful about a chance to reconnect and get back on better footing after my successful chicken-themed soiree. But this time our destination was none other than the country music capital of the world.

Whoever thought Kenny Chesney was lying about sexy tractors never met the heir to the country's biggest tractor manufacturer. Harrison Holt was quintessential rural chic. Good looking with long side-swept bangs, big blue eyes, and an immaculate oxford shirt fit. Few women could resist his Southern drawl, charm, or bank account.

This rang true for his bride, Graham Carter, whom he met his freshman year at Ole Miss and who equaled him in beauty and net worth. The pair looked like they'd stepped straight out of a Nicholas Sparks novel. Cedric had dubbed their wedding "*Steel Magnolias* on steroids."

Though Harrison and Graham both lived in Dallas, Harrison was originally from Nashville. Graham's family was from somewhere in Georgia where her family owned a carpet empire. The couple's marriage would be the merger of two Southern dynasties—and the event of the Nashville social season.

The couple had insisted that they marry outside Nashville at the Grafton Woods, an enormous antebellum mansion that was now a museum and private event space. It was a hub for large, swanky weddings in the area, and the couple wanted theirs to rival the best. With the budget we were given by the bride's parents, I didn't imagine that would be difficult.

Prior to our arrival, I had only seen pictures of the estate from a computer screen. Mary Ellen hadn't set foot on the property either. This was not standard procedure, but due to scheduling conflicts, one of Cedric's former employees who lived in Nashville had previewed the potential location. All the planning had been done in our Dallas office with the couple or virtually, and now it was the Thursday before the event. Mary Ellen and I were managing the full installation, and after checking into a boutique hotel downtown, we headed over to the site.

Much of the original property had been sold off and developed into affluent suburban neighborhoods, but vestiges of its history remained. A carriage house and stable—originally used for breeding thoroughbred horses—remained and could be used as individual venues. But the crown jewel was the columned Greek Revival mansion, which dated from the mid-1800s, along with the manicured boxwood gardens that would serve as the backdrop for the couple's ceremony.

Of course, everything was not only very traditional but also a standard to what one might imagine an over-the-top Southern wedding to be. As I said, "*Steel Magnolias* on steroids." The ceremony would take place outdoors in the garden, but large custom peach-and-white scalloped umbrellas were placed throughout the rows of bamboo folding chairs to shade the guests. Magnolia blossoms and vintage lace adorned the ends of the aisles.

White, trellis-covered bars flanked the entrance to the gardens where guests could select from a cucumber cooler or spiked sweet tea to keep cool during the thirty-minute nuptials. It was still considered spring, but like Dallas, Nashville could heat up early in the year, and we were glad to be prepared.

By the time we arrived the tent was well on its way to completion, and rental deliveries were rolling in. The reception structure was located past the gardens near the enormous whitewashed former stable, and inside the ceiling was draped in countless yards of peach fabric with crystal chandeliers hanging above every dining table. Custom napkins with embroidered magnolias on them complemented the centerpieces' peach garden roses, lush greenery, and dried cotton stems. Cedric's carpentry department created floor-to-ceiling lattice walls covered in faux greenery and white wisteria blooms, a dreamy backdrop for the band.

Mary Ellen and I had a break before our meeting with the bride and her mother to go through final ceremony details. So after checking on all the vendors, we decided to explore the grounds.

"I don't know about you, but if this heat doesn't let up, I just might have to find one of those tacky neck fans to wear so I don't pass out," Mary Ellen said as we walked a tree-lined path.

"Thank God they coughed up the money for all the AC we'll be pumping into this space so guests don't start dropping like flies."

"Remember when we used to blame everything on El Niño instead of climate change or mercury in retrograde or whatever?" she quipped. "I kind of miss those days."

I laughed. The site looked as beautiful in person as it had in my online research. Lush, rolling green hills and beautiful homes surrounded the well-kept grounds. I mentally noted a burbling, rocky creek as a great spot for photos.

As we circled back, a pair of massive cannons stood on the lawn near the house. Mary Ellen ran her hand along one.

"These are going off once they're declared Mr. and Mrs. Holt," she said. "No cannonballs, obviously."

"Cannons are certainly a choice. Why on earth? Every time I think I've seen it all . . ."

"Well, you know *why* there are cannons here, right?"

Clearly not. She took my puzzled expression as a sign.

"It's an antebellum home, Lottie. Even if it was never a working plantation, many of these old estates have pretty, well, complicated histories. Like, was it a battle site? Probably. And who do you think *built* this house? You just never want to be surprised."

Nope, I definitely hadn't connected the dots. "What do you mean, surprised?"

"Oh, a couple of years ago in Georgia," she shrugged, "we were shocked when a bunch of Civil War reenactors showed up during cocktail hour. They'd missed the memo that the property—also once the site of a battle—was being used for a wedding that day. Men in blue and gray literally wandered around with bayonets while we tried to keep them away from the guests."

My eyes bulged.

"Yeah, we'll just say that the bride was . . . not amused," she said. "We were all horrified, in fact. It's something you have to be aware of when working in the South. Venues can come with a story, good and bad. We try and navigate venue selection the best we can, but it's not always easy or perfect."

She sighed, looking over the grounds. "Spots like this can be complicated, even thorny, but they can also be beautiful."

"It's not just the South. To be honest, sounds a bit like all of America."

This was a more perceptive side to Mary Ellen than I'd imagined possible. I continued to ruminate over her words. She tossed her hair—still irritatingly perfect despite the humidity—and we headed off to meet Graham and her mother near the two separate bars built for whiskey and wine tastings during the cocktail hour. One of the Jack Daniel's heirs was a close friend and guest, and since he'd provided all the liquor for the blessed festivities, there would be no shortage.

Graham and her mother, a matronly woman who smelled of pearls and the symphony league, were leaning against the wine bar. We said our hellos and then went through our checklist with them to make sure all wedding-day items were accounted for.

On Friday the rest of the installation for the event went off without incident, and before I knew it, it was time for the rehearsal on the grounds.

I wasn't sure what to expect when it came to the wedding party, but everyone seemed to be on good behavior. No amount of wealth would indicate whether the bride and groom's loved ones would act like adults or animals at a ceremony rehearsal. But thankfully the run of ceremony went smoothly, eased by Harrison's winking at the female relatives and Graham playing the "Oh honey, please just come stand over here" card with a few unruly groomsmen and wayward uncles. As they rehearsed inside a tent adjacent to the carriage house, the shade and AC kept us all from dripping. And of course, I had my trusty panty liners in.

After the rehearsal ended and we headed back to the hotel, I started to feel cautiously optimistic that we could breeze through this trip.

Saturday's wedding prep felt like a blur. It was a sunny but blistering ninety-seven degrees outside, but thanks to about $15,000 in air-conditioning for the ceremony and reception tent, the guests would be cool as North Carolina cucumbers.

"It feels a little weird to be doing an event this large without Cedric, doesn't it? But all has gone smoothly thus far," I said to Mary Ellen as we finished setting out the place cards. "Maybe I should knock on some wood and then do another check-in with the vendors."

"Listen, I appreciate all your hard work this weekend. It's a lot to handle." Mary Ellen gestured broadly around us. "Cedric trusts us, which is why he sent us. Today's going to be great. Let's confirm the ceremony musicians are in place, and then I'm sending you over to get the bride and her family. Almost showtime."

As I escorted the bride and her parents to the ceremony site, Graham turned to me and said, "I've decided to have both of my parents walk me down the aisle. We already told my brother he doesn't need to escort Mom to her seat."

Switching last minute was a bit unusual, but plenty of brides chose to have someone other than or in addition to their father escort them. I texted Mary Ellen about the change and moved on.

While a string trio played, the dusty peach-clad bridesmaids made their way down the path to the front of the boxwood garden. Graham took a breath, hooked arms with her parents, and began her stroll to where her groom waited. As she reached the front, she turned her back to him and faced the crowd of family and friends. I barely had time to register that this was absolutely *not* what we'd rehearsed. In fact, I'd never seen or heard about a bride turning around to face the guests until the very end of the service with her new husband beside her. My internal alarm system began blaring.

"Thank y'all so much for coming here today." She took a slow breath. "It has been a joy to spend time with family and friends this weekend. I've been reminded of how many people have been an important part of my life. What a gift that has been . . . But I'm ultimately so sorry for making you come.

"I learned quite recently—this morning, actually—that Harrison cheated on me with my maid of honor, Penny." Poor stunned Penny didn't even get a glance in her direction as Graham went on. "Obviously, our wedding is off, but I wanted you to hear it from me and to thank you for being here. I love . . . *most* of you and am truly grateful you came to celebrate and support me." Her composure finally started to crack as her mother squeezed her arm.

"Oh, Graham, wait, it's not—" Harrison finally recovered his wits enough to try and interject. But the bride shot him a look that could burn bacon, and he went silent.

"Now, we've already paid for dinner and the band—and Lord knows we all will need a drink after this," Graham continued. "So please, do stay as long as you'd like here today. Enjoy the food and have a good night."

With that she turned on her heel and exited past the bridesmaids, again without sparing Penny so much as a turn of her head. Harrison, who looked about to vomit, ran toward her, trailing behind her parents.

Chaos erupted in the seats. A haze of nervous laughter and noisy four-letter words permeated the garden. An elderly woman on the groom's side clutched the pearl buttons on her shirt front. Graham's great-aunt cackled maniacally. She had the right idea.

Thank goodness for the shot of adrenaline that pulsed through my body, otherwise I would've been frozen in position at the back of the garden for the rest of eternity.

"Mary Ellen," I whispered intently into my radio. "There's umm, been a development over here at the ceremony, and well, the bride just canceled the wedding."

At first I thought she hadn't heard me, as it was radio silent on the other end of my earpiece.

"Mary Ellen? Are you there? Graham just called it off in front of *everyone*."

"Yes, sorry," she replied. "Just making sure I heard you correctly."

"What do I do? The minister and wedding party are still standing up front in total shock, one of the bridesmaids has run off sobbing, and the guests are bewildered."

I recapped what Graham had said and then waited for Mary

Ellen's instructions, muttering a prayer that I was on some sort of "gotcha" TV show.

"Okay," said Mary Ellen. "First, make sure the staff knows not to set off the cannon now. That'll really send everyone into a panic. Then go down the aisle and tell everyone that yes, they can hightail it to the reception tent for dinner and drinks if they wish, but we will also go ahead and pull all of the shuttles around for those who want to go back to the hotel.

"After that, go find the bride and her parents to make sure Harrison isn't being strangled by Graham's father, and radio me your position. I'll meet you there after I rework a few things here at the reception tent to get ready for our new non-reception reception," she said.

"Roger that," I replied. When I gave the two cannon attendants the cut-throat signal with my hand, they gave me the thumbs-up. Then I mustered all my gumption and headed down the center aisle to the front of the ceremony. I didn't allow myself a moment of hesitation; otherwise, I'd never do what needed to be done here.

Taking the stage with the sweetest Southern smile I could muster, I asked to borrow the microphone from the minster, who was happy to hand it over.

I opened my mouth to relay the instructions to the guests, then, *boom!* The cannon went off. What I wouldn't have given for awkward silence. Another *boom!* resounded, echoing through the acreage.

The attendants evidently took my cut-throat gesture to mean light the fuse. Idiots. Dogs began to bark. Guests started an uproar again. And the local fife and drum band, whose cue was the cannon boom, began to play. All the dominoes were falling, it seemed. I attempted to shout into the microphone over the cacophony.

"Excuse me! So sorry for the news and for any confusion, but, as

Graham said, you're welcome to head over to the reception tent. We are also pulling the shuttles around." And with that, I gave up.

The guests started ambling either toward the reception tent or toward the valet/shuttle line. A few members of the wedding party started asking me questions, to which I gently replied that I'd already passed along all the information I had at the moment but would be happy to help them to their tables or their cars.

With the ceremony cleared, I headed in our runaway bride's direction. I found Mr. and Mrs. Carter together near the front of the property.

Mr. Carter was barking orders into his cell phone. Mrs. Carter saw me and hurried my way. "Lottie, we are so sorry for not looping y'all in on Graham's plans. We didn't learn about Harrison's indiscretions until an hour before the ceremony. Graham was already in her dress! It was a lot to take in, as you can imagine, and we wanted to respect her wishes."

Apparently Graham's wishes included Mr. Carter sparing Harrison's life, but Mr. Carter did tell him to go jump off a bridge as soon as they were out of earshot. Mrs. Carter said she last saw Harrison headed toward the wine-tasting room near the gift shop. I would deal with him later.

"Where is Graham now? Is she okay?" I asked. "Is there anything we can do?"

"No," replied Mr. Carter as he hung up the phone. "She's on her way to Signature airfield where our plane is. Her mother and I will meet her there shortly."

"Oh wow, okay. Glad she's getting out of here."

"We'll be at our vacation home on Sea Island if you need to reach us. So please, if you can just sort things out for the remaining guests, it'd be much appreciated."

Another cannon blared. I cringed. *Why are they still going off?*

"Of course. I'm so sorry about everything."

"Me too," said Mrs. Carter. "I still can't believe Penny and Harrison would do such a thing. And for Graham to find out on the morning of her wedding? My baby will never recover from this." She started to sob.

Mr. Carter pulled out his handkerchief and handed it to Mrs. Carter while gently ushering her toward their car.

"I'll be in touch in a few days," said Mr. Carter. "Y'all did a great job up until now, and I'm sorry it ended this way."

"Me too," I replied. "Feel free to call us for anything. Don't worry about the reception. We'll handle everything." I felt my nails digging into my palms. I was wound tighter than a girdle, as my mamaw would have said.

With that, the Carters disappeared into their Mercedes-Benz. I exhaled and rolled my shoulders back, then scampered off to find Mary Ellen. She was outside the tent. "Don't worry about the Carters. The parents are handling the situation remarkably well, and Graham is already gone. I'm not sure where Harrison is, but I guess he isn't our problem anymore. How about the guests? Did anyone actually come over to the reception tent?"

"Shockingly, yes," Mary Ellen said. "It's like the people who stayed couldn't care less about what just happened. At least half the tables are full, and I was going to release the band, but people are already on the dance floor, so they're going to continue playing. This is a first for me, which says a lot."

"Tell me about it. I still can't believe Graham had the nerve to address everyone like that after finding out such devastating news."

"I'm sure she'll fall apart now, if she hasn't already." Mary Ellen arched her manicured brows. "But yes, she's tough as a pine knot. She had a real Scarlett O'Hara moment up there. I guess she'll be thinking about it tomorrow at Tara—or wherever else that private plane is taking her."

"'Frankly, my dear, I don't give a damn,'" I added without being able to stop myself.

"Fair enough," Mary Ellen guffawed. "Cannons aside, you did a great job. Way to take control of the situation."

I filed the rare praise away for the next time she inadvertently stomped on my self-esteem. "Thanks, Mary Ellen. Though I hope this is the first and last time either of us experiences this kind of surprise. I have never been more ready for a wedding to be over."

"I know I've been hard on you at times, but it's because you seemingly just flounced into The Firm and stole Cedric's attention without really spending the time at the bottom. I know you worked with Abigail's company, but this is the big leagues. And you've got to be committed if you want to stay." She mock wagged a finger at me.

"I do," I said, surprised at Mary Ellen's words—and my own certainty.

"All right, then let's go finish up this mess and get the heck out of here!"

The rest of the evening went on without any other issues. The former couple's friends and family were all speculating about details, but all we cared to hear was that Penny and Harrison were both found (at different times and places) and had made it safely off the property.

We adjusted the schedule so everything wrapped up after the dinner service ended. Mary Ellen instructed the caterers to cut the cake and pass out pieces to the remaining guests while informing them that the event was now over. This was the earliest either one of us had ever left a wedding. Tiny blessings.

"How about we head back to our hotel and grab a bite at the bar before turning in?" Mary Ellen asked.

"Sounds great to me. Plus, I've heard the men's bathroom outside the bar area is outrageously decorated, and Elvis used to pee in there all the time when he was in town. It's got to be late enough at night for us to sneak a quick peek without anyone seeing us."

Together, we headed back downtown. It might not have been a successful ceremony—through no fault of our own—but we did our part. I felt so thankful for Mary Ellen and Abigail and the experience I had gained from both women. I could see, with the new office opening, the eventual splintering of Cedric's squad. But I hoped that no matter what, we could all work together for a long time.

TWENTY-ONE

I went from country to the blues. Fitting. The next morning I dropped Mary Ellen off at the Nashville airport and turned the rental car west to Memphis. I was long overdue for a visit home, even if it was only for a day or two. While no one thought of their parents as "normal," it would be nice to be around some familiar faces, especially after the past twenty-four hours. I wanted the comfort of home.

Matt had called a few times over the weekend, and I'd texted him that I'd give him a call back once I hit the road. He was in a great mood after one of his clients received a bigger signing bonus than expected. I filled him in on the weekend, and we made plans to get together again once I returned to Dallas. I didn't realize it, but when I hung up the phone with him, we had talked for over an hour.

Memphis never felt particularly small growing up, but the skyline as I crossed over the "Old Bridge" paled in comparison to the "Big D." But what *didn't* pale in comparison now to everything in Dallas? My hometown suburb, on the border of Tennessee and Mississippi, was anything but glamorous, but it felt good to drive the familiar streets.

There was nothing particularly special about the area, but its lower cost of living, good schools, and proximity to downtown made it an attractive place to live. At least that's what Mom always told me when I questioned their choice of lifelong residency. Didn't every kid fantasize, though, about moving someplace more interesting than where they were raised?

I pulled into the circle driveway of the small red brick ranch I had lived in my whole young life. On par with the gatehouses for most of our Dallas clients' homes, I noted. Our clients' houses were so over the top they didn't seem real. After spending that day with Griffin shooting for the Heart Gallery, I realized that a regular dose of reality was what I'd need to stay sane in this industry. It's hard not to want more when you're only surrounded by the metroplex glitterati, spending thousands upon hundreds of thousands on one celebratory day.

The drive had made me think of our road trip back from Austin, and I went to text him but then thought better of it. After our last hang, I wanted to respect his boundaries. Our friendship had become too valuable to me to mess up.

Griffin certainly had a point about the challenges of finding meaning in the world of high-end events. I understood, especially given his past, that it could seem beyond frivolous. But I also thought about helping brides like Cassie, my barrel-riding bestie, have a truly significant, magical day. Those were the events that made the craziness and drama worthwhile.

I was lost in thought as the car idled in the driveway. Mom came out of the house waving her arms in front of me, trying to get my attention.

"Hello, Lottie? You coming in?" she shouted. "Come give me a hug—it's been forever!"

I got out of the car and hugged her. "Hi, Mom. I've missed you."

"Your dad's gone to pick up barbecue from Corky's and will be back any minute. You made great time."

"Yeah, the drive from Nashville is way more tolerable than the one from Dallas." I moved to the trunk to grab my bag.

Dad arrived a few minutes later and greeted me with the same warm hug, but with the smell of pork on his shirt, which made my stomach growl.

"How about we eat first and then you can get settled in?" Mom said.

"Perfect," I replied. "I'm starving, and I've been dying for some pork barbecue. That beef brisket they call barbecue in Texas doesn't cut it. It shouldn't be allowed in the same category."

"Yeah, but they make up for it with Tex-Mex," Mom said.

"I can confirm this fact," I said. "If I wasn't working all the time, living on coffee and cake, I'd probably get tacos every day."

I started laughing but then realized it had taken me approximately twenty-six minutes to open a can of worms.

"Let's talk about that over dinner." Mom finished setting out the food on the counter. We made our plates and then took our seats at the kitchen table. The worn wood had been the site of so many family meetings, late-night chats, and homework sessions. I traced a familiar scratch with my index finger.

"How was the wedding you worked this weekend? Grafton Woods is supposed to be just breathtaking." My mom always loved historic homes.

"Honestly, it was a bit of a train wreck." I filled them in on Harrison's cruel indiscretions, Graham's shocking ceremony speech, and the cannon salute to no one.

"Hoo, boy," my father mused. "That sounds like a lot for one weekend."

"It sure is," Mom added. "So, do you think you'll stay at Cedric Celebrations?"

Ah, there it was. The inquisition I'd been anticipating. "To tell you the truth, I do. I actually got promoted a few weeks ago. I'm assigned my own events to plan now, and, aside from the totally unpredictable hiccups, it seems I'm surprisingly good at it."

"'Course you are, sweetie," said Dad, scooping out baked beans. "We're not surprised to hear that at all. You've always been so responsible. Congratulations on the promotion, but you haven't been making a lot of money. Has that changed?"

"Not much," I admitted. "I got a small raise, but I actually enjoy the work. That has to count for something." I bit into a heavenly spare rib.

He nodded. "It does. But last time you two spoke, your mother told me you were barely getting by."

"Well, I'm also up for an even bigger role because Cedric is opening a new office. That will help too." I wiped my already saucy hands on a paper towel.

"That's an interesting possibility," said Mom. "I can't imagine how expensive it is to live in Dallas. It's crazy what they charge for everything there . . . Oh, and your father and I had been wondering if you'd given the LSATs any more thought. There's certainly a lot more money in lawyering, I imagine."

I braced myself. "Actually, I did make a decision about that. I'm glad I ended up coming home so I could tell y'all in person. Even though I know it's not what you'll want to hear."

I was surprised neither of them jumped in.

"Truth is, I don't want to be a lawyer anymore. Truly. I'm sure I'm walking away from a lot more security than a job in events will provide, but that's okay with me. I just don't see myself going to law school."

"But you were once so set on it. And then you were bound and determined you'd be Brody's wife." Mom sighed. "Are you sure this is the right direction for you now?"

"Yes." It was the second time in so many days I'd been asked that question, and I felt more confident than ever in my answer.

I knew Dad wasn't going to say anything if Mom didn't. This discussion had always really been between the two of us.

"Well, Lottie, it's your life," she said.

I just about spit the baked beans out of my mouth.

"We only want you to find something you love. If you're going to spend your life on something and make the necessary sacrifices—work or marriage or parenting or what have you—you've got to love it. Everyone at this table knows how I gave up teaching when you were born."

Dad had certainly been made aware of this fact many times, but it didn't seem to bother him. I could never quite tell, but then again, they'd been together for decades, and he would know better than I if she was really content.

"I gave up everything to move here, raise you kids, and support your father's business. Looking back, it was always my choice, and the life we have and the years I've spent with you and your brother were worth it to me . . . That's why I always wanted you to at least finish what you started. You worked so hard and did so well in college, and you have to admit, no one saw a career in wedding planning coming."

"Of course not," I said, feeling relieved already. "Me neither, but it's going really well. I'm finding my way."

"Are you seeing anyone?" Dad asked, moving on to the next line of inquiry.

"Wow, all the big hits at once." I laughed. "There's not really anybody serious, but I've been going out with a guy off and on since

October." Mom's head visibly perked up, so I told them a little about Matt. "Work is so busy, and we don't want to rush anything."

Then I opened my big fat mouth. "Plus, there's another guy I'm friends with through work, which has been fun, helpful, and also more than a little inspiring and challenging, depending on the day." I painted the broad strokes of Griffin's background for them. "But we're just friends and plan on keeping it that way."

"I see." Mom pursed her lips. Always a sign. Never a great one.

"He has some reasons for not being interested right now in marriage or long-term relationships. And I get it. Seriously." *So mature.* I mentally patted myself on the back.

"Hmm. Well, I'm glad to hear you're getting out there. In some fashion," she said. "We know you're planning all these weddings when you always really wanted your own to happen, and that's got to be hard."

She started gathering the plates to carry them to the sink. I passed mine over, then began consolidating the leftover containers.

"You're right, it can be. But I'm trying to look at it as a way to channel some of those dreams I had, the hopes and visions, to use them to help *other* people."

"Like the Mother Teresa of wedding planning," my dad cracked. We all knew where I got my middle-aged-man sense of humor from.

"Funny enough, I'm actually part of the team planning Brody's wedding." Bound by my NDA, I couldn't tell them all the details—or the name of his bride—but I said what I could.

I also refrained from mentioning my hopes that some minor, disfiguring calamity would befall the bride and assured them my primary focus was on myself, my own future.

"Lottie, dear, I am so proud of you," my mom said. "That takes a lot of strength. You were so heartbroken after y'all broke up; I've worried about you."

"I guess Tom will probably give you the first grandchild at this point," I said, hoping to lighten the tenor.

"Oh! Before I forget, we got you some souvenirs in Japan." Mom started down the hall.

"Your brother is actually seeing someone," Dad said, "and it sounds serious."

"Um, what?!" Tom notoriously played the field when we were adolescents—no rushing to settle down for at least one Jones kid, I thought—and then spent his military years overseas, presumably not finding a wife.

"Her name is Eleanor, and she's a nurse in the navy. She works at a hospital on his old base in Japan, but she's getting transferred stateside soon too."

"She's darling," Mom added, returning with a beautifully embroidered set of silk linens. "And listen, as long as one of you gives us grandchildren, I'll survive."

"Well, that takes some of the pressure off me." I forced a laugh. "Who knows, maybe Matt is perfect for me, or there's someone else waiting around the corner. Clearly my whole life isn't anything close to what I'd planned out."

"Sometimes the best things in life are unexpected," Dad said. "We aren't really the best people to talk to about living some grand adventure, but we are at least trying to support yours."

"Thanks, Dad," I said, almost tearing up. "I appreciate it. It's just a lot right now, you know?"

"Well, it's been months since we've seen you," said Mom. "And I'm going to take full advantage of this brief time in person. Quick phone calls and texts wear me out, and don't even get me started on Facebook. All my friends find out what's going on in their kids' lives online before their children say a word to them. It's just awful."

"I'm too old—or too young—for Facebook, Mom. So you don't have to worry about that with me."

"Well then on the Instagram. You know what I mean."

That night I crawled under my childhood Laura Ashley floral comforter, surprisingly content. My parents had some valid questions and concerns, though I'd never say that aloud or while fully awake. But I felt like my new identity was slowly, finally crystallizing. This was the right path for me. They'd see.

~ ✳ ~

After breakfast Mom and I puttered around her garden. Well, she puttered in a flower bed while I sat in an ancient metal yard chair, propped my feet up on a side table, and let the sunshine warm my face.

Our small backyard was, as you'd expect from a landscaper, packed to the rafters with a rotation of stunning seasonal plants. There was always a corner or two in bloom, nearly all year. The scents of the herb and peppermint beds commingled on the soft breeze.

She filled me in on a couple neighbors, as well as some cousins in the area. Church gossip, friends who'd moved away. I updated her on Natalia's latest hobbies and Megan's wedding plans. The same comfortable drill.

Then, she sat back on her heels and wiped her forehead with one dirty glove. A smudge of soil remained, not that I'd mention it.

"Lottie, hon, I've been wondering. You've been sort of dating this Matt for months, so we're getting the sense that maybe, just maybe, you don't even like him that much. Are you interested in him? *Really* interested?"

"Sure, Mom. He's a really great guy."

"Then why does it not appear to be going anywhere?"

"Like I said, there's work—" My mom cut me off with a look.

"You seemed to light up a bit more when you mentioned that photographer guy . . . So why is it that your most compelling option is someone who told you he'd never be serious?" She held up a still-gloved hand. "Feels like you're allowing yourself to go after something that is unattainable or just not real. Again." I knew she was referring to Brody, my own personal Voldemort. "This guy has told you he's not interested in marriage. You've got to keep moving forward, sweetie."

"I am, I promise."

She went inside to wash her hands, and then the house phone rang. I loved that they still had our same landline. I closed my eyes.

She was right, I hated to say. At least about some of it.

I owed Matt a solid chance. He ticked all the boxes and was easy on the eyes. But after all these months the sparks on my end just weren't there. I knew if I genuinely encouraged him, he'd probably be all in again, and, barring disaster, we'd be engaged in a year. That's how things worked in our world. He wanted all the right things, but it was as though the path to the life I'd always wanted had presented itself—and now I wasn't sure I should take the step. If I wasn't certain, I needed to cut him loose.

And while I *could* admit to being attracted to Griffin, my mom wasn't spot-on there. We were just friends, and my heart was content with that. But if I was putting out some "into him" energy, it was probably best to stay at a distance for the time being. No need to complicate life any further.

They'd see. This was more than a phase; I could finally see a path to being the woman I wanted to be—the friend, daughter, worker, and hopefully someday, wife. It was all within reach. If my new dream was to be the best darn wedding coordinator that ever existed and land that Atlanta job, I would go for it 100 percent. No more wishy-washy Lottie.

TWENTY-TWO

"Home, sweet *home*!" I considered yelling as I waltzed past the row of staff at the resort in Los Cabos a few weeks later in early May. I opted against it but accepted a welcome cocktail with an umbrella instead. It was good to be back in a place where I belonged (at least in my fantasies). I could certainly grow accustomed to this aspect of Cedric's world. Although now that actual guests would be booking rooms, I knew not to hope for the same luxe accommodations.

Good thing I'd adjusted my expectations because, alas, this room didn't have its own private plunge pool. That was the only thing wrong with it. I was on the second floor of a villa, facing the ocean on one side and lush but perfectly manicured gardens on the other. My suite boasted a Jacuzzi, a minibar included in the cost of the room, and a monogrammed bathrobe that I got to keep. I would take any and all available amenities to get me through this weekend.

Harriet—well, her assistant, Tasha—had even added me to the list of people who got a welcome basket, which was nice, albeit hilarious, considering how I'd spent the last three weeks overseeing the interns who'd assembled them all.

I lit the custom Byredo candle, stripped, poured some in-house bath salts, and stepped into the hot bath to soak away the travel grime. Just as I was settling in, the room phone rang, and I shot up and raced for it. "Hello?" I said after four rings.

"Lottie, it's Mary Ellen. *Where* are you? I need you in the lobby bar to start triple-checking all the final details. We only have one day before guests start to arrive, and I'm totally stressed out."

She hung up before I could even grunt a reply. I was glad to see our recent camaraderie hadn't sharpened her edge.

I got dressed, then stormed down to the lobby lounge area, hoping she wouldn't notice my slightly damp hair. Mary Ellen was seated at a pair of chairs tucked into a corner. I took the empty seat.

"Here, take this." She slid a file folder across the coffee table with a nervous glance around the room. "It's the site list and final run-of-show."

"You mean I'm going to know what happens before the ceremony starts? Goody!"

"Oh, I see we're taking a tone today? In that case give me the folder back."

I clutched it to my chest, then started to open it.

"Not here!" she whisper-yelled. "Read it when you get back upstairs."

I was baffled. Why didn't she just have me meet her in her room? What were we—Russian spies?

"We need to go over all the food and beverage orders and make sure they are updated to our latest numbers."

After a mind-numbing hour of checking off menus, delivery invoices, and making sure everything made it through customs, I went upstairs, folder in hand. Lucky me. A night alone in my beautiful suite overlooking the Sea of Cortez and a very lengthy schedule to memorize.

I had enough minutiae to focus on that I put off dwelling on the greater reality. But once in bed I tossed and turned. My Ambien wasn't cutting it. Brody was marrying a gorgeous global superstar. This weekend. And my literal job was to make it happen. My stomach churned as if at sea. The thought of seeing Brody again, this time with his stunning fiancée, made me queasy, roiled my insides.

That would be the first and, in some ways, biggest of a thousand cuts. Smaller, still painful, would be seeing his family and some of our friends from school. I could imagine their unintended jabs with questions about my career and relationship status. Other brutal moments that would surely remind me of the nuptials I'd imagined and the one Brody was now having. And then the final, excruciating cut of seeing him say "I do." I had to somehow stay focused and ignore the agony throughout.

The next morning, Thursday, I woke up to the ringing of the bedside alarm. I was still cross-eyed from lack of sleep and going over every last detail of the schedule, but Mary Ellen expected me in the lobby for a walk-through of the ceremony and formal portrait locations in fifteen minutes.

I pulled my honey-blond hair off my neck, regretted not refreshing my highlights before the trip, put on a tad more makeup than usual, and gave myself a few minutes to drink a cup of coffee on my terrace and *breathe*. I just had to get through the next couple days, watch my first love marry a glamorous celebrity, and then return to my significantly-less-glamorous life in Dallas. I didn't want anything to screw up my progress with Cedric. Even if it meant hiding in the bushes every now and then to cry it out.

But I'd kept it together for one day thus far. *Small victories*, I told myself.

Mary Ellen stood near the lobby entrance, tapping the sole of one

Jimmy Choo wedge on the ceramic tile. At least she had the sense not to wear stilettos for our trek through the equatorial underbrush. Next to her stood a small group of vendors waiting to start a pre-event walk-through, including Griffin. I'd completely forgotten he was getting in this morning and not tonight with the remainder of the advance team. His garish blue Tommy Bahama Hawaiian shirt managed to look ironically stylish on him.

He winked at me as I walked up, and my heart lifted ever so slightly. He, of course, had no idea of my resolve to keep him at arm's length.

We walked through the resort, Mary Ellen pointing out locations for photos and important moments.

"Here is where they're doing the first look." She dismissively pointed at a stone grotto lined with hibiscus bushes.

Standing in this spot, I could envision Brody seeing Harriet so clearly. Anxiety and dismay swirled. My fortifications threatened to crumble.

Griffin puckered his lips and made an exaggeratedly surprised face behind Mary Ellen's back. I tried to muster a grin.

"Lottie, are you okay?" He stepped closer.

"Yeah, I'm fine. Totally fine. Just tired."

"You sure?" he whispered, tugging on my hand as Mary Ellen kept walking. "What's going on?"

I looked down at our loosely joined hands. "It's not a big deal, really . . . Do you know whose wedding this is?"

"Yeah, Harriet Devore and one of the Rams players. Didn't you? Why?"

"Yes, but I kind of dated that Rams player, Brody Stevens, in college."

"Wowza. Wait, is this the guy you almost married? Definitely didn't know that fun fact."

"It was."

"And you're working his wedding? That feels like kind of a big deal, right?"

"Yeah, I mean, no. I guess sort of?"

"I see. Have you said hi yet?"

"Of course not!" I squeaked. "We dated for a long time and then it wasn't pretty at the end. I haven't spoken to him since graduation."

He crossed his arms and shook his head. "That's it? Doesn't sound like there was really any closure."

"No, not really. We all just scattered and he went on to this life."

"That sucks, but it was years ago. And this is the first time you've brought him up, so why are you being weird?"

"I'm not! I just, well, we were pretty serious. I did tell you I had a longtime college boyfriend. It's all just sinking in, I guess."

By then Mary Ellen and the others had continued down the path from us, oblivious that we weren't hanging on her every word.

"I think your emotions are getting the best of you," Griffin said with a shake of his black curls. "You were, what? All of twenty-two when y'all broke up?"

He clearly didn't understand. The pent-up anxiety and uncertainty over the past months cascaded out of me. "We were going to get married! And now he's marrying someone else! And not just anyone else but freaking Harriet Devore. He's *supposed* to be settling. He's supposed to never find someone as amazing as me. Instead he's found the weird hybrid of Julia Roberts and Charlize Theron."

"So you're jealous? Come on. I know this was a long relationship, but I was *actually* married and can tell you that's much harder to move on from. You're being a tad dramatic. This was your college boyfriend. You've both probably dated a dozen people since then. I know he has—I read *People* and *Sports Illustrated*. I can't believe you're this hung up on it still."

"You just don't get it! He was the one who—"

"Lottie, do you still have feelings for this guy? After all this time?"

I didn't know what to say. I just stood there, staring down at the gravel path glinting in the hot sun.

"I mean, it's not my place or anything, but . . . wow. You need to work some stuff out." He turned around to go back to the main resort.

I knew he had a point, though I'd never admit it. I obviously wasn't hoping to marry Brody anymore. But being there, the reality of his marriage finally in front of my face, was dredging up long-buried feelings. I had imagined every detail of this day—with me the one in white. I could project a ghostlike hologram of my own abandoned dreams on top of each special moment. I could still feel the vestiges of who I was back then, that girl who'd contorted herself to fit some version of Brody's life, only to get rejected. How was I supposed to shake this all off and help him marry someone else? I needed to prove myself to Cedric and Mary Ellen, but I just wanted to puke and get the hell out of here.

Pull yourself together, Jones. I took a few deep breaths. *Just put one foot in front of the other, and you can do anything.*

I trudged after the group, who were now standing a couple yards off the path near a stunning ocean vista.

"Where did Griffindor go?" Mary Ellen noticed I was alone.

"Oh, um, I'm not sure. He did mention earlier that he had to check on some equipment deliveries," I lied. "But I'm drawing up a map for him with all the locations for the bride and groom. I'll make sure he's got all the notes."

"If you say so. But if you guys screw this up and the bride and groom aren't happy with their portraits, we'll *all* be screwed. Remember that."

"I thought they wanted this all to be a supersecret and private affair," I said.

"Yes, but it's all a part of controlling the narrative. Privacy is like a luxury good in the age of social media," she said, as though this were a life-or-death situation. "If your wedding leaks as tacky iPhone pics, you're never getting invited to the Met Gala, and you might as well hand over your Soho House card. Bad placement can ruin you. The biggest stars keep a lid on things as long as possible, but Harriet's first Rams game will probably blow that."

"Mmhmm," I muttered.

She could tell I'd taken more interest in a huge lizard I saw climbing a nearby bush. "Lottie, I know you think this stuff is silly and stupid, but it's important. You've got to know how to navigate the celebrity world or you'll never make it to the next level."

She let me chew on that while we walked back to the main building. In reality I was agonizing about Brody and Griffin and how the heck I was going to make this all right again.

Near the conference rooms of the main building, Cedric's on-site team had commandeered an unused ballroom for their mission control. It was the rallying point for all the wedding-day items we brought with us from Dallas. A stockpile of Gatorade and Red Bull awaited dehydrated or "low energy" workers. Those not lucky enough to be staying at the actual resort but at the nearby motel could also stash their stuff while working the event.

In addition to Mary Ellen and myself, Abigail and a couple interns had made the trip to represent the planning division. (Most of the Trustie interns' parents had covered their flights so they could gain "work experience" and probably spend an additional week afterward lounging on the beach.) Travis was manning the office, God bless him.

Mary Ellen and I ducked inside the door as Cedric walked toward a podium that looked better suited for speeches during corporate conferences. Today it was the platform for the design gods. I spotted Griffin across the room near the videographer and Val's other assistant, but he wouldn't meet my eyes. This wasn't the time or place to try and explain myself, and I was thankful for a bit more time.

"Hear ye, hear ye," Cedric said, flourishing a palm frond–printed scarf. "By now, you all know what wedding we're here for. I wanted to thank you for the discretion I know you'll exercise while we are working this weekend—and I wanted to remind you of the nondisclosure agreements you've signed and the threat of legal reprisals should you so much as tweet the bride's shoes or her fandom's hashtag. Just think about how accommodating the local authorities might be and consider whether I would actually leave you here." Somehow he managed to deliver the most threatening of messages with a smile.

"These clients have asked for—and paid for—the utmost secrecy," he continued. "Now that means they're asking for that level of secrecy from their guests too. Your job is to ensure guests have an incredible time yet don't ever feel the need or opportunity to post anything online. We will be confiscating cell phones and even Wi-Fi-enabled video cameras upon check in. No exceptions. Not even the bride's parents. If any guests have an issue with that, send them to me. But if you spot a stray iPhone or even an iPod touch, it is your job to apprehend it. Repeat after me: if you see something, say something."

An awkward chorus of voices parroted his words, unsure if he actually expected us to repeat him.

"Good. Now that the tacky stuff is out of the way, let's talk about the gorgeous details!" He went on to outline the schedule of events, a couple highlight moments, and a layout of where everything was and needed to be. I zoned out and half listened. The reality that Brody— and his future wife—were about to be in front of me was now making me full-on dizzy. But I wasn't going to repeat last night's insomnia, fingers crossed. I didn't want to greet the happy couple with bags under my eyes. I needed to be sharp and on my A-game, for both personal and professional reasons. I would act unaffected and like the total pro I knew I was. That would have to be enough for now.

Cedric wrapped up his litany of instructions. "And finally, I don't say it enough, but this couple is getting the finest event production and coordination team in the *world*. I should know; I hired all of you. You are some of the best I've ever worked with in this industry. High-profile events like this can be stressful, but you wouldn't be here unless I had the utmost confidence in your abilities. From the most efficient and organized planners on my staff"—at this he glanced at Mary Ellen—"to the breathtakingly creative designers"—a nod to Abigail. "From the dedicated young interns to the hard-core security personnel, you're our A-team. So *do not let me down*. Or you will regret it. Cheers! Hooray! Yay weddings and all that. Now get out of my face and go shower before guests start to arrive."

TWENTY-THREE

Guests started checking in late that afternoon. I was helping in the main lobby, making sure that the concierge had the right welcome bags for each person, when I looked up—right into a familiar pair of twinkling golden eyes. "Hiya, Lottie," Matt said with a grin.

"What are you doing here? I thought you were in New York." Was I dreaming? Did I miss something? Our uncomfortable phone call on my drive back from Memphis felt like yesterday. After leaving home, I'd taken my mom's advice (though I'd never tell her as much) and told Matt I was only interested in him as a friend. We'd never really labeled our relationship, so I kept things as casual as possible. I likely blamed it too much on work.

He said he was disappointed but understood—and would still love to grab dinner and drinks when he was in town. I agreed, fully knowing that I'd ghost him again. But with Brody's wedding rapidly approaching, I gave myself a pass to deal with Matt later if needed. This was, apparently, my punishment.

"I hope this is a good surprise. I had a feeling you might be working this wedding, but I didn't want to say anything, since I wasn't sure I could make it—and, of course, the whole thing was pretty hush-hush. Our New York client let me postpone my trip so I could come here, and I thought it would be fun to surprise you."

"Oh, well, you definitely surprised me. I didn't see your name on any of the guest lists. Sorry—I'm a bit overwhelmed with everyone arriving today." That wasn't the half of it. I set down some amenity bags and gave him a hug. "My mind is all over the place."

"Well, it's probably my boss's name on the lists because he's technically Brody's manager. I hope it's not a problem that I'm here instead. When he found out I could make it to the wedding, he let me come since Brody and I go way back and the original invite was for me. He's been with our company since his rookie days. I used to crash with him whenever I was in LA, and he was just starting on the team. Anyway, he's the best."

"Yes, the *best*." I feigned joy and went to hand him his custom guest gift bag with his boss's name all over it. Perfect. Now Griffin, Brody, *and* Matt were all here together. I remembered Brody and Matt hanging out in college, but Brody had a ton of friends. Some were actual close friends and some just wanted to be in proximity to the athletes. Of course, I had no idea who Brody befriended since, and it was just my luck that he and Matt had become buddies.

One more headache for me in paradise.

However, this particular headache was going to get the cold shoulder for the weekend. For now, he was just another guest and I was *not* interested in losing my cool or focus any more than I already had.

"Here are all the guest instructions and information you'll need this weekend along with all kinds of overly priced amenities."

"Does this have all the details for the wedding party too? See, I'm an usher. Brody asked me to step up when he found out I could make it."

"Really? That's so lovely." What fresh torture was this? I'd been put in charge of wrangling the men in the wedding by Mary Ellen, likely as punishment for sassing her last weekend at a Four Seasons ceremony. I hadn't bothered to check her list yet, but I was going to be seeing a lot of his handsome face. And Brody's, of course. Had they ever discussed me? Not that I cared, precisely, but it was the principle of the thing.

I slipped the folder for the bridal party into his goodie bag, confiscated his cell phone, and sent him to his suite. Soon after, I dashed off to my own. I still hadn't seen the bride or the groom, but I wanted to put off seeing them—or anyone else I knew—as long as possible. I needed to get my emotions in check with a *serious* restart. And I needed to fix my hair.

I ran into Abigail on my way to my room.

"Abigail!" I just about leapt into her arms. Professionalism be damned; it was good to see a friendly face.

She almost dropped me as she started laughing. "What in the world, Lottie?"

"You are never going to believe who's here. It's my ex's wedding, which I probably should have told you, but I didn't want Cedric to boot me off the event. Now it's also like my entire little black book is at this resort. I'm about to have a heart attack." Tears started to form.

"Oh honey, take a deep breath. I think my room is right next to yours. We've got an hour or so to get ready before we need to set up for tonight, so come with me and tell me everything."

"I think I love you," I said as she walked me to her room.

A bit later, with a much-needed pep talk and a face full of concealer to fortify me, I faced the evening's event—an all-white décor and dress party on the southern beach of the resort. Attire was casual chic: white designer sundresses for the ladies and linen slacks with white shirts and rolled-up sleeves for the men. Women checked their stilettos at the sidewalk and slipped into custom monogrammed flip-flops so they could more easily prance about the sand in their resort attire. Cedric even allowed our team to wear white so we didn't stand out, a concession that most certainly pained him.

Even though it was a "casual" affair, we still pulled out all the stops for this welcome party. Indigenous Cochimí dancers wore feathered headdresses and tiny bikinis or shorts with shells and claws. Ankle bracelets rattled and chimed as they danced to the live band. White cabanas dotted the shoreline with fluffy white pillows piled underneath for lounging, and guests circled a wide fire pit dug into the sand.

The sun set over the water as everyone ate fresh sushi, local fruits, and steak skewers. Once the sun went down, torches provided the only light. The atmosphere would have been intoxicating to anyone not scrupulously avoiding a bevy of friends, flames, and exes.

The moment I most dreaded came midway through the evening. I'd managed to stay busy with Abigail, who reminded me periodically to stay focused and keep my eye on the ball. Together, we avoided the central lounge area where Brody and Harriet were holding court. I helped organize the waitstaff in a nearby tent so I didn't have to help guests, many of whom were Brody's family members I'd met when we were together. If they remembered me, it would be awkward. But to be forgotten would, in a way, be worse.

When Brody and I had dated, his mother had taken me under her wing. She worked as a receptionist at their church, and Brody's dad was, naturally, a high school football coach. Even then, she always looked put together as if they had millions. Some people were born with style. Others were just Southern.

I'd often wished my own parents would take inspiration from the Stevenses. Feminine and poised, Mrs. Stevens had always wanted a daughter in addition to her two football-playing sons. Whenever she came to Fort Worth, we would grab lunch at La Madeleine and browse at Neiman's. All these years later I still found myself making mental notes of things to tell her. I missed her. I'd spent four years thinking she might be my mother-in-law, and the loss lingered like the memory of her Dior perfume. She chatted with Brody's cousins near the sashimi station, so I took an alternate route to check in with Mary Ellen.

I turned the corner around the catering tent and instead found myself face-to-face with the happy couple, who were walking from the fire pit to the dessert table. My heart caught in my throat.

"Lottie!" Not surprise but a twinge of another emotion flitted across Brody's face. His nose now crooked slightly to the left, broken and healed sometime in the last couple years. His dark hairline had started to recede, but he wore it longer than in college. His blue eyes were the same guileless pools. He grabbed me for a quick bear hug before I knew what was happening. I caught a whiff of his cologne, bittersweetly noting that he still wore the same one.

"Hi, Brody." I gave him my best attempt at a relaxed smile as we parted. Then I took a breath and turned to the bride. "Hi, Harriet, I'm Lottie Jones, one of the wedding planners on Cedric's team. It's nice to meet you."

She waited a beat, then looked at Brody for a moment. Her manicured hand took mine in a surprisingly solid grip. "Lottie, it's so great to finally meet you! Brody has told me such great things, and Tasha *raved* about working with you. It's a real treat to know we're in such good hands."

She had a Kentucky accent like barbecue and whiskey. I then understood they had prepped for the possibility of meeting me. It was no secret where I worked, and someone must have connected the dots. I felt sheepish that the people whose movements were covered on gossip blogs had a better sense of my potential whereabouts than I did theirs, but I assumed it was part of the celebrity machine.

A junior publicist in Los Angeles probably had a dossier on all of Brody's ex-girlfriends in the event somebody came out of the woodwork to ruin his reputation someday. I was simply one liability to be weighed and cataloged. If that was the case, Brody would've known I'd likely be here all along but wasn't allowed to reach out to me ahead of time. And I sure as heck hadn't reached out to him before this weekend, even if he hadn't changed his phone number. This was the only way for us to interact now—as a coordinator and a client.

"It's truly been my pleasure. I'm so happy for y'all," I said, desperate to slip away. "Please let me know if you guys need anything or have any questions during the weekend. We want everything to be perfect for you."

I'd gone into work-robot mode. I could pretend they were just any other clients. Clients who needed to have the most perfect wedding in the world so I could get my new promotion and new life and never again have to think about how I once loved the groom.

My escape came quickly, in the form of Teddy Ramone. Although young enough to be his daughter, Harriet had played his love interest two years ago because, well, Hollywood. I dashed away as the seersucker-clad actor clapped Brody on the back and kissed Harriet on the mouth.

Though the wedding was considered small, the guest list was stacked with A- to D-list celebrities. At least three famous country singers mingled with their platinum-blond, Instagram-famous wives. Like many country artists, they loved football players and spent their offstage time on some sideline cheering on their team. I occasionally questioned how much of that love was purely platonic.

Then there were all of Harriet's actor and actress friends who hadn't made it as big; they looked familiar, but I couldn't exactly place them. Like the girl who always played the quirky best friend? And like *that* kid from *that* show we used to watch about vampires. Remember him?

This wedding certainly had a wide range of characters, but they all seemed eager to be here—despite giving up their cell phones—to rub elbows with the other beautiful, influential people.

I saw Griffin a couple times, hovering near the fire pit where the light was most interesting. He'd captured the details of the décor before guests arrived and spent the rest of the night taking candids of partygoers. At one point we caught each other's eye, but he quickly turned away as I took a step toward him. Okay, fine. Let him be touchy.

Sometime that afternoon my emotions had gone from feeling sorry for him and the way I acted to feeling annoyed at him for the way he acted. We were just friends, after all. I was the one suffering over this awkward weekend and could have used moral support. Yes, compared to a divorce, my college breakup wasn't the end of the world. But I was allowed to have my feelings. He was being so dramatic.

I found Abigail again and thanked God for the hundredth time that she'd been reassigned to this wedding at the last minute. She'd had to endure Cedric's constant hovering over her floral team since this was such an important event to him, but she'd get a nice commission and had a luxe room to herself for the weekend.

"How's it going?" Abigail asked as she rearranged some wilting peonies on a table. "I take it you saw, um, the groom just now?"

"Yes, I saw Brody . . . And it was bearable." I mean, I did still want to gag at the thought of him marrying someone else, but it was more a knee-jerk reaction than anything based on who he was today. I briefly considered that I had no idea who he was today. "Still, I'll be so ready when this one is over."

"We just have to get through tomorrow and then the wedding Saturday. You got this."

"Yep, exactly. Organize a gorgeous ceremony and reception and then get the bride down the aisle to the groom without my trying to steal him back or throw up on anyone. Should be easypeasy."

Just then, Abigail got a call on the walkie and dashed off to help deal with one of the arrangements that had been knocked off a table by one of Harriet's aunts. It was the first event of many for the weekend, and the guests were already getting wild.

I stood there a moment, surveying the crowd. A deep knot festered in my gut about all this weekend would hold, but I tried to tamp the feeling down. I could treat this wedding like any other. I could forget that half of these people would have been at *my* wedding, in another lifetime. Well, I could try. The stakes were too high not to.

Just then, a hand waved at me from a gap in the curtains of the closest cabana. I peered over, and the hand gestured even more frantically.

"Lottie! Psst!" I heard as I walked across the sand. Sweet Lord, it was Harriet. I resisted the urge to turn on my heel, then kept walking toward my most important client.

I clenched my fists, bunching into my dress. I exhaled. "Are you okay?"

She had a frantic look on her face like a cornered animal. *You and me both, hon.*

"Have you seen Teddy Ramone lately?" she asked.

"Um, I think he was last surrounded by a throng of Brody's cousins, regaling them with tales of Hollywood and his 'bad boy' days. Why?"

"Good, let's hope he stays there!" She surprised me with her vehemence. "He's been coming up behind me all night, squeezing my butt when no one's looking, and saying, 'You're not married yet.' I think he's still pissed I never hooked up with him while we were filming."

"I'd imagine you'd be one of his only costars never to fall for his charms," I admitted.

"Probably, but he's too drunk to take a hint at this point. And the last thing I need tonight is Brody to go all caveman and punch Teddy in the face. He gets so territorial."

I had some vivid memories of at least two occasions when Brody's primal instincts took over on my behalf too. He definitely put his exceptional size to use when he felt his woman was threatened. "Ugh, I know," I said without thinking.

But Harriet paused a moment, gave me a funny look. "I guess I don't need to explain that to you . . ."

Thankfully she trailed off and didn't elaborate on what precisely she knew about our history. I'd prefer to never know.

"So how can I help?" I said quickly, trying to rescue us both from the awkwardness.

"Can you be my lookout? Just until the coast is clear and he heads for the bar. Then I promise to go back to mingling with everybody." She pulled me into the cabana so no one else could see me. We sat there on the cushions for a few minutes in surprisingly comfortable silence. Then she broke it. "Tell me about the wildest wedding you've ever worked. I imagine there have been some big ones."

If she only knew . . . I thought about the past year, remembering several of the barely averted mishaps like the snake and the boys choir or the evil model daughters who tried to bust up their now-stepmom's wedding to their father. But most of what came to mind were the happy moments like the brides who sobbed in my arms from gratitude before they jumped in their departure cars or the fathers who slapped me on the back and told me I was worth every penny the whole thing cost them. I had truly enjoyed setting couples up for happily ever after. I didn't say any of that to Harriet, of course, but instead regaled her with a couple of the more ridiculous details.

"I can't believe that bride let her groom jump out of a helicopter!" Harriet said with genuine delight, handsy actors forgotten for the moment. "That's just so *beyond* . . . To be honest, I never thought I'd have a big wedding at all."

I couldn't help myself. "Really, what did you envision?"

"I don't know, something small and quiet. Even before I became an actor, I imagined I'd get married at my grandparents' farm back in Kentucky. I always envisioned a small wedding on their land, with the rolling hills in the background. Mostly family and a couple friends."

Her description sounded an awful lot like the wild places I'd roamed growing up too. "Why aren't you getting married there Saturday?"

"Oh, you know . . . This"—she waved her hands at the beach and the resort behind us—"is what they expect of me." She sounded so defeated.

I didn't have the heart to tell her she'd played right into those expectations by marrying a hot NFL player.

"Even though we've kept it quiet, my publicist wants to make sure we release two photos on social media and sell a couple to one of the magazines, get ahead of the story of our relationship, and 'craft the narrative.'" She made air quotes with one hand. I'd never been more grateful to be a middle-class nobody from Memphis.

Before I could come up with something suitably encouraging, she continued. "Not that this isn't my dream wedding, of course! You guys have done a beautiful job on everything. And all the people I love are here—as well as a few others for strategic reasons." She laughed bitterly. "But the most important thing is marrying Brody. He's truly unlike anyone I've ever known. He's thoughtful and respectful, so unlike all the actors I've dated over the years. And he's the most generous person I've ever met. You know we met at a charity function, one where they provide mobility options for kids in wheelchairs? What kind of guy takes his only day off during the week to do something like that—when there's no photographers around to prove he did it?"

"Yeah, his cousin was paralyzed when they were in middle school," I said without thinking. "It's always been a passion of his."

"Wow, I didn't know that. But it makes so much sense . . . That day, I really noticed him because he spent so much time just plopped down, sitting on the floor, and talking to each of the kids for a really long time. It was so sweet, and he seemed genuinely interested, this hulking athlete hanging out and tossing the football with kids who don't usually get to do that kind of stuff."

I could tell she wanted to bond over this man that we both cared about. The truth was, I'd been apart from him nearly twice as long as I'd been with him. Sure, I knew all his ancient history—but Harriet held his future. "I'm just glad to see that he's in a position now to really make a difference for kids like his cousin," I said.

I risked another glance out the curtain. No sign of Ramone. I asked Harriet if she needed anything for the evening, and then we split off on companionable terms. As Harriet walked back toward Brody, I felt marginally better. The dreaded meeting with them was over. I had survived it. And, annoyingly, I didn't hate Harriet. In another world I might have even wanted to be her friend.

At the end of the party, I slunk over to the waiting double-length golf cart and manned my position. After my successful wedding at Sarah's chicken ranch and navigating the nightmare that was

Nashville, I'd assumed I'd be given a plum assignment this weekend. Instead, Mary Ellen got to assist/hang out with Harriet and her coterie of leggy, famous bridesmaids while I was assigned to groomsmen duty. My role was to ensure they all made it to major events on time, weren't injured in ways that would show up in photographs, and didn't do anything that would get them arrested and stuck in Mexican jail. Simple stuff. If you weren't dealing with thirty-year-old toddlers.

Matt and four groomsmen piled into the back of the golf cart, and we bumped along to the villa where they were all bunking together. He sat on the seat immediately behind me and leaned over my shoulder. I could smell the tequila on his breath. "Hiya, Lottie. You having fun yet? Y'all did such an amazing job with this party."

Before I could answer, he went on, waving his hand at the guys sitting behind him. "You remember Hank and Jordan, right? Say hi, guys!"

Great. Of course I remembered Brody's freshman roommate and his football team "big brother." I waved without looking back, grateful that the darkness and their lack of sobriety could hide my discomfort. I floored the gas pedal, desperate to drop this crew off at their bungalow for the night.

On Friday morning Abigail invited me on a trip to the beach. I figured if I wasn't in my room and Mary Ellen tried to reach me, I wasn't technically dodging her calls. It wasn't my fault that our phones had also been confiscated and the walkie talkie wasn't in range.

We lay on the warm sand and pretended for a moment that we were simply on vacation. And that a mob of rowdy Southerners and B-list movie stars weren't waiting for us in the resort. The waves occasionally sprayed my toes, and a slight breeze kept us from baking in the midmorning sun. For a moment I thought about the beach trips my family used to take every August to Destin, Florida. We'd book the Best Western or similar accommodations and go for a week. Tommy and I would run rampant on the beach; my parents would lounge under umbrellas reading books and sipping cocktails at 11:00 a.m. If I closed my eyes, the same heat poured from the sand into my feet and shoulder blades.

"How are you holding up?" Abigail asked without looking at me.

"Oof, I'm hanging in. Feel a little pathetic, frankly, to be this wrecked over something that happened a lifetime ago."

"College is the perfect intersection of freedom and possibility. Stuff that happens can still loom large, be a big deal, for a long time."

"Yeah, we've both moved on, dated other people, all that. But I dunno, seeing him with his freakishly perfect fiancée is just driving it all home again. What I thought was possible that came crashing down."

"I get it," replied Abigail. "I'm sure you also wonder if you'd both stayed single if there would've been a chance. Although Brody doesn't seem like the kind of guy you'd want to be with now anyway. I'm not sure any form of 'normal life' is possible for most NFL players."

"That kind of attention and pressure all the time would be a nightmare. Which might make Harriet a great fit. They can both play the fame game together," I added because I couldn't help myself.

"Ha! Not to jinx them or be cruel, but these kinds of marriages don't usually work out. I'm glad it's not you I'm helping get married tomorrow."

"Me too, Abigail. Me too." I was getting to be a good liar.

Friday night's event was a more formal affair. Mary Ellen ran point on this one while Cedric acted as the conductor to Abigail's team, which was still working on floral arrangements. And by conductor, I mean he literally hovered over everyone, waving his arms around, looking very stressed out but never picking up an actual instrument slash flower himself. Abigail likely stood behind him, shaking her head periodically to let the team know which instructions to disregard.

Griffin had always been scheduled to be off-site during the dinner, taking photographs of the extended property and then ensuring the camera crew's equipment would be completely prepared for the next day. Val notoriously stocked up on extra supplies, from lenses to battery packs, as a contingency plan. She made sure everything was charged and ready the night before—and then required a second set of supplies be kept at an alternate location, in this case her hotel in town, in the event of a natural disaster, power outage, or other act of God at the venue. In short, Griffin was babysitting a bunch of battery packs and likely watching Netflix all night.

I wanted to see him, but I also wasn't sure what I'd say other than to ask him for an apology or defend myself, neither of which were the most productive ways to patch things up. Plus, I needed to be focused. One night down, two to go.

Harriet and Brody were very specific that they didn't want a traditional rehearsal dinner. I didn't understand initially, but now it made perfect sense: the last thing Brody and Harriet needed were their drunk friends (or wannabe friends) trying to deliver toasts that could possibly contain embarrassing and image-damaging stories. No open mics or childhood photo video montage for these two. I found myself surprisingly grateful for this fact—and that Cedric always prohibited our alcohol consumption until after send-off. It certainly kept me from making a career and social life–ending mistake by making a toast myself to the man who once drop-kicked my dreams.

Without toasts, only the strum of an acoustic guitar and the sounds of conversation could be heard on the terrace of the resort's gorgeous old white stucco chapel. Guests and family members enjoyed cocktails and mingled while the bridal party rehearsed at the top of the chapel stairs.

The chapel itself was too small for the ceremony, but it provided a breathtaking backdrop for the couple, and the following day, rows of bamboo folding chairs would be added for the guests where they were currently dining.

Thankfully I was spared from watching Brody and Harriet run through their vows. Mary Ellen had swapped positions with me so I could monitor the cocktail party and start of dinner service.

We'd hired chefs to cook lobsters and fresh fish on an open flame, which proved to be a big hit with guests. Jalapeño margaritas and citrus sangria flowed, and after a successful and brief dinner, the happy couple headed to their respective suites for some beauty rest—not that they needed it—before the big day.

That didn't mean The Firm's work was anywhere near done. Every evening's party was followed by a trip to one of the resort's bars, the only part of the property that remained open past 11:00 p.m. As soon as our planned events concluded, most guests would pile into deluxe golf carts and speed over for more drinking and cavorting under the stars.

I drove Matt and a coterie of ushers and groomsmen over to the bar near the infinity pool where they'd heard there was a TV showing a Rangers baseball game. Matt, of course, settled into the seat of the golf cart next to me.

"Hi, Lottie, how's it going?"

"Same as last night," I said a little too fast.

"Hey, just because we're not going out anymore doesn't mean this has to be weird." He slung one arm behind my seat. "I'm here for you. I mean, you and Brody were together for a long time, even if that was ages ago."

Matt was being a little annoying, but I appreciated that he was sympathetic to my plight, even if he didn't get the real source of my unease. "Yes, it's weird. I mean, I'm over him, of course, but it's still not the most fun experience to see my ex getting married. Especially not to someone like Harriet."

"I could see that . . . She's great though, isn't she?"

Sure, if you like boring stuff like sweet, gorgeous, rich, and talented. Instead I spoke the truth. "Yes, she's pretty fantastic."

We pulled up at the bar. "Want to come grab a drink? I've missed you, and I know you've got work to do and a lot on your mind, but I'll do my best to distract you and cheer you up. And I won't keep you long." Matt looked so cute when he pleaded.

"Thank you, but I'm still on the clock." Plus, I already had my eye on the restocked minibar in my room, not that I'd admit it.

"Well, once we're back in Dallas, I'm comin' for ya. I don't give up so easily. And don't worry about us tonight." He nodded toward the other guys. "We'll find our way back to our rooms." With that he gave me a wink and jumped out of the cart.

After reminding slash threatening him and the other ushers and groomsmen that they needed to behave and get some sleep before tomorrow, I headed back to mission control to check in one last time before bed. I'd be lying if I didn't admit that I relished the attention from Matt. Too bad I couldn't commit to the thought of the two of us really getting serious.

And it wasn't Brody on my mind either as I drove my cart along the path surrounded by lush, tropical greenery with a blanket of stars overhead. It was Griffin I couldn't shake. I considered going out to search for him to see if he was still stuck at Val's. But I couldn't do it. Maybe a good night's sleep would give me the energy and courage I needed to smooth things out with him in the morning. I enjoyed his companionship way too much to muddle things up with my own drama.

TWENTY-FOUR

Brody's wedding day dawned. I woke up super early, unable to fall back asleep. Happily ever after had, in fact, led me to paradise, but not remotely the way I'd envisioned. I tossed back the dregs of my coffee, popped my neck, and got to it. No more delaying the inevitable.

I radioed Mary Ellen that I'd started my duties for the day, which included putting out all the paper goods for the ceremony and reception. Between the ceremony programs, escort cards, place cards, and menus, I'd be tied up for a while.

Soon Cedric called a meeting with the planners to check in for any last-minute changes and double-check our positions.

"Remember, *no* phones, cameras, or i-anything allowed today," Cedric barked. "Beware of sneaky guests trying to slip something past us."

The secrecy was beginning to seem a bit overboard in my opinion. I mean, did anyone really care? Not to mention, Harriet and Brody would need to get used to the spotlight together. I could only imagine what life would be like for them once married. They'd be living with cameras constantly in their faces. Not the kind of life I'd want. And truly, I meant it.

The interns helped with random tasks, oversaw the start of the ceremony, and made sure all guests found their seats in a timely manner. For this lavish event, a program was placed on the back of each chair and held in place by a beautiful white satin ribbon tied around it. A few weeks before, we took a seminar on how to tie the perfect bow. (Yes, it was an actual class, and yes, I now considered myself an expert.)

The ceremony consisted of vibrant pink, purple, and coral details that complemented the rustic wood and lush green vines climbing up the chapel. Abigail's team constructed an arbor made entirely of drooping orchids and palm fronds that framed the wooden doors perfectly. The aisle was lined with thousands of coral-colored rose petals and more orchids spilling over the end of every row of seats. It was a tropical dream.

In the middle of all the brilliant colors stood Griffin. He had been tasked with taking detail shots for this wedding, while Val worked as the primary photographer. However, I couldn't imagine him not getting a promotion after this wedding, as there was so much to shoot and so much riding on the images turning out well.

"Griffin!" I pretty much yelled from the bottom of the chapel stairs. "Where the heck have you been?"

"Working and hauling over the rest of the equipment. Where else would I be? Lying out on the beach?"

Crud. How did he know Abigail and I had slipped out?

"Are you spying on me?" I tested the waters.

"You wish. I'm trying to get candid pics of the guests, but I found you instead. Don't worry, though. I didn't take any of you so there's no proof of you slacking on the job."

"For once, could you give me a break in that department?" I kept trying. "I thought you, of all people, would appreciate that I took a moment for myself amid all this."

I didn't fully notice it, but as we were talking, I had walked up the chapel stairs, and now he and I were standing directly under the arch of orchids where Brody and Harriet would stand just hours later.

"So are you still mad at me?" I moved closer. "I wondered if you'd call the room phone last night while you were on duty . . ."

"I owe you an apology," he started. "But I wanted to tell you in person."

"Oh, no, I think I'm the one who needs to apologize."

We both stood there staring at each other for a beat under a canopy of flowers while the warm, salty air whipped around us. My heart started racing, and his gaze dropped to my lips. He stepped closer . . . as the sound of Mary Ellen's voice came blaring from my hip.

"Lottie!? Lottie, are you there? Is your radio on yet? Have you fallen in the ocean?" she screamed through my radio, which was indeed on—with the volume turned up all the way.

Griffin laughed out loud as I floundered to turn it down and put on my earpiece. The woman had consistently fantastic timing.

"Yes, yes, I'm here, Mary Ellen. What's up?"

"We need to get the wedding party lined up near the chapel. I'm heading that way. Can you meet me there?"

"Yes. I'm here now checking on the setup."

"Well, I guess we'd better get going," he said as I turned back to him, the moment broken. "This wedding could be huge for both our careers. And I'm not going anywhere. Well, I mean, I need to go shoot the details over at the reception site real quick—but, you know what I mean. See you later."

"Yeah," I said blushing. "Good luck tonight."

"You too, Lottie."

And with that he jogged down the stairs, only looking back once to flash me that single-dimpled grin.

As part of my groomsmen duties, I headed for the lavish suite where Brody and his party awaited the ceremony.

The gaggle of annoyingly handsome groomsmen were scattered around the common area of Brody's palatial suite. They all looked to be dressed and ready, except for their jackets, which were laid out on various pieces of furniture to keep from wrinkling. I was impressed (and shocked) at their ability to follow instructions. A few of the men ate off the sprawling buffet of snack foods displayed on the dining table, and the rest gathered around a card table playing poker. The ushers were already in position at the ceremony site for any early guest arrivals. Matt's absence made me feel less anxious about facing Brody again.

I took a breath and knocked on the door to the groom's room.

"Come in," he called. He stood by the window, gazing out at the ocean.

Brody looked nothing short of amazing. I didn't see him anymore as "my Brody"—my youthful college sweetheart was gone. He was older, for starters. Time had been good to him, though, and he appeared genuinely happy.

"Hey. You ready?"

"Yeah, I think so . . . except for this bow tie. I cannot get the dang thing straight."

"Here, let me. I happen to be a certified bow-tie tier." I stood in front of him, focusing on the cloth at his neck and holding my breath. *Stay relaxed.*

"Y'all have really done a great job this weekend," he said over my head. "I know it can't be easy. I mean it's probably a little weird, but you know, I'm glad you were one of the people who helped us with this wedding."

It was sweet, how much he was trying to reassure me. He'd

probably smelled my near panic attack on Friday and hoped to avoid a reprise.

I finished pulling the ends of the bow even and stepped back to admire my handiwork. "It *has* been a little weird, I'll admit, but I'm glad I was here too. Even if I used to think it'd be me at someplace like this with you."

"Yeah, me too . . ."

I adjusted one side. "You know, I used to imagine what our wedding would be like. Hypothetically, of course."

He blew out a breath. It smelled like spearmint gum, as ever.

"Lottie, I knew about the chapel date . . . back in college." He took my expression of shock and horror to go on, but gently. "You listed me as the groom. The coordinator called me during the spring semester when you stopped replying to her emails. It wasn't hard to figure out."

"Oh my gosh, I could just die right now."

"No, I don't mean to put you on the spot. I guess, a little. But it was a turning point for me."

"How so?" I was poised to jump out the open window and swim for it.

"I knew that if you'd really wanted to marry me, if you'd known in your heart that it was the right thing for us, you would have said something already. You wouldn't have let it get so close . . . and I knew that if I'd really wanted to, I would have already proposed to you. Instead I was surprised by some secret contingency plan you'd put in motion."

"Again, please kill me now. There is a cheese knife over there that would do the trick."

He laughed. It was either a laugh or cry situation. "Seriously, I think we both knew we were meant for different lives. Not one better than the other, just different. Separate."

I stilled, paused my adjustments, absorbing. "If I can get over being horrifically, completely mortified, I might agree. But why didn't you say anything?"

"The whole thing woke me up, made me realize we needed to break up. Telling you I also knew about the chapel felt like adding insult to injury."

"How kind."

"Come on, I was what you thought you wanted. I don't think I was *actually* what you wanted. You were too ambitious to follow me around the country and just wait for me to come home from practice every day. There's nothing wrong with that for some players' wives, but seeing you here, managing the chaos, bossing people around, keeping up with more details than an NFL playbook, making it all look beautiful . . . This seems like where you were meant to be."

I soaked it in. What felt like devastating rejection had perhaps, in some way, freed me to find myself again, separate from my fears about the future and the manic desire for a storybook ending. I made a mental note to unpack that one later.

"Wow, Brody. Thanks—I think." I stifled a laugh. "I'm beyond humiliated that you know all those details, but you're also right. About all of it. Sadly, it's taken a while for me to figure out what I really want for myself, but I'm beginning to. And following you around after college wouldn't have been it. Looks like we both ended up in the right places."

I continued, handing him his jacket to put on. "And who would've thought that me acting like a psycho and booking the chapel for us would be my first real act as a wedding planner? Guess we got to plan a wedding together after all."

We laughed softly and then stood there, looking at each other. I smiled and blinked rapidly, willing my eyes not to water.

"I *am* sorry for how it all ended," he said.

"I understand. And I'm sorry for many things as well. But our past is, well, the past. We can both be grateful for that and move forward, look to the future . . ." My eyes met his again, and I cleared my throat. "But enough with this trip down memory lane. Time to get you ready to tie the knot for real. Do you have the rings?"

"Yeah. Here they are." He handed me the two small boxes.

"Okay." I glanced at my watch and walked back through the open door. Then I channeled Cedric. "We have to head down to the chapel," I said to the men. "Everybody ready and in a condition to stand upright for the next thirty minutes?"

Brody and the groomsmen obediently followed me down the steps and over to the chapel. Mary Ellen and I were assigned to processional duty. While I lined up the family members and the wedding party, she stayed back just out of sight with Harriet and her dad.

I gazed at Brody, so handsome in his tux, and wanted to be mad at him. But I was only mad at my younger self, at who I passively became in my quest to marry him, at what I set aside that no one ever asked me to abandon, and at how long it had taken me to find myself again.

As I lined up Brody's parents and grandparents, I was happy that they were happy. I'd once considered them family. Everyone had a nice golden tan after two days in Mexico, and the tropical breeze made the whole thing feel like a fairy tale. It wasn't *my* fairy tale, but in that moment I was authentically glad to be a part of it.

Brody ambled over to me, awaiting orders of where to stand.

"You look great," I replied cheerily, as I straightened his white orchid boutonniere. It still felt odd to touch his jacket like he was any other groom.

"You look good too. I meant what I said. It's been cool to see you rock this planning thing."

"Thank you. And I'm thrilled you found Harriet. Of course, I don't know her well, but if she's anything like what she seems, you're really lucky."

"Thanks, Lottie. That means a lot. I can't believe all this is happening, especially not so fast."

"Me neither, Brody. Me neither. But not only is it happening, it's happening *right now*. Time to take the walk." I ushered him to his spot in front of the best man.

With that, the prelude music concluded, and the string quartet began the first song of the formal processional.

Closure. How ridiculous was it that I felt utter and complete closure from the man I'd thought I would marry in the same moment I sent him down the aisle to wed another woman? The timing was laughable.

The maid of honor was halfway down the aisle when Mary Ellen, Harriet, and her dad came around from behind the bushes near the front of the aisle. Harriet was glowing and looked like every man's dream. She was perfect in her custom Vera Wang gown and tulle veil, and I stood across from Mary Ellen to fluff the train and send Harriet on the most important walk of her life. As she started to make her way down the aisle, I turned and headed to the reception without looking back.

I never wanted to look back toward Brody again.

<hr />

Mary Ellen radioed that the ceremony went off without a hitch and that the guests were on their way to cocktail hour. She stayed with the wedding party and family members for postceremony pictures, while the rest of us braced for guest arrivals by the pool.

Dinner took place on the deck overlooking the main infinity pool that disappeared into the Pacific Ocean. The sun had nearly set, and the lights from the sky and candles twinkled on the water. The entire scene was impossibly beautiful, beyond anything Cedric himself could have created.

All seventy-five guests were seated at one very long table that was covered in cream linens with thousands of soft pink and green flowers and candles running the entire length. I mentally applauded Abigail for making the blooms to appear so fresh despite the day's heat. That woman was a genius in her own right too. There was hardly room for the custom china or cut-crystal stemware, but as the sun reflected off the candles and glass, the whole table sparkled. The temperature had dropped since the start of the ceremony, so on each female guest's chair rested an ivory cashmere wrap that was custom monogrammed with her initials. Every detail was perfect.

The menu cards were hand-calligraphed with each guest's name in gold ink, and I made sure that the interns were helping everyone find their seats. (As an intern you get really good at holding grandmothers' elbows and directing drunken uncles without getting within arm's reach.)

As the last guest sat down, I could see Griffin finishing up shots of the beautiful table décor. He paused and lowered the camera, which covered the bottom half of his face. Our eyes met over the lens. He winked and mouthed something I couldn't make out. I arched a brow, puzzled.

He tried again: "Sorry, talk to you after?" I nodded and smiled in confirmation.

Griffin turned to head toward the ballroom, where guests would go following dinner. He didn't want to miss a thing, especially the hundreds of orchid garlands suspended over the dance floor that created a fantastic purple canopy of flowers. Val popped up here and there, snapping candid photos of guests mingling and looking festive.

Guests cheered for the newly married couple as they arrived at dinner, and wine flowed as everyone enjoyed steak, scallops, oysters, caviar, and other decadent courses. I snagged a bite of caviar on a piece of toast from where the caterer was plating everything, just to make sure it was as delicious as it looked. Spoiler: it was not. Give me barbecue over fish eggs any and every day of the week.

I stood to one side of the pool deck, letting the salty breeze cool my face. My insides felt jittery, like too much adrenaline was coursing through my body and was now slowly releasing. I'd been so tightly wound about today, it would take a while to come down. My mind wandered as guests ate their $300 meals. To Griffin, to Atlanta, to the Chloé handbag I hoped to purchase with this commission. I wouldn't get too far ahead of myself. But the future seemed bright.

Once dinner concluded, Mary Ellen took Brody and Harriet to change and have a moment alone before everyone relocated for cake and dancing. A mariachi band started up as soon as the newlyweds left dinner, and Abigail, the interns, and I gathered the guests to follow the band to the ballroom.

Most celebrity weddings include a celebrity performance at the reception. However, Brody and Harriet just wanted a fun party band that everyone could dance to. They'd already seen or had access to every famous musician out there, so a very good but traditional eighteen-piece group from LA was flown in to play the reception. Known for reading crowds well and getting everyone to the dance floor, they also had been coached to roll with it if any of the various country stars got tipsy and wanted to sing a song or two.

They were already playing onstage when the first guest stepped inside the large ballroom with glass windows overlooking the ocean.

The stars twinkled across the entire wall of windows. After a few minutes Mary Ellen ushered in the happy couple, and the bandleader welcomed them in as husband and wife.

Griffin knelt in front of them, slightly off to the side. No more hiding behind screens for him. As ever, his jeans pulled tight in all the right places while he moved. Broad shoulders hunched in position. His long hands moved, adjusting angles and capturing frames. His dark hair ruffled in the slight breeze as he worked. Not a bad view.

Harriet had changed into a short Monique Lhuillier lace dress with vintage Gucci heels. Brody stayed in his khaki suit but had taken off his jacket and rolled up his sleeves, exposing his perfectly tanned and muscular forearms. They really did look like the perfect couple, as their fans would most certainly call them. I found myself so swept up in pondering what their Brangelina name would be that I missed the official announcement of Mr. and Mrs. Brody Stevens. Barriet? Harridy? Brodiet? Could we include *Dirty* somehow? I was cracking myself up at the possibilities, all equally tragic.

I watched them dance. She'd picked "Bless the Broken Road," a fitting if clichéd song. I might've still low-key hated her for her perfection, and he had once end zone spiked my heart. But I could objectively say this week had brought me satisfaction. I enjoyed weddings. I was good at them. Even if I never got my own first dance song, that was something, at least.

The night was an out-of-body experience. Everything went according to script and was like a stream of tiny good-byes: cake cutting, first dances, toasts, bouquet toss, dance party, like everything and nothing I'd imagined. I had never realized how tightly I still held to that crushed dream, that shattered vision of my life, until it was slowly pried from my grip one finger at a time. Six months ago I would've sworn that I'd be hiding in a corner, standing in a puddle of my own tears. But I wasn't. I was helping Harriet with her lipstick and pulling up the chair for the garter toss, as I did for every other client.

Later, Mary Ellen sent the newlyweds off in their black car to the resort down the street, Las Ventanas. I didn't think it was possible for a spot in Mexico to be more luxurious than our current location, but yet again I was wrong. The über-chic Las Ventanas boasted the highest quality of everything, from the service to the sheets. It was also very secluded and private, to the extent that guests rarely saw other guests on the property unless they dined in one of the restaurants. Harriet and Brody planned to spend a week in their suite, relaxing in private away from the lenses of the paparazzi until it was time for them to return to reality and face the press—literally.

As the guests' departure sparklers burned out and the newlyweds' car disappeared into the darkness, the night had finally come to a conclusion. We were rather proud of ourselves as planners for pulling off such an elegant affair in Mexico's heat—and keeping it all top secret. Cedric, who got to keep his phone "to keep up with Twitter," frequently updated us that so far we had succeeded in fending off the paparazzi or any social media leaks.

Thank goodness. I was physically and emotionally exhausted and ready to return to Dallas. However, the guests were all still having a riotous time. The reception didn't end until nearly midnight, and the usual post-hangout bar was closed. Now, it's not like the guests were deprived of any alcohol at the wedding. In fact they were all pretty near smashed by the end of the night, and I had to drive several off to their rooms via golf cart, while keeping a firm hand on them so they wouldn't spill out onto the pavement.

After an especially quick drop-off, I steered the golf cart back toward the ballroom to pick up more guests. For those wanting fresh air, a lounge area with chairs and cozy benches had been set up around a fire pit just outside. A few partygoers lit sparklers from the flames and waved them around, drinks in one hand, glittering lights in the other. They had the haphazard look of the happily exhausted and slightly buzzed. Naturally, Griffin was capturing the moment. I parked the cart and moseyed over.

He took a couple more shots before acknowledging me, but Griffin turned my way with a tired grin. "Sorry we got interrupted earlier. Today's been madness. But looks like your team pulled it off. How are you holding up?"

"Better than expected. I feel like this might have been the best thing that could've happened to me—being here and all."

"Really?"

"Yeah. I'm sorry for earlier. I didn't want to get back together with Brody or anything, but I'm not sure I felt the closure you need to really allow yourself to move on. We hadn't spoken in years, but my heart was so torn up after our breakup, I don't know that I ever really let go of my vision of the life we could have had together. Making this wedding happen, actively choosing to face it, might have been the final piece I needed."

"I'm glad to hear that and glad it's all over, Lottie."

No one looked quite ready to leave the party, so I grabbed a seat on one of the benches. Griffin plopped down next to me, camera on the bench at his side. "I wanted to apologize too."

"It's okay, you were right. I needed to hear it."

His shoulder pressed on mine in the warm night. We stared at the fire.

"Maybe, but that wasn't the only reason why I got upset. I had no right to be jealous of Brody, but I was. You caught me off guard, and I handled it like a jerk. You know about my history, but we haven't really talked much about *your* exes. Forgive me for not being sensitive to how you felt. Though I for one am grateful you guys never did get married. And not just because walking back that kind of bad decision absolutely sucks."

I opened my mouth but closed it as he turned to face me. The sharp panes of his profile almost shone in the dim light. He took a breath.

"Because, well, what matters is now. How we both feel now. I know I've told you a lot of stuff about marriage and how I'll never do it again. I've pushed you away over and over again. I'm not saying that I want to marry you, please don't freak out," he said in a rush. "But you've made me realize that it might not be terrible if you're with the right person."

"Oh wow, Griff . . ." I was caught off guard, didn't know what else to say.

"I really like you . . . and as more than just a friend, obviously."

I had spent months telling myself that we were just buddies, tamping down any hopes about a future and crushing embers of attraction. But at his words they blazed back.

I gathered my courage. "You don't know how much I've wanted to hear that. I feel like I've been alternating between throwing in the towel on our friendship and arguing with you over why you should be willing to take a risk on me. Because I, well . . . I like you too."

We sat there, grinning stupidly at each other. Unsure what to do or say next, he solved it by pulling me into his arms.

"We can talk more about all this when we're back in Dallas, you can bet on it," he said into my hair. Which probably smelled of campfire, though I no longer cared.

We pulled apart, then sat in comfortable silence as the festivities wound down. Eventually, he slipped his arm around me again. I felt about fourteen years old, but in the best way possible.

"You know, Val pulled me aside earlier," he said softly.

"Oh really? Did she want to talk about what a great job you've been doing?"

"Sort of. Seems like she's booked a big *National Geographic* shoot and is thinking about getting back into nature photography."

"Really?"

"Yeah, I guess she's been trying to get back into it . . . But since she's not quite as agile as she used to be, she asked me to consider going as her assistant photographer."

This was big news. "Congratulations! Where is the shoot?"

"Well, that's the thing. It's in Alaska, starting in August and going through the fall."

"Still, that's amazing. Truly."

"But I meant every word I said, Lottie." His voice rose. "I really like you and would love for us to give this a shot. This Alaska thing won't last long, or it may fall through altogether."

"Don't say that." I squeezed his hand, which was currently resting on mine. "This sounds like an incredible opportunity for you. You should take it. I'll probably be right where you left me when you get back."

"You'd better be," he said, with a look in his eyes that sent chills up my spine.

I rolled my eyes at him and bit my lower lip. Then I reluctantly stood and straightened the hem of my dress. The group next to us had gotten louder once their sparklers burned out, and it was time to get them to their rooms while they were still somewhat coherent.

"Looks like my babysitting duties are almost over." I glanced toward the golf cart. "See you in the morning?"

"You mean *later* this morning?" He laughed.

"Ugh, don't remind me. I think I'm delusional now, I'm so tired from this whole weekend."

"Well, be safe, Lottie. And get some well-deserved rest."

"You too, Griff."

Finally, after a few more golf-cart trips, I slunk back to my room. The minibar would be restocked by now, and I was officially off the clock until brunch later that day. I'd earned myself a glass of tequila, hopefully a promotion, and some much-needed sleep. I was wired.

After a drink, I rang Griffin's room—still no cell phones—but he didn't answer. I wanted to talk to him more, but I had a feeling he was stuck downloading images to a hard drive or packing up equipment, so I left him a voice mail. Maybe the flashing light would beckon him to me.

I was greeting my second itsy-bitsy bottle of Jose Cuervo when I heard a commotion outside by the garden pool. Sipping my glass, I peered out the window. About a dozen groomsmen and male wedding guests were smoking cigars and drinking on the deck below. I spotted Harriet's father among them. I'm sure he was glad the whole "circus" was over and he could head back to small-town Kentucky until he and Harriet's mother were summoned again for a movie premiere or awards show. (She always thanked her parents for everything, which was awfully nice and awfully Southern of her.)

My room suddenly felt stuffy. I opened up the window and stepped onto the Juliet balcony. The name had always struck me as funny. I understood that Juliet stood at her window, talking to the moon and to a boy she could never have, but I was positive that villas in Verona must have had better balconies than this tiny railing and mere inches of standing room.

Something about weddings made a normal man who had been assigned the position of groomsman behave like he had one night left to live. Maybe it was the unlimited booze available at all hours. Maybe it was the single, desperate female guests available who made them lose their minds. Or maybe it was the personal desperation the bachelors felt realizing their buddies were leaving them behind. Whatever the reason, I'd already seen too many groomsmen behave like wild animals.

In hindsight I should have seen this coming. Los Cabos was basically the Vegas of Mexico. Wherever there was stifling heat, open bars with tequila, and wedding guests, someone was bound to get taken to jail, impregnated, or worse. The groomsmen at this wedding were from various Southern cities (or sports teams) and were surprisingly well behaved—contrary to the reputations that had preceded them. A few were overtly flirtatious, but I'd have been lying to say I didn't enjoy their sparkling smiles and Southern accents at least a little.

The ocean breeze tousled my hair as I watched from the shadows. Matt was among the guys passing around a flask. After about ten minutes, I slipped back inside to get ready for bed before I passed out in all my makeup. I wouldn't even be able to blame the tequila. The sheer exhaustion from the past three days was crashing over me like the waves down below.

I'd barely slipped under the covers when I heard a thump against my window. When it became too persistent to ignore, I threw my hair into a ponytail, grabbed the first T-shirt I could find, and drew back my curtains. I was already groggy, but I could make out a flock of groomsmen standing below my second-story balcony, beckoning me to "come out and play."

Flattering as it was, I was in no mood for shenanigans. I only wanted sleep. I stepped back onto the balcony to let the six of them—Matt and the father-of-the-bride included—know I would not be joining. I'm not sure which of my deranged Romeos surprised me more, and clearly the FOB was hammered because he was cackling right along with them. Gross.

As I was trying to convince them that I surely was not coming down and asking that they kindly refrain from throwing any more tequila-covered ice cubes at my window, Matt started to scale the side of the building. I watched in a kind of half-asleep awe as he climbed up the trellis on the side of my villa.

He hoisted himself over the railing, and, worried that he would tumble to his drunken death, I pulled him inside. I could feel his pulse racing in time with my own at the rush of risk. He could have fallen. He shouldn't be in my room. I was exhausted and *so* over tonight.

He whisked himself past me into the room and promptly collapsed on the sheets I'd been in just moments before. After a moment's hesitation, I decided I didn't have any fight left in me. With no better idea, I climbed in next to him and passed out myself.

TWENTY-FIVE

I was underwater, and one of the fish from *The Little Mermaid* was playing the drums. Sebastian sang, but I couldn't understand what he said. In the way that dreams blended into reality and day slowly dawned, I pulled the pillow from my head. The knocking persisted.

Matt lay sprawled next to me, shirtless. I glanced quickly under the covers, pleased to see he was at least still wearing his tux pants. I remembered nothing happened, but it never hurt to double-check.

Half awake, I cracked open the door, wearing only my T-shirt, and was chagrined to see Griffin standing outside. Crap.

"Hey," he said.

"Hey."

"I brought you coffee from downstairs." He handed it to me.

"Gosh, you're so sweet. What time is it?" I stood awkwardly in the doorway, blocking the room with my body.

"It's still early, I just—wait, what the hell, Lottie?"

I turned and saw Matt's shirtless torso disappear into the bathroom. "Oh, him? Griff, I can explain. It's hilarious, actually."

"You mean you got lost driving him home last night?"

"It was a stupid dare. He was drunk and climbed in through my window. Nothing happened, I swear!" It looked bad. *So* bad.

"Doesn't look like nothing. I thought after last night you and I were on the same page."

"We were, we *are*," I said urgently. "This is all a misunderstanding. I dated him awhile back, but he just climbed in and slept here, nothing happe—"

"Wait, you dated a guy who's been here this whole time? At your ex's wedding? You've got quite the love triangle going on here, huh?"

"Hey, that's not fair."

"No, this . . . this isn't fair." He motioned toward the inside of my room. He turned, threw his coffee cup in a trash can outside my door, and stomped down the hall.

But before I could bemoan the loss of a good latte, put on some shorts, and chase after him, Cedric thundered around the corner. He brandished his iPhone in my face. "What. The. Hell. Happened?" I grabbed his hand and took a closer look at his phone.

On his screen Harriet and Brody held hands on a cliff, the very spot Mary Ellen and I had staked out for their postnuptial portraits. Even if the picture was taken with a telephoto lens, it was very clearly them. And the angle of the shot was too close and too good to have been taken inside a helicopter or a boat. Someone had been on the property to snag this pic.

Above the image the headline blared: *Exclusive Images! Dirty Harry's Secret Romance—and Wedding!* The subhead went on to describe her hush-hush wedding to sexy NFL star Brody Stevens. The callout speculated that she might be pregnant. My eyes glazed over. How *did* this happen?

"I'm waiting for an answer." Cedric's voice had gone icy. I wasn't sure why he had assumed it was my fault, but I was too shocked with everything happening to really analyze at the moment.

"I don't know, sir." I wracked my foggy brain.

"Well, you were one of the only people with the property locations and schedule. I trusted you. I expect you to find out how this happened—or I'll assume you were the one responsible."

At that he turned on his heel and strode back down the hall. For the moment I couldn't do any damage control on the photos. But I could kick out the crasher who'd slunk back in my bed.

"You, *out*." I yanked the covers back, averting my eyes at the last second out of courtesy, though I wasn't sure what kind of courtesy should be extended to someone whose shenanigans were wrecking my day.

"C'mon, Lottie, come back to bed." Matt pulled a pillow over his head with one hand and blindly felt around for me with the other.

"Not a chance, buddy." I sat on the edge of the bedspread, careful to stay out of his reach, furiously pondering scenarios. Any number of people, from our team to the resort staff, could have tipped off the press as to who was getting married. It could have just been a lucky break that they managed to snag a shot of the couple getting their portraits done. But that still meant they needed property access, if not awareness of the exact location.

And the photos I'd quickly seen on Cedric's phone were too good quality, too well angled, to have been taken from a drone or as the result of a happy accident. No one stumbled upon the perfect spot to capture Harriet kissing her groom in the setting sun.

That meant someone must have helped the photographer. But who? Griffin wasn't capable of doing something so underhanded. I wondered if Mary Ellen was, but she didn't seem likely to throw

Cedric and The Firm under the bus. Wedding planning was her entire life. I doubted she'd risk that. And her salary was too good to be tempted by whatever paltry payment a photo agency offered for tips.

Abigail hadn't gone scouting with us, but she could have easily guessed a couple prime photo spots. But I hated to imagine my mentor as selling out the company. There also didn't seem to be much of an upside to it for her. I mentally scrolled through the other team members who'd come with us, discarding each as a potential suspect.

Instead of continuing the uncomfortable process of blaming my coworkers, I decided to apply my deep love of Olivia Benson to a good cause. I'd play detective.

"Um, guess I'll see you later, Lottie?" Matt stood awkwardly in front of me, his rumpled shirt finally back on. I'd completely forgotten he was still in the room.

"Yeah, see you at the brunch, Matt."

"I'm really sorry if I did something to get you in trouble with whoever was yelling at the door. That your boss? I really don't know what happened last night, but I do know all I did was sleep. More like, I blacked out next to you."

Thank goodness. "It's okay, it's not really your fault." I blamed myself. And the minibar.

"I shouldn't have climbed up in here, I know that."

"That is correct, Matthew."

"But I meant what I said the other day. I like you, Lottie. We'd be good together. I know standing here in my rumpled suit and morning booze breath isn't really selling that, but just know my door is open. I'd love to see you around."

"Thanks, Matt. Truly. Last night aside, you've been wonderful, and you need someone who is ready to build an amazing life with you. I'm just not sure anymore if that's me . . . But I really need to do some work now, so if I can call you later, that'd be great." I basically shoved him out of my room. "I'll see you soon."

With that I closed the door behind him and returned to my sleuthing. I brewed a cup of coffee in the in-room Nespresso machine and flipped open my laptop.

The photos had been exclusively published in *In Touch*, and the photography agency was credited in the image caption. That seemed like a good place to start.

A few more minutes of online digging and I had the photographer's name: Gerald McManus. I doubted ol' Gerry was answering calls or emails in Mexico, so I might have to wait until we were back in Dallas to track him down.

Meanwhile, #dirtyharrywedding and #dirtyharrytouchdown had started trending on Twitter, and the photos had gotten picked up everywhere. We were pretty screwed.

I glanced at the clock. I had to do something about my humidity bedhead before brunch. More detective work would have to wait. And I figured that Cedric would at least let me finish this wedding before firing me. Fingers crossed.

The brunch on a private terrace was the kind of low-key affair one would imagine with half the guests hung over (tequila rarely settled well) and with the bride's family threatening to sue. Pretty typical stuff. I spotted Harriet's manager in a corner near the table of huevos rancheros and bourbon-drizzled French toast, wagging her finger in Cedric's face.

"I assure you, madam, no one from my team would have done something as shady, as uncouth, as selling your client's photos." He dodged a manicured finger. "I would personally vouch for all of them. But we will get to the bottom of this. I understand your anger. This was not supposed to happen."

As she began to launch into a screed about how bad these rumors would be for Harriet's career, he cut her off.

"Actually, ma'am, when I planned Ellen Dove's wedding last year—you remember she married that major record producer?—they'd kept it a secret. We didn't release her photos either, but the groom had a sister who secretly streamed the ceremony on Facebook Live 'for her grandparents.' Of course, it was found and copied everywhere. That turned out to be a brilliant PR move because before long, actresses were lying and claiming they'd attended for months afterward. No one wanted to admit not only that they didn't get invited but also that they didn't even know she had a boyfriend. She was invited to the Met Gala that year and her per-film fee went up 30 percent. Everybody wants to be friends with the secretive, cool girl. This could be the best thing that happened to Harriet since her Golden Globe win."

It was a low blow to mention the Globes since Harriet was snubbed by the Oscars that year, but Cedric's point nonetheless hit home. Her manager was mollified for the moment.

I assumed that Cedric was just blowing smoke to appease the clients and that he'd still be furious with me, so I tried to be helpful and unobtrusive during brunch. As I was instructing the caterers to clear the last of the serving ware, Griffin came up to me. I braced for whatever he was going to say.

"Well, looks like the surprises keep getting better today. I'll be sticking around Dallas indefinitely, it seems."

"Wait, why?"

"Because I got *fired* over those pictures, Lottie."

"That doesn't make any sense. You wouldn't do something like that. You didn't, right?"

"Cedric and Val needed a scapegoat, and I took the actual portraits.

Val says that even if I didn't sell them out to the paps, I should have picked a less obvious or accessible spot."

"Does she not know Mary Ellen and I technically picked the spot—or that it was hidden by trees and on the literal edge of a cliff?"

"Nope, and I don't think she really cares. They just need deniability."

I wilted at this news. "I'm so sorry, Griffin. Sorry about your job, and for this morning, and not telling you about Matt before you found him in my room. Where, again, *nothing* happened."

"Lott—" Griffin tried to say, but I interrupted.

"I'd never want you to get fired, and I refuse to lose my job over this whole mess either. We need to find out who leaked the information and make all of this right."

I explained to him that I'd found the photographer's name responsible for taking the images for *In Touch*. We hatched a plan to try to comb through his social media and see if we could track him down before everyone left Mexico. An interrogation was in order.

As we prepared to head back to our respective suites and pack, neither Griffin nor I knew what to do about "us"—if there was even such a thing at this moment. We didn't get into more details about Matt's presence in my room, and I knew this wasn't the time to clear up our personal stuff. Cedric had just dropped a bomb, and the mess had to be sorted out before we could sort out our feelings for each other.

We awkwardly hugged. "See you around."

"Bye, Griffin."

Once everyone's cell phones were returned from confiscation, I spent a few hours trying to track down any information I could. It was hard to focus, though, with all the wedding-day items I needed to gather and ship back to Brody and Harriet's new house in the Hollywood Hills.

Griffin apparently struck out, too, since he was swamped packing up Val's photography equipment and saving all their images to backup hard drives before he headed back to Dallas.

The odds weren't looking to be in our favor.

And with that, one of the most eventful weekends of my life came to a pitiful end.

TWENTY-SIX

At the desk next to me, Claire was talking loudly on her AirPods about a fund-raiser for the Daughters of the American Revolution. She'd apologized twice about the volume, but everything grated on my nerves. I rubbed my eyes and resisted the urge to bang my head on the desk.

Two weeks had passed since Los Cabos, and I was still trying to track down Gerald McManus. Did he live in Mexico under an alias? He was a social media phantom. Fortunately, redeeming my career prospects was at least a distraction from my nonexistent love life.

The wedding scheduled after Harriet and Brody's wasn't mine, but I often got roped in as an extra set of hands. Not this time. That weekend, Cedric had let me sit and stew. He'd asked me every day for a week if I had any leads on the leak. Short of water torture, I wasn't sure how I'd get a mole inside The Firm to crack. And Anonymous wasn't about to pull off a hack for a Dallas wedding planner. After that first week, Cedric stopped speaking to me entirely.

I'd gone from all-star recruit to benchwarmer in a flash.

One afternoon Abigail came by my desk. "How you hanging in there, hon?"

"Oh, you know. Grateful not to be unemployed yet. But I'm totally baffled at what happened in Mexico. The usual. You?"

"I know all this sucks. But I'm sure this will blow over. Remember the swan boat? Cedric's memory is pretty short about these things."

"Maybe, but it does seem like I've at least missed my chance to be a part of the new Atlanta team."

"Even if that's the case," she patted my hand, "there will be other jobs and other promotions. I promise. You'll see."

And with that she sashayed to get her afternoon cup of coffee, leaving me feeling at least slightly better.

Until my phone pinged. It was Griffin.

> Call me. I may have a lead.

We hadn't spoken much since Mexico except for a few texts here and there, all about trying to uncover the leak. I didn't want to take the call anywhere at work, deeming the women's restroom or glass conference rooms unsafe. The moment I left and climbed behind the wheel of my car, I dialed him.

"What's going on?" I skipped the small talk.

"I found McManus. He's based out of Los Angeles, so I can't sneak attack him at home. But I think I tracked down a way to reach him."

McManus always covered the same summer film and music festivals, so one of Griffin's photographer buddies had agreed to try and chat him up at BottleRock in Napa. It was a long shot but currently the only shot we had. We strategized a little more before the conversation stalled.

"Well, I'll let you get back to work," he said. "I've got to update my portfolio site to send out for some applications."

I couldn't really read his tone, and I was still upset that he hadn't brought up our conversation from Mexico, even though I knew I could've done so too. It just never felt like the right time. And trying to fix our professional lives seemed more urgent—and controllable—than our personal. Deep down, I was still pretty upset he hadn't believed me about Matt. He gave up on me too easily.

"Okay, good luck," I said. "Keep me posted on what you hear."

"Will do. Bye."

With that he was gone. I sat staring at my blank screen and empty calendar, pretending to have work to do through the end of the day.

That night, Natalia and I went out to Mia's for Tex-Mex. Over frozen margaritas and chips, I filled her in on the latest.

"And I'm just so frustrated," I said. "I've busted my tail this year to get Cedric and Abigail and even Mary Ellen to notice my work. No matter who got the Atlanta spot, you know, my promotion seemed inevitable once the teams shifted around. Now that's in the toilet."

"I'm so sorry," Natalia said. "I'm sure it will get better soon, though!"

"Not sure how, but thanks . . . And on top of everything, the whole Griffin saga is still such a mess."

"Just rough, hon, just rough." She motioned to the waitress for more chips like a true friend.

"In Mexico I had a bit of a revelation at least," I continued.

"Oh, *that's* what they call it when a drunken man climbs into your bed?"

"Har har. No, seriously."

Natalia just looked at me and arched her eyebrows knowingly. "Have you thought some more about what Brody said?"

"I've tried to think about the painful awkwardness of that conversation as little as possible, thank you very much. But, yes, that's what I mean." I took a sip of my drink. "It was freeing to let Brody go, to say good-bye once and for all to that version of my life. But I realized I hadn't figured out why I became that person in the first place."

"Yeah, we know no rational person books the chapel and plans a wedding without a proposal."

"Thanks for telling me that at the time, by the way—oh, wait. So, when I think about college, it's like I lost myself. All along I let my path be dictated by others' expectations. My parents wanted me to be a lawyer. I wanted to marry my college sweetheart because it was like, gosh, an identity I could step into. I held on to Brody because I didn't know who or what else life had for me. But was it what I truly wanted? And I fell into wedding planning because it was the only thing I'd put any legit effort into."

"You did have some really great Pinterest boards."

"Thank you. I'll forever owe you for helping me translate those into something useful."

She gave me a double thumbs-up, the goofball.

"Maybe it was insecurity or, I don't know, social pressure. Or just not knowing myself yet. Whatever the reason, I planned an entire wedding to a person who hadn't proposed. Looking back, maybe I just enjoyed the process. The planning. The imagining. The details."

"Exactly," she said. "You're great at it. So like, what it is you want? Because you can make it happen. Who cares if Cedric never assigns you to another wedding? We're millennials. We're supposed to keep changing jobs and careers, right? So you pivot. On all fronts."

She was right. I may have blown it with Griffin, but I still believed I'd get there someday, with someone. And if I never did, I'd found something I loved to do. I got to make people blissfully happy for at least one day—the rest was up to them. "You know, I hear there has been a lot of upheaval at *The Talk*. Have you ever thought about making a pivot yourself?"

"Oh, absolutely," she quipped. "But the suburban moms of the Midwest just aren't ready for what I've got to bring them. Plus, I need to start Botoxing before I'm camera ready."

We cracked up and ordered another round of margaritas.

TWENTY-SEVEN

The next day I sat at my desk, downing Excedrin Migraine and cursing the tequila gods. Still, I felt more clearheaded than ever. I picked up the phone and called Griffin.

"Hey." He picked up after two rings. "Sorry I didn't call yesterday. I wanted to have news for you before I did, and I still haven't heard anything from my buddy," he said, clearly bummed.

"Yes, I know. But about that morning in Mexico, I wanted to explain," I started.

"It's okay, you don't owe me anything."

"Maybe not, but I'd like to at least clear the air. I'm only interested in you, Griffin. No one else. Also, for what it's worth, I told you the truth. Matt just climbed into my room on a stupid dare and then passed out. I tried to wake him up, but he was blacked out, and I couldn't move him. I slept on top of the covers while he drooled all over my sheets. Nothing happened, I promise."

"I believe you. To be honest I was just jealous and had no right to be. I think I needed to lick my wounds a bit. I was the one dragging my feet with us this past year, and you had every right to date whoever else you wanted to. Still do. I kept pushing you away, but all I wanted to do was get closer to you. When I saw you with that other guy, I was madder at myself than with you. And I really want to see where this thing goes with us, whatever the next couple months or years look like. I mean, we may both end up with a lot of time on our hands to hang out if we can't salvage this Mexico debacle."

"Oh, don't say that! We can salvage this. We have to."

We made plans to grab dinner on Friday and talk more, since I didn't have to worry about a rehearsal dinner this week. Regardless of what happened, I missed Griffin, and I knew that seeing him would make me feel better.

After killing time for a few hours, I got up to stretch my legs, grab another coffee, and see if Travis had any intel about the current mood of the office. I knew he listened in on most calls, "for the purpose of taking notes."

"Oh, muffin." He shook his head.

"That bad?"

"I mean, Cedric has been madder than a hornet about those photos, but it's mostly because he can't figure out who did it. Thank goodness our contract protects The Firm from legal action by Harriet and her new husband. From a purely marketing standpoint, the extra publicity never hurts, but Cedric hates a mole."

"So at least Harriet isn't planning to sue The Firm?" I knew Brody wouldn't initiate anything against us since I was still technically here. I'd consider it his final parting gift to me.

"No. I think we're safe on that end. I heard she just announced a couple new projects, so I imagine it's not hurting anything other than her ego. Must be nice to have someone like her hot new husband to help massage out any aches and pains, right?"

Clearly, Travis was not as up on *all* the office gossip as he thought, if he'd missed my history with Brody. I wasn't about to fill him in.

I headed back to my desk and decided to reorganize my wedding vendor files yet again to give me something to do while still in limbo. Claire was out of the office picking up linen samples from a showroom nearby, so I was alone in our shared workspace.

"Where is that stupid label maker," I muttered as I sifted papers around in my desk drawer.

Had Claire put it in her desk? I started rummaging through her drawers too. It never occurred to me that I was invading her private space since we weren't allowed any personal effects in the office. Not to mention we basically sat on top of each other.

Claire was, for the most part, extremely organized, yet another trait that set her apart from the other Trusties. No doubt she would make a great planner one day if she decided to stick to this career path. Her future certainly looked brighter than mine in that regard.

I finally found the label maker in the back of a drawer, where I also discovered the corner of a manila envelope wedged behind other files. I'm not sure what made me do it, but I pulled out the envelope along with the label machine. *Splash News* was written on the outside, and my stomach turned upside down.

I looked around to see the area had cleared out. I knew I shouldn't open up the envelope, but Splash News sounded familiar. My curiosity got the best of me.

Inside was a single piece of paper, an invoice. The one line item just said, "Location Scouting, $500." The date was the same as Brody's wedding. I couldn't believe what I saw. Why would Claire have this?

I anxiously looked around the room again, then quickly googled and confirmed that Splash News was indeed a paparazzi agency. I felt sick. I pulled out my phone and took a picture, then put the envelope back where I'd found it.

For months I thought Claire had my back. She'd been so nice to me and helped me fix one predicament after another. We literally held up a toppling cake together with our bare hands. Had I been wrong this whole time thinking that Mary Ellen was the "bad guy"?

I thought back to all the weddings we worked together and realized how often Claire mentioned that Mary Ellen wasn't on my team. But in reality, it was Claire who wasn't on my team.

I just couldn't fathom throwing someone under the bus like she had done, even if she didn't like the person. As I stood there, alone in the office, I decided to unleash the *Law & Order* part of myself. It was time to put Claire on trial. This might not be enough for a total conviction, but it was certainly enough to cause reasonable doubt for me and let me off the hook. Look at me using some of my ancient prelaw knowledge.

Once Claire returned from her errands, I did everything I could to avoid talking to her for the rest of the day. It wasn't easy, but between my AirPods and countless trips to the bathroom, I managed. I'm sure the interns thought I had some horrible stomach issues, but who cared.

Unfortunately Cedric left the office for the day before Claire did. I kept my cool. Telling Cedric the next morning would be better anyway. Time to prep for court.

———— ✳ ————

I had just changed out of my work clothes and was about to text Griffin about setting up dinner—as well as the Splash News invoice— when someone knocked on my door.

I opened it to find Griffin standing there, sweating and panting like he'd just finished a run. He held a piece of paper in one hand and a cluster of gorgeous pink peonies in the other. "Hi," he said, still catching his breath. "Can I come in?"

"Of course. Was I supposed to meet you somewhere? Did I completely flake on plans?" I asked as he came inside.

"No, sorry. I wanted to catch you here if possible. I know it's crazy, but I couldn't wait any longer to tell you what I really should've said on the phone earlier, but now I'm glad I get to do it in person."

"Okaaay," I said drawing it out. "Do you want something to drink first?"

"No, I'm good. Just come sit down over here with me."

We both moved over to the sofa, and he put the flowers and paper on the coffee table. "Oh, those are for you."

"They're beautiful, and my favorites." I picked up the peonies to smell and admire and then set them back down on the table for now. I gave him props. It was always a bold choice to buy flowers for a florist, even a former one.

"I remembered that they are," he said. "Listen, Lottie. I've been a total idiot these past few weeks. There's no excuse, and I just needed to say all this to you before I muck it up any more."

He blew out a long breath. "I'm totally falling for you. And it scares me to death because I haven't felt anything more than just friendship with someone since, you know. We may be moving to different states, who the heck knows? But I'm tired of letting my head dictate everything in my life now. Just because my marriage didn't work out doesn't mean it wouldn't work out with you. I'm not asking you to marry me or anything, but I'm just saying . . . I don't see that *not* happening in my future anymore.

"You make me want to change my mind, to try again, to hope with every piece of my sad, cynical heart that we could have a different story."

This was a new side to Griffin. It was like his *The Notebook* moment, minus the dementia. "Griffin." I was beaming from ear to ear. "I feel the same way."

"I can't stop thinking about you. It's almost miserable how much I do." He laughed. "I love the way you have a backup plan for every possible problem and still manage to get in a mess, despite trying so hard to avoid every bad scenario. I love how you take care of people and how you tell jokes like a middle-aged man. I love how you'd go to the mat for Natalia or your family but you don't always fight for yourself sometimes. I suppose, in sum, I want to fight alongside you—and probably with you—and see where this thing goes."

I reached over and took hold of his hand. "These past months, knowing you, working here, I've changed. In good ways, I hope. You've made me laugh, made me think, and made me believe I could do something with meaning, purpose, whatever you call it—whether it's planning weddings or having one of my own someday. I've never felt more in control of my life or more fully myself than when I'm with you. I like that feeling. A lot. We don't have to have all the answers. Just the next step."

And before I could say more, he leaned in and finally kissed me. Softly at first, then deeper. He pushed me back against the couch and it was like someone tickled my spine and punched me in the gut at the same time. I was intoxicated as I combed my hands through his dark hair and pulled him in even closer. My head swum by the time he finally pulled back.

"This day is really turning around for me," I said when I came up for air.

"Oh, yeah? Did someone else stop by and tell you he wanted to be with you?"

"Ha! No, but I think I finally have the proof I need to clear us of the Mexico mess."

"Really? Because I thought I was bringing that proof over to you now." He picked up an envelope from the coffee table.

"What are you talking about?"

"What are *you* talking about?" he asked.

"I found a pay stub for a paparazzi photographer in Claire's desk. I think it's enough to prove she was the one who tipped them off about the wedding."

"Well, now you will have a totally open-and-shut case." He handed me the piece of paper. "I heard back from my buddy who went to BottleRock with McManus. I guess the guy owed him a big favor because somehow, he got him to reveal that his source was Claire. She's your intern, right? Here's a copy of one of the emails between them going over location details."

I shook my head, still not believing Claire was our perp. Then I read over the email. "Aside from the money, why would she do this? I thought she was doing so well at The Firm . . . I thought we were close." This one cut deep.

"Who knows? Maybe she was jealous? She probably gets everything she wants in life and didn't want you in her way for a promotion? Whatever the reason, she can't deny it. We have an embarrassing amount of proof. Hopefully you'll be back in Cedric's good graces and on the Atlanta shortlist again." Those big brown eyes bored into mine.

"You know, I'm sure they need photographers there too."

"I do love a good art and music scene, and Atlanta has one of the best," he said, stroking a thumb across my cheek and kissing me again.

Yep. My day had decidedly turned around.

EPILOGUE

I slammed the trunk of my Prius shut and walked back to the front door of our apartment building. I'd never be able to see out the back window with the meager contents of my life overflowing the backseat, but I could still make it the ten and a half hours to Atlanta.

Natalia stood on the curb, watching me with a gloomy look on her face. We'd lived together for almost a decade, and this would be a sad and strange transition.

"You sure you're going to be able to sleep at night without me?"

"Probably not. But I'm excited to no longer have to count and label my yogurts or cans of LaCroix," she said, laughing. "Seriously though, I think having a place of my own will be good for me. It feels like a step in the right direction."

Natalia was moving into a studio in the same high-rise where we'd been living, so at least very little else had to change about her life. And I liked that I could still envision where she'd be, even if I no longer got to see her on the daily.

After we'd shown Cedric the photos and email, he was like a caged tiger, ready to pounce the instant Claire returned to the office. Their conversation occurred behind the glass of his office walls, but everyone could see enough to get the gist of it. Moments later, she hustled out the red lacquered doors.

"Hey Claire, hold up," I gasped as I caught up with her in the office parking lot.

"I really need to go." She sniffled a bit.

"Listen, I just need to know *why*. I thought we were becoming friends. I really liked working with you. What happened?"

"Friends?" Claire asked. She opened the driver's side door and tossed her purse in. She then turned to me sans tears, but with a giant smirk on her face.

"Lottie, we were never friends. I mean, I like you fine. I was always nice to you because you were nice to me, but the last thing I need are more friends. What I need is a job. A real one. Not some stupid assistant role that I was clearly going to be stuck in with you already clawing your way to the top of the food chain."

"Um, but I'm sure that wouldn't have been the case. There were so many new opportunities—"

"Save it. Cedric couldn't be bothered to notice me. It's typical, really. My dad has zero respect for me and what I'm capable of too. He thinks I'm just a massive mooch, especially compared to my over-achieving older sister. I don't need to live in anyone else's shadow on a daily basis. There's only so much grunt work I can take."

I was speechless. I never expected anything like this from Claire. Apparently I was not the best at reading people.

I stood there in silence, with nothing to say in response that would do either of us any good. Then Claire slammed the door of her Range Rover and took off. I guess we had both been right at that miserable wedding we worked together last summer. There was still nothing more terrifying than a pretty girl with a boatload of cash.

Later that day, Cedric announced that Mary Ellen and Abigail would be running his Dallas office and that I was going to help a team launch in Atlanta. He and Geoffrey would be officially splitting their time between the two cities. This part, at least, I couldn't have planned out better myself.

And here I was, ready to go. Time for a big step forward. I turned to say my good-byes to Griffin, and Natalia casually stepped over to a nearby bench to give us a moment.

"You really don't need someone to drive with you?"

"What are you talking about? Atlanta isn't that far. It's certainly closer than Alaska, right?"

"Good point. We'll see what happens there," he mused. Once Cedric had finished his office reorg, he gave Val Trujillo a call. He not only cleared up the leaked photos, but he also raved about Griffin's solo work at a couple events. Griffin was offered the Alaska gig that very day. Unfortunately he'd spent his weeks of unemployment reevaluating his own trajectory and wasn't sure he still wanted to go.

I hoped some of that had to do with me now. He didn't have to move to Atlanta, but not moving to Alaska was great with me. He knew for certain he wouldn't be returning to event photography no matter where he landed. "Either way, I don't think I was ever really cut out for weddings."

"I hope you only mean that professionally," I said without thinking.

"I do." He pulled me into a hug. "Everything else is on the table."

I stood for a moment, savoring the feeling of his arms and the piney smell of his detergent. "So, this is it, huh?"

"We'll figure it out." He gave me a final squeeze. "In the meantime you're going to conquer the Atlanta wedding scene."

With that he kissed me good-bye, gently at first and then more hungrily. I clung to him, knowing it had to last me for a while. After we finally parted, Natalia came over to give me one last long hug. We both pretended not to be wiping away tears.

Minutes later, I was driving away—once again looking ahead instead of behind. Okay, well, maybe with a glance over my shoulder.

Years ago, back on those chapel steps, I thought I'd lost everything. In some ways, I had. My entire perfect life. The wedding of my dreams and the guy who frankly only existed in my imagination. And that version of me contorted to fit something that wasn't right. But the path I was set on, packed with broken glass and collapsed cakes, twisting and twirling like a first dance, had become my own. Along the way, it became a choice and not a chance.

Yes, I'd come so far. I was rebuilding the Lottie that I'd dismantled back then, but better. Small pieces of myself had somehow snapped back into place. My hopes. My ambition. My strengths. My love. All mine, not perfect but not dependent on anyone or anything else.

And now, literally and figuratively behind the wheel, I held the future solely in my hands. It was time.

A NOTE FROM THE AUTHORS

We met as college freshmen in Texas, crammed in the back of an SUV during sorority recruitment. We spent four years navigating the highs and heartbreaks, living together in closet-sized dorm rooms and exploring (read: freaking out about) the possibilities of our futures. By the time this book is published, we will have been friends for half our lives; we're grateful to have gotten to see each other find our ways, building careers and families.

What you hold in your hands is a work of fiction. While it's peppered with real places and memories loosely inspired by some real events, it's purely a novel and our attempt to convey even a fraction of the wonder and hilarity and awkwardness of young adulthood. We can't believe it exists, and we hope it brings you joy, laughter and a bit of fantasy.

XOXO
Asher + Mary

ACKNOWLEDGMENTS

As the saying goes, if you want to make God laugh . . . But truly, for two "planners," neither of us could have imagined what life would hold. And for that, we're abundantly grateful.

We would like to thank everyone who supported, loved, and believed in us while we wrote this novel together. A special thank you to our other "roomies": to Erin Sioco for your eternal optimism and selfless cheerleading, and to Maggie Gormly for your storytelling expertise and unshakeable faith. Thank you both for reading early drafts, letting us borrow your anecdotes, and remaining friends with us afterward.

We owe a massive debt to agent Nena Madonia Oshman for your insight and advocacy, even when all we offered was a scattered collection of outlandish stories. Thank you to the entire Dupree Miller team.

Thank you to editor Jocelyn Bailey, for your vision, humor, wordsmithery, and occasional tough love. You helped us navigate a writing and publishing process from across the country and during a pandemic/general dumpster fire of a year. To Becky Monds for jumping in with us—we can't wait for the next round together. To Amanda

Bostic for seeing the spark in our half-baked idea and giving us a shot. To Kerri Potts, Margaret Kercher, and the whole Harper Muse crew, thank you for the support and space we needed to bring this story to life.

I (Mary) would know nothing about this wacky and wonderful world of weddings without Dr. A Thompson, Mary, Sara Fay, Abbie, Leah, Jason and, of course, Todd. You all inspired me, taught me much of what I know, and brought immeasurable joy into my work-life. Thank you to the countless vendors and clients who allowed me to work with them over the past decade and trusted me with their events. Wedding planning is my passion, and it's been my honor to participate in so many lovely couples' road to the altar. I hope this book brings you many laughs, as no one will truly understand planning a wedding like someone who's been through it.

Thank you to Nita and John Hollis for showing me what marriage really looks like—the good and bad, the very ugly and the very beautiful. Your prayers, support and encouragement mean the world to me, and this book would not have been possible without you both. I'm one very lucky daughter.

Thank you to my children, G and JA, who bring so much joy to my life and gave me the space I needed at times to write this book. It's an honor and pleasure to be your mom, and the thought of each of you getting married one day already brings tears to my eyes. Don't worry, I have a planner in mind to help you.

Paul, not only is this book dedicated to you, but I want to thank you for loving me so well and for supporting me since the day I said my very own "I do" to you. You've been with me since the beginning of my wedding career and proved to be the rock I never knew I needed to grow personally and professionally. Thank you for listening to all my crazy stories, for helping me with last-minute tasks, for holding down our fort while I worked countless weekends and for rubbing my feet after 16 hours in heels. You're my everything and living proof that God's plan for my life is far superior to my own.

I (Asher) owe a lengthy list of authors, journalists, and English professors my gratitude for teaching me about storytelling, pruning my prose, and toughening up my shoe leather and thin skin. For starters, Jim Kelly, Liz McNeil, Donna Goeglein, Molly Reardon, Heather Landy, Paula Span, Michelle Tan, Devin Tomb, and Kevin Carr O'Leary—I learned invaluable lessons from each of you as a writer and a human. To Suzy Evans, thank you for the book swaps, the Nora Ephron nights, the wine, all of it. To Jill Atkinson for sticking with me the longest, for reading early and staying late, always.

Our partnership would not have been possible if not for the many people who pitched in with both of our children while we stole moments to write. Thank you to Mary Callahan for uprooting your life and being the TallPaul for a season. And a heartfelt thanks to Carissa Payan for loving my kids, knowing them so well, sharing your considerable expertise, and keeping us all organized. Our family would have been lost without you.

Thank you to my parents and grandparents, for sharing your own stories, for walking the winding paths of marriage, and instilling an appreciation for the South. It will, in many ways, always be home. And Mom, words can't express my gratitude for bestowing your love of books and shaping me into the reader, writer, and woman I am today. Marmee still tells the best stories.

To Mary, thank you for always being unapologetically yourself, for inviting me into this journey with you, for pushing me to finish, and for never suffocating me in my sleep.

And finally, Emerson, Sullivan, and Montgomery—you have sacrificed heaps of time with me for the sake of this book and for my dreams. (I'll always have those pitch calls from Monty's hospital delivery room.) Being your mother is the greatest job and deepest joy in the world. Y'all are my heart. Justin, there's much to be said, but, my love, somehow you always already know. I'm really glad you asked me, all those years ago. Someday, we'll do it all over again just for fun, in my old dress and your new tux. Thank you for fighting for my dreams as much as your own, for reading fiction for me, and for this life, this family. Nothing would be possible without your constant belief and love. You remain my North Star.

DISCUSSION QUESTIONS

1. We meet Lottie when she's a newly single recent graduate. What was your first impression of her?

2. Have you ever gotten carried away by your own ideas about what should happen and (to whatever degree) lost hold of reality? Have any of your plans for your future completely fallen apart?

3. Conversely, have you ever found yourself somewhere—whether it's a relationship, a job, a home, etc.—and felt like you just stumbled into it, the way Lottie did with wedding planning? If so, did you stay?

4. Many of the weddings in the book were inspired by real couples' events—and mishaps. Which was your favorite wedding?

5. As the event planners know, every couple has the one major "must" at their wedding. If you're married, what was it for you? Or, if you've never been married, what would it be if you had a wedding?

6. Lottie struggles at different points to find significance and purpose in her work. Whether you work in or out of the home, does that resonate with you?

7. Matt represents so much about the life and relationship Lottie always believed she wanted. Did you ever think Matt stood a chance? Would you have given him a shot?

8. You may not have planned a wedding to someone who never proposed, but have you ever thrown yourself into a plan/goal only to realize it wasn't actually the right thing for you?

9. Lottie and her friends discuss the challenges of balancing life and work, especially as women. For Natalia, none of the women higher up in her company have personal lives she thinks she'd aspire to. Would you see that as a challenge or as a sign to find another career/company/job?

10. Several characters proved to be different than Lottie's initial assumptions about them. Which character do you identify with most? Were there any who frustrated you? Who was your favorite?

11. Did you expect Lottie to be betrayed by Claire? Have you ever felt blindsided by someone you thought had your back?

12. Both Griffin and Lottie felt swept up in an expectation, real or otherwise, that they had to find a spouse in college. Have you ever felt pressure from yourself or your surroundings to hit certain life benchmarks by a certain age? How did that impact you?

13. If you're married, what was the biggest disaster that occurred surrounding or during your wedding?

14. As he and Lottie work together more, Griffin keeps dropping negative comments about marriage. We eventually learn that Griffin divorced after a brief marriage to his college sweetheart. Why do you think Griffin would rather not try again?

15. Even if it was based on a fantasy, Lottie bought into the idea of who she was with Brody. Why do you think she gave up her dreams and identity for him? Have you ever let a relationship—romantic or otherwise—so define you that you lost yourself? How did you move forward?

16. The story ends with Lottie and Griffin finally together, but about to move to separate cities. Do you think they're going to make it long-term?

ABOUT THE AUTHORS

Mary Hollis Huddleston

Photo by Abigail Volkmann @abigailvolkmannphotography

Mary Huddleston is the cofounder and creative director of Please Be Seated, the premier event rental company in Nashville, Tennessee. Mary and her husband started the business in 2014 and now have more than thirty employees servicing events nationwide. Mary started her career as an event coordinator in Dallas, Texas, initially at Diamond Affairs Weddings and Special Events, and later at the nationally recognized Todd Events, where she helped launch their wedding division. In 2018 Mary established Mrs. Southern Social, a lifestyle platform focused on modern entertaining at home. She has more than seventy thousand Instagram followers and has been featured in *Southern Living*, *Southern Lady*, StyleBlueprint, and *Nfocus*.

Visit her online at mrssouthernsocial.com
Instagram: @mrssouthernsocial

Asher Fogle Paul

Photo by Jenny Anderson

Asher Fogle Paul is a human interest and entertainment journalist. Most recently, she served as digital features editor at *Good Housekeeping*. She's also held posts at *Us Weekly*, *People*, and *Reader's Digest*, and her work has been published in *Marie Claire*, *Cosmopolitan*, *Esquire*, *House Beautiful*, *Elle*, and *W*, among others. Asher has an MS in magazine journalism from Columbia University and a BA in English from Texas Christian University. She lives in New York City with her husband and three young children. *Without a Hitch* is her debut novel.

Instagram: @asherpaul